Praise for Marta

"Marta Perry delivers a strong story."
—*RT Book Reviews*

"An excellent mystery that's certain to keep you in constant suspense."
—*RT Book Reviews* on
Season of Secrets

"An exceptionally written story in which danger and romance blend nicely."
—*RT Book Reviews* on
A Christmas to Die For

"*Tangled Memories*...is captivating...readers will want this book on their keeper shelf."
—*RT Book Reviews*

"You are not going to want to put Marta Perry's suspenseful book down, not even for a second."
—*RT Book Reviews* on
Land's End

Marta Perry

SEASON OF SECRETS
and
A CHRISTMAS
TO DIE FOR

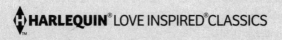

Recycling programs
for this product may
not exist in your area.

ISBN-13: 978-0-373-60974-1

Season of Secrets and A Christmas to Die For

Copyright © 2014 by Harlequin Books S.A.

The publisher acknowledges the copyright holder of the individual works as follows:

Season of Secrets
Copyright © 2006 by Martha Johnson

A Christmas to Die For
Copyright © 2007 by Martha Johnson

www.Harlequin.com

Printed in U.S.A.

CONTENTS

Marta Perry has written everything from Sunday school curricula to travel articles to magazine stories in more than twenty years of writing, but she feels she's found her writing home in the stories she writes for the Love Inspired lines.

Marta lives in rural Pennsylvania, but she and her husband spend part of each year at their second home in South Carolina. When she's not writing, she's probably visiting her children and her six beautiful grandchildren, traveling, gardening or relaxing with a good book.

SEASON OF SECRETS

For now we see in a mirror, darkly, but then
face to face; now I know in part, but then
I shall know full, even as I am known.

—1 Corinthians 13:12

This story is dedicated to my granddaughter,
Greta Nicole Wulff,
with much love from Grammy.
And, as always, to Brian.

Chapter One

"Why is he coming back now?"

Aunt Kate put her morning cup of Earl Grey back in the saucer as she asked the question for what had to be the twentieth time since they'd heard the news, her faded blue eyes puckered with distress. December sunlight streamed through the lace curtains on the bay window in the breakfast room, casting into sharp relief the veins that stood out on her hand, pressed to the polished tabletop.

"I don't know, Aunt Kate."

Love swept through Dinah Westlake, obliterating her own fears about Marc Devlin's return to Charleston. She covered the trembling hand with her own, trying to infuse her great-aunt with her own warmth. Anger sparked. Marc shouldn't come back, upsetting their lives once again.

"Maybe he just wants to sell the house since the Farriers moved out." Aunt Kate sounded hopeful, and she glanced toward the front window and the house that stood across the street in the quiet Charleston historic block.

Annabel's house. The house where Annabel died.

Dinah forced herself to focus on the question. "I suppose so. Do you know if he's bringing Court?"

Her cousin Annabel's son had been three when she'd seen him last, and now he was thirteen. She remembered a soft, cuddly child who'd snuggled up next to her, begging for just one more bedtime story. It was unlikely that Courtney would want or need anything from her now.

"I don't know." Aunt Kate's lips firmed into a thin line. "I hope not."

Dinah blinked. "Don't you want to see Courtney?" This visit was the first indication that Marc would let his son have a relationship with his mother's kin that consisted of more than letters, gifts and brief thank-you notes.

Tears threatened to spill over onto her great-aunt's soft cheeks. "Of course I do. But that poor child shouldn't be exposed to the house where his mother died, even if it means I never see him again."

"Aunt Kate—" Dinah's words died. She couldn't say anything that would make a difference, because she understood only too well what her aunt felt. She, too, had not been back in that house since Annabel's funeral.

Except in the occasional nightmare. Then, she stood again on the graceful curving staircase of Annabel and Marc's house, looking down toward the dim hallway, hearing angry voices from the front parlor. Knowing something terrible was about to happen. Unable to prevent it.

"Everyone will start talking about Annabel's death again." Aunt Kate touched a lacy handkerchief to her eyes, unable as always to say the uglier word. Murder. "Just when it's forgotten, people will start to talk again."

Something recoiled in Dinah. It seemed so disloyal never to talk about Annabel. Still, if that was how Aunt Kate dealt with the pain, maybe it was better than having nightmares.

She slid her chair back, patting her aunt's hand. "Don't worry about it too much. I'm sure people are so busy getting ready for the Christmas holidays that Marc will have been and gone before anyone takes notice."

Her aunt clasped her hand firmly. "You're not going to the office today, are you? Dinah, you have to stay home. What if he comes?"

It was no use pointing out to her that Dinah was going to police headquarters, not an office. Aunt Kate couldn't possibly refer to her as a forensic artist. In Aunt Kate's mind, a Charleston lady devoted herself to the church, charity and society, not necessarily in that order.

"I thought I'd check in this morning." As a freelance police artist she only worked when called on, but she'd found it helped her acceptance with the detectives to remind them of her presence now and then.

"Please, Dinah. Stay home today."

Her hesitation lasted only an instant. Aunt Kate had

taken care of her. Now it was her turn. She bent to press her cheek against Aunt Kate's.

"Of course I will, if that's what you want. But given the way he's cut ties with us, I don't expect Marcus Devlin to show up on our doorstep anytime soon."

Was she being a complete coward? Maybe so. But she'd fought her way back from the terror of the night Annabel died, and she had no desire to revisit that dreadful time.

Please, God. Please let me forget.

That was a petition that was hardly likely to be granted, now that Marc Devlin was coming home.

After helping her aunt to the sunroom that looked over her garden, where she would doze in the winter sunshine, Dinah cleared the breakfast dishes. It was one of the few things Alice Jones, her aunt's devoted housekeeper, allowed her to do to help.

Alice was nearly as old as her great-aunt, and the two of them couldn't hope to stay on in the elegant, inconvenient antebellum house on Tradd Street if she weren't here. She wasn't even sure when she'd gone from being the cosseted little girl of the house to being the caretaker, but she didn't see the situation changing anytime soon, and she wouldn't want it to.

A sound disturbed the morning quiet. Someone wielded the brass dolphin knocker on the front door with brisk energy. It could be anyone. Her stomach tightened; the back of her neck prickled. Instinct said it was Marc.

Heart thudding, she crossed the Oriental carpet that

had covered the hall floor for a hundred years or so. She turned the brass doorknob and opened the door.

Instinct was right. Her cousin's husband stood on the covered veranda, hand arrested halfway to the knocker. A shaft of winter sunlight, filtered through the branches of the magnolia tree, struck hair that was still glossy black.

For a moment, Dinah could only stare. It was Marc, of course, but in another sense it wasn't. This wasn't the intent, idealistic young prosecutor her teenage dreams had idolized.

"Dinah." He spoke first, his deep voice breaking the spell that held her silent. "It's been a long time."

"Not by our choice," she said, before thinking about the implication.

The lines around his firm mouth deepened. "I know." He quirked one eyebrow, and the familiar movement broke through her sense of strangeness. "Are you going to let me come in?"

She felt her cheeks warm. What was she doing, keeping him standing on the veranda like a door-to-door salesperson? No matter how much his return distressed Aunt Kate, she couldn't treat him as anything but the cousin-in-law he'd always been to her.

She stepped back. "Please, come in." She grasped for the comfort of ingrained manners. "It's good to see you again, Marc."

He stepped into the wide center hallway, the movement seeming to stir the quiet air, and she had to suppress a gasp as pain gripped her heart. Forgotten? No, she hadn't forgotten at all. His presence brought her ten-year-old grief surging to life.

Was being here doing the same for him? She thought it might—his face had tightened, but that was all. He was better at hiding his feelings than he used to be.

She had to say something, anything, to bridge the silence. She took refuge in the ordinary. "Did you have a pleasant flight?"

He shrugged. "Not bad. I'd forgotten how warm South Carolina can be in December."

"That just shows how much of a Northerner you've become. Everyone here has been complaining that it's too cold."

His face relaxed into a half smile. "Wimp. You should try a Boston winter sometime to see what cold really is."

"No, thanks. I'll pass."

He had changed. He was ten years older, of course. Ten years would change anyone. He looked—successful, she supposed. Dress shirt, dark tie, a tweed jacket that fit smoothly over broad shoulders, a flash of gold at his wrist that was probably an expensive watch. Being a corporate attorney instead of a prosecutor must suit him.

But it wasn't so much the way he was dressed as the air about him—the air of a successful, accomplished man.

"Well?" He lifted that eyebrow again. "What's the verdict, Dinah?"

She wouldn't pretend to misunderstand him. "I was thinking that you talk faster than you used to."

He smiled. "I had to learn because no one would stick around long enough to hear what I had to say."

The smile was a reminder of the Marc she'd known. *Dear Father, this is harder than I'd imagined it could be. Please, get me through it.*

"Come into the parlor." However much she might wish he'd leave, she couldn't stand here in the hall with him.

She turned and walked into the small, perfectly appointed front parlor. He'd find this familiar, she supposed. Aunt Kate hadn't changed anything in seventy years, and she never would. Anything that showed wear was replaced with an exact duplicate. Aunt Kate didn't bother to decorate for Christmas much in recent years, but the white mantel bore its usual evergreen, magnolia leaves and holly, studded with the fat ivory candles that would be lit Christmas Eve.

Dinah sat on the Queen Anne love seat, gesturing to the wing chair opposite. Marc sat, leaning back, seeming very much at ease. But the lines on his face deepened, and his dark eyes hid secrets.

"You've changed." His comment startled her, but it shouldn't. Hadn't she just been thinking the same about him? No one stayed the same for ten years.

"I'm ten years older. That makes a difference." Especially when it was the difference between an immature teen and an adult woman.

He shook his head. "It's not just that. You're not shy anymore."

"I've learned to hide it better, that's all."

Marc *would* remember the shy, gawky teenager

she'd once been. She could only hope he'd never noticed the crush she'd had on him.

"It's easy to see that you're blooming. How is Aunt Kate?"

And how, exactly, was she going to explain the fact that Aunt Kate wasn't coming in to greet him?

"She's...older, obviously. She'd deny it vehemently, but she's begun to fail a little."

"So you're taking care of her."

"Of course."

That's how it is in families, Marc. We take care of each other. We don't walk away, the way you did.

He frowned slightly, and she had the uncomfortable sense that he knew what she was thinking.

"Is she too frail to see me?"

Her careful evasion had led her just where she didn't want to be. "No. She just—"

She faltered to a halt. There wasn't any good way of saying that Aunt Kate didn't welcome his return.

"She just doesn't want to see me." His mouth thinned. "Tell me, does she think I killed Annabel?"

The blunt question shook her, and mentioning Annabel's name seemed to bring her into the room. For an instant Dinah heard the light tinkle of Annabel's laugh, caught a whiff of the sophisticated fragrance that had been Annabel's scent. Grief ripped through her, and she struggled to speak.

"I—I'm sure she doesn't think that." But did she? With her firm avoidance of the subject, Aunt Kate had managed never to say.

His dark gaze seemed to reject the feeble words. "What about you, Dinah? Do you think that?"

Before she could find the words, he shook his head.

"Never mind. I don't suppose it matters."

She found the words then, at the pain in his voice. "I don't think you could have hurt Annabel."

How could anyone have hurt Annabel, have struck out and destroyed all that life, all that beauty?

His face seemed to relax a fraction. "Thank you. I'm selling the house. I suppose you guessed that."

"We thought that was probably why you'd come back," she said cautiously, not wanting to make it sound as if that was what she wanted.

"It's time. Having the Farriers rent the place all these years let me drift, but when they decided to move, I knew I had to do something about the house."

"You won't be here long, then." She was aware of a sense of relief. He would go away, and the terrible wound of Annabel's death would skin over again.

His brows lifted. "Are you eager to see the last of me, Dinah?"

"No." He was making her feel like that awkward teen again. "I just assumed you'd be in a hurry to get the house on the market and go back to your life, especially with the holidays coming."

"The holidays," he repeated, something a little wary in his voice.

"I suppose you and Court have all sorts of plans for Christmas." She was talking at random, trying to cover her embarrassment.

"Well, he's past the Santa stage, but he still gets excited."

"Does he?" For a moment she had a vivid image of the three-year-old he'd been—big dark eyes filled with wonder at the smallest things—a butterfly in the garden or a new puzzle she'd bought him, knowing how much he loved working them. "I'd love to see him."

Again the words came out before she considered. Marc had made his wishes clear all these years, limiting their contact to cards and gifts. Just because he'd come back didn't mean anything had changed.

"You'll get your wish," Marc said abruptly. "He's over at the house now, unloading the rental car."

She could only stare at him. "You've brought Court here, to the house where—" She stopped, unable to say the words.

"You think I'm crazy to bring Court back to the house where his mother died." Marc's voice was tinged with bitterness, but he could give voice to the thought she couldn't.

"I'm sorry." She sought refuge in platitudes. "I'm sure you know what's best for your son."

"Do I?" Vulnerability suddenly showed in his normally guarded eyes, disarming her. "I wish I were sure. I thought I knew. I thought the best thing for Court was a whole new life, with nothing to remind him of what he'd lost."

"So you kept him away from us." Did he have any idea how much that had hurt?

"Away from you, away from this place."

Marc surged to his feet as if he couldn't sit still any

longer. He stalked to the window, then turned and came back again. The room seemed too small for him. He stopped in front of her.

"I did what I thought I had to," he said uncompromisingly. "And it worked. Court was a normal, bright, happy kid, too happy and busy to worry about the past."

She caught the tense. "Was?"

"Was." He sat down heavily.

She waited, knowing he'd tell her, whatever it was. She didn't want to hear, she thought in sudden panic. But it was too late for that.

"Maybe this would have happened anyway," he said slowly, sounding as if he tried to be fair. "He's thirteen—it's a tough age. But when school started in September, one of his teachers assigned a writing project on family history. He started asking questions."

"About Annabel."

He nodded. "About her, about her family. About our life here in Charleston. He became obsessed." He stopped, as if he'd heard what he said and wanted it back. "Not obsessed—that's not right. I don't think there's anything unhealthy about it. He's curious. He wants to know."

She swallowed, feeling the lump in her throat at the thought of Annabel's child. "I remember. He was always curious."

"Yes." His face was drawn. "He has to know things. So he told me what he wanted for Christmas."

He paused, and she had a sense of dread at what he was about to say.

"He wanted to come back to Charleston. That's all

he asked for. To come back here and have Christmas in the house before I sell it."

"And you said yes."

"What else could I do?" He leaned toward her, his dark eyes focusing on her face, and that sense of dread deepened. "But it's more complicated than I thought."

"What do you mean?"

His hand closed over hers, and she felt his urgency. "I realized something the moment I saw the house again—realized what I've been evading all these years. I have to know the truth about Annabel's death."

He had shocked Dinah, Marc realized. Or maybe *shock* wasn't the right word for her reaction. His years as a prosecutor had taught him to find body language more revealing than speech, and Dinah was withdrawing, protecting herself against him.

Protecting. The word startled him. Dinah didn't have anything to fear from him.

He deliberately relaxed against the back of the chair, giving her space. Wait. See how she responded to that. See if she would help him or run from him.

He glanced around the room with a sense of wonder. It hadn't changed since the days when he'd come here to pick up Annabel, and he'd thought it caught in a previous century then. Clearly Kate preferred things the way they had always been.

But Dinah had changed. He remembered so clearly Annabel's attitude toward her shy young cousin—a mixture of love and a kind of amused exasperation.

She's such a dreamer. Annabel had lifted her hands

in an expressive gesture. She's impossibly young for her age, and I don't see how she's ever going to mature, living in that house with Aunt Kate. Let's have her here for the summer. She can help out with Court, and maybe I can help her grow up a little.

His heart caught at the memory. *I feel it more here, Lord. Is that why I had to come back?*

Dinah had certainly grown up. Skin soft as a magnolia blossom, blue-black hair curling to her shoulders, those huge violet eyes. He couldn't describe her without resorting to the classic Southern clichés. Charleston knew how to grow beautiful women.

Dinah seemed to realize how long the silence had grown. She cleared her throat. "I don't know what you hope to accomplish at this late date. The police department considers it an unsolved case. I'm sure someone looks at the file now and then, but—" The muscles in her neck worked, as if she had trouble saying those words.

"They've written it off, you mean. I haven't." He wasn't doing this very well, maybe because he hadn't realized what he really wanted until he'd driven down the street and pointed out the house to his son. "Court hasn't."

Dinah's hands were clasped in her lap, so tightly that the skin strained over her knuckles. "There's nothing left to find after ten years. No one left to talk to about it."

"There's you, Dinah. You were there."

Her face went white with shock, and he knew he'd

made a misstep. He shouldn't have rushed things with her, assumed she'd want what he wanted.

She pushed the words away with both hands. "I didn't see anything. I don't know anything. You, of all people, should know that."

A vivid image filled his mind, fresh as if it had happened yesterday—Dinah's small form crumpled on the staircase of the house across the street, black hair spilling around her. He'd found her when he'd come home in the early hours of the morning from a trip to track down a witness in one of his cases.

He'd rushed downstairs to the phone, shouting for Annabel, and seen the light in the parlor still burning. He'd pushed open the half-closed door—

No. He wouldn't let his thoughts go any farther than that. It was too painful, even after all this time.

"I know that you fell, that you had a concussion. That you said you didn't remember anything."

"I didn't. I don't." Anger flared in her face, bringing a flush to her cheeks that wiped away the pallor. "If I knew anything about who killed Annabel, don't you think I'd have spoken up by now? I loved her!"

The words rang in the quiet room. They seemed to hold an accusation.

"I loved her, too, Dinah. Or don't you believe that?"

She sucked in a breath, as if the room had gone airless. "Yes." The word came out slowly, and her eyes were dark with pain. "I believe you loved her. But there's nothing you can do for her now. She's at peace."

"The rest of us aren't." His jaw tightened until it was difficult to force the words out. "Court knows I was a suspect in his mother's death. My son knows that, Dinah."

"Oh, Marc." The pity in her face was almost worse than her anger had been. "I'm sorry. Surely he doesn't believe you did it."

"He says he doesn't." He tried to look at the situation objectively, as if he were a prosecutor assessing a case again. "Most of the time I think that's true."

But what if there was a doubt, even a fraction of a doubt? Could he stand to see his close relationship with his son eroded day by day, month by month, until they were polite strangers?

"I'm sorry," she said again, looking at him as if she knew all the things he didn't say. "I wish I could help you. I really do. But I don't know anything."

He studied her troubled expression. Dinah certainly thought she was telling the truth, but there might be more to it than that. She'd been there, in the house, that whole summer. There far more than he had been, in fact. If there'd been any clue, any small indication of trouble in the events of that summer, Dinah could have seen.

He wouldn't say that to her, not now. He'd shaken her enough already, and if he wanted her cooperation, he'd have to step carefully.

"I understand." He stood, seeing the relief she tried to hide that he was leaving. He held out his hand to her. After a moment she rose, slipping her hand in his. Hers was small and cold in his grip. "But you can still be a friend, can't you? To me and to Court?"

She hesitated for a fraction of an instant before she produced a smile. "Of course. You must know that."

"Good." He made his voice brisk, knowing he had to pin her down while he could. "Come and see us tomorrow. We should be settled enough by then to entertain a guest. I want you to meet Court."

Again that slight hesitation. And then she nodded. "I'll see you tomorrow."

It wasn't much, but it was enough to start with. If Dinah knew anything, eventually he'd know it, too.

Chapter Two

"I just wish you wouldn't go over there." Aunt Kate followed Dinah to the front hall the next day as if she'd bar the door.

Dinah stopped, managing a smile for her great-aunt. "I wish I didn't have to." She hadn't told Aunt Kate about Marcus's intention of looking into Annabel's death. That would only distress her more.

"Well, then—"

"I must, don't you see?" Obviously Aunt Kate didn't, or they wouldn't be having this conversation again. "You're the one who taught me about the importance of family."

Aunt Kate's lips pursed into a shape reminiscent of a bud on one of her rosebushes. "Marcus Devlin is not a member of our family."

"Annabel was." She struggled to say the words evenly.

Aunt Kate's eyes misted. "Does he know you haven't been in that house since Annabel died?"

"No. And you're not to tell him." She clutched Aunt Kate's hand. "Promise me."

"Of course, dear. But if it bothers you that much, it's all the more reason not to become involved with Marcus's visit."

"This isn't about Marcus. I have to go over there for Court's sake."

Aunt Kate gave in at that—she could see it in her eyes. It was a good thing, because Dinah couldn't bear to argue with her.

"I suppose if you must, you must." She touched Dinah's hair lightly. "You're as stubborn as I was at your age."

"I'll take that as a compliment." She bent to kiss her aunt's cheek.

"We'll deal with the gossip somehow, I suppose." Her aunt tried one last volley.

"Darling, you know they'll gossip anyway. What I do or don't do won't change that."

"I suppose. It's just…" She caught Dinah's hand as she opened the door. "Be careful, Dinah. Please."

The intensity in her aunt's voice startled her. "Careful of what?"

"Marc. Just be wary of Marc. There may be more to his return than he's telling you."

Dinah could think of nothing to say to that. She slipped outside, closing the door quickly.

Aunt Kate, through some instinct, seemed to know more than she'd been told. Marcus did have an agenda, and it certainly wasn't one of which Aunt Kate would approve.

Well. Dinah stood on the piazza for a moment, pulling her jacket a little tighter around her. How had Aunt Kate stumbled upon that? Had she sensed something from Dinah's reaction?

She'd tried to hide her feelings after Marc had left the previous day. This idea of his that he'd look into Annabel's death—well, it might be understandable, but she couldn't help him. She had to make him see that.

She went out the brick walk to the gate in the wrought-iron fence that enclosed Aunt Kate's house and garden. The gate, like most of the others on the street, bore a wreath of magnolia leaves in honor of the season.

She touched the shining leaves. Maybe Court would like to make one, if he was determined to observe a real Charleston Christmas. Charlestonians were justifiably proud of their Christmas decor.

Crossing the quiet street, she had to will her steps not to lag. She took the step up to the curb, facing the gate in the wrought-iron fence. Marc's gate was similar to Aunt Kate's, but the black iron was worked into the shape of a pineapple in the center—the traditional symbol of Southern hospitality.

The house beyond, like Aunt Kate's and most other old Charleston houses, was set with its side to the street, facing the small garden. According to local lore, the houses were laid out that way because in the early days of the city, home owners were taxed based on how many windows faced the street. The truth was probably that they'd been clever enough to place the piazzas to catch the breeze.

Open the gate, go up the brick walk. Her breath came a little faster now. Ridiculous, to hear her heart beating in her ears because she neared her cousin's house. She should have faced this long ago. If Aunt Kate hadn't sent her away so quickly after the tragedy—

She stopped herself. Aunt Kate had done what she thought was best when confronted with the death of one great-niece and the emotional collapse of the other. She couldn't be blamed.

Dinah had come back to Charleston as an adult. She could have gone into the house at any time, but she'd successfully avoided every invitation.

Her first instinct had been right. Marc's return would change all of them in ways she couldn't imagine.

She reached for the knocker and then paused. In the old days, she'd run in and out of Annabel's house as if it were her own. She shouldn't change things now. She grasped the brass knob, turned it and let the door swing open.

Please, help me do this. Slowly, she stepped inside.

The spacious center hallway stood empty, the renters' furniture gone with them. Weak winter sunshine through the stained-glass window on the landing cast oblongs of rose and green on the beige stair carpet. The graceful, winding staircase seemed to float upward.

The space was different, but the same. Even without Annabel's familiar furnishings, it echoed with her presence, as if at any moment she would sail through the double doors from the front parlor, silvery blond hair floating around her face, arms outstretched in welcome.

A shudder went through Dinah, and she took an involuntary step back.

"I know."

She turned. Marc stood in the doorway to the room that had once been his study. He'd exchanged the jacket and tie he'd worn the previous day for jeans and a casual ivory sweater. His eyes met hers gravely.

"I know," he said again. "I feel it, too. It's as if she's going to come through the door at any moment."

"Yes." She took a shaky breath, oddly reassured that his memories were doing the same thing to him. "I thought it would seem different to me, but it doesn't."

He moved toward her. "I thought I'd already done all my grieving." His voice roughened. "Then I found the grief was waiting here for me."

She nodded slowly. For the moment, the barriers between them didn't exist. Her throat was tight, but she forced the words out.

"I haven't been in here in ten years. I couldn't." Her voice shook a little. "Or maybe I was just a coward."

Marc grasped her shoulder in a brief, comforting touch and then took his hand away quickly, as if she might object.

"You're not a coward, Dinah. It's a natural reaction."

Ironic, that she'd just done what she'd told Aunt Kate not to do. Still, the confession of her weakness seemed to have eased the tension between them.

"What about Court? Is he having trouble with being here?"

He shook his head. "He doesn't seem affected at all. It's unnerving, somehow."

It would be. She had a foolish urge to comfort Marc. "He was only three, after all. He slept through everything. He doesn't have the memories we do."

"No." He took a deep breath, his chest rising and falling. "I'm grateful for that."

"Maybe that makes it right that you kept him away from us." She couldn't help the bitterness that traced the words.

His jaw tightened. "I thought it was best for him."

"Obviously." Unexpected anger welled up in her. Both Marc and Aunt Kate had done what they thought was best, regardless of the consequences. "Are you sorry for the pain that caused us? Or do you just not care?"

Marc looked as startled as if a piece of furniture had suddenly railed at him. His dark eyes narrowed, and she braced for an attack.

Footsteps clattered down the stairs. They both jerked around toward the stairwell.

"Hey, Dad, can I go—"

The boy stopped at the sight of her, assessing her with a frank, open gaze. She did the same. Tall for thirteen—he had his father's height, but he hadn't broadened into it yet. He had Marc's dark eyes and hair, too, and for a moment she thought there was nothing of Annabel about him.

Then he trotted down the rest of the steps and came toward her, holding out his hand. "I know who you are." He smiled, and it was Annabel's smile, reaching out to clutch her heart.

"I know who you are, too." Her voice had gotten husky, but she couldn't help that. "Welcome home, Court."

Marc still couldn't get over how quickly Dinah had bonded with his son. He finished dusting the desk he and Court had carried from the attic to his study and put his laptop on it. That's where Dinah and Court were now, happily rummaging through the attic's contents to see what should be brought down for their use over the next few weeks.

At some point, he'd have to take a turn going through the attic. The thought of what that would entail made him cringe. He hadn't sorted a thing before he left Charleston. Now the reminders of his life with Annabel waited for him.

And, as Dinah had pointed out, he should make the house look furnished if he intended it to show well to prospective buyers. That hadn't occurred to him, and he could see already that Dinah would be invaluable to him. And to Court, apparently.

Court surely couldn't remember her. He'd only been three that summer. Still, Dinah had spent a lot of time with him. Maybe, at some level, Court sensed that they already had a relationship.

He opened his briefcase and stacked files next to the computer. The vacation time he'd taken to come here had been well earned, but it was impossible to walk away completely from ongoing cases. He'd have to spend part of each day in touch with the office if he expected to make this work.

His mind kept drifting back to that summer, unrolling images he hadn't looked at in years. Annabel hadn't felt well much of the time, and she'd been only too happy to turn Court over to Dinah. Face it, Annabel had been annoyed at being pregnant again, and each symptom had been a fresh excuse to snap at him about it.

He should have been more sympathetic, and he knew that painfully well now. He'd been absorbed in prosecuting a big case and relieved to escape the tension in the house by the need to work late most evenings.

What he hadn't expected was how devoted Dinah became to Court, and how well she'd cared for him. Maybe she'd loved him so much because she'd always been alone, the only child being raised by an elderly aunt, shipped off to boarding school much of the time.

That was one thing he'd been determined not to do with Court. The boy had lost his mother, but his father had been a consistent presence in his life. He'd thought that was enough for Court, until the past few months.

"Are you stacking those files, or shredding them?" Dinah's voice startled him.

He glanced down at the files he'd unconsciously twisted in his hands. He put them down, smoothing the manila covers.

"I was thinking about something other than what I was doing. Where's Court?" He turned away from the desk, the sight of Dinah bringing an involuntary smile to his lips. "You have cobwebs in your hair."

She brushed at the mass of dark curls. "He found the boxes of Christmas ornaments, and he's busy going through them. Your attic needs some attention."

"That's just what I was thinking." He crossed to her, reaching out to pull the last wisp of cobweb from her hair. Her curls flowed through his fingers, silky and clinging. "I can't close on a sale until I clear the attic."

"I guess it has to be done." The shadow in her eyes said she knew how difficult that would be.

"Maybe you could help sort things out." There was probably every reason for her to say no to that. "There might be some things of Annabel's that you would like to keep as a remembrance. I'm sorry I didn't think of that sooner." He'd been too preoccupied with his own grief to pay sufficient heed to anyone else's.

She made a gesture that he interpreted as pushing that idea away with both hands. "I don't need anything to help me remember Annabel."

Once he'd been amused at how Dinah idolized his wife. Now he found himself wondering how healthy that had been.

"You might help me choose some things to keep for Court, then," he said smoothly. Court was probably a safe way to approach her. She'd been crazy about him when he was small, and he'd certainly returned the favor. "I remember him running down the hall full tilt, shouting 'Dinah, Dinah, Dinah.'"

A smile that was probably involuntary curved

her lips. "I remember him singing 'Someone's in the Kitchen with Dinah.' You taught him that to tease me."

They were smiling at each other then, the image clear and bright between them. He leaned forward.

"You see, Dinah. We do have something in common."

Her eyes darkened. "If anything, too much." She took a breath, as if steadying herself. "Court really wants to have Christmas here."

He nodded. He was playing dirty pool, getting at her through Court, but he'd do what he had to. Any excuse to keep her in the house might help her remember.

"A Charleston Christmas with all the trimmings." He grimaced. "Thanks to the Internet, he has a calendar of every event through to First Night. If I try to skip a thing, he'll know it."

"Blame the tourist bureau for that." Her smile flickered. "They wouldn't want to miss a single visitor."

"Anyway—" He reached out, thinking to touch her hand, and then thought better of it. "Anyway, will you help me do Christmas, Dinah? For Court's sake?"

Aunt Kate had schooled her well. No one could tell from her expression the distaste she must feel, but somehow he knew it, bone deep.

"For Court's sake," she said. Then, cautioning, she added, "But we'll have to work around my job."

"You have a job?" He couldn't help the surprise in his tone.

"Of course I have a job." Her voice contained as much of an edge as she probably ever let show. "Did you think I sat around all day eating bonbons?"

"No. Sorry." He'd better not say that he'd assumed she'd been like Annabel, doing the round of society events and charity work until she married. "I am sorry. I guess I'm still thinking of you as a schoolgirl."

"I haven't been that in a long time." She seemed to accept the excuse, but those deep violet eyes were surprisingly hard to read.

"Sorry," he said again. "So, tell me what you do."

"I'm a forensic artist. I work for the Charleston Police Department primarily, but sometimes I'm called on by neighboring jurisdictions."

He couldn't have been more surprised if she'd said she was a lion tamer, but he suspected it wasn't a good idea to show that.

"That's—"

"Surprising? Appalling? Not a suitable job for a well brought up young lady?"

Her tone surprised him into a grin. "That sounds like what Aunt Kate might say."

"Among other things." Her face relaxed. "She still has trouble with it. She doesn't think I should be exposed to—" She stopped suddenly, her smile forgotten on her face.

"To violence," he finished for her. "It's too late for that, isn't it?"

"Yes. Much too late." It sounded like an epitaph.

If she let herself think about Marc's intentions for too long, Dinah could feel panic rising inside her. She'd forced herself to hold the subject at bay but now, driving to police headquarters the next day, she took a cautious look.

How could Marc possibly expect to learn anything new after ten years? Did he really think he could find the solution that had eluded the police?

Obviously, he did. In a sense, she could understand his determination. He saw a possible harm to Court in the unanswered questions, and he'd do anything for his son.

Ten years ago he'd loved his son, of course, but he'd been so preoccupied with his work that he hadn't been as available to Court as he should have been. Apparently, after he left Charleston, he'd turned his priorities around completely. She had to admire that.

But she wasn't so sure he was right about Court. Knowing more about his mother's life was admirable, but knowing more about his mother's death could only cause pain. She should know. She'd lived with that pain for too long.

What if Marc imagined she knew something about the night Annabel died that she'd never told? Everyone else had long since accepted the fact that she hadn't seen or heard anything. The dream was just that, a dream.

But Marc tended not to accept something just because everyone else did. She remembered that about him clearly. It had made him a good prosecutor. She wasn't sure it made him a safe friend.

She pulled into a parking place near the headquarters building on Lockwood Boulevard. Across the street, the black rectangular monument to fallen officers gleamed in the winter sunshine, making her heart clench. She pushed Marc into the back closet of her mind. She'd go inside, find Tracey, and concentrate on some complicated police case instead.

She hurried inside, clipping her identification to the pocket of the blazer she wore with tan slacks. She still smiled at the memory of Detective Tracey Elliott taking one look at her the first time they'd met and telling her not to come to headquarters again looking like a debutante.

At the time, Tracey had resented having a civilian artist foisted off on her by the chief of detectives, who'd been influenced in turn by an old friend of Aunt Kate's on the city council. Dinah had never regretted using influence to get in the door. She could prove her abilities only if they gave her a chance to try.

Nodding to several detectives who'd eventually accepted her, she wove through the maze of desks and file cabinets to where Tracey sat slumped over a thick sheaf of papers.

"Good morning."

Tracey shoved one hand through disheveled red curls, her green eyes warming with welcome. "Don't tell me it's good unless you've got some decent coffee stashed in that bag of yours."

It was a long-standing joke between them. Dinah set her tote bag on the desk and lifted out two foam cups, handing one to Tracey. She sat in the chair at the side of the gray metal desk and opened hers.

Tracey inhaled, seeming to gain energy just from the fragrant aroma. "You're my hero."

"Not quite. Just a hardworking forensic artist. Do you have something for me?"

She hoped. It had been a longer than usual time between assignments, and even though she didn't have to depend on her income from her work, that occasional paycheck gave her a sense of accomplishment, validating her professional status.

Her relationship with the department was still prickly. Some officers viewed any civilian on their turf with suspicion. The fact that she produced good results with difficult witnesses didn't necessarily change that.

"I'm not sure." Tracey frowned, shoving a manila folder over to her. "We have a witness to a knifing, but she's all over the place. We know she has to have seen something, but she's not admitting it."

Dinah scanned through the file, relieved to have something to think about besides Marc. "Is it gang-related?"

"Could be, but there's something about it that doesn't fit. The victim was a sixteen-year-old—parochial schoolkid, no gang involvement. The witness is her best friend. They were on their way home from a movie and took one shortcut too many."

She nodded, registering the site of the crime. It wasn't an area where she'd walk at night, alone or with a friend.

"Will the witness talk to me?"

"That's the problem." Tracey's expression spoke of her frustration. "Yesterday she would. That's why I called you. Today she says no. She knows nothing, saw nothing. And her friend won't be going to any more movies."

The words might have sounded flippant, but Dinah knew they weren't. She and the rough-edged detective had developed a friendship that probably surprised Tracey as much as it did her, and she knew the depth of pain that any death brought Tracey.

"I'm sorry." She wanted to say more, but knew she shouldn't cross that line. "Maybe she'll change her mind. Call me anytime."

Tracey nodded but gave her a probing look. "I thought you might be too busy since your cousin-in-law is back in town."

"How on earth did you hear about that?"

"He was a suspect in an unsolved murder. Word gets around, believe me."

"He didn't kill Annabel."

Tracey raised an eyebrow. "You sure of that?"

"Of course I am."

"Nice to be sure."

She swallowed irritation. "All right, Tracey. What's this all about? Did you get me down here to talk about Marc?"

"No." She shrugged. "But you're here. I couldn't help asking what you think about Marcus Devlin's return."

The irritation faded away. Tracey was just being Tracey. She couldn't blame her for that.

"I was surprised." That was honest. "I didn't think he'd ever want to come back, because of the tragedy."

"Why did he?"

"His house has been rented all these years. The renters recently moved out, so he came to make arrangements to put it on the market."

"A good Realtor could have taken care of that for him."

"You're like a dog with a bone, you know that?"

Tracey grinned. "That makes me a good detective. Why did he really come back?"

"Because of Court. His son. My cousin's son. Court wanted to see the house before it was sold. They're staying through the holidays. Not that it's police business."

"It's an open case," Tracey said gently. "Dinah, you must know that most often, a pregnant woman is killed by a husband or boyfriend."

"Not even you can believe Marc would bring his thirteen-year-old son back to that house if he killed the boy's mother. Besides—" She stopped.

"Besides what?" Tracey prompted.

"Marc wants to find out the truth."

"I've heard that line before."

"Tracey, he didn't kill Annabel. He couldn't have."

"In that case, why does his return bother you so much?" Tracey held up her hand to stop a protest. "You're not that good at hiding your feelings."

"I was in the house that night," she said slowly. "I suppose you know that."

Tracey nodded. Of course she knew. She'd probably read all about the case before she'd ever agreed to work with Dinah.

"I don't want to have to relive the pain again. I loved Annabel. I want to protect her memory."

"Why does her memory need protecting?"

Dinah could only stare at Tracey, aghast that the words had come out of her mouth. She wasn't even conscious of thinking them, but now that she'd spoken, she knew it was true.

She wanted to protect Annabel's memory. And she didn't know why.

Chapter Three

"We need to get a big tree, Dad. One that reaches the ceiling, okay?" Court leaned forward in the back seat of Marc's car, propping his arms on the back of Dinah's seat.

Marc didn't take his eyes off the road, but Dinah saw the slight smile that touched his lips. She thought she knew what he felt—that it was good to see Court enjoying himself so much.

She'd like to think so, too, but this tree-buying trip could turn out to be a disaster. She eyed Marc. Did he really not know what he could be walking into?

"How exactly do you expect to get a tree that big back to the house?" Marc asked, as if it were the only concern on his mind.

"We can tie it on top." Court twisted to look out the side window, bouncing Dinah's seat. "Hey, is that the water over there?"

"Charleston's a peninsula—we're practically sur-rounded by water. Your dad is taking us to the Christmas tree sale via the scenic route." As far as she was concerned, the longer it took to get there, the better. "Fort Sumter is there at the mouth of the harbor. We should take the boat trip out one day while you're here."

"Cool." Court pressed his face against the glass for a better look.

His absorption in the view gave her the opportunity for a carefully worded question aimed at Marc. "Are you sure you want to go to this particular tree sale?" she said quietly. "There are several others."

Marc's jaw tightened until it resembled a block of stone. "The Alpha Club sale still benefits charity, doesn't it?"

She nodded, not wanting to verbalize her concerns within Court's hearing.

"Then that's where we're going." Marc's tone didn't leave any room for argument.

Stubborn. He had always been stubborn, and that hadn't changed. He'd been a member of the Alpha Club once and active in the civic and charitable activities of the group of young professionals. They'd been fellow attorneys, fellow Citadel graduates, movers and shakers in Charleston society. Did Marc think he'd find a welcome there now?

Her stomach clenched. She wanted to protect both him and Court from any unpleasantness, but she could hardly do that if he insisted on walking right into the lion's den.

Protect. She'd told Tracey she wanted to protect Annabel's memory. The truth probably was that she couldn't protect any of them, including herself.

Fortunately, or perhaps unfortunately, they drew up then at the parking lot that had been transformed into a Christmas tree paradise—decorated trees, garlands, lights, live trees, cut trees, trees of every shape and size. The Alpha Club did its sale in style.

"Wow." That seemed to be Court's favorite expression. He slid out of the car as soon as it stopped. "I'll find just the right one." He loped into a forest of cut trees, disappearing from sight.

Dinah got out more slowly and waited while Marc came around the car to join her. "He definitely hasn't lost his enthusiasm, has he?"

"Not at all." His smile was automatic, and she thought some other concern lay behind it. "He was asking me questions today about your family history," he said abruptly. "I tried to answer him, but I'm probably not the best source for Westlake family history."

She knew what he was looking for. "Aunt Kate is." Aunt Kate was the repository of family stories that would be lost when she was gone unless someone cared enough to hear and remember them.

"I know she doesn't want to see me." The words were clipped. "Do you think she'd talk to Court about the family?"

She could only be honest. "I don't know. I'll ask her."

"Thanks, Dinah. I appreciate it."

His hand wrapped around hers in a gesture of thanks. It lasted just for an instant. It shouldn't mean anything. It didn't mean anything. So why did she feel as if the touch surged straight to her heart?

It was nothing. A hangover from the teenage crush she'd had once. She took a breath, inhaling the crisp scents of pine and fir, and shoved her hands in her jacket pockets.

"We'd better find Court, before he picks out a twenty-foot tree."

They moved into the mass of trees. And mass of people, too. It seemed half of Charleston had chosen this evening to search for the perfect tree. Surely, in this crowd, it would be possible to find a tree and leave without encountering any of Marc's one-time friends.

They rounded a corner of the makeshift aisle through the tree display, and she saw that she'd been indulging in a futile hope. Court, pointing at a huge fir, was deep in conversation with a salesman. The man didn't need to turn for her to recognize him. And judging by the quick inhalation Marc gave, he knew him instantly as well.

He hesitated, and then he strode forward, holding out his hand. "Phillips. You're just the person I was hoping to see."

Phillips Carmody turned, peering gravely through the glasses that were such a part of his persona that Dinah couldn't imagine him without them. Then his lean face lit with a smile.

"Marc." He clasped Marc's hand eagerly. "How good to see you. It's been too long."

"It wouldn't have been so long if you'd come to Boston to see us."

So Phillips had been welcome to visit, while Annabel's family had not. Anger pricked her, and she forced it away as she approached the two men and Court, who looked on curiously, the tree forgotten for the moment.

"Phillips can't leave Charleston," she said. "The city's history would collapse without him."

She tilted her face up to receive Phillips's customary peck on the cheek. He always seemed to hesitate, as if remembering that it was no longer appropriate to pat her on the head.

"Dinah, dear, you're here, too." He focused on Court. "And so you must be Courtney. Annabel's son." His voice softened on the words. "I'm Phillips Carmody, one of your father's oldest friends."

Court shook hands. "I'm happy to meet you, sir." He gave the smile that was so like Annabel's, and she thought Phillips started a bit. It came as a shock to him, probably, as it had to her.

"How long are you staying?" Phillips glanced at Marc. "I heard you were putting the house on the market."

"I see the grapevine is still active." Marc seemed to relax in Phillips's company, his smile coming more easily now.

Dinah felt some of her tension dissipate as the men talked easily. It looked as if her fears had been foolish.

Marc had handed over a shocking amount of money and they'd negotiated when the tree would be delivered when the interruption came.

"Phillips! What are you doing?"

Dinah didn't have to turn to know who was there. Margo Carmody had an unmistakable voice—sugar-coated acid, Annabel had always said. How someone as sweet as Phillips ended up married to a woman like that was one of life's mysteries.

Dinah pinned a smile to her face and turned. "Hello, Margo. Are you working the sale as well?"

Margo ignored her, the breach in etiquette announcing how upset she was. Margo never ignored the niceties of polite society. Except, apparently, when confronted by a man her acid tongue had proclaimed a murderer.

"Look who's here, my dear." Nervousness threaded Phillips's voice. "It's Marcus. And his son, Courtney."

Margo managed to avoid eye contact with both of them. "You're needed back at the cash desk, Phillips. Come along, now." She turned and stalked away, leaving an awkward silence behind.

"I'm sorry." Faint color stained Phillips's cheeks. "I'm afraid I must go. Perhaps I'll see you again while you're here. It was nice to meet you, Court." He scuttled away before Dinah could give in to the temptation to shake him.

"That woman gets more obnoxious every year." She could only hope Court would believe Margo's actions were motivated by general rudeness and not aimed at them. "How Phillips stands her, I don't know."

"He seems to come to heel when she snaps her fingers." Marc's dry tone was probably intended to hide the pain he must feel.

"Would you expect anything else?" The voice came from behind her.

Dinah turned. Not James Harwood. It was really too much that they'd run into both of the men who'd been Marc's closest friends in the same night. Still, James and Phillips ran in identical social circles, and they were both mainstays of the Alpha Club, regulars at the elegant old building that graced a corner of Market Street near The Battery.

"Hello, James." This time Marc didn't bother to offer his hand. It was clear from the coldness on James's face that it wouldn't be taken.

"James, I—" A lady always smoothes over awkward situations. That was one of Aunt Kate's favorite maxims, but Dinah couldn't think of a thing to say.

"You shouldn't have come back." James bit off the words. "You're not welcome here."

Court took a step closer to his father. The hurt in his eyes cut Dinah to the heart. Court shouldn't have to hear things like that. Marc should have realized what might happen when he brought him here.

"I'm sorry you feel that way." Marc's tone was cool, the voice of a man meeting rudeness with calm courtesy. But a muscle in his jaw twitched as if he'd like to hit something. Or someone.

"I think we're ready to leave now." She'd better intervene before they both forgot themselves. "We have what we came for, don't we, Court?"

Politeness required that Court turn to her, and she linked her arm with his casually. "Ready, Marc?"

Please. Don't make matters worse by getting into a quarrel with James. It's not worth it.

Whether he sensed her plea or not, she didn't know. He flexed his hands, and she held her breath. Then he turned and walked steadily toward the car.

* * *

"Hey, wouldn't it look cool if we strung lights along the banister?" Court, standing halfway up the staircase, looked down.

Struck by a sudden flicker of resemblance to Annabel in his son's face, Marc couldn't answer for a moment. Then he managed a smile.

"Sounds great. What do you think?"

He turned to Dinah, who was dusting off the stack of ornament boxes they'd just carried down from the attic. In jeans and a faded College of Charleston sweatshirt, her dark curls pulled back in a loose ponytail, she looked little older than the sixteen-year-old he remembered.

She straightened, frowning at the stairwell. "What do you think of twining lights with an evergreen swag along the railing? I think I remember several swags in a plastic bag in the attic."

"I'll go see." Court galloped up the steps, managing to raise a few stray dust motes that danced in the late-afternoon light. A thud announced that he'd arrived at the attic door.

Marc winced. "Sorry. Court doesn't do much of anything quietly."

"I'd be worried about him if he did." Dinah glanced up the stairwell, as if following Court in her mind's eye. "At least he's not showing any signs that being here bothers him. And if he's not upset after what happened last night—"

"I know. I guess I haven't said you were right, but

you were. We should have gone somewhere else for the tree."

"I wish I hadn't been right." Her face was warm with sympathy.

Maybe it was the sympathy that led him to say more than he intended. "I expected antagonism from Margo. She never liked Phil's friendship with me, and she and Annabel were like oil and water."

"I remember." Dinah's smile flickered. "Annabel had a few uncomplimentary names for her."

"Which she shouldn't have said in front of you." He ran a hand through his hair. "Margo doesn't matter. But Phil and James—"

He stopped. No use going over it again. No use remembering when the three of them had been the three musketeers, back in their Citadel days. He'd thought the bonds they'd formed then were strong enough to survive anything. Obviously he'd been wrong.

"Phillips is still your friend. He's just not brave enough to stand up to Margo. He never has been."

"Maybe." He'd grant her Phil, and his patent knuckling under to the woman he'd married. But… "James thinks I killed Annabel." He checked the stairwell, but Court was still safely out of hearing, rummaging in the attic.

Dinah started to say something. Then she closed her mouth. It didn't matter. Her expressive face said it for her.

"You think I should have been prepared for that. You tried to warn me."

"I thought it might be awkward. I didn't expect out-right rudeness."

She sounded as primly shocked as Aunt Kate might have, and he couldn't suppress a smile.

"You don't need to laugh at me," she said tartly. "They were all brought up to know better."

"Next you'll say that their mothers would be ashamed of them."

"Well, they would." She snapped the words, but her lips twitched a little. "Oh, all right. We're hopelessly old-fashioned here. I suppose James has been in poli-tics too long to have much sense left. And besides, you know how he felt about Annabel."

That startled him. "Do I?"

She blinked. "Everyone knows he was crazy about her."

"I didn't." Had he been hopelessly stupid about his own wife? "How did Annabel feel about him?"

"Oh, Marc." Dinah's eyes filled with dismay. "Don't think that. It never meant anything. Just a crush on his part."

"And Annabel?" Dinah wanted him to let it go, but he couldn't.

"Annabel never had eyes for anyone but you. She just—I think she was flattered by James's attention. That was all. Honestly."

She looked so upset at having told him that he didn't have the heart to ask anything else. But he filed it away for further thought.

He bent to pick up the stack of boxes. "We may as well take these to the family room. If I know my son, he'll drag everything out, but he won't be as good about putting things away."

Dinah went ahead of him to open the door to what would be the back parlor in most Charleston homes. They'd always used it as a family room, and he and Court had managed to bring down most of the furniture that belonged here. By tacit agreement, they'd avoided the front parlor, the room where Annabel died.

"Court looks so much like you. Looking at him must be like looking at a photo of you at that age."

He set the boxes down on the wooden coffee table that had been a barn door before an enterprising Charleston artisan had transformed it. "Funny. I was thinking that I saw a little of Annabel in his face when he looked down from the stairs."

"I know." Her voice softened, and he realized he hadn't done a good enough job of hiding his feelings. "I see it, too—just certain flashes of expression."

He sank onto the brown leather couch and frowned absently at the tree they'd set up in the corner. He'd told Court it would be too big for the room. The top brushed the ceiling, and he'd have to trim it before the treetop angel would fit.

"Maybe it's because we're back here. My memory of Annabel had become a kind of still photo, and she was never that."

"No, she wasn't." Dinah perched on the coffee table, her heart-shaped face pensive. "I've never known anyone as full of life as she was. Maybe that's why I admired her. She was so fearless, while I—" She grimaced. "I always was such a chicken."

"Don't say that about yourself." He leaned forward almost involuntarily to touch her hand. "You've been through some very bad times and come out strong and whole. That's something to be proud of."

"I'm not so sure about that, but thank you."

For a moment they were motionless. It was dusk outside already, and he could see their reflections in the glass of the French door, superimposed on the shadowy garden.

He leaned back, not wanting to push too hard. "Being back in the house again—has it made you think any more about what happened?"

"No." The negative came sharp and quick, and she crossed her arms, as if to protect herself. "I don't remember anything about that night."

"That summer, then. There might have been something you noticed that I didn't."

She shook her head. "Do you think I didn't go over it a thousand times in my mind? There was nothing."

And if there was, he suspected it was buried too deeply to be reached willingly. Dinah had protected herself the only way she could.

He'd try another tack. "You're connected with the police. If there's any inside information floating around, people might be more willing to talk to you than to me."

Dinah stared at him, eyes huge. "Someone already talked to me. About you."

"Who?" Whatever had been said clearly had upset her.

"A detective I work with."

He was going to have to drag the words out of her. "What did he say?"

"She. She said…"

He could see the movement of her neck as she swallowed.

"She reminded me that the case is still open. And that you're still a suspect."

He should have realized. He, of all people, knew how the police mind-set worked. And this detective, whoever she was, wanted to protect one of their own. Wanted to warn her off, probably, too.

"Dinah, I'm sorry."

"For what?"

"I didn't think. I've put you in an untenable position. I shouldn't have. If you want to back off…" He shook his head. "Of course you do. I'll make some excuse to Court."

As if he'd heard his name, Court came into the room, arms filled with evergreen swags. "I found them," he announced happily. "But we don't have nearly enough lights, Dad. We need to go get some more before we can do this. Want to come, Dinah?"

She stood, smiling at Court. "You two go." She glanced at Marc, the smile stiffening a little. "I'll unpack the ornaments while you're out. I'll be here when you get back."

He understood the implication. She wasn't going to run out on them, although she had every reason to do so. He felt a wave of relief that was ridiculously inappropriate.

"Thank you, Dinah."

* * *

Was she crazy? Dinah listened as the front door clicked shut behind Marc and Court. Marc had understood. Or at least he'd understood the spot he'd put her in professionally, if not personally. He'd given her the perfect out, and she hadn't taken it.

She couldn't. She may as well face that fact, at least. No matter how much she might want to stay away from Marc and all the bitter reminders, too many factors combined to force her to stay.

She'd been thirteen when he married Annabel, the same age Court was now. With no particular reason to, he'd been kind to her, putting up with her presence when he'd probably have preferred to be alone with his bride, inviting her to the beach house at Sullivan's Island, even teaching her to play tennis. She'd told herself she didn't owe Marc anything, but she did.

And Annabel—how much more she owed Annabel, her bright, beautiful cousin. She'd loved her with a passion that might otherwise have been expended on parents, siblings, cousins her own age. Since she didn't have any of them, it all went to Annabel.

Finally there was Court. Her lips curved in a smile, and she bent to take the cover off the first box of ornaments. Court had stolen her heart again, just as he had the first time she'd seen him staring at her with unfocused infant eyes when he was a few days old.

Whatever it cost her, she couldn't walk away from this. All her instincts told her Marc was wrong in what he wanted to do, but she couldn't walk away.

She began unpacking the boxes, setting the ornaments on the drop-leaf table near the tree. They were an odd mix—some spare, sophisticated glass balls that Annabel had bought, but lots of delicate, old-fashioned ornaments that had been in the family for generations.

One tissue-wrapped orb felt heavy in her hand, and an odd sense of recognition went through her. She knew what it was even before she unwrapped it—an old, green glass fisherman's weight that she'd found in an antique shop on King Street and given to Annabel for Christmas the year before she died.

For a moment she held the glass globe in her hand. The lamplight, falling on it, reflected a distorted image of her own face, and the glass felt warm against her palm. She was smiling, she realized, but there were tears in her eyes.

She set the ball carefully on the table. She'd tell Court about the ornaments, including that one. That kind of history was what he needed from this Christmas in Charleston.

She'd been working in silence, with only an occasional crackle from a log in the fireplace for company, when she heard a thud somewhere in the house. She paused, her hand tightening on a delicate shell ornament. They hadn't come back already, had they?

A few quiet steps took her to the hallway. Only one light burned there, and the shadows had crept in, unnoticed. She stood still, hearing nothing but the beat of her own heart.

Then it came again, a faint, distant creaking this time. She'd lived in old houses all her life. They had

their own language of creaks and groans as they settled. That had to be what she'd heard.

She listened another moment. Nothing. She was letting her nerves get the better of her at being alone in
the house.

A shrill sound broke the silence, and she started,
heart hammering. Then, realizing what it was, she
shook her head at her own foolishness and went in
search of her cell phone, its ring drowning out any
other noise. Marc hadn't had the phone service started.
She'd given him her cell-phone number in case he
needed to reach her.

The phone was in the bottom of her bag, which she
finally found behind the sofa in the family room. She
snatched it up and pressed the button.

"Hello?" Her voice came out oddly breathless.

"Dinah? You sound as if you've been running. Listen, do you think a string of a hundred white lights
is enough? Court put two strings in the cart when I
wasn't looking."

Her laugh was a little shaky. "You may as well get
two. If you don't use the second one, you can always
take it back."

"I guess you're right." She heard him say something distantly, apparently to the cashier. Then his voice
came back, warm and strong in her ear. "Is everything
all right? You don't sound quite yourself."

"It's nothing. Really. I was just scaring myself,
thinking I heard someone in the house." When she
said the words, she realized that was what she'd been
thinking at some deep level. Someone in the house.

"Get out. Now." The demand was sharp and fast as the crack of a whip.

"I'm sure I just imagined—"

"Dinah, don't argue. Just get out. And don't hang up. Keep talking to me."

Logic told her he was panicking unnecessarily, probably visited by the terrible memory of coming into the house and finding Annabel. But even if he was, his panic was contagious.

Holding the phone clutched tightly against her ear, she raced across the room, through the hallway and plunged out the door.

Chapter Four

Dinah slid back on the leather couch in the family room, cradling a mug of hot chocolate between her palms, and looked at Court. He'd collapsed on the couch next to her into that oddly boneless slouch achieved only, as far as she could tell, by adolescent boys. His mug was balanced precariously on his stomach.

"More cocoa?"

He shook his head, the mug wavering at the movement. "I'm okay." He watched her from under lowered lids. "How about you? You feeling okay? Anything you want?"

He was attempting to take care of her, obviously. The thought sent a rush of tenderness through her. She tried to keep the feeling from showing in her face. He wouldn't appreciate that when he was trying so hard to be nonchalant about the prospect of an intruder in the house.

Marc's footsteps sounded, far above them. He was

searching the attic, probably. She was convinced he wouldn't find anything. She'd simply overreacted to being in the house alone, and, in turn, he'd overreacted. There'd been no one in the house.

It was probably best not to talk to Court about that. She nodded toward the bare tree, propped in its stand in the corner. "Do you always have a big tree at home?"

The corner of his mouth twitched, making him look very like his father. "Not big enough. We have a town house. It's plenty big enough for the two of us, but Dad always says there's not room for a big tree." He sent a satisfied glance toward the tree. "This is more like it."

"Aunt Kate—well, I guess she's actually your great-grand-aunt—hasn't had a real tree since I grew up. She's content with a little artificial one on a table."

Court's great-grand-aunt. Aunt Kate had to be made to see that she must talk with Court about his ancestors. She didn't have to discuss his mother, if she didn't want to, but she couldn't deny a relationship with the boy.

"Yeah, that's what my grandma and granddad do, too. They say real trees are too expensive in Arizona, anyway."

"Do you see them much?" Marc's parents had left Charleston within a year of Annabel's death, moving to Arizona supposedly for his mother's health. It might have been that, of course, but she doubted it. Did they feel they were living in exile?

"We were out for Thanksgiving." Court maneuvered himself upright, letting the mug tip nearly to the point of no return before grasping it. "Maybe I should go see if Dad needs any help."

"I don't think—"

"Dad doesn't." Marc came in on the words. "Everything's fine."

Dinah sensed some reservation behind the words, and her stomach tightened. There was something he didn't want to say in front of Court.

"You sure? I could check the cellar." Court obviously considered that he should have been included in the search.

"Already done." Marc glanced at his watch. "If you want to email your buddies before we call it a night, you'd better go do it."

"How about the tree? I thought we were going to decorate."

"Tomorrow's time enough for that. Dinah has to go home."

"Okay, okay," he grumbled, but went toward the door. "You'll help tomorrow, won't you, Dinah?"

She was absurdly pleased that he wanted her. "I have to go into work in the morning, but I'll come and help in the afternoon."

Court lifted an eyebrow in Marc's characteristic expression. "I wouldn't mind seeing police headquarters, you know."

"Dinah's going to work, not giving tours." Marc gave him a gentle shove. "Go on, and don't stay online too late. I'm walking Dinah home."

Court disappeared across the hall, raising his hand in a quick goodbye. Dinah waited until the office door closed behind him.

"Did you find anything?"

"Nothing to take to the police." His level brows drew down. "Anyone could have popped the back door with a screwdriver, though. I blocked it tonight with a two by four, but I'll put a new lock on tomorrow." He picked up her jacket, holding it for her. "Come on. I'll walk you home."

"That's not necessary." She slid her arms into the jacket. He adjusted it and then clasped her shoulders.

"Maybe not, but I'm going to."

The sense of being protected and taken care of was entirely too tempting. But she wasn't the little cousin any longer. She was a big girl now. She took a deliberate step away, putting some space between them.

"You're overreacting. All that was wrong was a creaking old house and my overactive imagination. There was no need for you to come rushing back here like a…a superhero, out to rescue the damsel in distress."

"Is that what I did?" His face had gone still.

"Yes." Marc had to understand that their relationship had changed. They were never going back to the way things had been between them. "I didn't need rescuing."

He frowned at her for a long moment. Then he seemed to come to a decision. He pulled something from his pocket and held it out to her.

"Probably you're right. But I didn't feel like taking it for granted after reading that."

She smoothed out the crumpled sheet of yellow tablet paper. The message on it was printed in pencil, in block letters. It informed Marc, with the embellishment of considerable profanity, that he was a killer and that he would be punished.

She resisted the urge to drop it and scrub her hands. "Where did you get it?"

"It was shoved in the mailbox sometime today. Luckily I found it, not Court."

"In the mailbox—not mailed?"

"No." His expression became grimmer, if that was possible. "That means the author of that missive was on my veranda today. If I overreacted when you thought someone was in the house, I had good reason."

"I guess I would have, too. But people who write anonymous notes don't usually act on them."

"Is that the police consultant speaking?" He shook his head, taking the paper back and tucking it into his pocket. "Sorry. I know you mean well. I know what you say is true. But it's not easy to be rational when—"

She knew what he was going to say. "When someone you love has been killed in this house."

He gave her a baffled, angry look. "Exactly. Irrational or not, that's what I felt. And maybe it's not so irrational. The person who killed Annabel is still out there, remember?"

"I'm not likely to forget. But if he has any brains at all, he'll stay as far away from you as possible."

"Maybe so. Still, I'm not taking any chances. So tomorrow I'll put a new lock on the back door. And tonight I'll walk you home."

There was more that she wanted to say, but she didn't think he was in the mood to hear it. So she went ahead of him to the front door, stepping out onto the piazza where she'd fled so precipitously earlier, listening to him lock the door carefully.

The air was chilly, and she stuffed her hands into her pockets. A full moon rode low in the sky, sending spidery shadows across the walk. She heard Marc's footsteps behind her, and he reached out to push the gate open when she reached it.

She paused on the walk. "You could just watch me to my door, you know."

"I could. But I'm not going to." He slid his hand into the crook of her arm.

The street was still and deserted. She glanced up at him as they crossed. "Are you sure you want to stay, after all this?"

"Court would never agree to leave now. And I keep my promises to my son. Besides—"

He paused, and she couldn't make out his expression in the moonlight.

"Besides?"

He shrugged. "I told you. Now that I'm here, I know I can't go back to being content with the status quo." His fingers tightened on her arm, and she felt his determination through their pressure. "Do you know why I went into a private firm when we moved away?"

The change of subject bewildered her. "Well, I suppose I thought you wanted a change. Or to make more than you could as a prosecutor."

"There's certainly that." There was a certain grim humor to his tone. "I've done far better financially. But that's not why. I went into a firm because no prosecutor's office or state's attorney's office would have me. Not with the shadow of my wife's murder hanging over me."

The bitterness in his tone forbade any facile answer. For a moment she couldn't say anything at all.

"I'm sorry," she said finally. "I didn't realize. I should have." She hesitated, feeling her way. "I guess I've continued to look at what happened then as if I were still sixteen."

"You're not sixteen anymore." They'd reached the gate, and he opened it for her. "Now you can face what happened as an adult."

Marc sounded very sure of that, and he didn't seem to expect a response. That was just as well, because she wasn't sure she could give one.

"Good night, Marc."

He nodded. "Sleep well."

She doubted that. She very much doubted it.

Marc wasn't sure how long it had been since he'd seen his son so thoroughly happy, so completely unclouded. Since before he'd started asking questions about his mother, probably.

"But Dad—" Court hung over the stair railing, looking ready to take flight. "Some colored lights along the porch would look really cool."

"Piazza, not porch." Nobody had a piazza in Boston, and the old Charleston term had come back to him.

"Piazza, then. We could get the kind that blink."

Much as he liked seeing Court happy, he had to draw the line somewhere. The decorating was getting out of hand.

"I'm afraid not." Dinah intervened before he could come up with a way to nix blinking lights. "There are regulations on the types of decorations you can have on houses in the historic district. No blinking lights." She smiled up at Court from where she sat on the floor, attaching the bottom of the garland around the newel post. "There should be a crèche somewhere in the attic. It was your mother's when she was a little girl."

That was all Court needed to hear. "Good deal." He galloped up the stairs.

"Thanks, Dinah." He hooked the garland on the small nail under the railing. "I don't know what he'd have come up with next."

"Reindeer on the roof, probably." She smiled, but her eyes seemed shadowed, somehow. She turned away, as if she felt his gaze, dark hair sweeping down to hide her face.

"Probably," he agreed. He focused on the garland. "Is it bothering you? Being here?"

"Not at all." The response came too quickly.

"Something's wrong." He leaned his elbow on the newel post, looking down at her. "Can't you tell me what?"

She stretched, slim shoulders moving under the deep purple sweater she wore. "It's work. You wouldn't be interested."

"I would definitely be interested," he said. "Come on, talk." He still had trouble picturing Dinah in a police setting. A cotillion, yes. Police headquarters, no.

"Tracey Elliott is a detective who often calls on me. She's working a case where a young girl was killed.

The only witness is her friend, a girl only a couple of years older than Court." She shook her head. "I have to struggle for my detachment every time I'm called in, but this one—" She shrugged expressively. "It's hard."

"Can't someone else take this case?" The instinct he had to protect her was probably ridiculous. She wouldn't thank him for it.

She stiffened. "It's my job. I don't want anyone else to take it. Besides, it's going to sound conceited, but I can do this if anyone can. She'd shut down completely for a uniformed officer with a computer identification kit."

"I guess I can see that." Naturally a scared, traumatized teenager would rather talk to someone like Dinah. "Are you getting anywhere with her?"

"She keeps backing away, insisting she didn't see anything. But the evidence shows that she had to have witnessed the crime. So we keep trying. She's agreed to see me again tomorrow morning."

"And that makes you tense." He was still trying to get at the cause for the shadow in her eyes.

"Doing it is hard. But it's worth it if I get something that leads them to a killer, don't you think?"

She looked up at him, dark curls flowing away from her heart-shaped face, and he was struck by several feelings at once. That Dinah had grown into a woman to admire, doing something important, and that he was stuck in a job that, however rewarding financially, didn't measure up to his dreams.

"Yes, I guess it is."

Dinah stood, her hands full of strings of lights.

"We'd better get on with this, or Court will think we're not doing our share."

He went onto the first step. "Just feed the lights up to me, and I'll attach them. By the way, I almost forgot to tell you. Remember Glory Morgan?"

"Of course. She was your housekeeper. I run into her once in a while."

"She's agreed to come in and work a few days a week while we're here. I thought that would be a help in getting the house ready to sell."

"I see." Her brows arched. "Are you sure that's your only reason?"

She was entirely too quick. "You know, there's something to be said for not jumping to conclusions."

"I'm a grown-up now, remember? You're hoping that having Glory here will somehow help you. But if Glory knew anything, she'd have talked long ago. She's as honest and forthright as they come."

"She'd have told anything she knew about Annabel's death. I'm hoping there may be something else, something that happened that summer that will give me a lead. The police would have found anything obvious. I'm looking for something that's not obvious."

Dinah nodded. "I guess I understand, but I'm not sure anything will come of it. Still, it'll be worth having Glory here just to taste her corn bread again."

"She'll give Court a taste of some real Charleston cooking, that's for sure. Maybe I ought to look up the yardman, too. I don't suppose you remember him. Jasper Carr."

"I remember him. Annabel didn't like him."

For an instant it didn't register. Then he looked down at her. She was busy with the lights, and she'd spoken almost absently.

Careful. Don't scare the memory away.

"What makes you say that she didn't like him?"

Apparently he hadn't been casual enough with the question, because Dinah looked up, her eyes wide. "I don't know. I don't know why I said that."

Don't rush her. "You must have noticed something Annabel said or did that showed you she didn't like him."

He tried to say it easily, not to let too much interest show in his voice. This was what he'd hoped, that Dinah would remember something no one else had noticed about that summer.

She sat back on her heels, the lights forgotten in her lap. Her dark eyes seemed to be looking far away. No, far inward would be more accurate.

"Annabel came in from the garden. She'd gone out to pick some flowers for the table. She said something like, 'That Carr. Marc should get rid of him. I don't like the way he sneaks around.'" She blinked, then focused on him. "Didn't she ever tell you that?"

"Not that I can remember."

"Well, maybe she didn't want to bother you. You had that big case going on and you were out most of the time."

He'd been out most of the time. Dinah said it in a matter-of-fact way. She wasn't accusing him.

But he accused himself. He hadn't been there. He'd

been too wrapped up in his work to notice what was happening in his own house.

"Marc, what's wrong?" Dinah stood, her hand on the banister. "Do you think Carr had something to do with Annabel's death?"

"He wasn't the person I was thinking of. I don't think the police paid much attention to him. There didn't seem any reason to."

"The fact that Annabel didn't like him isn't a reason for murder."

"No, it's not. But that may not be all there was to it. She didn't say anything else about him to you?"

Dinah shook her head. "What are you going to do?"

"I think I'll have a talk with Glory about Carr. Annabel may have said something to her." He put his hand over hers on the railing. "Thanks, Dinah. You've given me something to look into, at any rate."

She was frowning. "What did you mean when you said Carr wasn't the person you were thinking of?"

He hadn't intended to tell her, but maybe she had the right to know. He'd already involved her more than he'd intended. "There was someone else. Someone I'd prosecuted who'd made threats. His name was Leonard Hassert."

"But if you prosecuted him, wasn't he in prison?"

"He should have been. They let him out early—good behavior, so they said." Bitterness rose like bile. Hassert shouldn't have been running around loose.

"Surely the police investigated him."

"They checked him out. He had an alibi. Three people were prepared to swear he couldn't have been any-where near here that night."

"But if so—"

"People do lie, Dinah." His tone was gently mock-ing. "I'm not satisfied, even if the police were. I think it all bears looking at again."

"I suppose so." Her hand closed on his. "But—"

"Hey, aren't you done with those lights yet?" Court's voice sounded from above them. Marc looked up, to see his son hanging over the railing.

"We're working on it."

Dinah snatched her hand free. "Do you think we've been loafing? We'll be finished in a jiffy. I'll take the lights up to the top and work my way down."

She darted past him up the stairs. Uneasiness moved through him at the sight.

"You don't need to…" he began.

Dinah turned, the string of lights in her hand. The smile ebbed from her face, like sand washed by the outgoing tide. She looked down, toward the hall, her fair skin paling. She grabbed the railing.

He reached her in a millisecond. He hadn't thought. He'd been stupid. "Dinah, are you all right?"

She took a breath and straightened, her hand falling away from the railing. "I'm fine." Her gaze evaded his. "Let's get this finished."

"Right. We will." He took the string of lights from her. "You go down and tell me if I'm getting them even, okay?" It was the only thing he could think of to get her off the stairs without Court noticing anything.

She nodded and went on down the steps. It must have taken an effort not to hurry.

He wanted her to remember. But in his need to know, he hadn't thought about what remembering might do to Dinah.

Chapter Five

Dinah sat bolt upright in bed, a cry strangled in her throat. She clapped her hand over her mouth. Had she actually cried out, or had it been only in the dream?

No, not dream. Nightmare. Shivering, she clutched the quilt around her. She was cold and perspiring at the same time, her heart still pounding with remembered fear.

Breathe in, breathe out. Concentrate on your breath, let your pulse slow, your heartbeat steady. How could a mere dream, a product of the mind, produce such violent physical symptoms? She couldn't have been more terrified if she'd been in actual danger.

She drew her knees up and wrapped her arms around them. The soft, much-washed cotton of the quilt was as soothing as her mother's caress. She was all right. She was safe in the room that had been hers since she'd come to live with Aunt Kate when she was nine. The double-wedding-ring quilt had been her mother's; the sleigh bed had been her father's.

She looked automatically toward the bedside table. It was too dark to make out their features in the silver-framed photograph, but she didn't need the light. She knew how they looked—always young, always laughing, always holding each other—the way they'd looked before Hurricane Hugo tore apart all their lives.

She plucked the robe she'd left across the bottom of the bed, pulling it around her as she slid from the cocoon of covers. Her toes curled into the hooked rug that lay over the polished heart of pine floor, the touch grounding her.

She was all right. She wasn't trapped in the dream, standing on the staircase in Marc and Annabel's house, looking down at the dimly lit hallway. Seeing the sliver of light from the front parlor, hearing angry voices, being afraid without knowing why.

A shudder went through her, and she gritted her teeth until it faded. She always woke from the dream at that moment. She never saw the rest of it, but maybe that was God's providence, protecting her from something too terrible to be borne.

She knew how the story ended, in any event. It ended with Annabel, her beautiful cousin Annabel, dead on the floor in front of the Adam fireplace in her elegant parlor.

She took another long, shaky breath and crossed the room. Her eyes were growing accustomed to the dimness, touching one familiar object after another. Aunt Kate had created this space for her when she took Dinah in, seeming happy to trade the peace and comfort of an elderly spinster's quiet existence for the trials of raising a distraught, grief-stricken child.

Reaching the window, Dinah slid down to her knees, pushing up the sash so that she could prop her elbows on the low, wide sill. The chill night air touched her face. The quiet, dark street slept. She was twenty-six, not sixteen, and she wasn't afraid.

Marc's house slept, too. For ten years it had been rented to a busy professional couple whose brisk lives and genteel parties had routed any shadows left from the tragedy that happened there. Still, despite repeated invitations, she'd avoided going inside. She'd thought she'd been doing the right thing, dealing with her grief in her own way. Instead she'd just been delaying the inevitable.

It didn't take too much effort to figure out what had brought on the nightmare tonight. That moment when she'd run heedlessly up the stairs and then turned—

Her heart was thudding again, and she took another deep breath, forcing herself to be calm. She would not relive that moment, staring down at the hallway, feeling her vision darken as her ten-years-younger self filled her mind.

Marc had known, of course. She couldn't miss the pity in his face when he'd reached her, made an excuse to get her off the stairs.

A little flare of anger went through her. Why should he pity her? It was his idea, after all. He wanted her to remember.

I can't remember, Father. I don't know anything. Why can't he understand that?

If I did know anything—

Her mind backed away from that thought. She didn't. She didn't.

She covered her face with her palms. Even in prayer, she couldn't go that deeply.

You know. She pressed down the welling tide of panic. *You understand, Father. This is how I cope. Isn't it going to be enough?*

Maybe not.

She rose slowly, stretching cramped muscles. From the bedroom alcove, a light blinked on her computer. Copies of the forensic drawings she'd done were stacked neatly on her desk, next to the case with her sketching materials, ready to go at a moment's notice.

Ironic, wasn't it? Her sketches had helped crime victims deal with their traumatic memories, but she could do nothing about her own.

A wave of revulsion went through her. She didn't want to do anything with her own. She wanted to bury them so deeply she'd never think of them again.

Please, Lord. She passed the oval-framed mirror, a pale ghost in her white nightshirt, and climbed back into bed. *Please let me forget.*

Trying not to think about what was crunching under her feet, Dinah climbed the stairs of the run-down tenement. Tracey forged ahead of her, seeming to be unaffected by the dirt and the smells.

"Do you think the girl will actually go through with it this time?" Dinah didn't really need an answer, but the distraction of hearing Tracey's voice might keep her from tensing up too much as she approached the interview.

"We live in hope." But nothing about Tracey's expression, as she glanced back, suggested hope. Tracey had her game face on. Maybe that was how she coped with what they were about to do.

"You're sure she must have seen something?" She made it a question, although she knew the answer.

"Positive. There's no way she stood where she says she did and didn't see the attacker." Tracey's expression softened slightly. "Poor kid. She's immature for a fifteen-year-old. This is going to make her grow up fast."

"Too fast." She knew only too well that experience. It had been hers.

Tracey stopped in front of a door and rapped. "Here we go. Are you ready?"

She nodded, wishing her stomach didn't tie into knots each time she did this. But if it didn't, that might mean she had hardened herself to the victim's pain, and she never wanted to reach that point.

In comparison to the filthy hallway, the inside of the small apartment was almost painfully clean. A threadbare rug covered the floor in the living room area, with flimsy modern furniture placed carefully on it. A large television sat on a metal stand in the corner, and the end tables bore identical vases of plastic flowers atop white doilies.

The girl's mother ushered them inside, almost wringing her hands in anxiety. Tracey had prepped the woman, so she knew to leave them alone with her daughter.

Dinah scanned the living area. "The kitchen table will be best," she murmured to Tracey, who nodded. Tracey understood that putting a physical barrier like a table between Dinah and the victim would help to make the girl feel safe.

Talking reassuringly, Tracey walked the mother toward what must be a bedroom, while the girl came reluctantly toward Dinah.

So young—that was all Dinah could think. With her parochial school uniform, thick dark braids and slight, undeveloped figure, she looked like a child.

"It's nice to see you, Teresa." Dinah slid onto one of the kitchen chairs, gesturing toward the seat across from her. "I'm Dinah."

Thin lips set in a straight line, dark eyes avoiding contact, the girl nodded and sat down, folding her arms. Behind the girl, Tracey moved quietly to a chair in the far corner of the room, out of Teresa's line of sight.

It wasn't going to be easy. Everything about Teresa screamed that she wasn't going to cooperate. Tracey knew that as well as she did. Still, they had to try.

She looked around for something to serve as a conversation starter. Three framed school photos hung on the wall behind Teresa—a different Teresa, smiling and eager, a smaller sister with a gap-toothed smile, an older brother, doing his best to look serious in his school blazer and tie.

"I see your mother has your latest school pictures up. My mom always did that, too."

Teresa's shoulders moved in a shrug that could mean anything.

"What are your brother's and sister's names?"

"Margaret. And Joseph." Her mouth clamped shut again.

Clearly small talk was out. Dinah fingered the drawing pad and pencil on her lap, out of Teresa's sight. She might not have a chance to use it.

"Teresa, I'd like to go back to the morning of that day. Will you do that for me?"

A nod.

"Okay, let's start with breakfast. Do you remember what you had to eat?"

They'd have to do this slowly. Taking the witness through the day, letting her recall nonfrightening events, sometimes helped to put her at ease.

Keeping her voice soft and her questions unobtrusive, she led Teresa through the events of the day— breakfast with her family, walking to school with her little sister, classes, lunch.

She didn't look at Tracey, knowing she could count on Tracey not to interrupt. Tracey understood the process, unlike many officers. Teresa had to be led gently to remember, not to guess at eye color or nose shape. This couldn't be rushed, and the wrong question could send them back to square one, perhaps contaminating the memory beyond any hope of accuracy.

Teresa closed her eyes occasionally to visualize what the teacher wrote on the board, what she'd taken from the lunch counter. She glanced to the left, signaling that she was using the remembering part of her brain.

Good. Dinah was there with her, taking a scoop of

macaroni and cheese, looking around the lunchroom
for a friend. Sitting down with Jessica, who only had
hours left to live.

Through supper, the movie, what they talked about
as they came out of the theater. Teresa was tensing now,
and it was hard not to tense with her. Trauma engraved
the scene on the victim's mind, but it also made access-
ing it wrenching and painful.

"You turned into the alley," she said gently. "Tell
me what you saw."

"Dark." Teresa's neck muscles worked, her breathing growing heavy. She crossed her arms, protecting
herself. "It was dark. I couldn't see."

She felt, rather than saw, the sharpening of Tracey's
attention. The alley hadn't been dark. If it had, the girls
probably wouldn't have turned into it. But a streetlight
overhung it, making it look safe.

"Teresa—"

"No!" She shot out of the chair so abruptly that it
toppled over. "I didn't see anything! I didn't!" Bursting
into tears, she ran from the room. The bedroom door
slammed, shuddering from the impact.

"Well." Tracey's eyebrows lifted. "I guess there's
nothing on your pad."

Dinah mutely showed her the blank sheet.

"So we got nothing. It happens." Tracey rose.

"We got something." Dinah got up, reaching for her
bag, feeling as if she needed something to hang on to.
"She may never tell us, and you can't take it to court,
but she knows who killed her friend."

Tracey's brows lifted a little higher. "You're sure of that?"

Dinah didn't question how she knew. Some combination of instinct, experience and guidance, probably. But she knew.

"I'm sure. But we may never get it out of her. She doesn't want to remember."

She knew what that felt like, only too well.

"Sorry I couldn't get any closer." Marc strolled beside Dinah from the parking space he'd found a block from Marion Square. They were about to tackle the first item on Court's lengthy list of Charleston Christmas events, the lighting of the city Christmas tree.

The cool evening breeze lifted Dinah's dark curls, and she tucked her hands into the pockets of her wool jacket. "This is fine. Do I look as if I can't walk a block?"

Court was several yards ahead. Either he found their pace too slow, or he wanted to give the impression he was alone. It was tough to tell with a teenager. At least he could speak freely to Dinah.

"You look as if you're exhausted. Haven't you been sleeping?"

"I'm fine." She dodged a stroller, shooting him an annoyed look. "Please don't hover. I get enough of that from Aunt Kate."

He shrugged, unconvinced. "If you say so."

The crowds grew thicker as they approached. Families, teenagers and elderly people poured into the area, roped off for the occasion. He remembered Marion

Square Park as a bit shabby and run-down, but the city had clearly made an effort to improve things.

He couldn't begin a serious conversation with Dinah in the middle of a holiday crowd, but sooner or later they had to talk. The way she'd looked those moments on the stairs with her white, strained expression still haunted him.

He had to find a way to reassure her that he wasn't going to press her about what happened. Sure, he hoped she might remember something useful, but not at the cost of her well-being. And she'd already given him a possibility, with her revelation of Annabel's attitude toward Carr, the gardener. He hadn't found Carr yet, but he would. He might need to use the firm of private investigators he'd taken the trouble of looking up.

Court slowed his pace and let them catch up with him as they approached the immense Christmas tree at the center of the square. "Have they always done this, Dad?"

"I don't know about always, but I remember going to a tree-lighting when I was a kid. I'm not sure it was in this park, though."

"There are tree-lightings all over the area." Dinah smiled at Court, some of the tiredness easing from her face. "And it's not just to draw tourists, really. Folks like to celebrate, and we're proud of our city, aren't we, Marc?"

He nodded, because to do anything else would provoke an argument. *I'm not part of the city any longer, Dinah. You must realize that. People don't want me here, and I don't belong anymore.*

That shouldn't give him such a lonely feeling, but it did.

"There's Phillips." Dinah raised her hand to wave across the crowd. "He's working one of the charity stands tonight. We should go over and say hello."

He slid his hand into the crook of her arm, anchoring her to the spot. "Later. Looks as if the program is about to start." And he didn't need his son exposed to any more snubs.

He watched Court's face as the tree-lighting ceremony progressed. They'd been to plenty of tree-lighting events over the years, so why did this one impress him so much?

Court stared, rapt with attention, as the Magnolia Singers performed folk carols, and clapped along with the Charleston Community Band. And when the mayor flipped the switch and the sixty-foot tree lit with lights, Court's eyes were as big as they'd been at four or five.

He suspected he knew the answer. This was Court's heritage, just as it had been Annabel's and his. That was what made the difference. In keeping Court away from the possibility of pain, he'd also kept him away from his roots.

When they'd sung the last carol, Court turned to him. "Wow, that was great. How about some hot chocolate? Watching made me thirsty."

Dinah laughed. "I can see how it would." She linked her arm with his. "There's a stand across the way— let's go."

So apparently he was going to see Phil tonight whether he wanted to or not. Dinah didn't even question that—of course they'd go to the stand where Phillips was working. He'd opened this up when he'd insisted on going to the Alpha Club tree sale, so they both knew Phillips was still a friend, in spite of his wife's attitude.

When he saw them approaching, Phil's face broke into the singularly sweet smile he remembered from when they were boys together.

"Hey, it's good to see you." He swung around to fill foam cups with coffee from an urn. "Let me just take care of these customers, and then we can visit."

The moment that took gave him a chance to study his old friend for the second time. In the glare of the unshaded lightbulb that hung from the top of the booth, Phil's face had lines that aged him, and his hair was more gray than fair.

Still, he, Marc, probably looked older, too. Bitterness had a way of showing on the face.

Otherwise, with his lean, ascetic face and thick glasses, Phil looked like what he was—a historian more comfortable in Charleston's past than the present.

"There now." No one waited for service but them. "What can I get you? It's all for charity, remember, so don't be stingy."

"Hot chocolate all around," he said. Margo was nowhere in sight, and Phil obviously felt free to be friendly without her intimidating presence.

Phillips poured the chocolate and handed the cups across the counter. Dinah wrapped her fingers around the cup as if seeking its warmth.

"I'm glad I had a chance to see you again." Phil's

eyes fixed anxiously on his face. "I wanted to say I'm—I'm sorry about what happened the other night. Margo gets these ideas in her head, and nothing can get them out."

She thinks I'm a murderer. Nothing to be gained by repeating the obvious. "It's not your responsibility, Phil. I just hope Margo doesn't speak for you."

"No, of course not." Phil flushed slightly. "I know you didn't hurt Annabel. The very idea is ridiculous."

"James doesn't think so." That still stung. He and James and Phil had been like brothers when they were cadets at the Citadel. He'd thought then that nothing could ever come between them. They were going to save their beautiful city together—Phil as historian, James as politician, he as crusading prosecutor.

"I know." Phil's gaze dropped, as if he didn't want to admit how deep the breach went. "James has changed since, well, since you left Charleston. I thought once we'd be friends for life, but now we don't seem to have a thing in common. I wish life didn't—"

Before he could finish the thought, a bevy of teenage girls came giggling and nudging each other to the counter.

"Sorry, I'll have to take this." Phil checked his watch. "My helper should be here by now. He's late."

"Would you like me to help, sir?" Court set his cup down on the counter. "Just till he gets here?" Court glanced at him. "It's okay, isn't it, Dad?"

He suspected the presence of several cute girls had something to do with his son's sudden altruism. "Dinah may want to get home."

"I'd like to stay," she said quickly. "Let's find a bench and watch Charleston go by until Court's ready. Court, we'll be right nearby, so come and find us."

He nodded, and while Court hurried into the booth, he and Dinah walked down the path to the nearest bench.

It was surprisingly private, screened by azalea bushes, even though it was just a few feet away from the booths. Dinah sat down with a little sigh and sipped at the chocolate.

"You look wiped out," he said bluntly. "Don't tell me to mind my own business, Dinah. Is our being here upsetting you that much?"

She looked at him, eyes wide and startled. "It's not you and Court. It's the case." She shrugged, lips curving in a rueful smile. "Was I rude earlier? I'm sorry. Aunt Kate fusses over me so, and Alice—you remember Alice Jones, her housekeeper?"

"Round, comfortable, the best pies I ever ate. She's still there?"

She nodded. "A little rounder, probably. She keeps offering me chamomile tea. Says it's good for the nerves."

He propped his arm along the back of the bench, leaning toward her. "Okay. I promise not to offer you any chamomile tea. Can you tell me about the case, or is that a breach of protocol?"

"Probably, but there's not much to tell. She broke the interview off today before we could get what we need." Dinah seemed to be looking back, probably weighing whether she'd handled the girl right. "I guess I'm disappointed not to come away with a lead."

"It's more than that, isn't it?" He touched her shoulder lightly. "You identify with this girl. Her experience is too similar to yours."

Dinah stared out across the park, as if mesmerized by the thousands of twinkling white lights draped from the trees. "I feel empathy for her, I suppose. But there's one big difference. We're sure she must have seen something, if she can just let herself remember it. I didn't see anything."

He knew better than to question that. It was what Dinah believed, and arguing wouldn't change that.

"Still, a case like this, with a young girl, must be especially painful."

She nodded, still not looking at him. *Talk to me, Dinah. Please, talk to me.*

She tilted her head back, dark hair flowing across the collar of her cream wool jacket. "I guess that's part of it. Her mother doesn't know what to do to help her, any more than Aunt Kate knew."

"Your aunt sent you away."

"To her cousins in New Orleans. Bless their hearts, they didn't know what to do with me, either." She smiled faintly at the memory.

"Still, you got through it somehow." She should have had more help. Professional help. He should have insisted, though he'd had no right or say.

"Going to art school was the best thing that could have happened to me. In a way, I painted out all my grief and anger. I think I started to find my way once I'd done that."

Have you found your way, Dinah? Or are you still hurting?

He didn't dare to ask the question, but he probably already knew the answer. She was hurting, and his presence made that pain worse. He couldn't even comfort himself with the idea that it would be best for her to face the past, because that wasn't his motive. He was using her, and that was an ugly thing to find in himself.

"Dinah—" He wasn't sure how to put his feelings into words. "Court and I can't leave here with so many questions unanswered. But maybe you should back away." He shook his head. "That wasn't what I wanted to say to you, but you're forcing me to be honest. And maybe what's honestly best for you is to stay away from us."

She turned toward him, her cheek brushing his fingers with a touch soft as a snowflake. She gave him a grave, sweet look. "A few days ago I might have agreed. But now—it's too late for that, Marc. I'm in this thing with you and Court. All the way."

His throat tightened. "Thanks, sugar." The Southern endearment came to his lips without thought. "I'm glad you're on our side."

He'd gotten what he wanted. He should be happy. But all he could think was that now he was responsible for Dinah, too. If this situation hurt her, which it very well might, then he was to blame.

Chapter Six

Dinah perched on a stool at the kitchen counter, watching as Glory rolled out crust for chicken pot pie. She might have been a teenager again, escaping to the kitchen for a quick chat with Glory.

Escaping? She took a closer look at the word her subconscious mind had chosen. She'd loved staying in the house with Annabel and Marc that summer, helping to care for Court. Why on earth would she have wanted to escape that?

She hadn't. That was all. Her mind had made a silly misstep. She picked up a scrap of dough and rolled it idly through her fingers.

"So." Glory's black eyes were bright with curiosity. "What you think about Mr. Marcus coming back here like this?"

The soft Gullah cadences of Glory's speech were soothing, even though the question wasn't.

She hesitated. She could trust Glory, but what did

she really think about Marc's return, underneath her concern for Aunt Kate and Court and Marc himself?

"I think he had to do it," she said finally. "He had to put things to rest here. I just wish I knew what other things his coming will stir up." James Harwood's animosity flickered through her mind. That had to hurt Marc, as close as they'd been.

"Always a danger of that." Glory's strong brown arms wielded the rolling pin like a weapon. "Folks don't like prodding into the past for a lot of reasons— some good, some not so good."

Dinah had twisted the fragment of dough into a tortured shape. She tossed it into the waste can and dusted her hands. "That's what I'm afraid of, I guess. That he'll stir up something he can't control."

Glory's lips twitched. "Don't know as anybody gonna stop him, though."

"Certainly not me."

Although she probably had as much influence over Marc now as anyone did. Odd. At first, he'd tried to treat her as if she were still that sixteen-year-old, but the more they were together, the more that wore away. Now they talked like friends, for the most part. Except when she tried to get in the way of what he wanted.

No, no one would stop Marc.

The kitchen door swung, and he came in. Glory sent him a smiling glance. "Ain't no use you coming in here now, looking hungry. Supper won't be ready for an hour, and I cook faster without a lot of people cluttering up my kitchen."

"Dinah's here." He smiled at her and leaned against the counter next to her. "Doesn't she bother you?"

"Dinah knows how to make herself useful." She slid a baking tin toward Dinah. "You go on and make some cinnamon crisps out of that leftover dough. Maybe that'll keep these boys from starving till supper's ready."

Marc's lips twitched at being referred to as one of the boys, as if he were no older than Court.

"What's the matter? Doesn't your housekeeper in Boston order you around?" She obediently began rolling out the dough scraps, trying to get the dough as thin as Glory did.

"We don't have a housekeeper now. Just a cleaning service that comes when we're both out and does its work invisibly."

"Sounds a little impersonal."

"I'm sure that's how they prefer it." He seemed to be watching Glory slide the pot pie into the oven, but his expression indicated that his thoughts were elsewhere. "You didn't make pot pie that last summer we were here, did you?"

Glory closed the oven door and wiped her hands on her apron. "Pot pie's not a summertime dish, to my way of thinking. Heats up the kitchen too much. You want things that cook faster in the summer."

Clearly Marcus wanted Glory to talk about that summer. So Dinah would steer the conversation in that direction, even though her instincts were to do anything but that. "Or cold dishes. You still make the best potato salad on the Peninsula?"

Glory grinned. "Child, I make the best potato salad on both sides of the Ashley and the Cooper," she said, naming the two rivers that bound old Charleston into itself. "Maybe even in Charleston, Berkeley and Dorchester counties all put together."

"I remember that potato salad," Marc said. "Sometimes we had Sunday lunch out on the veranda—potato salad and cucumber sandwiches and crab salad."

"Stop, you're making my mouth water. And Glory won't make us potato salad. It's not summer."

It wasn't any summer, but especially not that summer, ten years ago, when they'd lunched on the veranda, laughing at Court's attempts to catch one of the butterflies that hovered over the buddleia bush. There hadn't been any shadows of impending tragedy over those lunches, had there?

Glory straightened, hands on her hips. "No sense you talking about potato salad, Mr. Marc. You want to ask me something, just come right out and ask it. You know I'd do anything at all I could for you."

That was a vote of confidence, and she hoped Marc appreciated it. Glory believed in him.

"Thank you." His voice softened a little. "It's not any one question I want to ask you. It's that I hope you'll think about what it was like here that summer. Think about any little things that happened that didn't feel quite right, even if they don't seem to have to do with my wife's death. We don't know what might be important."

Glory nodded, her eyes shadowed. "Reckon I've spent plenty of time on my knees about it. There's nothing that pops into my head, but I'll think on it some more."

"What about Jasper Carr? Do you remember anything about him?"

Dinah had put Carr into his mind with her simple comment about Annabel not liking the man. She hadn't meant anything by the words—they'd just popped out, and Marc had seized on them.

His single-mindedness chilled her. If Marc did find evidence that implicated someone in Annabel's death, what would he do? Turn it over to the police, or try to take matters into his own hands? She hadn't thought that far, and she should, before she said anything else that might make him suspect someone.

Glory was shaking her head slowly. "Can't think of anything, except that time I found him in the kitchen. But you already know about that."

"Found him in the kitchen?" His voice was sharp, his prosecutor's voice. "What are you talking about?"

"Why, that one evening I came back for my purse. I'd gone off without it. Everyone was out, and there Carr was right here in the kitchen."

"Doing what?" Marc leaned forward, intent.

She shrugged. "Nothing that I could see. He said the back door was open and he just come in for a drink of water, but I didn't buy that. I spoke to him pretty sharp and sent him off with a flea in his ear, I can tell you that."

"Why did you say I knew about it? I didn't."

"I told Miz Annabel the next day." Distress caught at her voice. "Had to do something, didn't I? She said she'd talk to you about it. Said you'd have to give him his notice. Didn't she tell you?"

"No. No, she didn't tell me." He swung toward her. "Did Annabel tell you about it?"

"I don't think so. Not that I remember, anyway."

Impossible to tell what he was thinking, but something implacable hardened his features, turning him into a stranger.

He zeroed in on Glory again. "When was this? Do you remember?"

"I couldn't forget it." Her voice went low and mournful. "It was just a few days before Miz Annabel died."

"Court, if you eat any more of that raw cookie dough, your stomach is going to explode." Dinah tried to sound severe, but judging by the grin on Court's face, he wasn't intimidated.

"That's an old wives' tale, isn't it?" He put another dollop of sugar-cookie dough in this mouth and spoke indistinctly around it. "There's nothing in them before they're baked that's not there afterward."

He perched on the edge of the solid oak table in the kitchen, no doubt getting flour all over his jeans. Well, that didn't matter. Jeans could be washed, and at least the Christmas cookie baking could keep both of them from brooding about where Marc had gone.

"Maybe not, but that's what Aunt Kate always told me. And since she's the one who taught me to make sugar cookies, the advice comes with the cookies."

"Not your mom?"

So few people ever mentioned her parents anymore

that Court's innocent question raised an unexpected pang of grief. Everyone else knew what had happened to them, so she never had to explain.

She forced a smile. "My mother wasn't much of a cook. She was more into outdoor things like riding and sailing." Always alive, so alive, with her dark hair blowing in the wind and her eyes sparkling.

"She and your dad both died, didn't they?" Court's mobile face went somber.

Not the happiest of conversations to distract him, but she couldn't tell him anything but the truth. "I was nine, the year Hurricane Hugo hit Charleston. We had a cottage out on Isle of Palms then. My parents were trying to save it."

Foolish, so foolish. None of those houses had been saved from the fury of that storm. They'd risked their lives for a thing of nails and boards, leaving their daughter alone.

"Where were you?"

"They'd brought me in to stay with Aunt Kate." The image of her mother's face was clearer than her own, reflected in the dark glass of the microwave on the countertop. She'd gone out the door laughing and waving.

We'll be back soon, Dinah, and we'll tell you all about it. Be a good girl.

But they hadn't come back. Others had come to tell the story of the cottage collapsing. But she had done her best to be a good girl, hadn't she?

She shook her head. She'd intended to keep his mind off his father, not plunge him into another sad tale.

"Okay, let's get back to these cookies. How are you at decorating?"

"Don't know. I never tried. What do I do?" Court bounced off the table, the tea towel he'd tied around his waist flapping.

"You can be as creative as you want with these." She plunged a small spatula into a bowl of icing and coated the surface of a Christmas-tree-shaped cookie. "There's icing in tubes and sprinkles in different colors, too. Have a ball with it. Just remember people might actually want to eat them."

"Gotcha." He wielded a spatula enthusiastically. "Dad doesn't have much of a sweet tooth, but I'll bet he'll eat a couple when he gets home." Court glanced at the clock. "You think he's going to be much longer?"

"I don't know."

She hoped not. Of course it was inevitable that he'd go looking for Jasper Carr, after what Glory had revealed the day before. And it was probably equally inevitable that he'd brush off her suggestions to discuss it with the police or turn it over to the private investigator he'd talked of hiring.

She couldn't protect Marc from himself, and she didn't seem to be doing a very good job of protecting Court from worrying about him.

"I'm sure he's fine. He said he'd be back for supper, didn't he?"

Court nodded, apparently intent on the cookie he was decorating. "He should have let me go with him. I'm not a little kid."

What could she possibly say to that? Fortunately she didn't have to reply, as the front doorbell began to peal.

"I'll get it." She pulled off the oversize apron that belonged to Glory.

"It can't be Dad. He has his keys with him."

She pushed through the swinging door into the hallway. Funny, that was probably the first time she'd heard the doorbell since Marc had come back. Charleston hadn't been beating down his door coming to call.

The frosted glass panel on the front door distorted the figure beyond. She swung the door open, her eyebrows lifting in a polite question when she saw that the man was a stranger. "May I help you?"

"Devlin. Mr. Devlin. I want to see him." He clipped the words off, and one hand beat a tattoo against his leg.

She didn't know him. Did she? Tall, painfully thin, with sunken cheeks and sparse gray hair. Nothing rang a bell, but still something about him seemed faintly familiar, like an old photograph she couldn't quite recognize.

"I'm sorry, but he's not here right now. May I give him a message for you?"

"No. No message. I'll wait." He took a sudden step toward her, and it was all she could do not to retreat.

"I'm sorry. You'll have to come again another time." She swung the door toward him, feeling her pulse quicken. This wasn't right. The intensity that came flooding from the man wasn't normal.

He swung one arm up, blocking the door and sending shock waves through her. "I have to see him." He shoved. Her feet slid on the polished floor as her pulse notched upward. He was going to come in. She couldn't stop him—

"No!"

Court's voice was so like Marc's that for an instant she thought he was there. Then his strong young hands grabbed the door and shoved. The door slammed shut. She snatched the dead bolt and twisted it. Safe. They were safe.

Thunderous blows hit the door, making the glass tremble. She winced away.

"Come on." She grabbed Court's hand. "We've got to call the police."

They ran together back to the kitchen, where she grabbed the cell phone she'd left on the counter, punching in 911.

"An intruder is trying to break into the house." She could only hope she sounded calmer than she felt as she gave the address.

"Officers are on their way." The dispatcher's voice crackled in her ear. "Don't hang up. Keep talking to me."

"He's coming around the house." Court hung on the sink to look out the side window. "He's going to try getting in the back."

"He's coming to the back of the house." She relayed the words, heart thudding. Court—she had to keep Court safe. *Please, Lord, show me how to keep Court safe.*

"Go to an inside room and lock the door." The dispatcher's voice was sharp. "Don't come out until you know the officers are there."

She swung around. "Someplace with a lock." Maybe Court's mind was working better than hers was. Not the pantry—it didn't lock. Her mind cringed at the idea of being trapped in the cellar.

"Powder room," Court said. He seized her hand and grabbed the wooden rolling pin from the table. "It locks from the inside."

She had a quick image of the man's face, framed in the back window, as they raced back through the swinging door, into the tiny powder room under the stairwell. Slam the door, lock it, switch on the light.

Court's face, in the glow of the overhead light, was excited. Not afraid. Excited.

"Wow, Dinah. Nothing like this ever happens at home."

"Trust me, it doesn't usually happen here." She was still clutching his hand, and she wasn't about to let go. "That's generally considered to be a good thing." She pressed the phone to her ear. "We're locked in the powder room. I can hear him banging on the back door. If he gets in—"

"The patrol car is nearly there. Just hang on a few more minutes."

She nodded, then realized how ridiculous that was. The woman couldn't see her.

But Someone Else could. Heedless of how Court would react, she put her arm around him and closed her eyes.

"Dear Father, put Your protection around us now.

Keep us safe from harm." Another volley of crashes against the back door came, and she winced. *"We trust in You, Lord. Amen."*

"Amen," Court echoed softly.

Please, Lord—

The wail of a siren punctuated the prayer. The police were here.

Marc screeched to a halt in front of the house, heart pounding, mind whirling with fear and jumbled prayers. *Let them be all right. Please, let them be all right.*

Neighbors clustered on the walk, defying the genteel traditions of Tradd Street by craning their necks to watch the police load a man into the back of a black-and-white. Leonard Hassert.

Marc's stomach clenched as he recognized the man and remembered his angry, shouted threats at the prosecutor when the jury convicted him.

He ran up the walk, brushing past the uniformed officer on the veranda and raced inside. "Court! Dinah!"

Court exploded out of the family room and into his arms. He held his son tightly, heart twisting in his chest. He couldn't lose Court, no matter what, he couldn't. *Thank You, Lord.*

"Where's Dinah? Is she all right?"

"I'm fine." Dinah stood in the doorway of the family room. She managed a smile, but fear still haunted her eyes. "We're both fine. If I ever have to be locked in a powder room with someone while a maniac pounds on the back door, I'll take Court."

Court freed himself, flushing a little. "Hey, you were pretty tough yourself."

"I wasn't the one who thought of the rolling pin as a weapon. I'm just glad we didn't have to use it."

"He didn't get into the house?" His mind started working again, now that the primal need to protect them had eased.

"No, thanks to the new lock you put on the back door."

"The police got here in time." Court grinned. "Boy, was I ever glad to hear that siren."

"Not as glad as I was," Dinah said, smiling at him. "You thought the whole thing was thrilling—admit it."

Dinah and Court had moved to an entirely new plane in their relationship. That was what facing danger together did for them, apparently.

But they shouldn't have had to. It was no thanks to him that they were safe. God had answered his prayer, but left him with a load of guilt. He hadn't protected them.

"Do you know who that guy was, Dad? The police want to talk to you about him."

He owed Court an honest answer. But not, perhaps, too many details.

"His name is Leonard Hassert. I sent him to prison, back when I was a prosecutor."

Hassert. The name echoed in his mind. Hassert had threatened him. Hassert had been out of jail, pending appeal, when Annabel died.

"Did he—"

Dinah stopped Court's eager questions with a hand

on his arm. "The detectives are waiting to talk to your dad, remember?"

"Oh, right." Court jerked a nod toward the family room. "They're in there. Come on."

Dinah's fingers tightened. "I think they want to see him alone. Let's go clean up that mess we left in the kitchen, okay?"

She looked back, her eyes meeting his, as she and Court started down the hallway. Funny. He almost felt that she was telegraphing him a warning.

No warning was needed. For the first time in years he was looking forward to talking with the police. Adrenaline pumped through him as he headed toward the family room. After this, they'd have to admit that Hassert was a suspect in Annabel's death.

He stopped short in the doorway, eyes on the man who rose to meet him. Draydon. Lieutenant Alan Draydon had been in charge of the investigation into Annabel's death ten years ago. He'd made no secret of the fact that he'd thought Marc as guilty as sin, even though he couldn't find enough evidence to take it to trial.

That was then. This was now. Now he wasn't in a state of shock over his wife's death. Now he could make Draydon see that Hassert was a viable suspect.

"Lieutenant Draydon." He didn't bother to offer his hand. The man wouldn't take it. Ten years hadn't changed Draydon all that much. A few more pounds, a little less hair. He still had a vague resemblance to a bulldog with those drooping jowls and sleepy eyes.

The sleepiness was misleading. Draydon was an aggressive detective—probably a good one, even though he'd been wrong in Marc's case.

"Mr. Devlin." Draydon's lips winced in what might have been intended for a smile. "So you've come back to Charleston. I always thought you would, eventually."

He chose to ignore what was probably meant as a veiled threat. "I'm back. And that seems to have stirred up Leonard Hassert."

"We'll investigate him. Probably take another look at your wife's death." Draydon gestured toward a chair. "Have a seat, Mr. Devlin. I've been looking forward to talking to you since I heard you were back." He smiled, and this time he actually seemed to be getting some enjoyment from the situation. "It's always good to have another chance to close an open case."

Dinah had been right to send him that look of warning. Draydon wasn't focused on Hassert. He had zeroed in on the husband, just as he had ten years ago.

He hadn't succeeded then. Now, Draydon clearly thought he had another chance to prove Marc guilty of Annabel's death.

Chapter Seven

Dinah crossed the street slowly the next afternoon, aware of subtle changes in the atmosphere of the block. Some of the houses seemed closed to the neighborhood, their drawn shades proclaiming their noninvolvement. At others, lace curtains twitched as her neighbors watched her approach the gate to Marc's garden and push it open.

Well, they'd get over it. Wouldn't they? Surely they couldn't hold a grudge against her forever for her association with the disturbance the day before.

One positive thing had come out of it, Court was even now having tea with Aunt Kate, at her invitation. She wasn't sure Court appreciated the tea, but he seemed engrossed in Aunt Kate's stories of the family. She had it all at her fingertips, back to the first Westlake who'd come from London to the fledging colony in 1697. Her cheeks had been pink with excitement at having a new audience for her tales.

While Court was pleasantly occupied, she had to

talk to Marc. There had been no chance the previous day. He'd obviously not wanted to discuss the police reaction in front of his son.

But she'd seen the worry he tried to hide. His conversation with Lieutenant Draydon hadn't gone well. Not that she thought it would. She'd sensed Draydon's animosity only too well.

She walked through the house, expecting to find Marc in the study. It was empty, as was the family room.

She found Glory in the kitchen, slicing onions on the counter. Glory gave her a long, serious look.

"Hear y'all had some excitement here yesterday."

"Too much excitement. Believe me, I could have done without it."

"So could the neighbors, I reckon." Glory jerked her head toward the back door. "Mr. Marc's out there. Some no-count left a message on the garage."

"Oh, no." It didn't seem a strong enough response. "People don't do things like that here."

Glory's knife thudded against the wooden cutting board. "Looks like they do now. He didn't want Court to see it, but there's not much gets past that boy."

"I'd better go and talk to him."

She went out the back, trying not to think about Hassert standing there, pounding on the door. A few steps took her to the garage. She rounded the corner and stopped, stunned. Glory had warned her, but she still hadn't been ready to see the word *Murderer* in foot-high red paint on the back of the garage.

Marc, in jeans and a faded Citadel sweatshirt, was painting over the letters.

It took a moment to find the right casual tone. "It looks as if it will take a couple of coats."

"Afraid so." Marc's even voice didn't give anything away, but his jaw was tense and he didn't look at her.

"Marc, I'm so sorry. It shouldn't have happened." She took a step toward him, not sure how to deal with the anger he had under such iron control.

"Obviously the neighbors didn't care for the police cars on their doorstep. I can hardly blame them."

"Let me help." She bent to pick up the second brush that lay next to the paint can.

He shook his head sharply. "Leave it alone, Dinah. You'll get dirty."

"I don't mind—"

"Leave it, I said." His voice roughened. "Consider this thing a warning for you, too."

She took a breath. "Are you telling me to stay away from you?"

"I should." He put the paintbrush down and swung to face her, planting his hands on his hips. "I put you in danger yesterday just from being in my house." His jaw twitched. "And my son."

"You weren't responsible for that man's actions."

"I should have realized something might happen."

He couldn't seem to let go of his guilt. And there was nothing she could do to help him.

"What did Draydon say? What's happening to Hassert?"

"He's in jail at the moment, but he probably won't

stay there for long. They'll plead it out. After all, he didn't actually get into the house."

"And Draydon?"

"You already know what Draydon thinks, don't you? You saw that yesterday."

Yes, she'd seen. "He'll investigate. He's a good cop, Marc."

"Yes. He is." Marc slapped paint on the garage wall. "He won't let his personal belief keep him from investigating thoroughly. But at rock bottom, he believes he knows who killed Annabel. Me."

She didn't know what to say at the pain in his voice. "Marc, maybe you and Court should just go back to Boston."

"I can't. It's too late for that. It's opened up again now. I have to go all the way." He shook his head. "I tried to convince Court to join some friends on a ski trip for the holiday. He won't go."

Of course he wouldn't. "He's just like his father. Stubborn."

His mouth twisted. "I have to keep him safe. And you. I can't let what happened yesterday happen again."

What would it take to make him understand? "You're responsible for Court, but not for me. I make my own decisions. I'm one of the grown-ups now, Marc."

"So was Annabel." He swung toward her again, and her breath caught. His face was ravaged with pain. "Don't you see? If Hassert killed Annabel, it was because of me. So, in a way, Draydon's right. I am responsible for Annabel's death."

* * *

Marc hesitated as they came out the red door of the church, wondering if he should offer his arm to Kate Westlake. Or would that be presuming too much? She had invited him and Court to attend services today, but her attitude toward him still verged on the frosty.

Kate, as if she'd measured his thoughts, linked her arm firmly with Dinah's and went carefully down the steps to the sidewalk. Court had been looking at a brochure on the Circular Church's history as he exited the sanctuary, but now he caught up with him.

"Hey, Dad, did you know this church has been here since 1681?"

Dinah, overhearing him, smiled. "Well, not this building. This congregation. This is actually the third building on the site."

"Westlakes have attended services here since the earliest settlers." Kate tapped him on the arm. "That's part of your roots, too, Courtney."

"I'll remember, Aunt Kate." Court gave her the sweet smile that was so like Annabel's.

Her faded blue eyes glistened briefly. "You're very like your mother. You know that, don't you?"

Court nodded, probably a bit embarrassed to bring on so much emotion.

Kate might not have accepted Marc, but she'd accepted his son. Or did she just think of Court as Annabel's son?

The fierce family pride of hers might have something to do with her sudden thawing. Either Court had won her over, or she was announcing to the neighbors that the Westlakes were not to be trifled with or in-sulted.

Well, either way, he was glad Court had a chance to get to know her. Kate was a piece of family history herself, the classic repository of all the family stories and legends. It would have been wrong to prevent Court from appreciating that.

To his surprise, Kate had actually talked to Court about Annabel. Court had come home from their little tea party clutching photographs she'd given him of his mother as a young girl. He'd had to struggle to hide his feelings. It probably wasn't cool, at thirteen, to be moved by having some mementos of your mother.

They walked down Meeting Street, thronged with Sunday morning churchgoers, toward the car, Court now holding Aunt Kate's arm, Dinah beside him. Would Kate talk to him about Annabel, if he asked her? About that last summer? She'd made her attitude toward him so clear that he hadn't even thought of it, but maybe since Court had bridged the gap, she'd be more open. It was worth a try.

"You're supposed to talk to the lady you're escort-ing," Dinah said primly. "Or have you forgotten all you learned about Charleston etiquette?"

"I still remember those Saturday afternoon dance classes, if that's what you mean." The boys pretend-ing to choke at wearing white shirts and ties, the girls preening in their dresses and white gloves. "Court doesn't know how lucky he is to have escaped those."

She looked up at him, smooth brow furrowing. "Has something else happened? You looked worried."

"No, not at all. Well, not any more than I was." How could he be? He wouldn't tell Dinah that he wanted to talk to Kate about that summer. He had no doubt that she'd disapprove strenuously.

They reached the car, and Kate turned toward him. "We always have just a cold lunch after Sunday services. You and Courtney are very welcome to join us, if you'd like."

Kate was thawing, actually speaking to him directly.

"Why don't you allow us to take you two ladies out to lunch instead? I have reservations at Magnolia's, and I'm sure they'll be able to squeeze two more chairs at the table."

He deliberately mentioned the restaurant. Magnolia's was one of the places to see and be seen in Charleston. Kate would really be making a statement if she were willing to go there with him.

Her hesitation was infinitesimal. Then her chin went up. "That sounds delightful. Dinah and I would enjoy accompanying you."

He drove sedately over to East Bay. Kate, who seemed to have appointed herself tour guide, contributed tidbits of history about the buildings they passed. If Court was losing interest, he managed to hide that fact.

Well, he had Kate's company, but getting her alone to have a serious conversation would be considerably more difficult. Between her dragon of a housekeeper and Dinah, they kept her well protected.

He was lucky enough to find a parking space near the entrance. As they approached the door, they found a caroling group in Victorian dress singing to a small crowd that had gathered on the sidewalk. Court stopped, curious as always. Marc nudged Dinah.

"Why don't you and Court enjoy the music for a few minutes? I'll take your aunt in and get her settled. I'm sure she doesn't want to stand." Before any of the three of them could raise an objection, he took Kate's arm and hustled her inside.

The hostess swept them to a white-covered table by the window in one of the elegant dining rooms, with Kate nodding regally and exchanging greetings with at least half the people they passed. Charleston was a small town at its heart, when one disregarded the tourists and the students. Everyone in Charleston society knew everyone else. They'd attended those Saturday afternoon dance classes, gone to the same schools, woven a tight, virtually invisible bond.

He seated Kate, helping her to arrange her formidable fur stole over the back of her chair. "Comfortable?"

"Fine." Her gaze met his. "I assume by all this manipulation that you wish to talk with me."

"I—"

"That's fine, because I wish to speak with you. Does that surprise you?"

He nodded in wary agreement. Never underestimate the power of little old ladies, especially one like Kate Westlake, with generations of Charleston tradition behind her.

"I know that my return has raised talk. I'm sorry if that's distressed you."

A flicker of humor showed in her face. "That

wouldn't stop you, however." She waved away any answer he might make. "There's no point in regretting. You're here, and we have to face that."

The waitress interrupted with menus. She announced that the brunch specialty was shrimp and sausage with tasso gravy over grits, and disappeared again to bring the extra place settings he requested.

"Did you have something specific in mind?" He lowered his voice, speaking under the noisy conversation of the tourists at the next table.

"Just this. The sooner this situation is resolved, the better. For Dinah's sake, as well as the rest of us."

"I don't want to hurt Dinah."

"You might not be able to help it. The truth comes at a cost." She shook her head, her fingers trembling a little as she toyed with her spoon. "You wanted to ask me something. What is it?"

She was giving him a chance he hadn't expected. "Yes, I do. Was there anything you noticed that summer, or anything that Annabel told you, that seemed unusual? Anything, no matter how small. A quarrel with someone, someone hanging around the house, anything."

She shook her head slowly, not looking at him. "Nothing that comes to mind. It seemed like any other summer, except that Dinah was staying with Annabel. She'd run in every day, of course, always full of stories about Court."

Dinah, not Annabel. "Annabel didn't talk to you about anything that was going on?" He felt a sense of futility. If Hassert had been the killer, there might not have been anything to notice.

"No." Her voice lowered to hardly more than a whisper, and it was as if she were talking to herself. "I failed her. I didn't mean to, but I failed her."

His attention sharpened. "What do you mean? How did you fail Annabel?"

"Annabel?" She looked up, eyes wide and startled, and he had the sense that for a moment she'd forgotten he was there. "No, I didn't mean—" She pressed a handkerchief to her lips. "Not Annabel. Dinah. I shouldn't have sent Dinah away."

"You said Annabel." He leaned toward her. "Kate, what did you mean?"

She put the handkerchief down and looked around. "What's taking them so long?" Her tone was querulous. "We should be ordering."

He sat back in his chair. He couldn't badger an elderly lady in public. Or in private, for that matter. If he drove Kate to the verge of tears, Dinah would have his head.

He'd have to let it go for the moment. But while they debated the relative merits of tomato bisque with fresh crabmeat or lobster salad, he mulled over her words in the back of his mind.

She hadn't made a mistake or confused the two girls. For those few moments she'd been back in that summer, grieving over some way she felt she'd failed Annabel. She knew something about that time that she wasn't ready to say, and he'd dearly love to know what it was.

* * *

Dinah tried to relax as she walked with Marc across the campus of The Citadel that evening, Court a few steps ahead of them in his excitement. She wasn't sure spending the evening at the Christmas concert was such a good idea, with suspicion circling around them like no-see-ums on a summer night.

Still, what else could they be doing that would be more helpful? Once Court had gotten his father reminiscing about his undergraduate days at The Citadel, their attendance was a forgone conclusion.

Court had what Aunt Kate would call a whim of iron. Annabel had been like that, too. Once she'd decided she wanted something, there was never any talking her out of it.

"That's where the cadets stage the Retreat ceremony every Friday during the school year." Marc waved toward the expanse of lawn between the buildings.

"Can we come?" Court asked, predictably.

She could easily read Marc's expression, even in the growing dusk. He didn't really want to relive old school days, not under the present circumstances.

She could spare him that, at least. "I'll call and see if it's on for Friday," she said. "I'm not sure when the holiday break starts. If they're doing it, you and I can come." The long gray lines, marching in precision, the flags fluttering and bagpipes keening—of course Court wanted to see it. Any boy would.

"That'd be great, Dinah." He linked his arm with hers, and the unexpected gesture of affection touched her heart.

Marc's frown grew deeper as they approached the white pavement of the courtyard, The Citadel's battlements rising like a fortress around them. White Christmas lights sparkled from the buildings, and the courtyard was thronged with Charlestonians dressed in their best and cadets in uniform. It pleased her to see females among the cadets. Not many, it was true, but once that had seemed impossible.

She moved a little closer to Marc. Did he have the same wary, on-guard sense that she did? Coming here was entering into the heart of Marc's past, where he was likely to run into any number of people he knew, and have just that many occasions to be snubbed by them.

Marc was well armored, probably, but Court wasn't. She didn't want Court's bright, cheerful self-confidence to be dented by anything that happened here.

The chapel was filling up quickly. Did she just imagine it, or did the buzz of conversation take on a different tone as they went down the center aisle, guided by a cadet in dress uniform?

A lady never shows her feelings in public. Aunt Kate's maxims might seem outdated in today's world, but they were there to fall back on in situations like this. Head high, she slid into the pew next to Court.

They might have been wedged in with a shoehorn. She leaned across Court. "I'm going back to the vestibule to hang my coat up. It'll give us a little more breathing room. Don't give my seat away."

Court grinned. "I'll throw myself across it if anyone tries to sit here."

She worked her way back the center aisle, against traffic, seeing faces where before she'd concentrated on getting down the aisle behind the usher. Phillips and Margo sat in the last pew. Phillips glanced up and gave her a shy smile. Margo looked studiously across the rows of people, as if searching for someone she'd misplaced.

Well, she'd get through life very nicely if she never had to speak to Margo again. But she could feel her cheeks burning as she reached the vestibule.

The coatracks were jammed, of course, but she finally found an empty hanger and stuffed her coat in, heedless of wrinkles. She swung around and found herself staring directly at the Citadel tiepin of the man who stood behind her.

"Why are you cooperating with him?" James Harcourt spoke in a furious undertone, his fingers closing around her wrist. "Have you no loyalty to Annabel? She was your cousin."

Anger spurted through her control. Maybe Aunt Kate could live up to her maxims. It looked as if she couldn't.

"Annabel was my cousin," she said. "And Marc was your friend."

"Was. He forfeited that when he hurt Annabel." For the briefest of instants, fierce grief replaced the polished politician's aura that James wore so well. "Annabel would hate you for this."

His intensity, so at odds with the public James, shook her, and for a moment she was almost afraid.

Nonsense. She was letting this situation get to her, and she wouldn't do that.

"James, wake up. That's ridiculous. Annabel would laugh if she heard you say that. Marc didn't hurt her. He couldn't. How are you going to feel when the killer is found and you've already condemned one of your closest friends without even a trial?"

She wrenched her hand free and, not looking to see the effect of her words, she hurried away.

By the time she reached her seat, she was able to smile at Marc and Court in what she hoped was a normal way. It must not have been quite as convincing as she'd hoped, because Marc leaned toward her, a questioning look on his face.

Before he could speak, the organ music swelled, capturing them. She sat back, watching the procession of cadets. She'd enjoy the concert. She would not let the ugliness of suspicion taint what should be a beautiful experience.

Her own intentions probably couldn't have achieved that. But when the young voices rose in the old songs of rejoicing at the Savior's birth, she was so filled with that spirit that there was no room left for anything else.

Perhaps choir directors grew weary of doing the same music year after year, but nothing could have brought Christmas more surely into her heart than this. When a young female cadet stepped forward to sing "Silent Night" with candlelight glowing on her fresh face, tears spilled over. Good tears—the kind that washed away pain and left her feeling free.

The music ended with the final verse of "Silent

Night." There were stars in Court's eyes when they stood. "Wow," he murmured.

She smiled. He used that one word to cover a lot of emotion. "It was, wasn't it?" For a moment they smiled at each other, perfectly in accord.

She'd turned to start back up the aisle when it hit her—a wave of uneasiness so strong it made her pause, clutching Court's arm. Someone, somewhere in the crowded chapel, was looking at them with such dislike, even hatred, that it was palpable.

She tried to shake it off. She was imagining things, surely. But she found herself scanning faces as they moved along the aisle. *Was it you? Or you?*

They stopped at the coatrack while she retrieved her coat. She slipped it on, nodding and smiling as the crowd flowed around them. With a little luck, they'd be out the door without incident.

James stepped into their path. Her throat seemed to close. If he was going to create a scene here, of all places...

Marc stood still, hand on his son's shoulder, waiting for James to make the first move.

James nodded finally, the movement as jerky as a marionette. "Marc." Having gotten that far, he seemed unable to get any farther.

She couldn't stand this. With an abrupt movement, she seized his hand. "Merry Christmas, James."

He looked at her, startled, as if he'd forgotten she was there. Then his face twitched in what was probably meant to be a smile.

"Merry Christmas, Dinah." He looked at Marc.

"And to you, Marc. And Courtney." He turned quickly, as if that was all he could manage. "Good night."

"Well." Marc glanced at her. "That was a surprise."

She nodded. "Let's go home."

Chapter Eight

She was on her way to work, and she absolutely wasn't going to give in to the temptation to check on Marc and Court this morning. Dinah pulled her hair back into the low knot that she considered her "work look" and gave herself a final quick survey in the dresser mirror.

Fine. She looked perfectly normal. A little concealer did wonders to hide the telltale signs of a sleepless night.

No, not entirely sleepless. She'd had the nightmare again, and she'd wakened with her mouth dry and her heart pounding. She'd switched on the bedside lamp and reached for her Bible, seeking solace. It had fallen open to a familiar verse.

For now we see in a mirror dimly, but then face-to-face.

The verse echoed in her mind as she picked up her handbag and the portfolio that contained her drawing supplies. Well, that verse was certainly true enough of the current situation. It was impossible to see clearly what she should do or where the danger lay. The sensation she'd had at the concert, of inimical eyes watching them, sent a fresh shiver down her spine.

Enough. She stared at the silver-framed photograph on her night table, and her mother's face smiled back at her. Lila McKenzie Westlake had never been afraid of anything in her life. What would she think of a daughter who let herself be panicked by an imagined stare?

Imagined, that was the key word. She'd probably just been feeling guilty over having spoken as she had to James.

She went quickly from her room and started down the stairs, running her hand along the polished railing. That outburst had been out of character for her, but maybe it had done some good. At least James had been civil to Marc afterward.

Marc wouldn't let it show, but the defection of people who'd been his closest friends had to hurt so much. In the old days there'd been a photo in his study— Marc, James and Phillips in their gray Citadel uniforms, arms around one another's shoulders, laughing. Their young faces had been like the young faces in the choir. Odd that she remembered that picture so clearly after all this time.

Aunt Kate still sat at the breakfast table when she came down. Dinah bent to give her aunt a quick hug. Aunt Kate had been in an odd mood since the Sunday brunch with Marc. She wasn't sure what was going through her mind.

"I'll bring the newspaper in for you, and then I'm off to work."

"You won't forget to check on the availability of ca-
terers, will you, Dinah?"

"I'll take care of it," she promised, suppressing a
sigh. Aunt Kate's sudden decision to hold her Christmas tea this year was going to mean a flurry of decorating and cleaning. Still, if it made her happy, it was
a small price to pay.

Getting to know Court had thawed her attitude considerably, and Dinah thought that once she'd talked
to Marc, she'd no longer been able to imagine him a
killer. But it was the paint on the garage door that had
roused Aunt Kate's fury. What was the world coming
to, when one of her neighbors could be so uncouth?

So Aunt Kate was throwing down the gauntlet to
her friends. Come to my Christmas tea and be polite to
my nephew-in-law, or lose my friendship. Once she'd
decided to put herself on Marc and Court's side, there
was no stopping her.

Dinah went quickly out the walk and then paused
in the act of reaching for the newspaper. The magnolia wreath that she and Court had made and hung on
the gate was no longer there. Instead it lay in the gut-
ter next to the curb.

The anger that swept through her surprised her with
its strength. She'd best not let Aunt Kate know about
this. She went quickly out the gate and across the street,
seething. Maybe she could get it fixed and up again before Court saw. Really, who would do a thing like that?
Her Christmas spirit was taking a beating this year.

The wreath didn't look as bad as she feared when
she picked it up. The vandal had simply ripped it from

the gate and tossed it, not taking the time to pull it apart. She turned it over. The wire loop they'd put on to hang it from was undone, but she could twist it back into place again.

"Ms. Westlake. Sure is nice to see you again."

The voice startled her. She glanced up to find a man sauntering toward her. A ruddy weather-beaten face, thickly curling reddish hair, a patched denim jacket that strained over a paunch—he looked faintly familiar, but she couldn't place him.

"Good morning." One last twist did it, and she hung the wreath back on the gate. "I'm sorry. I'm afraid I don't remember who..." She left the sentence open-ended, hoping he'd rescue her.

"Don't remember me, do you?" He stopped a few feet from her. "I reckon there's no reason you would. But I remember you."

He leaned against the fence, and something in the movement brought a memory back. Annabel, looking out the window at the garden and shaking her head.

"That man does more leaning on the fence and talking than he does working. I'll have to speak to Marc about him."

"You're Mr. Carr. You were the gardener for my cousin and her husband."

And Marc had been looking for him unsuccessfully. She sent a glance toward the house. Was Marc home?

"That's right. You were just a kid then. Here you're all grown up now." Both the smile and the way his regard lingered on her were a shade too familiar.

"I know Mr. Devlin would like to speak with you."

She put her hand on the gate, pushing it open. "Won't you come in?"

Carr took a step back. "I heard that. Thought maybe I'd come by. Then I thought maybe I'd like to know what he wants to see me for first."

She couldn't let him get away now that he was here. She made an inviting gesture toward the gate. "He's been talking with people who were here the summer his wife died. I'm sure it won't take long."

"I don't know as I want to get mixed up in that." He shrugged. "Never does a man with a business any good to get mixed up with the police."

"There's no question of the police." At least, not yet. "He'd just like to talk about what you remember."

"Nothin'." He said quickly. "I don't remember nothin' about that night."

Her attention sharpened. Why did he assume she meant the night Annabel died?

"You might remember something that happened that summer that would be helpful."

"I don't." The movement of his eyes gave lie to his words. "But if someone did happen to know something, what do you s'pose it might be worth?"

It was like being handed a live bomb. Carefully. Handle this very carefully.

"If someone knew something about a crime, the best thing he could do would be to talk to the police. If you try to sell information—"

He stepped back farther, eyes widening in an un-convincing expression of innocence. "Hey, I didn't say nothing about selling no information. I don't know anything. Don't you go putting words in my mouth."

She'd gone too far, and she tried to repair the damage. "Just come in and talk to Mr. Devlin, all right?"

"No, ma'am." He spun on his heel. "I don't have nothin' to say." And he went off down the street at something approaching a jog.

She stared after him, frustrated. She'd blown it. She'd have to go and tell Marc that Carr had been here and she'd let him get away. Still, what more could she have done?

She went quickly up the walk and in the door before she could think of some reason to evade the task. She came to a dead halt in the foyer, feeling as if she'd walked into a wall. Or into the past.

The marble-topped stand Annabel had brought from her parents' house stood against the right wall again, opposite the doorways to the front parlor and the family room. The gold-framed mirror that had been a wedding gift hung over it once more, just as it had when Annabel lived here. And the vase on top of the stand held arching sprays of jasmine, Annabel's favorite flower.

Her mind whirled, the aroma touching memories she hadn't looked at in years. Annabel bending over her infant son, blond curls falling forward, laughing as Court's baby fingers reached for them. Annabel triumphant and alive in evening dress, as she and Marc got ready for the bar association dinner—sparkling in black and diamonds, Marc, dashing in a tuxedo, eyes only for his beautiful wife.

Dinah took a strangled breath and turned to see

Marc standing in the door to the study, watching her. She cleared her throat, fighting for calm.

"I see you've brought some more furniture down." Best if he not see the effect it had on her.

He nodded. "I had a talk with a real estate agent yesterday about putting the house on the market. She looked around and repeated what you said—it will show a lot better if it looks lived-in."

"Did she give you the idea of buying the flowers?" The scent seemed to clog her throat.

"After we brought the stand down, I remembered that Annabel always had flowers there." He touched the jasmine gently. "She liked the way they reflected in the mirror."

"I remember." She wrenched herself away from the past. "I just saw Jasper Carr. He spoke to me, out on the street in front of the house."

"What?" Marc started toward the door. "Why didn't you bring him in? Is he still there?"

"Don't bother. He's left already. I'm sorry. I tried to persuade him to come in and talk with you, but he wouldn't."

He turned back, giving her a quizzical look. "Don't look so tragic about it, Dinah. It's not your fault. It was a slim chance that he'd have anything useful to say, in any event."

"That's just it. I think he might." She hated saying this, knowing it was the one thing that would make Marc determined to find him.

"What do you mean?" He covered the distance between them in a couple of strides, clasping both her hands in his as if she might try to run away. "What did he say? Tell me, Dinah."

"I'm trying." She was. It wasn't Marc's fault that the warm grasp of his hands on hers had robbed her of the ability to think straight, let alone speak. His intensity seemed to be an engine, driving her heart to pound out of her chest.

"Sorry." He loosened his grip but still held her wrists gently in his hands. He'd be able to feel her pulse racing, if he bothered to notice. "I didn't mean to shout. Just tell me what he said. Why did he talk to you?"

Maybe better not to mention what had happened to the wreath. "I was adjusting the wreath on the gate when he walked up and started talking to me."

"I see." He looked as if he saw more than she'd said. But he couldn't know about the wreath.

"He recognized me," she said hurriedly. "I didn't know him right away." She went back over that odd conversation. "He said he'd heard you were looking for him, so I asked him to come in. But then he started being—well, *evasive* is the only word."

"Did he say he knew something about Annabel's death?" It had to cost him to keep his voice that even.

"It was odd. First he said he hadn't noticed anything that summer and there was no point in talking to you. Then he said what if someone had noticed something, would you be willing to pay for information."

"You're sure that's what he said?"

"That was the gist of it." She looked into his face. "That's when I blew it. I said if he knew anything, he had to come forward. He denied saying it, insisted he didn't know anything, and off he went. Marc, I'm sorry. I should have been more tactful."

"Don't beat yourself up over it." His dark eyes were intent, focused on a goal she didn't see. "I'll take it from here."

"But he denies knowing anything."

His lips tightened. "It sounds as if he could be persuaded to remember something if the price were right."

"You can't pay someone for information."

"I'm not the police. I'll do whatever I have to."

She didn't like the way he said that. "You don't know where he is."

"The investigator I hired tracked down some of his favorite haunts. I'll find him." He focused on her. "Look, it won't be much use doing that until fairly late in the evening, and I don't want to leave Court alone here. He wouldn't tolerate the idea of a babysitter, but could you think of something the two of you could do together tonight, just to keep him occupied?"

"Marc, can't you just leave it to that private investigator? Isn't that why you hired him?"

"No. I can't." The words dropped like rocks.

Nothing she might say would change his mind. Trying would be an exercise in futility.

"All right. I'll think of something to do with Court." Now it was her turn to clasp his hand firmly. "But, Marc, you be careful. Promise me you'll be careful."

She was going to be late at headquarters, but maybe a peace offering would help. She swung by Baker's Café, parked and hurried inside, wishing she had time for one of their signature poached-egg dishes. Instead she ordered an assortment of scones and muffins and surveyed the breakfast crowd while she waited for the order.

Charleston was a small town at heart—she'd always known that. And Baker's Café was popular with the locals, which probably explained why Phillips and James were sitting at a small table a few feet from her, engrossed in conversation. Just a friendly get-together, or were they talking about Marc's return?

She took the few steps that separated them. "James, if you eat Eggs à la Bakers every day, you'll need new suits the next time you run for office."

She'd surprised him into a smile as he looked up from the plate of poached eggs, shrimp and andouille sausage. For a moment he seemed like the old friend she'd known for years, but then his expression frosted over as he remembered their last encounter.

"Dinah." Phillips got up quickly. "How nice to see you. Won't you join us?"

She shook her head. "I'm on my way to work. I just stopped by for some muffins."

James's eyebrows lifted. "Balancing the police department's interests with Marc's must be quite a job."

"On the contrary. We all want justice, don't we?" So James still felt convinced of Marc's guilt, even though her lecture at the concert had seemed to soften him up. A fragment of memory teased her. "By the way, didn't you used to use the same gardener Marc and Annabel did—Jasper Carr?"

"Carr? I remember him. One of a long series of unsatisfactory gardeners we hired. But he left Charleston long ago, for good, I thought."

There was a piece of information she hadn't had. "Do you remember when that was?" Shortly after Annabel's death, perhaps?

He shrugged. "I don't keep track of people like that. Anyway, he's gone."

"Not anymore. I saw him this morning. He spoke to me."

Phillips put down his coffee cup. "Dinah, honey, seems to me the man had an unsavory reputation. You shouldn't be talking to him. Where did you see him?"

That was Phillips, of course, still thinking she was a little girl who had to be protected. Still, maybe it was as well not to give the gossip mill any more fuel. "I just ran into him on the street." She glanced at the counter. "I must go. It's been nice seeing you all."

Politeness dictated she say that, but she wasn't sure "nice" exactly described her feelings as she hurried back to the car. James had given her food for thought, though. It might be worth finding out when Carr had left Charleston, as well as when he'd returned.

"It's frustrating." Tracey slapped a file down on her desk blotter, the sound masked by the usual hum of activity in the office late that afternoon.

Once again they'd had a futile visit with their witness. Teresa would go so far with Dinah but no further. Before Dinah could put a line on paper, she'd dissolve in tears and run from the room.

The case, frustrating though it was, at least distracted her from the disturbing encounter with Jasper Carr, Marc's equally disturbing intentions, and the revelation that Carr had left town sometime after Annabel's death. Maybe, if she put it to her correctly, Tracey could be of help.

"You know what's going to happen, don't you?" Tracey ran her hand through her hair, adding to her wild woman look. "I've got half-a-dozen other cases to work. If we don't get something soon, this will be pushed to the back burner. Somebody will look at it once a year, and that's it."

"I know." Dinah closed her eyes for a moment, picturing the spotless apartment, the work-worn mother, the haunted look in the girl's eyes. "If that happens, she'll never heal. Never."

"That sounds like personal experience talking." Tracey leaned toward her.

She shook her head. "Not really. I've gotten past the trauma."

"Dinah, you wouldn't say that if you could see your face when you talk to Teresa. Every time you look at that girl, it's like you're looking in a mirror."

"No." She pushed that away with both hands. "Anyway, it's not like that. It's just on my mind because I'm concerned for Court."

"Are you sure it's not Marc Devlin you're concerned about?"

"I'm sure." She took a breath. Just ask. "You know, you could do something for me that would help resolve this situation."

Tracey's eyebrows shot upward. "Something I could lose my job for?"

"No, of course not. I just want to locate someone. Jasper Carr. He used to be my cousin's gardener. He apparently left town after her death, but I know he's back, and I'd like to find him."

"That sounds like a bad idea."

"Will you do it?" She knew Tracey well enough to know that she might disapprove, but she wouldn't let her down.

Tracey gave an elaborate sigh. "I suppose. But Dinah, I'm telling you this for your own good. Take a couple steps back from Devlin."

"I can't. I—"

"She's giving you good advice, Ms. Westlake."

She hadn't heard Draydon approach. He stood over them. He'd shed his jacket, his tie was askew, and he looked as if he hadn't slept in a while.

She straightened, feet crossed at the ankles, hands folded in her lap, spine taut—typical Southern lady posture, drilled into her practically from birth. "I don't know what you mean."

"Marc Devlin. Ms. Westlake, you don't want to get drawn in by him." That was surely sympathy in his face.

"Marc did not kill my cousin."

He sighed. "I guess you really want to believe that. But you've been involved in police work long enough to know that the obvious is true more often than not."

"Not this time." She would not let herself respond to

the concern on their faces. "Anyway, what about Hassert? He certainly acted like a guilty man."

"Guilty, maybe, but not of this crime," Draydon said. "We checked and double-checked his alibi for the night of the murder before we let him go."

"You let him go?"

He shrugged. "He's out on bail. He's smart enough to stay away from Devlin now, I'd say."

Marc wouldn't be surprised. He'd predicted this outcome, but she hadn't wanted to believe it. "I wish I could be as sure as you are. He didn't look very harmless when he was trying to break into the house."

"Look, Ms. Westlake, I'm only talking to you like this because you're one of us. You're not in any danger from Leonard Hassert." He leaned toward her, his face intent. "It's Marc Devlin you need to watch out for."

Marc pulled his rental car into the garage, trying to shove away the frustration that was eating at him. He'd have to walk into the house and act as if everything was fine. Dinah had been upset enough earlier over her encounter with Jasper Carr. He didn't want to aggravate that by his failure to locate the man, even though he itched to question her again for every single word Carr had spoken.

He walked quickly around the house. Not that he expected to find anything or anyone, but it seemed an instinctive protective measure. The bear, prowling the area around his cave for foes.

Unfortunately, his problems were human, not animal. Nothing disturbed the serenity of the garden. The white lights Dinah and Court had hung from the low branches of the live oak sparkled like stars in the chill air. The veranda light shone on the magnolia and holly wreath on the door, and the window candles seemed to call a welcome.

Welcome. He hadn't thought about that word in connection with this house in a long time. He put his key in the lock, tapping lightly on the door. No point in alarming Dinah and Court.

But when he walked into the hallway, only Dinah came from the family room to meet him.

"Where's Court?"

Her eyebrows lifted. "Hello to you, too. Court went up to bed a while ago. He said to tell you thanks for asking me, but he doesn't need a babysitter."

"Sorry. Hello, Dinah. I hope he didn't take out his antibabysitter attitude on you."

She smiled, but he thought he detected strain in the fine lines around her eyes.

"Not at all. He was charming company. We went out to Citadel Mall and did some Christmas shopping and then ended up with hot chocolate and pepperoni pizza." She shuddered a little. "His combination, not mine."

"I figured that." He crossed to the family room, shedding his jacket and tossing it on the nearest chair. "That kid has a cast-iron stomach. You wouldn't believe what I've seen him put away for breakfast."

She'd followed him into the family room, and she nodded at the logs glowing in the fireplace. "When we got home he insisted on starting a fire in the fireplace. He wanted to toast some marshmallows, just to top things off, but luckily there weren't any."

"I'm glad for your sake." He sank onto the leather couch, suddenly aware of how tired he was, and patted the seat next to him. "Now sit down and tell me what has you looking so stressed, other than Court's strange tastes in food."

"Nothing." She sat, but her eyes evaded his. "What happened tonight? Did you find him?"

"No." He stretched his legs toward the blaze. He'd have said it wasn't cold enough to start a fire, but it was comforting anyway. "I went to one dreary dive after another in the part of town the chamber of commerce doesn't advertise to tourists. It was the same story everywhere. Carr is a regular, but they haven't seen him in a couple of nights."

"Then he's changing his regular habits." Dinah seized on that immediately. "That must mean something."

"Maybe that he doesn't want to see me." He studied her face. That delicate profile might have been etched on a cameo. "Come on, sugar. I can see something's wrong. You may as well tell me."

"If you go back to Boston and call people 'sugar' they'll have you arrested."

He resisted the urge to smile. "You're stalling."

"It's nothing." She shrugged, focusing on the hands she had clasped in her lap like a schoolgirl. "I shouldn't let it upset me. It's the jasmine."

For a moment it didn't compute. Then he realized

she was talking about the flowers on the hall table. "The jasmine? What about it?"

"The scent gave me a headache, for one thing." She rubbed the tips of her fingers between her brows. "But it also made me remember things. Is that why you bought it? Because scents stimulate the memory?"

"I bought it because Annabel used to put jasmine in that vase, that's all." Questions burned on the tip of his tongue, but he had to proceed carefully. "Did the jasmine bring back memories of Annabel?"

What do you remember, Dinah? What memories are buried so deeply you never want to find them?

She nodded slowly, her lips tensing. "It made me think about that summer. Mostly I remember the quarrels. I'd forgotten that." She looked at him then, with what might have been accusation. "You weren't around much, but when you were, it seemed you and Annabel were always arguing."

She was being fair. It was irrational to feel pain at the look in her eyes.

"Yes." He had to take a breath before he could go on. "Sometimes I think that's all I can remember of that time. The arguments. The heat. The pressure at work to succeed."

He stared into the heart of the fire, remembering. There had been pots of flowers in the hearth the day Annabel had thrown a Dresden china shepherdess against the fireplace. Shards of china had sprayed over the flowers.

"What did you fight about?" Dinah's voice had gentled, as if she felt his pain.

"Everything." He shrugged. "Annabel didn't want to be pregnant again, did you know that?"

She shook her head, eyes wide. "But she loved being a mother."

"She did. But we hadn't planned another baby just then. I thought, seeing how she loved Court, that it would be all right. That once the baby came, she'd forget how she'd felt."

"She would have." Dinah's words were quick and warm. "Of course she would have."

He shrugged. "Maybe. But at the time, she hated it. Every symptom was another reason to rail at me. And she hated my job."

"You were such a good prosecutor. I always thought—"

"What?" He put his hand over hers where it lay on the couch between them, wanting to know what that serious-eyed child had thought of them.

"I thought you were a hero, going out to battle the bad guys every day."

"With a writ in one hand and a subpoena in the other." He had to take it lightly, because he'd like to be that hero Dinah imagined.

"I'm sorry you lost that, Marc." She seemed to read right past his words to his heart. "It's not fair."

He shrugged. No point in talking about what couldn't be cured. He'd made a satisfying career for himself, even if it wasn't what he'd dreamed it would be.

"Annabel wanted me to give up prosecutorial work for something more prestigious. I was away too much,

I wasn't consorting with the right kind of people—you name it, it became a quarreling point. I'm sorry you heard us."

"I never realized what the quarrel was about. I just knew things weren't right between you. Was that why she wanted me to stay that summer?"

He met her gaze, startled. "I don't know. I never thought of that."

"She may have thought I'd be a distraction. Or a buffer." Her face clouded with sorrow. "I wish I'd been able to give her what she wanted."

He tightened his grip, wanting to reassure her. "That wasn't your job. You were just a kid. It was my job." His throat tightened with the words he didn't want to say. "I hated the quarrels, so I stayed away from the house more than I had to."

"Marc, don't." She turned toward him, violet eyes bright with unshed tears. "You can't blame yourself."

"If I had been here, it wouldn't have happened." He said out loud the words that had festered in his soul for ten years. "I know that, Dinah. I failed her."

"No. No, you didn't." In her eagerness to comfort him, she took his hand between both of hers. It seemed he could feel all that was good and true in Dinah through the pressure of her fingers. "That's survivor guilt. All of us have felt that, but it's not true."

"Not for you. But it is for me."

A tear spilled over onto her cheek and glistened there. He touched it to wipe it away. Somehow it seemed very important that Dinah not cry over him.

Her skin was warm and smooth against his fingertips, and her eyes shone with caring. For him. All that warmth and caring and honesty that was Dinah drew him toward her until it took all his strength not to pull her against him and cover her soft lips with his.

He couldn't. He shot to his feet and covered the space to the fireplace in a few short strides. The room wasn't big enough. He needed to be farther away from her than this.

The mirror above the fireplace reflected the cozy room—the furniture Annabel had chosen, the Christmas tree that Court and Dinah had trimmed. And Dinah, sitting where he'd left her, a lost look in her eyes.

Feeling anything but a cousinly fondness for Dinah would be a recipe for disaster. A relationship between them in the shadow of Annabel's death would be enough fodder for the gossip mills to last a lifetime. Aunt Kate would die of the shame of it.

Dinah wasn't a child any longer, but she wasn't the tower of strength she'd like to think she was. He'd brought her enough grief already. He couldn't bring her any more.

Chapter Nine

Aunt Kate's Christmas tea was in full swing, the hum of conversation rivaling a swarm of bees. Dinah pinned a smile to her face and carried a fresh tray of ham-asparagus rolls to the light buffet that had been set out on the dining-room table. She'd almost persuaded Aunt Kate to use a caterer, but Alice had taken great offense at the idea of someone else preparing food to be served in this house.

Several traumatic discussions later, Dinah had accepted defeat. She had finally convinced them to let her bring in some cream puffs and a few savories from a bakery they trusted. Everything else Alice had made, with the help of a niece to do the prep work.

Dinah scanned the table to see if anything else needed replenishing. The cheese bennes were going quickly, of course. No one had the light touch Alice did with the delicate cheese and sesame wafers. She'd been begging Alice for years to let her help make them, but Alice insisted no one else could slice them to the exact thickness of a dime. She'd probably carry her secret recipe to the grave.

She switched the tray for one she had waiting on the sideboard. One good thing about being this busy—she had a reason not to go anywhere near Marc.

He'd barely spoken to her for the past few days. Ever since that night when they'd been so close, to be exact. Her cheeks warmed at the memory of those moments. He'd nearly kissed her, before he'd jumped up and practically run away.

Had he seen something in her eyes that precipitated it? That idea was too humiliating even to consider.

He'd opened up to her, showing her his pain, and she'd responded. That was all. That had to be all. He would never look at her as anything but Annabel's little cousin.

She couldn't think about that now. She had to keep smiling, keep being the perfect hostess. No one must see anything in her face when she looked at Marc.

The pleasant hum of conversation as guests eddied between the parlor and the dining room assured her that everything was going as it should. People had turned out in force this afternoon, a testament to the power the Westlake name still had in Charleston society.

Court, in a navy blazer and gray slacks, hovered next to Aunt Kate's armchair, ready to fetch anything she needed. She was introducing him to everyone, her tone calm and commanding.

"Say hello to my great-grandnephew, Courtney. Annabel's son."

Aunt Kate's words put Court securely in his proper

place in Charleston's social strata, and people responded to that. She'd already overhead several invitations to Court to meet this young person or that, participate in one event or another.

As for Marc, well, people were at least being civil to Marc. Etiquette demanded that. She let herself glance at him. He was standing by the bay window, a cup of fruit punch in one hand. Phillips stood next to him, looking as relaxed as she'd seen him lately.

She began to weave her way through the crowd, offering a tray of sweets—tiny cream puffs and éclairs, Alice's rich triple chocolate brownies, pecan tassies. Phillips swerved away from Marc and stopped her, picking up two of the brownies.

"Margo's not here to chastise me, so I'm going to eat what I want."

Dinah raised her brows. "Does she really have a sick headache?"

"Now, sugar, you know better than to ask a man to tell on his wife. Your aunt accepted her excuse."

"My aunt would never let you know if she didn't."

But Dinah had read behind Aunt Kate's smile. Sooner or later, Margo would regret this affront to Westlake family pride. Aunt Kate might no longer take an active role in the complex web of Charleston's social structure, but she still had power. A telephone call, a word dropped in someone's ear, and some committee appointment or invitation that Margo coveted would be inexplicably out of her reach.

"I just wanted to thank you, Dinah." Phillips's gray eyes warmed behind his glasses. "Without you, I probably never would have renewed my friendship with Marc, and I'd have been the poorer for it."

"I'm not sure I had anything to do with it, but I'm glad, for both your sakes. Have you been reminiscing about your Citadel days?"

"We surely have. I tell you the truth, I'd never have gotten through those first weeks without Marc and James. The two of them dragged me bodily through more than one obstacle course. Seems a long time ago, I'm afraid. I couldn't even walk an obstacle course now." He shook his head, smiling. "Maybe I'll get some coffee to go with this brownie."

He headed toward the silver coffee urn on the sideboard, and she smiled after him. It was good to see that relationship mended, if nothing else could be.

"Old friends getting back together, I see."

She turned. James stood behind her, balancing one of Aunt Kate's bone-china cups in his hand. His smooth, polished air was perfectly intact, but there'd been something a little off-key in his words, hadn't there?

"It's nice to see you, James." She hesitated, then spoke impulsively. "Why don't you go and join them? It's not the three musketeers without you."

His cool blue eyes studied her face for a moment before he gave a chilly smile. "What a nice child. You want everyone to shake hands and be friends."

"I'm not a child." Although denying it probably sounded childish. People who had been Annabel's friends would always think of her that way. Including

Marc. Something seemed to squeeze her heart. "I just think it's past time for people to move on."

"Can you forget that easily? I can't."

Shaking him was not an option at Aunt Kate's Christmas tea. "I'll never forget Annabel, if that's what you mean." She kept her voice low, although no one seemed close enough to hear. "But Marc is innocent."

"We're none of us as innocent as all that, Dinah." His blue eyes, intent on her face, were like shiny marbles, giving away nothing of his feelings. "Are we?"

"I don't know what you mean." Had she been guilty, with her teenage crush on her cousin's husband?

He shrugged, looking away from her as if losing interest. Or as if disappointed in her. "Some things can't be forgiven, you know. They're too deep a betrayal for that."

"James—"

He thrust the cup and saucer into her hands. "Please make my excuses to your aunt. I'm afraid I'm due at another engagement."

He worked his way through the crowd so quickly he might be escaping, without a single glance in Marc's direction.

Well. She deposited the cup and saucer on a side table. That was odd. Was James talking about himself? Or Marc?

Betrayal. It was an ugly word for an ugly deed. But who had been betrayed, and why?

She found herself moving through the crowd toward Marc without having made a conscious decision to do so. She was a few steps away when he saw her.

His eyes warmed for an instant. Then, very deliberately, his expression changed to something else. Friendly but distant, as if she were a waitress descending on him with her tray of desserts.

"You're not going to offer those to me, are you? Phillips is the one with the sweet tooth."

"And I've had my share," Phillips said quickly. "Dinah, don't you get to sit down and enjoy the party?"

"When it's over." She forced a smile. "Then I'll relax." And then she'd let herself listen to what her heart was telling her.

That she was only kidding herself when she insisted she didn't have feelings for Marc. And that he saw, and knew, and was warning her off.

Whatever impulse had made her decide to brave King Street traffic to get some Christmas shopping done had definitely led her astray. Dinah sat at the light, drumming her fingers on the wheel as pedestrians, laden with far more packages than she'd managed to purchase, made their way across the street.

King Street was dressed in its finest for the holiday season, with lights everywhere and Christmas trees in every window. She should be enjoying this outing, instead of fretting.

Truth was, she'd thought to distract herself from her feelings about the situation with Marc. Unfortunately, she wasn't succeeding.

She should have talked to him about that odd conversation with James Harcourt. But he had made it all but impossible, managing never to be alone with her even when he and Court had stayed to help clean up after the guests had left. She'd thought about going to the house this morning, but turned coward at the thought. So she'd gone shopping instead.

The cell phone interrupted the thoughts that didn't seem to be going anywhere. She checked the number before answering. Tracey. "Hey, Tracey. What's up?"

"Not much." But she sounded harried. "You remember that information you asked me to get for you?"

Her heart beat a little faster. Information on Jasper Carr, the elusive gardener. "Did you find anything?"

A long pause. "Listen, this information isn't going out to any unauthorized person, is it? Because that could bring me grief."

To Marc, in other words. Naturally Tracey would feel that way. "No, it's just for me. I promise."

"Okay, then. He doesn't seem to be at the address that's listed for him, but he's working out at Magnolia Gardens. It's a temp job, just for the Christmas season. You can probably find him there."

"Thanks, Tracey. I appreciate the help."

"What are you up to, girl? Something I should know about?"

"Nothing that has anything to do with the police. I just want to talk to him, that's all."

"Well, you be careful." Her voice was concerned. "Don't do anything stupid."

"I won't."

She hung up, elated. Something, at last, was breaking her way.

Marc would say she should come straight to him

with this information. He was the one who needed to talk to Carr. But she'd promised Tracey, and she couldn't go back on that.

So the obvious course was to drive out to Magnolia Gardens and talk to the man herself. She'd been caught by surprise the last time, and she hadn't said the right things to him. This time he would be the one to be surprised, and she'd persuade him, somehow, that he had to talk to Marc.

The light went green. She flicked on her turn signal and made an abrupt right turn, leading to annoyed drivers venting their feelings with their horns. She'd take the expressway over the Ashley River and head up 61.

She had no idea what time gardeners left for the day, but Magnolia Gardens should be open until five. She'd be in time.

Or not. She hadn't thought about how crowded the commercial strip on the west side of the river was this time of day. At least it was moving faster than downtown traffic. Strip malls gradually gave way to housing developments, and the road became what Aunt Kate reminisced that it used to be—oak-lined, moss-draped, low country. The Ashley River gleamed through the trees off to her right now and then.

Once this road had been lined with plantations, their mansions facing the river, until Union troops marched down the road toward Charleston, burning as they went. Now only three were left—Drayton Hall, Middleton Place and Magnolia. They'd all been familiar to her since childhood, but Magnolia was her favorite. Carr had been lucky to find work there.

She took the turning toward the river at the Magnolia Gardens sign. Aunt Kate used to bring her every year to see the camellias at Christmastime, and again in the spring to see the azaleas.

She parked the car. The lot was nearly deserted, probably too late in the day for most visitors. She hurried to the ticket booth. Only one other car pulled in behind her.

"Just an hour till closing, miss," the woman warned as she took the bill she held out.

"That doesn't matter. I just need to locate one of your employees. Jasper Carr. Do you know where he might be working?"

She consulted a clipboard. "Should be down by the Biblical Garden, if he's doing what he's supposed to." She sounded doubtful.

"I'll find him. Thank you." She hurried down the path, buttoning her jacket. The wind was chilly, and she hadn't dressed for this. She could only hope that, for once, Carr would indeed be where he was supposed to be.

The White Bridge over the lake was strung with evergreen swags and wreaths along its railing, and in the distance, she could see the glow of the camellias. She really should try to bring Aunt Kate out while the camellias were blooming.

She went quickly down the path toward the Biblical Garden. It was a favorite spot of Aunt Kate's. She'd been there so often that she no longer needed to walk around and read the signs that described the plants, but simply sat, drinking in the still atmosphere.

Well, Dinah would do no sitting today, at least not if she could help it. Find Jasper, persuade him to cooperate. Maybe she should hint that Marc would be willing to pay for information. Marc had certainly given her the impression that he might.

Hurrying her steps, she rounded the hedge into the Biblical Garden, rehearsing the words she'd say. She stopped abruptly. A long-handled rake leaned against an empty red wheelbarrow. No one was there.

She hadn't realized how much she wanted to find the man. The disappointment was like a blow to the stomach.

Well, his equipment was there, so surely he was around somewhere. "Mr. Carr?" Her voice echoed emptily. No one answered.

She stepped back onto the path outside the Biblical Garden, looking in both directions. Nothing. Still, he hadn't come past her. She'd go on. He wouldn't have left the hoe and wheelbarrow there if he'd quit for the day.

The path led on to the maze. Magnolia's designer had modeled his maze on the one at Hampton Court, but instead of boxwood, it was planted with hundreds of camellias. She walked toward it, captivated as always by the sight.

She stood for a moment, feasting her senses on the delicate blossoms and the dark leaves of the holly bushes that were interspersed with the camellias.

"Mr. Carr?" she called again. No reason to believe he'd gone into the maze. He was probably hiding out somewhere, though, perhaps having an illegal cigarette.

"Mr. Carr?" She called again, starting into the maze. The blossoms surrounded her, closing into what had always seemed a magical place.

Christmas camellias, she called them as a child, thinking everyone had camellias blooming for Christmas. She stopped. Was that a step she heard?

"Hello? Is anyone there?"

Again there was no answer, but something brushed against the far side of the bushes on her right.

She froze, apprehension sending chills snaking down her spine. She opened her mouth to call out and then closed it. If someone was there, he hadn't responded to her previous calls. Instinct told her he wouldn't answer this time.

She ought to feel angry. She didn't. She felt afraid.

No point in standing here, waiting and wondering. She'd go back to the ticket booth, find out where Jasper checked out when he left for the day, and wait for him there.

That was a sensible, practical solution. So why did she feel compelled to creep away like a thief? She took a careful step back from the hedge of camellias, then another. Her breath was soft and shallow as if even breathing might draw too much attention to herself.

I'm being silly, Lord. Or am I? Please, surround me with Your protection.

She reached the entrance to the maze and took a deep breath. It was going to be all right. It was.

She walked quickly along the outside of the maze, breath still coming too quickly. Foolish, to let herself be spooked by being alone here. She wouldn't let her wayward imagination ruin a place she'd always loved.

A few more steps and she'd reached the corner. She'd just go back—

A blur of movement from the corner of her eye, an arm, a sleeve, someone grasping her, a hand over her mouth. She tried to scream, but the hand was choking off her voice. She struggled, kicking at him, trying to swing her handbag at him. Struggle, fight, don't give in—

"Ms. Westlake, please. Please, don't scream. I won't hurt you."

Please, Lord, please, Lord.

"I won't hurt you, I won't. I just want to talk." He sounded as if he were on the verge of tears, and somehow that seemed to get through the fear.

She twisted around to see his face. Jasper Carr? No. It was the man she'd last seen trying to get into the house. Leonard Hassert.

She pushed away the fear. Fear led to panic, and panic would do no good.

"Please, Ms. Westlake." His voice was trembling, and she realized his hands were trembling, too. "Just don't scream, all right? I'm going to take my hand away."

He moved a step back. She took a breath, the air sweet. Her muscles shook with the effort it took not to run.

"What do you want?" Her voice rasped on the words.

"Not to hurt you," he stammered. "Not that. Please, you have to believe me."

"You picked an odd way to convince me of that."
Give me the right words to handle him, Father.

"I'm sorry, I'm so sorry. I thought you wouldn't see me if I came to your house, so I followed you."

He was certainly right to be cautious. She'd call the police at the sight of him. He looked so pitiful, standing there with tears in his eyes, that her fear ebbed away.

"All right, I'm here now." She clenched her handbag tightly. "Say what you have to say."

"I have to talk to him—Mr. Devlin. I know he doesn't want to see me. I thought maybe you could talk to him for me. Get him to see me."

She took another step back, and he made no move to stop her. She slipped her hand into her purse, relieved when her fingers closed over her cell phone.

"I'm doing this all wrong." He rubbed his forehead, looking and sounding like a petulant child. "I think about it, but then I don't know what to do."

"Why do you want to talk to Mr. Devlin?" Impossible to go on being afraid of someone who looked so hangdog.

"I wronged him."

"What do you mean?" Her heart jolted. Maybe she'd been too quick to think him harmless. Was he talking about Annabel's death?

"I wronged him," he said again. "I have to tell him. I have to make amends." He reached in his pocket, and she tensed. But his hand came out with a small white card. "He can reach me here. Please, please—"

His voice broke. He turned away, tears spilling over, and lurched into a shambling run down the path and out of sight.

Chapter Ten

"I think it would be best if you and Court went over to your house." Marc said the words without any real expectation that Dinah would listen to him.

Sure enough, she shook her head. "I'm staying here." She planted her hand on the hall table, as if to anchor herself. "If Court would like to go keep Aunt Kate company this evening, I'm sure she'd appreciate it."

"No way." Court flushed slightly. "I mean, I like her a lot, but if Dad's going to entertain a murderer, I'm not leaving."

"I doubt very much that Hassert is coming here to confess to murder."

But what was driving the man? His behavior had been odd to the point of dangerous, first trying to force his way into the house and then accosting Dinah that way at Magnolia Gardens. Marc was reminded yet again of her recklessness.

"You shouldn't have gone out there after Jasper Carr alone. It was too dangerous."

Dinah's chin lifted at the implication that she couldn't take care of herself. "I didn't even find Carr. And I've told you, Tracey gave me that information in confidence. I shouldn't have told you at all, but after what happened with Hassert, I didn't have much choice." She glared at him as if it was his fault.

"You were alone, that's the point. Hassert was obviously following you—" He stopped, because if he thought of how the man had frightened Dinah, he'd be more inclined to punch him than to listen to him.

"If it hadn't been there, it would have been someplace else." She shrugged her shoulders eloquently. "I can't stay inside the house all the time. I won't change my life because of Hassert or anyone else."

"Well, I've agreed to see him. I hope that will end it." He glanced at the grandfather clock. It was nearly eight. "He should arrive soon. I'll hear him out, and then I'll make it clear to him that if he comes near any of us again, he'll be back in jail."

Dinah nodded. "That would do it for any sensible person. Hassert hasn't impressed me as being especially sensible so far."

She'd put her finger on the heart of what bothered him, of the thing that had his stomach churning when he thought of the man being too close to Dinah and Court.

"That's been his pattern, as far as I can tell." He had to speak coolly, rationally, even though what he wanted to do was pick her up and carry her bodily out of the house. "He acts on the impulse of the moment and regrets it afterward. I looked up his case again before we came south. He's not a career criminal."

"Let's hope he doesn't plan to start."

The doorbell rang, and Dinah jerked. In spite of her determined facade, she was nervous.

Without thinking about it, he caught her hand to reassure her. The simple gesture set up a longing to hold her that was anything but simple. He let go as if he'd touched something hot. *You're not going to do that, remember?*

Dinah looked away from him and grabbed Court's arm. "We'll be in the family room with the door ajar, listening. If we hear anything odd, we're calling the police."

"If I had a baseball bat—" Court began.

Dinah pulled him toward the family room. "No baseball bats. Your father can take care of himself."

Did she really think that? She was afraid, but he wasn't sure whether that fear was for him or Court or herself.

Maybe it didn't matter. The point was it existed, and he'd exposed Dinah to that by coming here and forcing her to choose sides.

He shoved his concerns about Dinah to the back of his mind as he approached the door. He'd have to worry about Dinah later. Right now he needed to focus on dealing with Leonard Hassert.

He yanked the door open with such force that Hassert looked startled. He tried to arrange a less-forbidding expression on his face. If he hoped to get anything out of the man, it would be best not to scare him.

"Hassert. I understand you want to talk with me."

"Yes—yes, sir, I do." He was practically stammering. "May I come inside?"

He took a step back, holding the door open even though his instinct was to slam it in the man's face. "Come in." He nodded to the study door. "In there."

Following Hassert to the study, he watched the way he walked, the way his hands moved, the way he held his head—all the things he would notice in a courtroom when a defendant took the stand. Hassert was afraid, that was certain. He also gave the impression of being embarrassed, hands fidgeting, eyes not meeting his.

Obedient to the promise he'd given Court and Dinah, he left the door ajar. He just hoped they had sense enough not to act prematurely and ruin things.

He nodded to the chair he'd placed in the pool of light from the desk lamp. "Have a seat." The chair behind the desk he'd reserved for himself. It gave him a nice wide expanse of solid mahogany between him and Hassert.

Not that that would help if the man were armed. Well, a person had to take a few chances if he were to accomplish anything.

"You've gone to plenty of trouble to see me." His fingers tightened on a paper knife, and he forced them to relax. "Let's hear what you have to say."

Hassert flushed, the color brightening his pale complexion for a moment, then fading. "I'm sorry. I told Ms. Westlake I was sorry, too. I didn't mean to scare her."

Relaxation wasn't working. "What did you think

would happen when you lunged out from behind a bush and grabbed her? Of course she was frightened. She could have you arrested for assault."

Hassert paled again at the threat. Obviously he didn't want to go inside again. "I said I was sorry."

"You acted on impulse, just like you did when you attacked that man in the bar. You jumped out and grabbed Ms. Westlake without thinking of the consequences."

"I didn't mean anything." He hung his head like a sulky child. "I just had to get you to talk to me. I know I did it all wrong." He looked up, and Marc saw that his pale blue eyes were filled with tears. "I'm sorry. I had to see you. I had to tell you how sorry I am."

He planted his hands, palms down, on the desk surface. "You mean you're sorry for killing my wife."

"No!" Hassert's voice soared, and Marc could only hope Dinah wouldn't be inspired to call the police. "No, I didn't do that. I couldn't do anything like that. You have to believe me!"

"Why?" He kept his voice cold. "Why would I believe you? You told Ms. Westlake you'd wronged me. That's the biggest wrong anyone ever did me."

"You don't understand." Hassert slumped in the chair, and it was hard to believe he'd be brave enough to raise his hand to anyone. "All my life I've had the same trouble. I've given in to anger or fear and done the wrong thing. I always told myself I couldn't help it."

"You threatened me when you were convicted. How do I know you didn't follow through on that threat and come after my wife?"

Panic flared in the man's eyes. Marc tensed. Maybe he'd pushed too hard.

"I didn't do anything to her. I had an alibi. The police checked it."

"Alibis can be faked." He'd thought that all along, but looking at Hassert, his conviction was seeping away. Hassert didn't look or act as if he had that particular sin on his conscience. It had been a long time since he'd practiced criminal law, but the instincts were still there.

"I don't know how to convince you, but I didn't." He shook his head, seeming to shrink in the chair.

"Then why did you say you wronged me? Why were you so eager to see me?"

Hassert's hands twisted together in his lap. What would Dinah say about his body language? She had to be expert at reading that, to do the job she did. Not that he was going to let her get anywhere near Hassert to find out.

"I threatened you. You were doing justice, and I threatened you." Hassert shook his head, seeming on the verge of tears. "When I was in prison, I finally had to face the truth about myself. All the excuses fell away, and the Lord made me see that I was a miserable sinner. But He forgave me." Hassert looked up, smiling through his tears. "I knew I had to try and right the wrongs I'd done. I wasn't able to find you, to tell you that, until you came back to Charleston."

He let out a long breath. Was this for real? It certainly sounded that way. "You went about it the wrong way. You know that, don't you?"

"I know. I'm sorry. I never meant to scare anyone. I just really needed to see you, so I could ask for your forgiveness." He leaned forward, face intent, and gripped the edge of the desk. "Please. I can understand if you don't want to, but please forgive me. I was wrong. I have to ask for your forgiveness."

He didn't want to give it. That was the rock-bottom truth. The man had haunted his dreams for years.

But he'd always trusted his instincts, and they were telling him that Hassert hadn't had anything to do with Annabel's death.

And if someone asked for forgiveness, what else could he do? *Forgive us our trespasses, as we forgive those who trepass against us.* It would be hard to go on praying that if he couldn't forgive.

His throat was so tight he wasn't sure he could speak. He stood, taking his time, studying the man who rose when he did and stood there with pleading on his face.

"I forgive you." He cleared his throat and held up his hand before the man could speak. "But I want your word that you won't approach my family again, and that includes Ms. Westlake. This closes the books between us. Agreed?"

"Agreed." Relief flooding his face, Hassert wrung his hand. "Thank you, sir. Thank you."

Marc nodded. He ought to feel relieved. But as he showed Hassert to the door, he could only think one thing. This meant that Annabel's killer was still out there, somewhere. Watching. Waiting.

* * *

"How soon is it going to start?" Court, impatient as he always seemed to be, leaned forward in the back seat, staring out at the Cooper River, serene in the dusk.

"The boats start moving at five o'clock, but it'll take them a while to get downriver this far."

Court had found the Christmas Parade of Boats on the internet, and he'd been fully prepared for nonstop nagging to get his father to agree to come. Dinah had been mildly surprised to be invited, since Marc seemed to be making a point of avoiding her, especially after the incident with Hassert. He had, she suspected, decided that he was going to protect her from her association with him, whether she wanted his protection or not.

"Are you sure Waterfront Park is the best place to watch?" Court fidgeted.

"We're sure," Marc said firmly. "Why don't you get out and walk around?"

"Instead of bugging you?" Court grinned. "Okay."

"Stay where I can see you," Marc warned.

"Chill, Dad." Court got out, grinning, and walked off toward the water.

Now it seemed Marc's turn to be jittery. He drummed his fingers on the steering wheel. The problem was that he was alone with her. He didn't want to be.

She struggled for the right words. How to do what she'd intended to do the next time she was alone with him? She had to do something to restore a normal relationship with Marc. They couldn't go on this way.

Her fault, she supposed. She'd let him see too clearly that she had feelings for him, and now he was torn between warning her off and protecting her.

"Maybe we ought to get out." Marc reached for the door handle.

"Wait a second." She took a steadying breath. If she let him get out now, she'd probably never muster up the courage to do it. "I need to talk with you."

He gave her a polite, noncommittal look. "Of course."

Her heart winced. He looked at her as if she were a stranger.

"I was a little surprised that you invited me tonight."

He blinked. "I don't know what you mean."

"Let's not pretend, Marc." It took an effort to keep her voice even. "We need to clear the air between us. You've been shutting me out."

He didn't deny it. "This has turned more difficult than I expected. I don't want to expose you to any more episodes like the one with Hassert."

"The situation with Hassert is cleared up."

"That doesn't mean something else won't go wrong." His jaw set with characteristic stubbornness. "I can't protect you all the time."

"I don't want you to protect me." Shouting at him would probably do no good, although she was tempted. "I'm all grown up, Marc. You have to stop thinking of me as a child."

His eyes seemed to darken. "I don't. Maybe that's part of the problem."

She caught back a gasp. That was more honesty

than she'd expected. Or wanted. But maybe that was
what was needed, that they be honest about their relationship.

"Something happened between us the other night—
connection, attraction—I'm not sure what it was." She
said the words slowly, feeling her way. "I didn't intend
to bring that up. I know it makes you uncomfortable."

"That's not quite the word I'd pick," he said drily.

She fought the longing to jump out of the car. "I've
done a great job of protecting myself since Annabel's
death, you know. Keeping everything on the surface,
never letting myself look too deeply. I told myself that
was my way of dealing with grief."

It hadn't just been the grief. She was beginning to
see that now. It was her relationship with other people,
with her job, even with God. One thing to recognize it,
but another to figure out what to do with it.

"I just want you to know—"

"Don't!" His voice was harsh enough to make her
wince. "Look, Dinah, we both know we can't be anything to each other than what we were."

She hadn't expected anything more, but his blunt-
ness hurt more than it should. She swallowed the pain.

"I know that. But I'd like to think we can still be
friends."

He wasn't looking at her. He was staring out the
windshield, as if he saw something fascinating out on
the moving water. "We'll always be friends, Dinah."

That sounded like a farewell. Her heart squeezed
painfully in her chest. Friends.

Court came darting toward the car, his face excited.

Maybe the boats had appeared. She could leave the car and put some space between herself and Marc.

"Dad, hey, Dad." Court wrenched the door open. "I saw him, that gardener guy you showed me the picture of."

Marc was already out of the car before she had a chance to react. "Where? Are you sure?"

She slid out her side of the car and hurried around to them.

"Over that way," Court pointed toward the crowd. "Sure, I'm sure. I looked at the picture, didn't I?"

Marc exchanged glances with her. "Let's have a look. You two stay together, will you?"

"Dad—"

"I want someone with Dinah," Marc said quickly.

"Oh. Right." Court subsided.

This time she didn't protest. Marc's expression had told her this was as much for Court's sake as for hers.

"Show me where you saw him." She refrained from taking Court's arm. He wouldn't appreciate that.

"This way." He plunged into the crowd, squirming through enthusiastically.

She followed with a bit less enthusiasm. Court was still a child, although he'd resent that furiously. He didn't remember his mother's death, and this whole business was more like a treasure hunt to him than anything else.

She grabbed his jacket to slow down his progress. "If you knock someone into the water, you're going to be extremely unpopular."

"He was standing right here." He nodded to the low

railing that separated the walkway from the river. "Do you think he knows we're after him?"

"That could be." Carr was being awfully elusive, for someone who'd hinted he had information to sell. "What was he wearing?"

The act of putting a description into words would blur the image of the man in Court's mind, but that couldn't be helped. It was the constant dilemma facing police officers in dealing with eyewitnesses.

"Faded jeans. Some kind of a dark jacket, maybe a windbreaker. I didn't notice the clothes so much. I just saw his face, and I knew it was the face in the picture Dad showed me."

She nodded, looking around. The crowd was thickening now, pressing toward the water, craning for the first glimpse of the lighted boats. "I don't think we're going to find him in this crush. Let's see if your dad had any luck."

But when they'd worked their way back through the crowd to Marc's side, he shook his head. "If he was here, he may have spotted us and slipped away."

"I should've gone after him myself, instead of coming for you."

Marc slung his arm around Court's shoulders. "You did the right thing. I never want you to do something like that on your own."

"You think he's dangerous? That maybe he's the one?"

"No, I don't." Marc spoke quickly. "He acts like he knows something, but that could just be an excuse to get money."

"Maybe he figures if he's hard to get, it'll raise the price," Court said.

"That's good thinking. It could be exactly what's on his mind. If so, he'll show up sooner or later." He squeezed Court's shoulders. "Don't worry about it, okay?"

"Right. Hey, look! The boats are coming." Forgetting the subject that quickly, Court pushed forward with the rest of the crowd.

She glanced at Marc's face. "Is that really what you think about Carr?"

"I don't know what I think." His voice had an edge of frustration. "But he can't stay out of sight forever." He took her arm. "Let's catch up with Court, before he ends up in the river."

Marc seemed able to dismiss Carr from his mind nearly as fast as Court did. They joined Court, who peppered them with questions as the boats, strung with lights and with Christmas music playing, began to pass by. They'd go down to the point, then up the Ashley on the other side of the peninsula, celebrating the holidays in a uniquely Charleston manner.

It was exactly like a dozen other Christmas boat parades she'd attended. But she hadn't felt this uneasiness at any of the others. She moved her shoulders, trying to shake off the sense of someone watching her.

Someone could well be watching her, but that didn't mean that person had ill feelings toward her. At least half of Charleston seemed to be here. She'd already seen a number of people she knew in the crowd. Likely the other half was down at the Battery, waiting for the boats to reach them.

A tourist, apparently feeling that Marc sounded like a native, asked him a question, and Marc turned away to answer the man. She looked around for Court. He'd moved close to the edge of the walkway, craning his neck for the best possible view of the boats.

He shouldn't be that close to the edge, although he'd dispute that if she told him so. Marc was already several paces away as the crowd ebbed and flowed between them. It was like being caught in the tide out at Sullivan's Island, thinking you knew where you were only to discover you'd moved with the current.

Instinct sent her toward Court. If he leaned out any farther, she'd grab him as if he were a two-year-old, whether he liked it or not.

She worked her way closer, frustrated by the crowd, which seemed to sense her desire and want to thwart it. She squeezed between two very large women who were engaged in a loud conversation about their Christmas shopping. Ignoring their annoyed looks, she spurted through like a cork popping from a bottle. A few more steps and she'd reach Court.

A white yacht, ablaze with lights, let forth a blast of Christmas music. The crowd pushed forward. Court, caught off guard, seemed to lose his balance, tipping forward toward the dark water.

Panic shoved her toward him. "Court!" She grabbed, her hand catching his jacket as he flailed on the edge. For an instant that seemed like an eternity they counterbalanced each other, but her feet were slipping on the damp surface and in a second they'd both be in the water—

"Hey, look out!"

Strong hands grabbed her arm, hauling her backward. Her fingers slipped on Court's jacket, but it was okay, someone else had him and he was safe.

"You okay, ma'am?"

"I'm fine. Thank you." *Thank You.* She managed to breathe again. "Court, are you all right?"

He nodded, white-faced but composed. "Yes. Sorry. Thank you, sir."

"Anytime."

Their rescuer faded back into the crowd, the whole incident over in less than a minute, probably unnoticed by most of the bystanders. Court was fine. Even if he'd fallen in, he'd have been all right—chilled from the ducking, but all right. There was no reason for the fear that snaked through her as she pulled Court close.

"You're sure you're all right?"

He nodded, not pulling away. "Let's find Dad." He looked at her, his eyes wide. "Dinah, I didn't just fall. Somebody pushed me."

Chapter Eleven

"Thanks, Glory." Dinah accepted the mug of coffee Marc's housekeeper handed her, sinking down on the leather couch in the family room. The Christmas tree lights were turned on, in spite of the sunshine that poured through the tall windows. Obviously Court didn't intend to miss a minute of the holiday.

"Mr. Marc will be down directly." Glory hesitated, as if she had a mind to say something more, but then she turned and went out.

That was just as well. Dinah had no wish to rehash the events of the previous evening. She'd already done that for too much of the night.

She wasn't sure she'd ever felt quite that absolutely visceral response of terror when she'd thought Court was in danger. And although she and Marc had taken turns playing it lightly in front of Court, she hadn't stopped shaking inside for hours.

She hadn't realized how much Court had come to mean to her. Oh, she'd known she loved him, of course:

But that absolute terror for him was something she'd never experienced before. It must be what a mother felt when her child was in danger.

Her mind flickered briefly to Teresa's mother, to that look she had of simply waiting for something too dreadful to describe to descend on her little family. She would understand.

Annabel would understand. Would she resent Dinah for feeling that way about Court?

She wrapped her fingers around the mug, taking comfort in its warmth. Surely not. Annabel would want them to be close, wouldn't she? To her horror, she didn't know the answer to that. Her teenage adoration for her beautiful older cousin seemed naive to her now. How could she say what Annabel would want? She'd never known her as a adult.

Somehow, in the darkest hour of the night, her prayers for Court had crystallized something she'd been barely aware of until now. For Court, she could open her heart to God, breaking down the walls she'd erected to protect herself. For him, she could be open to the possibility of pain.

By morning, she'd known what she had to do. She had to convince Marc to take Court and go away. That was the only solution. Court had to be kept safe, even at the cost of never knowing who killed Annabel. Even at the cost of never seeing him or Marc again.

She heard the footsteps on the stairs soon enough that she could wipe away the tears that hovered and force a smile to her face by the time Marc opened the door.

"Dinah." He crossed to the table, pouring a mug of coffee from the carafe Glory had put there. "I need this." He turned, his gaze raking her face, and then came to sit across from her in the big leather chair. "I don't need to ask how you slept. It's written all over your face."

"Don't remind me." She took a sip of the coffee, holding the mug to hide her face for a moment. "How is Court this morning?"

"He's fine. Top of the world, in fact. Apparently nearly falling in the Cooper River was worth about a hundred emails to his friends." He jerked his head toward the study. "That's where he is now, in fact."

"I'm glad he's so resilient." Too bad she wasn't. "Is he still convinced someone pushed him?"

"Yes." He examined his coffee. "He could be mistaken. It could have just been the normal movement of the crowd. There were plenty of people there, and you can't always account for what a crowd will do."

She'd like to believe that. "I know. They could have surged forward accidentally, throwing Court off balance. But you don't believe that, do you?"

"No." His face tightened. "I don't. I think someone meant it for a warning. To tell me that Charleston's a dangerous place for anyone connected to me."

"That's what I think, too." She took a breath, trying to stifle the pain. "So I think you and Court should leave."

"Run away?" His eyebrows lifted.

"I don't care what you call it." She set the mug on the

coffee table. The caffeine had stopped helping. "You can't risk Court's safety."

"I've been trying to convince him to go to a friend's place for the holiday. I promised I'd join him for Christmas." His smile flickered, but it held no amusement. "You'd think I could force him to go, wouldn't you?"

"Well, not unless you wanted to drag him onto the plane. He won't go unless you do, is that it?"

He nodded.

"Then you have to go, Marc." She leaned forward, as if her intensity could convince him if her words didn't. "You don't have a choice."

She couldn't read what his dark eyes were hiding. "That's what you've wanted from the moment you heard we were coming, isn't it?"

"No. Well, maybe at first." She struggled to remember how she'd felt about Marc's arrival just a few short weeks ago. "I didn't want to confront the past. I thought—" She shook her head. "It doesn't matter. Everything has changed. But you still have to admit that leaving is the only sensible thing to do."

"For Court's sake."

"Yes, of course." She'd love to know what was behind the mask he seemed to be wearing. "You can't let Court be in danger."

"No. You're right." He looked very tired all of a sudden. "We'll have to go."

The door opened on his words, and Glory came in. "There was a message for you, Mr. Marc." She held out a slip of paper. "It was that man we were talking about. Jasper Carr."

"What?" Marc lunged from the chair, snatching the piece of paper. "Why didn't you call me to the phone?"

"He didn't want me to." Glory's brow furrowed. "I don't like that man. Never did. He insisted I just give you a message." She nodded toward the paper. "Come to that address today at five. He'd meet you there."

"Was that all he said?" The question shot out in what she thought of as Marc's prosecutor voice.

"There was one other thing." She sounded reluctant.

"Let me guess. He wants me to come alone."

Glory shook her head. "Just the opposite. Said he didn't want to see you alone. He'll only meet you if Miz Dinah comes, too."

He did not want Dinah to go with him to meet Jasper Carr. And since arguing with her on the subject had done no good whatsoever, he was simply going to leave without her. He'd rather deal with the consequences of her anger than put her at any further risk, no matter how slight.

He walked quickly toward the garage. There was no doubt she'd be angry. Shy little Dinah had grown up, and the feelings he'd begun to have for her reflected that.

That didn't bear dwelling on. He couldn't explore any feeling for Dinah other than cousinly affection. Even if it hadn't been for the barriers created by the suspicion attached to him, it was impossible. No matter how she might try to break free, Dinah was tied by the past. She had idolized Annabel in a way that couldn't let her feel anything for him without a boatload of guilt.

As for him—well, Court had to come first for him. He couldn't even think about any relationship that could affect that. Court loved Dinah as a cousin, but that didn't mean he'd welcome a romantic attachment between her and his father.

He rounded the corner by the garage and came to a stop. Dinah, hugging her black leather jacket close to her body, stood waiting by the car.

"You're here." Well, that was certainly mastering the obvious.

"Somehow I thought you might decide to do this without me." She put her hand on the door handle. "It won't work, Marc. You should know that."

He glared at her over the roof of the car. "I don't know any such thing. And I don't intend to take you with me to see a character like Jasper Carr."

She yanked open the door. "Then you'd better be ready to throw me out of the car, because I'm going." She slid into the passenger seat.

Fuming wasn't doing much good. And his anger had to be at least partially frustration over the complex feelings she generated in him.

He got into the car, shut the door and fastened his seat belt. "Satisfied?"

She smiled. "I am, thank you."

He turned the ignition and began to back out of the garage. "And don't try the demure Southern belle routine on me, either. It doesn't fit with your sheer stubbornness."

"Southern ladies are always stubborn. How else would they deal with Southern men?"

"An unanswerable question." He turned out onto the street. "Do you know anything about the address Carr gave?"

"Only that it's in a neighborhood where I don't spend much time."

"All the more reason why you shouldn't be going."

She gave an elaborate sigh. "You know perfectly well why I'm going. It's not that I have any burning desire to talk to that man again, but he won't meet with you unless I'm there."

He glanced at her, to see her forehead wrinkle. "Wondering why?"

She nodded. "I can't imagine, unless for some strange reason he thinks a second person should witness your meeting. But that doesn't make much sense."

"It does if he's afraid of me." He voiced the thought that had been in the back of his mind since he'd heard Carr's terms. "If he thinks I'm a murderer, he won't want to be alone with me."

"That's ridiculous." Dinah's voice was as sharp as he'd ever heard it. "If the man knows anything at all about what happened that night, he certainly knows it wasn't you."

"Why, Dinah?" He looked at her, his hands tightening on the wheel.

She blinked. "Why what?"

"I didn't realize, until I came back, how many people are convinced I killed Annabel. But not you. Why aren't you afraid to be alone with me?"

"Well, I—I just know you too well. I know you couldn't do anything of the kind."

"That's not really an answer and you know it." He wasn't sure why it was so important to him to press her. "You were a kid then. You took me at face value."

"If you mean I took you for granted—of course I did. You were part of my family."

"Maybe you didn't know me as well as you thought you did. What does any sixteen-year-old know about the adults around her?"

"I'm not sixteen any longer. And I'm still sure." She shook her head, and he saw the fluid movement of her hair, blue-black against the black leather of the jacket. "Some things a person is just sure of. I don't have to analyze my feelings. I know."

"You were there that night." He paused for a heartbeat, praying he was saying the right thing. "Maybe you're sure about me for another reason."

She didn't speak, but he saw her hands clench together in her lap.

He had to keep trying. "Dinah, you had a head injury that night. You know as well as I do that sometimes people can't remember the things that happened moments or even hours before an accident like that."

"There's nothing to remember." Her voice was tight and strained. "I didn't see anything that night. I didn't."

He wanted to probe, to ask if she remembered coming out of her room, starting down the stairs. Something had made her fall. Surely that wasn't a coincidence.

But gut instinct told him he'd driven her as far as he dared for the time being. They'd come back to it again. They had to.

He checked the street sign and then pulled slowly to the curb. "This is it. Not very prepossessing, is it?"

The house had once probably been a charming Victorian single-family home. Now shutters hung lopsided, paint peeled, and a general aura of decay surrounded the place. Like so many houses of this era, it had been chopped up into small apartments. Presumably Carr lived in one of them or imposed on a friend who did.

Dinah's hand was already on the door handle. He reached across her to still the movement, bringing his face very close to hers.

Too close. He drew back a little. "Stay in the car, Dinah. Please."

"I don't think Carr will interpret staying in the car as coming with you." She pulled the handle up. "Let's get this over with."

The doorbell didn't seem to produce any sound, but the double doors, their etched glass now grimy and cracked, stood open. He stepped into the hall, motioning Dinah to stay behind him.

Silence, nothing but silence. Either the other apartments were vacant, or the tenants were extremely quiet. He started up the narrow stairwell, which probably replaced something that had once been grander. According to Carr's directions, he was on the second floor.

He felt Dinah close behind him. She wasn't putting her hand on the filthy railing, and he could hardly blame her.

"I'm having a bad feeling about this." He hadn't intended to whisper, but the silence around them seemed to suppress any noise. "Dinah, please go back outside, at least until I see if he's here."

Her fingers closed on his jacket sleeve. "If you think I'm waiting down there by myself, you'd best think again."

"Stubborn," he muttered, and quickened his pace. As she'd said, let's get this over with.

The door to 203 stood slightly open. "Carr? Jasper Carr, are you here? It's Marc Devlin."

Nothing. He glanced at Dinah. Her eyes were wide in the gloom.

"Carr?" He tapped on the door, and it swung open.

It took him a moment to register what he was seeing. Carr lay on a couch, legs sprawled half off. A bottle had fallen from one hand to the floor.

"He's drunk," he said, disgust in his voice. And then something about the stillness, the rigidity of the body, began to penetrate. "Stay here," he ordered Dinah, trusting that his tone left no room for argument.

He crossed the room until he stood staring down at the man. Reluctantly he put his fingers on Carr's throat, searching for a pulse. There was none. Whatever Carr had intended to tell him, he'd never hear now. The man was dead.

Dinah sat in the captain's office at police headquarters, not sure how long she'd been there. Long enough, at any rate, for the shaking to subside.

She took a steadying breath and then raised the foam cup of coffee to her lips. It was just as bitter as Tracey always insisted, but it did serve to warm her.

She found Tracey studying her. "This really is bad coffee." She tried to keep her voice light, tried to erase the worry that clouded Tracey's face.

"If I'd had more time, I'd have stopped for some of the good stuff." Tracey ran her hand through her hair in a characteristic gesture. "You feel any better?"

She nodded. She and Marc had been separated from the moment they'd arrived at headquarters. She'd been shown into the office, and Tracey had been hauled in to take her statement, probably out of deference to her status as a civilian police employee.

Marc had been shown no such consideration. He was in an interview room with Draydon. She could only hope he'd remembered his own training and refused to say anything until he called an attorney.

She shifted in the hard metal chair. "How can Draydon possibly think Marc had anything to do with Carr's death?" She shouldn't put Tracey on the spot, but she couldn't hold the question back. "I was with him when we found Carr. Or does he think I was involved?"

"Of course not. He doesn't know that it was murder. He's just trying to cover all the bases, that's all. I'm sure you'll both be free to leave soon."

Did Tracey really believe that, or was she trying to make her feel better?

"There was a pill bottle open next to him." She was driven to talk about it, even if Tracey couldn't respond. "It could have been an accidental overdose."

"We'll know more about it after the autopsy." Tracey surveyed the outer office, as if hoping someone would come to rescue her.

"Or it could have been suicide." Maybe the coffee was doing some good. Her mind seemed to be working again. "If it was, isn't that as good as an admission of guilt? Carr must have killed Annabel."

Tracey hitched her chair closer. "Listen, Dinah, you know I can't talk about it."

"I know." She reached out impulsively and grasped her friend's hand. "I know you're just here because we work together." A thought struck her, taking her breath away. "Or is that all over? Will they refuse to give me any more work because of my involvement in this case?"

"I won't lie to you, Dinah. It's not going to do you any good around here, at least not unless this business is cleared up quickly."

"So I'm persona non grata, is that it?" There was more bitterness than the coffee would produce. All the work she'd done to be accepted here was going to go for nothing.

"Look, don't worry about it this early in the game." She gripped her hand. "You know I'm not giving up on you."

"Thanks, Tracey." She shouldn't burden Tracey with her troubles. It wasn't fair to her, when there was nothing she could do.

"Let's talk about something else." Tracey sounded determinedly cheerful. "How was your aunt holding up when you talked to her?"

She'd called Aunt Kate the moment she'd been allowed to, afraid she'd hear something on the radio or television and panic.

"She surprised me, actually." She noted the sad-looking artificial Christmas tree on the corner of the captain's desk. "I tend to forget how strong she is. Just because she's physically weak now doesn't mean she's lost any of that moral fortitude. She has Court with her, and he'll stay there until we get back. She and Alice are teaching him to make taffy, whether he wants to or not."

"I can imagine how a teenage boy is reacting to that." Tracey smiled. "Your aunt—" The door opened.

Dinah's breath caught. It was Marc. "What happened? Are you all right?"

Tracey rose. "I'll just leave you alone for a few minutes." She went out, closing the door behind her.

Marc shook his head, his face grim. "It's hard to tell what Draydon thinks. He's predisposed to be suspicious of me, obviously." He sank into the chair Tracey had vacated. "I can't say I blame him. I'd react in the same way if it were my case."

"Unless he wants to believe I was in on it, he can't believe you harmed Carr. I was with you."

He shook his head, leaning forward but not touching her. "It's not that simple, sugar." The endearment seemed to slip out without his noticing it. "I don't know what the coroner will say, but Carr had been dead for a while. They could conclude that I killed him earlier and then came back with you, hoping that would allay suspicion."

"That's ridiculous." Anger warmed her. "Draydon's thinking is too convoluted for a police detective if he thinks that."

He shrugged. "Well, let's look on the bright side. I

didn't see a note, but that doesn't mean there wasn't one. If Carr committed suicide it will go a long way toward clearing me, even if he didn't leave a note." He reached out, his fingers closing over hers. "I just wish you hadn't been there. Aunt Kate will scalp me for involving you."

"Aunt Kate is fine. She—" The door opened again, and suddenly her heart raced.

Draydon stood in the doorway. Marc straightened, dropping her hand and rising.

"Did you want to talk with me again?"

Draydon looked as if he'd like to say yes, but instead he shook his head. "You and Ms. Westlake are free to go. For the moment."

She stood, grabbing her jacket, only too glad to get out before he changed his mind. But Marc hadn't moved. His jaw tightened.

"What does that mean?" He sliced off the question.

Draydon held the door politely. "The investigation has a long way to go. You should know that, Counselor. But I'm guessing we'll find that Carr knew something about your wife's death and was foolish enough to try and blackmail a murderer."

Marc shouldn't say anything. She grabbed his arm, her fingers digging in.

"You heard him, Marc. Let's go home." She tugged him toward the door, breathing a little easier when she got him past Draydon.

"Just one thing." Draydon dropped the words as they passed him. When they both looked at him, he smiled.

"Don't leave town," he said gently. "Either of you."

Chapter Twelve

Dinah's steps slowed as she and Marc approached Aunt Kate's front door. She paused, looking up at him. "Maybe we'd both best take a minute to put a smile on."

He lifted an eyebrow. "Do you honestly think we'll fool anyone?"

"I don't know." Her heart twisted at the thought of Aunt Kate's frailty. "But we have to try and keep Aunt Kate from realizing how serious the situation is. She gets so frightened for me."

His hand closed over hers. "She loves you. You're all she has."

"I know." She shivered as a breeze ruffled her hair, rustling the leaves of the hundred-year-old live oak they stood under. "She's all the family I have, too."

"We're family." His fingers tightened almost painfully. "Court and I. Even if we're not Westlakes."

Family. However much he might deny it, she was still Annabel's little cousin to him. "I know."

"It's probably best if Court doesn't know all the

details either," he said. "The difficulty will be keeping them from him. He's very resourceful. If I don't answer his questions, he'll look up the newspaper on the internet."

She had to smile at that. "I suppose he would, wouldn't he? Well, all we can do is try."

They stepped onto the piazza, and he reached for the door handle. "Odd, isn't it? My decision to leave town came just a little too late. Now we can't."

Draydon's words seemed to hang in the air. *"Don't leave town, either of you."*

Well, she had no intention of going anywhere, but Marc and Court should be safe back in Boston by now. The thought left an empty feeling where her heart should be. Sooner or later they'd leave, and she'd have to learn to get along without them. It wouldn't be easy.

Marc opened the door, and they stepped into the warm hallway, lush with a sweet aroma. Court plunged from the parlor to meet them.

"Hey, are you guys okay? What happened? Did you do CPR on the guy?"

Marc sent her a despairing glance over his son's head. "Yes, we're all right. No, we didn't." He wrapped his arm around Court's shoulders. "Listen, son, we don't want to upset Aunt Kate. Let's try not to talk about it just now."

Court's face was eloquent in his disappointment. "Bummer."

"Okay?" Marc prodded.

"Okay. But I think Aunt Kate's really getting a secret thrill out of it, even though she was worried about Dinah."

"Well, let's go in and assure her that Dinah's fine." He gave Court a quick hug before releasing him. "I'll talk to you about it later. Promise."

"Dinah?" Aunt Kate's voice wavered just a little. "Come in, please."

She hurried into the parlor, pinning a smile on her face. "I'm sorry, Aunt Kate." She bent to press her cheek against Aunt Kate's. "It took forever. I hope you didn't worry too much."

Her aunt's hand caught hers and clung, but she managed to smile. "Court did a wonderful job of explaining that naturally you'd have to tell the police everything you saw. I hope it wasn't too dreadful."

"Not at all." She hoped she'd be forgiven the small lie to save her aunt distress. "Goodness, it smells as if you all have been cooking up a storm. What did you make?" She addressed the question to Court, who grinned.

"They taught me how to make taffy. And then Alice and I made about a million of those little pecan cookies. 'Course I probably ate about half of them."

"No such thing," Alice said. She stood in the doorway, smiling at him. Court had obviously made a conquest. Alice didn't let just anyone into her kitchen. "You come and help me carry the trays in. Your daddy and Dinah must be starving."

"We don't need…" she began, but it was too late. Feeding people was Alice's way of coping. Well, it would keep Court busy, anyway. She glanced at Marc, suspecting that he was thinking the same.

He moved around the parlor, as if too restless to sit still after the events of the past few hours. He stopped by the mantel.

"I see you've done some more Christmas decorating. I remember these angels from years ago."

Startled, Dinah looked at the mantel. There, tucked among the greens, were Aunt Kate's Christmas angels, fragile china figures dating from a century ago at least.

"We haven't gotten the angels out in years. You always say they're too fragile."

Aunt Kate gave a little shrug, the lacy shawl she had around her shoulders moving against her green wool dress. "I thought it would amuse Court. And he's very dextrous, for a boy."

"I didn't break a thing." Court came in from the kitchen, carrying a tray with the coffee service.

"See that you don't start with the Meissen china," Alice said. She began putting plates of cookies, savories, and tiny sandwiches on the coffee table.

"Alice, that's far too much food."

"Speak for yourself, Cousin Dinah." Court snatched a chicken salad sandwich. "I'm a growing boy."

"Leave some for the rest of us," Marc said. "It's not often I get to have some of Alice's shrimp paste, and I'm sure it's still the best in Charleston."

Alice beamed. "I'll just bring out some of that hot chocolate young Courtney likes. Dinah, you should drink it, too. Better for you than coffee."

"I suppose it's pointless to tell you I'm one of the grown-ups," she said.

Alice paused in the archway, turning to deliver a parting shot. "You're not so grown-up as all that."

"Alice, you're under the kissing ball." Court grinned, putting his arm around her and kissing her cheek.

Alice swatted him, but her eyes glowed with laughter. "Just for that, you come along and carry the hot chocolate in."

"That boy," Aunt Kate said indulgently. "He spotted the kissing ball in one of the boxes and wanted to know what it was. Nothing would do but that he hang it up right away."

"I hope he didn't tire you out." Marc bent over to take one of the delicate china cups Aunt Kate held out to him. "It was good of you to have him here."

"Of course he'd come here," she said. "We're family."

There that word was again. Family. Aunt Kate would never see Marc as anything but Annabel's husband, and there was no changing that.

Well, at least the crises of the past few days seemed to have mended whatever reserve she'd held on to against Marc. She was treating him as she always had.

Court came back in with the hot chocolate and solemnly poured a cup for Dinah. As he bent to hand it to her, he grinned. "I'll get you some coffee, if you'd rather."

"You'd better not disobey Alice. She always gets her way. Although judging by that kiss, you've already figured out a way to her good side."

"You don't think she minded, do you?" His face grew serious. "I just wanted to distract Aunt Kate. I wouldn't want to upset Alice."

What a kind heart he had. "Court, no one could be upset at a kiss from you."

He seized her hands in his. "Then it's your turn, Cousin Dinah." He tugged her, laughing, under the kissing ball and planted a noisy kiss on her cheek.

She hugged him, smiling. She'd told Marc they mustn't upset Court and Aunt Kate, but it was really Court who'd managed to cheer everyone.

"Come on, Dad." Court grabbed his father's arm. "You have to give Dinah a kiss, too." He shoved him toward her.

A wave of panic swept through her when Court pushed them together. Marc's arms closed around her. He couldn't kiss her here, like this, in front of everyone. She looked up, hoping Marc would turn it away with a laugh.

But the laughter in his face seemed to slip away as he looked at her. His eyes darkened.

She was suspended in the moment, unable to speak, to move, to do anything to turn away the inevitable. Marc bent, it seemed in slow motion, and his lips found hers.

The kiss couldn't have lasted more that a few seconds, but truth could be seen in the momentary flash of lightning.

They'd managed to distract Court and Aunt Kate from the danger, but at what cost? She couldn't deny what she felt for Marc any longer, at least not to herself. She was in love with him, and there was no future in that at all.

"Dinah?" Aunt Kate called her name as soon as she came downstairs the next morning. "Is that you?"

"Of course." She hurried into the breakfast room, giving Aunt Kate a reassuring hug. "Who else would it be at this hour of the morning?"

"I'm being silly, I suppose." Aunt Kate fumbled with her teaspoon. "I just wanted to be sure you're all right."

"I'm fine." She poured a cup of tea and helped herself to a piece of toast. She didn't really feel like eating, but Aunt Kate and Alice would worry themselves to death if she didn't.

"You had a terrible experience." Tears glistened in her eyes. "I know all of you tried to make light of it, but it must have been dreadful, finding that man. Marc never should have taken you there."

"He didn't want to. I didn't give him a choice." If only there was something she could say that would allay Aunt Kate's fears. But she was afraid, too. Afraid for Marc, with the cloud of suspicion hanging over him. Afraid for Court, who must not face losing his father.

"I always thought Annabel was the stubborn one." Her aunt dabbed at her eyes with a lacy handkerchief. "You've changed since Marc came back."

"Don't think that." She put her hand over her aunt's. "I'm the same person I've always been. It's just that having to face things about Annabel's death has made me more—aware, I guess. Responsible."

"You've always been too responsible. Too serious. Even that summer, trying to take over with Courtney when Annabel—" She choked.

Dinah patted her, alarmed. "Don't, darling. Don't upset yourself this way. It's going to be all right."

Even to soothe Aunt Kate, she couldn't seem to make that sound terribly convincing. How was it going to be all right? What if Marc were charged? Her feelings were of small concern next to that very real possibility.

"No. It isn't." The strength in her aunt's voice startled her. "I failed. I failed Annabel. And you."

"Don't be silly. You've always been there when I needed you."

Aunt Kate gripped her hand with feverish intensity. "I should never have sent you away. I thought I was doing the right thing, but now I know it was wrong. We should have faced it together."

"You did your best. That's all anyone can do."

Aunt Kate had probably kept herself up most of the night, worrying herself into this state.

"I failed you both." She shook her head. "Even with Annabel right across the street, I couldn't keep her from grief."

"What happened wasn't your fault. It wasn't anyone's fault except the person who did it."

Her head moved tremulously from side to side. "I knew, you see." Her voice was hardly more than a whisper. "And I didn't confront her. I should have, but I was afraid. I didn't want to lose her."

"What are you talking about, Aunt Kate? What did you know? Something about Annabel?"

Her heart was suddenly beating in sharp, quick thuds, and she couldn't seem to get her breath.

Aunt Kate covered her face with her palms. "I knew, and I did nothing."

She didn't want to hear, didn't want to know. If Aunt Kate had been afraid, she was, too. She didn't want to know.

But she had to. For Marc's sake, and Court's.

She took her aunt's hands gently in hers, drawing them away from her face. "It's all right. Really, it is. Just tell me about it, and I'll take care of it."

Tears spilled quietly onto Aunt Kate's cheeks. "It was Annabel. That summer. I heard her. There was another man. She was seeing another man."

Her throat was so tight she couldn't possibly push any words out. But she had to. "Are you sure?"

"Yes." It was the barest whisper. "I'm sure. I heard her, talking to him on the phone. Her voice—it couldn't have been anything else."

She couldn't think, just yet, of all that implied. "She didn't know you heard her?"

"No. I slipped away. I should have confronted her. If I had, maybe it wouldn't have happened."

"You mustn't think that. There's no way of knowing. Talking to her about it might have made things even worse." Although how they could be worse, she didn't know. "Who was he? The man. Who was it?" Dread gripped her heart.

"I don't know. I never knew. I never heard his voice. Just Annabel's."

"You didn't have a guess?" She'd been an oblivious sixteen-year-old who'd seen nothing, even when it was right under her nose. But Aunt Kate had been an elderly woman, who'd surely seen enough of life to notice something—a look, a word.

"I didn't know. I didn't want to know. I thought I could pretend not to know. But it was so hard. And when Marcus came back—"

Marc. What was she going to tell Marc?

Aunt Kate pressed her hands. "You have to take care of it, Dinah. I can't. You have to decide whether or not to tell Marcus, because I can't."

He shouldn't have kissed Dinah. Marc moved restlessly around the house the next day, unable to settle to anything for very long. With everything else he had to worry about, he seemed fixated on that moment.

He'd expected to dream about finding Carr's body. Instead his dreams had been impossible ones of holding Dinah, laughing, kissing, with nothing to shadow their happiness. Impossible dreams.

He rechecked the locks on the back door and the cellar door. Court had to be safe. Draydon's demand not to leave town didn't apply to Court, so he could send him to friends. But if he did, he wouldn't be with him to protect him.

And Dinah—he rubbed the back of his neck, where tension had taken up residence. Dinah had to be kept safe, too. Being around him had endangered her. If she had any sense, she'd steer clear of him. But since even now he could see her approaching the front door, that seemed unlikely.

He flung the door open, torn between his need to be with her and his conviction that she was safer away from him. "What brings you here?"

Dinah blinked and walked past him into the hallway. "What a gracious greeting. I'm fine, thanks, and you?"

"Sorry." He had manners enough left to be embarrassed. "I'm afraid being suspected of yet another murder has eroded any Southern courtesy I had left."

Her brows drew together. "You don't really think that, do you?"

"Draydon didn't tell me not to leave town because he likes having me around."

"He told me that, too, but I don't interpret it to mean that he suspects me of murder."

"No. He just thinks you might be a witness." He gave in to the temptation to grasp her hand. "I'm sorry, Dinah. I never should have involved you in this."

"Seems to me I involved myself." She glanced toward the stairwell at the sound of several loud thumps. "What on earth is Court doing now?"

"Rummaging around the attic, I suppose. It's his current fascination. He appears periodically to announce a new Christmas decoration project, or to suggest that some other piece of furniture be brought down. He'd have everything out if we were here long enough."

"I suppose it will all have to be gone through, in any event. Where are you putting things?" She turned around, as if expecting to see furniture piled in the hallway.

"We brought the table down to the dining room. Court decided he needed it for some project he has in mind. And the drop-leaf desk that used to be in Annabel's room intrigued him. We put that in the front parlor." His voice became dry when he had to refer to the room where Annabel died.

Dinah seemed to become aware that he was still holding her hand and drew it away, her face composed. She did a better job of ignoring the currents between them than he did.

Or maybe that meant she was retreating, pulling that wall around herself again. If so, it was something else for which he was to blame.

"It almost sounds as if Court has decided to stay."

"I don't think it's that, exactly. Usually he tells me what he's thinking, but not this time."

"Has he asked you anything about what Draydon suspects?" Her eyes darkened with worry.

"No, but he's a smart kid. He's bound to figure out something is going on." He rubbed the back of his neck again. It didn't help.

"Marc, we need to talk—"

Court's footsteps thudded down the stairs. "Hey, I didn't know Dinah was here. Hi, Dinah." He swung around the newel post at the bottom. "You didn't bring any more cookies, did you?"

"Court," he said warningly.

His son grinned, unrepentant. "It's a compliment, Dad. Dinah knows that."

"I'll tell Alice," Dinah said. "I'm sure she'll send a care package over."

"Come on, I want you both to see what I set up in the dining room." He swung the door open. "I found Dad's old train set."

"I didn't know that's what you were up to." He followed Dinah into the dining room. "So that's why you insisted we had to bring the table down."

The train set took him back to his childhood, although his mother would never have allowed him to set it up on the dining-room table. It had always gone in the playroom. He'd saved it for Court and then forgotten it when they'd left Charleston. Well, it was one thing they wouldn't forget this time.

"I waited for you to be here before I tried it." Court picked up the extension cord. "Ready?" He shoved the cord into the socket.

With a faint hiss, all the lights in the house went out. Court stared at him, chagrinned. "Oops."

He shook his head, smiling. "I had a feeling that if you plugged one more thing in, you'd blow a fuse."

"Don't feel bad," Dinah said. "At least it happened in the daytime, when you can see to fix it."

"I'll get it, Dad."

"No, just go around and unplug a few things. I know where the new fuses are." He pushed through the swinging door to the kitchen, still smiling. Blown fuse or not, Court and the train set had distracted him for a few minutes, at least.

The drawer next to the stove held the flashlight and the fresh box of fuses. He snatched them up and headed for the cellar door. Even in the middle of the afternoon, it would be dark enough in the cellar to require a flashlight.

He could hear Dinah and Court talking in the dining room as he opened the cellar door. Dinah was good for Court. And maybe, in a way, Court was good for her, too. He'd been wrong to think keeping them apart was for the best. Regardless of what happened now, Court understood the power of family.

He switched the flashlight on, aiming it at the wooden stairs, and started down. If he—

The tread cracked beneath his foot. He lurched, off balance, reaching for something to grab, too startled even to yell. His hand closed on a water pipe, cold against his palm, and for a split second he thought he was okay.

Then the step broke, crumbling under him, his body dropping downward, his hand clenching at the pipe, slipping, losing it, knowing he was falling.

Chapter Thirteen

Dinah heard the crash, and for an instant she and Court stared at each other, uncomprehending. Pain flashed through her. "Marc!"

They bolted toward the cellar door, jostling each other in their hurry. Court reached the door a step ahead of her, charging through.

Instinct had her grabbing his arm before she thought through the danger. They teetered together on the tiny landing.

Daylight from the open door touched what was left of the stairs. Two steps clung to the landing. The rest of the stairway was a mass of jagged timbers.

Marc lay crumpled on the cement floor, the broken flashlight rolling away from his out-flung hand. He wasn't moving. Her heart ripped in two.

"Marc!"

"Dad!" Anguish filled Court's voice. "Dad, say something. Please, be all right."

He leaned forward as if he'd try to jump down, and Dinah yanked him back.

"The bulkhead door. We have to go around the outside to get to him. Hurry."

She shot toward the front door, pausing just long enough to grab her cell phone from the handbag she'd left on the hall table. The mirror above it reflected her white, frightened face.

Please, Lord, please, Lord, let him be all right.

She punched in 911 as they ran, gasping out the address and the circumstances. Court reached the slanted double doors first and pulled them open, plunging down the few steps to basement level.

She followed, heart thudding in her ears. *Please, let him be all right.*

Court dropped down beside his father. "Dad, Dad!"

"Easy, Court. Take it easy." She pulled him out of the way, putting her hand on Marc's chest, and relief flooded through her.

"He's breathing." Her voice choked on the words. "He's alive. The ambulance is on its way. They'll be here in a couple of minutes. It's going to be all right."

Thank You, God. Thank You.

"How bad is he hurt?" Court was trying not to cry, but his voice was choked. "Why isn't he saying anything?"

"Careful, don't bump him." She moved to touch Marc's head cautiously. "It looks as if he's knocked out." She ran her hands over his arms and legs. Nothing obviously wrong, but how did she know?

"We should get a pillow," Court said. "We can't just leave him on the floor."

"Best not to try and move him until the paramedics get here." She understood Court's urge to help. He needed to do something that would make him feel he was helping his father. "A blanket would be good, though."

Court shot to his feet. "I'll get one. Be right back." He thundered out of the cellar.

Alone with Marc, she smoothed his dark hair away from his face, allowing herself the luxury of letting a few hot tears fall.

"Be all right," she whispered. "You have to be all right, Marc. We can't get along without you."

Court ran back with the blanket just as she heard the wail of a siren. She grabbed the blanket.

"You'd better go and show them where we are."

Court nodded, his face white, and ran out again, reappearing a few seconds later with the team of paramedics.

Dinah put her arm around him, drawing him a few feet away from Marc so that they could work. "It's going to be all right," she soothed, wishing she knew that for sure. "Your dad's in good hands now. Let's go outside so they have room to work."

Nodding, Court rubbed his eyes with the back of his hands and followed her out into the chill winter sunshine. "Are you sure he's going to be all right?"

"I'm sure he is." *Please, Father.*

Neighbors had come out onto the street, and she saw

Alice lingering at the gate. Dinah motioned her in, and then went to meet her halfway.

"Tell my aunt not to worry," she said quickly, before the woman could launch into a hundred questions. "Marc fell on the cellar steps. They'll probably take him to the medical center to check him out, and Court and I will go along. I'll call her from there."

Alice's eyes were bright with curiosity, but she managed not to ask anything. "Take care of that boy." She turned and hustled back out the gate.

The paramedics were bringing Marc out of the cellar on a stretcher when she reached them. She clutched Court's hand as they followed the stretcher to the waiting ambulance. Poor kid—he didn't have anyone but his father. No wonder he looked terrified.

She gripped his hand tighter. "He's going to be okay, Court. You have to hang on to that. I'll be with you the whole time. You're not in this alone."

He nodded, tears welling in his eyes. They reached the ambulance, and he caught one of the paramedics by the arm.

"I want to ride with my dad."

The paramedic looked at her, as if for support. "That's not a good idea, son. We'll be working on him."

"I'll drive us," Dinah said quickly. "We'll follow them to the hospital."

Court shook his head. "I want to go with him."

The paramedic was shaking his head when Marc moved.

"Court." His voice was barely more than a whisper, but joy shot through her at the sound.

"Dad." Court launched himself at the stretcher, his voice breaking.

"I'm all right. Now don't be a pest. You ride with Dinah, you hear?"

Court nodded, clutching his father's hand.

"We'll see you there, Dad."

She understood, only too well, what Court felt. It was hard to watch Marc being slid into the ambulance, hard to see the doors close, shutting them out.

"He talked." Court turned to her, tears shimmering in his eyes. "You heard him. He talked. He's going to be okay, isn't he?"

"Of course." She forced strength into her voice. Court needed to know that he could count on her. "He's going to be fine."

She caught Court's hand as they hurried to the car, and he didn't pull away. Marc was going to be all right. She had to believe that.

She also had to know the answer to the question that hadn't seemed to occur to anyone else yet. What had made the stairs collapse when Marc was on them?

"I feel okay. I want to go home." Marc repeated the words for probably the twentieth time, this time to the attending physician in the emergency room. If he said them often enough, maybe they'd sink in.

He sat up on the narrow bed, pulling his shirt on and trying not to grimace at the pain in his bruised ribs.

The doctor raised her eyebrows. "Hurts, doesn't it? You'll really do better to let us keep you overnight, Mr. Devlin."

He managed a smile. "You wouldn't put it that way if you really thought it essential that I stay, now would you?"

"Probably not." She studied his chart, her eyes tired behind her glasses. "You're a lucky man, in my opinion. You fell eight feet onto a concrete floor and didn't break anything. Except for the bruises and a mild concussion, I can't find anything wrong."

"So I'll do fine at home." All he wanted was to get out of this sterile environment and be with Court, so he could reassure him. But he wasn't going to let his son see him lying in a hospital bed.

He clutched the edge of the bed and slid forward until he was standing on his own two feet. Maybe he wasn't a pretty sight, with bruises and abrasions down one side of his face, but at least he was upright.

The doctor sighed at his stubbornness. "All right, you can go. But only if there's a competent adult to stay with you tonight. I don't want you alone with only your son to look out for you. It's not fair to him."

"I don't need—" he began, but he didn't get any further.

"I'll stay with him and his son tonight." Dinah stood in the doorway, Court pressing behind her, his face screwed up as if he were trying not to cry. Dinah looked at the doctor, not at him. "Will that be satisfactory?"

The doctor gave her an assessing look before nodding. "I'll have the nurse give you a sheet of instructions." She went out, smiling at Court as she passed him.

He didn't want to bring Dinah in any deeper, but

who else would he call? Not elderly Aunt Kate. Glory lived clear out in Monck's Corners. Phil's wife would have a fit at the thought of his helping, and as for James—well, James seemed to have tried him and found him guilty. That caused a separate small pang. He'd shut all of his Charleston connections out of his life, one way or another, and only Dinah was left.

I've involved you enough, Dinah. I don't want to risk your getting hurt. But he couldn't say any of those things in front of Court.

"The nurse said we could come in." Her glance touched his half-buttoned shirt and skittered away. "Do you need some help with that?"

He nodded. "Court, be a buddy and button this for me. My ribs feel like a linebacker has been standing on them."

Court came to him in a rush, relief washing over his face. "You're really okay?"

Marc ruffled his hair. "I'm really okay. You taking good care of Dinah?"

"Sure thing." Court busied himself with the buttons, head down. "I'm glad you're all right." His voice was husky.

"Me, too, son." He looked over Court's head at Dinah, who stood just out of reach of his hand. "Thanks, Dinah. For everything."

Tears glittered in her eyes, and she didn't attempt to hide them. "My pleasure. Just don't scare us like that again."

For a moment he couldn't look away. Close, so close.

He wanted to reach out and draw her into his arms. But he couldn't. It wasn't fair.

He pushed himself away from the bed. "Look, about staying with us tonight, that's really not necessary. I'm sure we'll be fine."

"I'm sure you will, too, but that doesn't mean I'm going to leave you alone."

"I don't need a bodyguard, Dinah."

"Actually, maybe you do." She slung her bag over her shoulder. "Shall we get out of here?"

He nodded. He'd make another effort later, once Dinah saw that he could take care of himself and Court.

He took a step, winced, and threw his arm over Court's shoulder. "I guess I could use a little help."

They emerged into the waiting room. Dinah, who was just ahead of him, stiffened suddenly, as if presented with an unwelcome sight.

He moved past her and saw that he was right. Lieutenant Draydon leaned across the registration desk, apparently arguing with the clerk. At the sight of them the quarrel stopped.

"Mr. Devlin." He approached, giving him the once-over. "Looks like you're not hurt too badly."

"I'm all right." He clipped the words off. It wasn't any of Draydon's business, and how on earth had he found out about the incident so fast, anyway? "You'll excuse me. We were just leaving."

Draydon planted himself in his path. "I have a few questions about this accident of yours."

He gritted his teeth. Probably the fastest way to get rid of the man was to give him the bare facts. "It was just that—an accident. The cellar steps gave way, and I fell."

"Nobody else in the house at the time?"

"My son. And Ms. Westlake. Why does a household accident interest the police?"

He stepped around Draydon and moved toward the exit. He shouldn't have asked that question. It was one he didn't want answered in front of Court.

"Funny, that is. How problems seem to be dogging you since you came back to Charleston," Draydon drawled. "I'd just like to know why. Call it professional curiosity. I'm sure Ms. Westlake understands."

Dinah whirled, the fury on her face startling. "No, I don't understand. Mr. Devlin is in pain. He needs to go home, not stand here answering questions."

"Now, Ms. Westlake—"

"No!" Her voice cracked like a whip. "If you want to investigate something, why don't you investigate why that step broke?"

Her words seemed to hang in the air for a long moment. Then Lieutenant Draydon leaned toward her, his whole face sharpening with interest. "Now, what makes you say that, I wonder?"

Marc grasped Dinah's arm, but he suspected she didn't need the hint to say no more. "That's all," he said shortly. "We're done here."

Ignoring Draydon, he hustled Court and Dinah out into the parking lot. They were twenty feet from the door before he realized he didn't know where the car was.

He stopped. "Sorry. I didn't mean to give you the bum's rush."

"You did the right thing." Dinah's voice shook. "I'm sorry. I shouldn't have said that. I just—"

"I understand." He did. He understood that she cared for him, and that caring was leading her into a difficult, maybe a dangerous place. "I appreciate you defending me."

"I didn't do a very good job of it." She looked up at him, trying to smile, but her lips trembled.

Court had walked on toward the car, and for a moment they stood alone in the darkened parking lot, the faint glow from one of the overhead lights touching the upturned oval of Dinah's face.

His heart clutched. She was inexpressibly dear to him. He could never tell her that. He couldn't ask her to share the suspicion that was directed at him. And even if that were resolved, Annabel's memory would always stand between them.

He needed to lay the past to rest and push on into the future. But Dinah could never face it, so she could never let it go.

Dinah walked slowly down the staircase, running her hand along the rail. She no longer panicked on the stairs, but holding on seemed a wise precaution.

Court was asleep in his bed, oblivious to the concerns that plagued the adults in his life. His dad was safe and at home. That was all it took to give him uninterrupted slumber.

She couldn't hope for the same. In fact, she'd probably settle with a book on the sofa in the family room and stay awake for the duration. She'd be of small use to Marc if he needed her and she was asleep.

Besides, any sleep she had in this house was bound to be tortured by the dream again. A chill touched her, and she went quickly down the rest of the stairs.

"Marc?" He was supposed to be resting, but somehow she doubted it. She glanced in the family room. Empty.

"Marc?" She called again, softly. Waking Court wouldn't make this night any easier, and she had no desire to launch into reassuring him again.

Or reassuring Aunt Kate, for that matter. It had been all she could do to keep her elderly great-aunt from coming to the hospital to see for herself that everyone was all right. She'd developed a fierce, protective love for Court in the short time she'd known him.

Dinah started back down the hall to the kitchen. Maybe Marc had decided to get something to eat. She could fix him a sandwich—

She stopped, aghast. The cellar door stood open, and Marc's legs extended into the hallway.

She reached the door in a second, terrified at what she might find. "Marc!" She clutched at his legs.

He turned an annoyed face to her. "What are you doing?"

"What are *you* doing?" Relief and anger sharpened her tone. "You're supposed to be resting. I thought you'd collapsed."

"Sorry." He shook his head and winced at the movement. "I didn't mean to scare you. I'm just following your lead."

"My lead?"

"You're the one who told Draydon he should be looking into why the stairs collapsed."

"That doesn't mean I think you should be disobeying doctor's orders. Please go and rest."

She sat on the floor next to him, trying to peer over his shoulder. With the errant fuse replaced, she had a good view of the jagged timbers and the concrete floor. A shudder went through her. The image of Marc lying there would be fodder for a few more nightmares.

Marc played the flashlight he held over what remained of the top steps. Obviously he didn't intend to come out until he'd finished what he was doing.

She didn't want to know, but she had to. "Well? How does it look?"

He slid back into the hall next to her, raising himself to a sitting position. She could see by his expression it wasn't good news.

"The stairway was pretty rickety to begin with, braced by a couple of upright supports. It looks to me as if someone sawed almost all the way through the uprights. The first time anyone put any weight on the tread, he could bet the whole thing would come down. And he could have tampered with the fuse box at the same time."

Her mind raced, trying to imagine it. "But how could anyone get into the cellar? How could they have done that without being heard?"

Marc shrugged, his face hard. "I locked the door into the cellar, but not the bulkhead doors. I figured the only danger was someone getting into the house itself. My mistake."

"You'd have heard him, surely." His expression had begun to frighten her. Not for herself—for that unknown someone. "Even if he did it in the middle of the night, I'd think you'd hear something."

"We've been out a lot. There were plenty of times when the house was empty and someone could get in. And with it getting dark as early as it does, why would he bother coming in the middle of the night?"

She digested that. "You think you know, don't you?"

He shook his head. "Somebody comes to mind. It's the sort of thing Carr might do, don't you think?"

"But he's—"

"Dead. I know. But this could have been done at any time. That's the beauty of it. Someone could do it and then just wait for me to have a reason to go down the cellar. No need to be anywhere near here when I fell."

"It might not have been you." A shiver went through her. "It could have been Court. Or me."

Would she have gone down into the cellar, if she'd been alone with Court and the lights went out? Of course she would have. Carr, if it had been he, hadn't seemed to care much who he hurt. But there was another possibility.

The secret Aunt Kate had confided hung heavy on her soul. She'd made the decision to tell him before the accident, but that had intervened. Now, she wasn't so sure. It might have had nothing to do with Annabel's death, and it would hurt Marc so much. And if Draydon found out, he'd think it gave Marc the perfect motive for murder.

"If he wanted me to leave Charleston, it probably didn't really matter to him who got hurt." His face was so tight it looked like a mask, but a muscle twitched under the raw abrasion at his temple.

She couldn't give him something else to worry about, not tonight. Surely bad news could wait a little longer.

She touched his arm, reassured at the feel of warm skin and hard muscle. "I know you don't want to talk to Draydon, but you have to tell him this."

"I know. I will." He closed his hand over hers for a moment. "But not tonight. Court needs time to get over his scare before we're plunged into having police in the house. In the morning is time enough."

"I suppose." But she certainly wouldn't be sleeping tonight.

Marc stood and held out his hand to her. She took it, and he helped her rise. Then he turned away to shut and bolt the cellar door. He spoke without looking at her.

"I think it's time for you to go home and get some sleep. We'll be fine." His tone was coolly dismissive, as if he talked to an employee.

Anger flickered through her, warming her. "Nice try. I promised the doctor I'd stay, and I haven't changed my mind."

"Dinah…"

"No!" Aware she'd raised her voice, she glanced up the stairs, but there was no sound from Court. "I'm going to make myself a cup of tea, and then I'm going to curl up on the couch in the family room. Please go to bed. I'll be checking on you through the night, just as the doctor ordered."

She waited for an argument. It didn't come. Marc just stared at her for a long moment. Then he turned and went quietly up the stairs.

She let out a shaky breath. It could have been worse, although what could be worse than having Marc look at her as if she were an irritating stranger?

Please, Lord. I don't know what to do about this. I'm afraid for Marc. I don't know where to turn. Please, hold us in Your hands tonight.

Somehow just the act of prayer calmed her fears. She went steadily across the hall to double-check the lock on the front door. Everything was safe.

As it had been safe the night Annabel died? She couldn't let herself think about that, or she'd never get through this night.

She walked quickly past the side table. The jasmine had been replaced with a spray of greens and holly. It didn't matter. It still reminded her of Annabel.

Chapter Fourteen

The night had been peaceful, but Dinah certainly didn't look it. She frowned at her reflection in her bedroom mirror the next morning. She patted some concealer on the dark shadows under her eyes and dusted powder over it. That would have to do for the moment.

She glanced at her daybook as she tucked it in her bag. Tomorrow was Christmas Eve. She seemed to have lost a few days from this Advent season in the turmoil of the past few days.

Well, Christmas would come whether she felt ready or not. It didn't depend on how many gifts she had wrapped.

Her cell phone rang, and she hurried to pick it up from the dresser, heart thumping. How long until she didn't react to every unexpected sound?

"Hello?"

"Hey, girlfriend, saddle up. Teresa's ready to talk to you." Tracey didn't bother to hide her exuberance.

"Seriously?" That was unexpected.

"You bet. How soon can you meet me there?"

"Half an hour. Frankly, I'm surprised the captain was willing to let you use me, after everything that's happened."

Tracey's hesitation gave her away. "Let's say that what the captain doesn't know won't hurt any of us."

"I don't want you to risk your job for me."

Tracey chuckled. "Don't worry. All I'm risking is a chewing out. And if we get anything, it'll be worth it. See you there."

If they got anything. Dinah grabbed her bag and headed for the stairs.

Please, Lord. Let us bring some closure to this situation, for Teresa's sake, at least.

Once she was in the car, fighting the morning traffic that was inevitable in a small city hemmed in by two rivers, she let herself think about Marc. He was meeting with Draydon this morning. She'd offered to be there and had been turned down so curtly that it was almost an insult.

Her feelings didn't matter. All that mattered was that Lieutenant Draydon see that someone was after Marc. That he take it seriously. Draydon might begin from the suspicion that Marc was guilty, but headquarters scuttlebutt said he was a fair man. That was the best they could hope for, wasn't it?

She pulled to the curb behind Tracey's car, greeted her and went back up the narrow, dirty stairs, her heart beating faster now, her hands clammy. Would this be the day they got something?

Once again the anxious-looking mother ushered

them in, and once again Dinah took her seat at the table across from the girl, pad in her lap. Teresa wrapped her arms around her thin body, staring down at the plastic lace place mat in front of her.

"I'm glad you wanted to talk to me again, Teresa." She kept her voice low. "Can we talk about that day again?"

Teresa shot her a dark, unreadable look. "Don't you want to ask me what he looked like?"

This was a little unusual for Teresa. Some witnesses jumped to that right away, but not the difficult ones. Not the ones she was called in on.

"If you want to tell me."

She shook her head. "I've told you and told you. I've told everyone. I didn't see him. Or if I did, I don't remember."

But her voice, her manner, cried out to Dinah's heart.

Please, Father. Help me to help her.

"Let's just talk about that day, then. Talk about what you did see."

Back to the beginning. Talk about the day her friend died, lead her through all the small, mundane happenings of the day, the things that seemed ordinary at the time but now took on new meaning, viewed from the context of what they knew had happened that evening.

Teresa began to relax—she could see it in the way her fingers unclenched. More detail crept into her narrative. Who had spoken to them at lunch, what they'd said, who'd already seen the movie they'd planned to attend.

Almost without her recognizing it, Dinah's pencil began to move. She held her breath, forcing herself not to stare down at the page. Sometimes it happened this way, as if God were letting her see through the words, see what the witness had seen, live it through her.

Hard. It was hard. Her breath quickened when Teresa's did. Her hands grew clammy, and her stomach lurched when the girls turned into the alley.

A dark figure, a scuffle, a scream—her own scream, or was it Teresa's? Fragments of details coming out almost without Teresa seeming to know it. A smell, the brush of fabric from a jacket, the sound of labored breathing. The knowing. *Close your eyes, don't look, you must never know—*

Dinah's pencil raced, emotion flooding through her body, into her fingers. Choking her.

Teresa stopped, as if a switch had been turned off. Her hands went to her mouth, her eyes glistening. "I can't." She started to push away from the table, ready to flee.

"Not yet." She didn't take her gaze from the girl. "Tracey, will you get her mother, please?"

Tracey moved. She heard the murmur of voices from the bedroom, their footsteps coming back. She held Teresa in place with sheer force of will.

When they were all there, she spoke. "Teresa." She lifted the drawing pad, heavy now with the weight of grief. "Is this the man?" She held it so the girl could see.

Teresa stared, face horrified. She let out an anguished cry, echoed by her mother. "Yes. Yes." She collapsed onto the table, sobs wrenching her body. Her mother gave a keening cry and held her.

Tracey's focus moved from the drawing to the school photos on the wall. "The brother?"

Her throat was so choked she could barely get the words out. "Yes. She'll tell you now. She'll tell you."

She turned and fled from the room.

Dinah could only thank God that she didn't have to deal with the aftermath of their discovery, as Tracey did. She pulled the car into the garage and hurried through the back gate into the garden. The sky, dark and lowering, seemed to echo her feelings, looking at if it would burst into tears at any moment.

Was I right to expose the truth, Father? She wrapped her jacket around her as she scurried toward the door. *It's going to bring so much grief for them. Maybe it would be better never to know.*

She didn't know. All she knew was that she wanted to collapse into bed and fall into a deep, dreamless sleep. That seemed very unlikely. Sleep, yes, but dreamless? She shivered as she pulled the door open. Dreams came with the territory for her.

She hurried into the dim hallway and nearly ran into Marc. Her breath caught, and she tried to arrange her face into something that wouldn't give away her feelings.

"Marc. I didn't realize you were here."

"Just checking on Court, but don't tell him I said so. He's in the kitchen with Alice and your aunt, helping them bake pies. Or getting in the way, I'm not sure which."

"They're delighted to have him, I know." She edged past him. If she could just reach the stairs without letting him get a good look at her face, she could escape.

"Dinah?" He caught her arm. "What is it? You look as if you've been hit by a truck."

She tried to smile. "That's an interesting comment coming from a man with your bruises."

His hand slid to her wrist, his fingers encircling it. Could he feel the way her pulse hammered? Probably.

"You're shaking." He checked around, seeming to know instinctively that she wouldn't want to run into Aunt Kate just now. "Come with me." He led her into the front parlor, closed the door and nearly shoved her into a chair.

He sat down opposite her, holding her hand wrapped in his. "Talk. What's going on?"

"I should go upstairs. I don't want Aunt Kate to see me. She has enough prejudice against my work already."

"Something happened at work. Tell me. Is it the case you were working on with the teenage girl?"

Clearly she wasn't getting out of the room without telling him something. "She agreed to see us again. This time…" She tried to control the shudder that went through her. "I can't explain it. Sometimes I just get so close to the witness that I react as much to the things they don't say as to what they do."

To her surprise, he nodded. "I know. That happens

to me sometimes when I'm questioning a witness or a client. You just know, even before you reason it out."

"You understand. That makes it easier. Some of the detectives look at me as if I'm crazy."

"They do the same thing, probably. They just call it a hunch, or a gut instinct." The gentle movement of his fingers on her hand soothed her. "So you identified the guy. That's good."

"Not so good. It was her brother." Her fingers strained against his. "I can't help but wonder if I did the right thing. What that family will go through—"

"Don't, Dinah, don't. It'll be rough, but they'll be able to heal now, don't you see?"

"I suppose. What a sad Christmas they'll have." Her eyes were hot with unshed tears. She shook her head. "I'm sorry. I need to go upstairs and lie down for a bit."

She stood, and he rose, too, his face drawn with concern.

"Believe it, Dinah. The truth is always better. Always. You were able to help that girl face it. If you—"

He stopped abruptly, but she knew what he wanted to say.

"Why can't I do the same for myself?" She swung away, hands clenching so tightly her nails cut into her palms. "That's what you mean, isn't it?"

"I guess I do."

She couldn't bear the pity in his voice. "I didn't see anything!" She heard an echo of Teresa's words in her own. "I didn't!" She bolted from the room, running up the stairs as if something chased her.

By the time she reached the top she was breathless.

She hurried into her room, shut the door and turned the lock. She never locked herself in her room. Never. But she had to be alone.

The impulse to throw herself on the bed and weep had been displaced by anger. She paced across the room. How could he do that to her? He'd seen how upset she was already. How could he try and make her face that again?

She stalked to the window, staring down at the street. Marc came out of the gate and walked across toward his house. His shoulders were stiff with tension.

She turned away, hot tears spilling onto her cheeks. Her anger slipped away, leaving in its place a frightening emptiness.

She sank into her desk chair, fingers touching the objects on the desk at random. She hadn't even asked him how it went with Draydon. She should have.

Burying her face in her hands, she reached out to God. *I'm sorry. I'm so sorry. Taking my fears out on Marc isn't fair. He just wants to know the truth. But I can't. I can't.*

That was what Teresa had said. She hadn't accepted it from the girl. She'd forced her to go deeper than she'd wanted to do, because they had to know the truth.

Justice. Tracey wouldn't use the word, but that was what drove her. The need for justice in a messy world.

Marc needed justice, too. He was in danger. Feelings didn't matter. She hadn't spared Teresa's feelings, had she? Why was she so protective of her own?

That's different, Father.

But it wasn't. It wasn't, was it? She picked up a pencil, fingers moving aimlessly. How did she justify sparing herself from pain?

She'd spent the past ten years praying to God to let her forget. *For now we see in a glass dimly...* She'd wanted to go on seeing dimly. Not knowing.

Was there anything to know? She took a deep, shaking breath. *Please, Father. If there's anything to remember, please let me remember. Let me see clearly.*

She probed delicately into her mind, as carefully as a surgeon with a scalpel. Was there anything? That day—the memories came slipping back as she opened the door to them a crack.

Annabel, irritated at Marc for working late. Irritated at everyone and everything, it seemed. Scolding Court for some small infraction until Dinah had scooped him up, carrying him upstairs for a bath and a story, snuggling with him as if that would make up for Annabel's mood.

Standing outside Court's door, listening. Annabel had been in the parlor. She hadn't wanted to see Annabel again, angry that her grown-up cousin had acted so childishly.

Why are you being such a nag? Marc had to work late. He couldn't help it. You shouldn't act that way toward Court. Don't you realize how sensitive he is?

Shocking, to think those things about Annabel, beautiful, loving Annabel, whom she'd idolized.

Her tears had spilled over. She could feel them on her cheeks now, hot and salty. She'd run into her room, thrown herself on the bed, cried out all the frantic, fervent emotions that tumbled inside her.

Later, much later, something had wakened her. She'd opened the door, standing there with her bare feet on the wooden floor, hesitating. Voices. Someone was with Annabel. Had Marc come home? Were they arguing about his working so much?

She'd crept to the stairs, her hand gripping the railing. She'd leaned over. And then...

Nothing. Her mind shrank back, wincing, closing over the wound. Don't go in, don't go in, don't go in.

She clenched the pencil so hard it snapped off in her hand.

Please, God. She stopped, not sure what to pray. And then she knew.

Please, Father. If it's Your will, let me remember. I'm open to whatever You have for me.

Slowly, very slowly, the tension drained out of her. She straightened, wiped her eyes then looked down at the paper on the desk in front of her. And saw what she'd drawn.

It was the Citadel crest, drawn over and over again across the page.

Marc pushed back from the computer, looking out the study window. It was getting dark already, and he was sitting here with only the glow of the laptop screen for company. He'd managed to lose himself in work for over an hour. He'd managed to forget so easily the pain he'd caused Dinah.

Rotten timing, that's what it had been. He'd known for days that he had to talk to her again about what she might remember from that night, but he'd kept putting it off, not wanting to cause a breach between them.

And now, because he'd been frustrated after that futile conversation with Draydon, he'd brought it up to Dinah at the worst possible moment. She'd already been used up by what must have been a terrible experience for her with the girl, and he'd barged in and trampled on her feelings.

He leaned back, rubbing the nape of his neck. Dinah was stuck in the past, able to help other people bring the memories out and face them, but unable to do the same for herself.

I'd like to believe I did it for her sake, Lord, but I know that's not true. I chose that moment because I'm desperate for something that will clear me. If I'm charged, what will happen to Court?

No excuses. He was making excuses, and there weren't any. *I was wrong. Forgive me. And please, show me what to do, because I'm at the end of my rope. I thought I knew what was right. Now I just don't know.*

He heard a key turn in the lock of the front door. Court, coming in ravenous for supper? Or Dinah? She was the only other person with a key.

He had reached the doorway when Dinah met him. She shoved past him into the study, thrusting a sheet of paper at him. Her face was nearly as white as the page.

"Dinah? What's happened?" He looked at her, not the paper in his hand.

"I tried." Her voice shook. "I tried to do what you wanted, and that's what happened."

He glanced down at the sheet. It was an image of

the Citadel crest, done over and over in Dinah's delicate pencil drawing, some a simple doodle of a couple of lines, others shaded and rounded.

"I don't understand." Instinct told him not to approach her. She looked as if she'd shatter like crystal at an unwary touch.

Her eyes, dark with shadows, focused on his face. She took a ragged breath and seemed to search for calm.

"I tried to remember. I opened myself to whatever memories I might have hidden away about that night."

Excitement surged through him, but he forced his voice to remain calm. "Did you remember anything?"

She was looking into the past, her eyes wide, the pupils dilated. "Playing outside with Court on the swings after supper. It was so hot, but he had to be outside. I pushed him. He kept saying, 'Higher, higher.'"

"What happened when you came inside?" *Gently. Don't startle her out of the memory.*

"He was all sweaty, his hair wet and curling on his neck." She smiled slightly. "I hugged him. We were laughing." The smile slipped away. "Annabel was upset. Angry with you, for not coming home. Angry with me, for letting Court run around outside in the heat. Angry with Court, for putting his dirty hands on her clean skirt."

"It didn't mean anything, sugar. It was really me she was annoyed with, not you and Court." She was hurting. He didn't want her to hurt. But he needed her to remember.

"I know." She shook her head a little, seeming to

come back to the present. "But I got mad at her. It seems so wrong, that I got mad at her and a few hours later she was dead."

"We all felt that way." He longed to put his arms around her in comfort, but he didn't dare. "Did you yell at her?"

She looked shocked. "No, of course not."

Of course not. Shy little Dinah would never have yelled at the grown-up cousin she adored.

"What did you do?"

"I took Court up and gave him a bath. We played, read stories. Afterward..." She hesitated for a long moment. "Usually, if you weren't there, I'd go down and watch television with Annabel. But I was still angry with her. So I just went in my bedroom, found a book to read and went to bed."

That explained why Annabel had been alone downstairs. But why had she been in the front parlor? That had never been explained. Then, as now, they used the family room almost exclusively unless they were entertaining.

"You woke up," he said quietly. "At some point, you woke. Do you know what woke you?"

She shook her head, black hair moving against the white cashmere sweater she wore. She'd come out without a coat.

"I was just awake. I thought I heard someone downstairs, so I went to the door. Opened it. I went to the top of the stairs." She stopped. "That's all. That's all I could remember." She closed her eyes for an instant.

"But there's something else. Something Aunt Kate told me yesterday."

His heart thudded. He'd been convinced Kate was hiding something from him. He'd been right. "What? What did she say?"

Her lips pressed together, as if she didn't want to let the words out. She swallowed, the muscles in her throat working. "She overheard Annabel on the phone. Talking to a man. She said…" She stopped, her mouth twisting.

Shock and pain clawed at his chest. "It can't be."

"She blames herself for not confronting her." Dinah's voice was thick with tears. "She's sure it's true that Annabel was involved with a man that summer."

Another man. How could he have not known, not guessed that something that serious was wrong?

"What about you?" The words came harshly. "Did you know?"

"Of course not. I never imagined anything of the kind."

There was something in her voice that caught at him. He grasped her hands, swinging her around to face him. "Tell me the truth, Dinah."

"I am! I just—" She wrenched her hands free, wiping at her tears like a child. "Ever since you came back, I've felt as if I had to protect her memory. Maybe, somewhere deep, I suspected. I don't know!"

He struggled to stop reacting and start thinking. A man. "Who? Who was around that summer?" He knew the answer to that. The usual group of friends—people he knew well, people he'd never dream would betray him. "This is crazy," he muttered. "She must have been wrong. Aunt Kate. She must have misunderstood."

"I'd like to believe that."

"But you don't." He shot a look at her, irrationally angry with her, as if she were to blame.

She shook her head tiredly. "I don't know, Marc." She nodded toward the crest. "But that has to mean something."

He finally got it. "You think this points to me, don't you? With Annabel's affair providing the motive."

"That's not what I said."

His stomach churned, his finger curling into fists, crumpling the paper. "You didn't have to." He shook the paper at her. "Your drawing says it for you. You identify me with the crest."

She seemed to be looking at him from a great distance. "You used to wear a Citadel tiepin whenever you wore a tie. It was gold. Annabel gave it to you."

"And you'll convict me on that." He wanted to shake her.

Anger flamed suddenly in her eyes. "You're the one who wanted me to remember. I tried, and that's what happened. Don't blame me because I couldn't come up with the answer you wanted."

He wasn't sure when he'd been this angry. Dinah, the one person he was sure believed in him, thought he was guilty.

Carefully he put the paper down on the desk. "You'd better keep this safe. Draydon might want to see it."

"Marc—"

He shook his head, grabbing his jacket from the

back of the chair. "I'm going out. Tell Court I'll pick him up later."

Later. As in after he regained control of himself. Without looking at her, he stalked out of the room and out of the house.

Chapter Fifteen

When the door slammed behind Marc, the house seemed to shudder in response. Dinah sank down in the desk chair and leaned back, head throbbing. Raw emotion still hovered in the tightness of her throat.

But she couldn't cry anymore. She was all cried out. She closed her eyes, tried not to think. She was tired, so tired. Too tired to get up, cross the road to Aunt Kate's, deal with the questions Aunt Kate and Court would have.

So she sat, unwilling to move, unwilling even to think. She'd just rest for a while. Try not to think. Just rest, until she felt able to cope again.

She wasn't sure how long she sat there before the images started to form in her mind. Against the blackness of her closed lids, she saw her bare toes curling into the stair carpeting. Saw her hand reach for the railing. Felt herself lean against the railing, looking down at the hallway.

The white tiles glowed softly in the dim light of the

small lamp Annabel kept burning. Voices murmured. The door to the front parlor must be ajar. She couldn't see it from where she stood, but light streamed out in a pale yellow band, crossing the tiles, touching the table, the jasmine, the mirror.

She shot bolt upright, a shudder working its way through her body. She was remembering. After all these years of insisting she'd seen nothing, knew nothing, she was remembering.

She was alone in the house for the first time in years, if ever. Was that why? She gripped the leather arms of the desk chair, holding on as if afraid she'd fall.

Alone in the house. Once this had been a second home, but after Annabel died she'd avoided it as she'd have avoided walking through a cemetery at midnight.

Then Marc and Court came back. That sense had faded, a little painfully, perhaps, but it had gone. She wasn't afraid here any longer.

Because of Marc. That was it. Because at the deepest level of her soul, she wasn't afraid of him. She knew he hadn't been with Annabel in the parlor that night. He hadn't struck out at her.

Whatever that image of the Citadel ring meant, it didn't mean that. Marc had jumped to the conclusion she was accusing him, but—

Wait. Why had she thought of it as a ring? She'd identified it to Marc as the crest, which could have been on any piece of jewelry or clothing.

The paper lay on the desk, where Marc had thrown it. She snatched it up and smoothed it, peering at the drawing in the glow of the computer screen.

She touched the most developed of the drawings, probably the one she'd done last. There—was that the suggestion of a curve, as if the crest were set in a curving band?

It wasn't evidence. Even if she generated a complete memory, which she had no idea if she could do, that wasn't evidence. But to her, it was better than evidence. It was proof. Marc hadn't worn any ring except his wedding ring. So whoever the drawing pointed to, it wasn't Marc.

She pushed herself out of the chair, and moved silently over the soft carpet. She'd go home, pull herself together and find some way of making Marc understand.

Judging by the way he'd rocketed out of the house, that wouldn't be easy. For the first time she realized she was standing in near-dark, with only the glow of the computer screen for light.

She reached toward the lamp, then drew her hand back. Go home. Marc would have to go there to pick up Court. She'd talk to him then.

She went quietly to the door, her feet making no sound on the soft carpet. She opened it and stopped, heart in her throat.

There was a light on in the front parlor. The door was ajar, sending a band of yellow light across the tiles.

A shiver went through her. No voices, not this time. But noise. Someone was in the room, moving around.

Marc? Could he have come quietly back to the house without her hearing him? Well, obviously someone had.

Somehow she didn't want to click across the tile

floor in her heels. She slid out of her shoes and picked them up. Then stood, torn with indecision.

If it was Marc in the room, she'd feel like a fool for trying to sneak out of the house without speaking to him. It couldn't be Court. He'd never enter the house or any other place that quietly.

No one else had a key. Whoever had rigged the cellar steps to fall hadn't needed a key.

She'd been a coward for most of her life. If she didn't at least try to see who was in the parlor, she'd be a coward for the rest of it.

Please, Lord.

She'd slip across the hall, staying in the shadow. Whoever it was, he obviously thought he was alone. Either it was Marc, in which case she had no need to fear. Or it was someone else, and she'd never forgive herself if she didn't try to find out who that someone else was.

Marc sat in his car, staring across the street at The Citadel. True to its name, in the dusk it looked like a medieval citadel, its pale walls glimmering. It had taught generations of cadets the meaning of discipline and honor. It had given him an excellent education and friendships he'd thought would last a lifetime. Now it had also given him a frightening puzzle.

He'd driven around the city in a haze of anger until he'd found himself here, face-to-face with his past. The anger faded, forcing him to recognize how futile and foolish it had been.

Dinah was right. She'd done what he asked, at who

knows what cost to her psyche. She'd told him the truth about Annabel, even though it ripped her apart with pain. And he'd repaid her with anger.

Somehow the idea that Dinah believed in him had become a part of his assumptions about himself. About her. The fear that she didn't trust him had rocked him more than he'd have believed possible.

Because he considered her his only friend here? No.

Truth time. It wasn't friendship he felt for Dinah. Without realizing it, his feelings for her had deepened over the past weeks into love.

Hopeless love, probably. He'd known from the first surge of attraction that there could be no future for them. The only thing he could do that might help Dinah to heal was to get to the bottom of this.

All right. Dinah had brought back some images of that night, and the crest was part of that. The only thing he had to work on, in fact. But he began with the knowledge that he hadn't killed Annabel. So the implication of the crest was that the person who'd been in the house that night hadn't been an ex-con like Hassert or a casual worker like Carr.

It had been a friend. Who? The man Aunt Kate heard her talking to?

His eyes closed. They'd entertained that summer, but not much. Annabel had said she was too tired much of the time. But when they did have people over, the crowd had inevitably included two people who had reason to wear a ring or a tiepin with that insignia. James. And Phillips.

His friends. The three musketeers.

But James could barely manage to be civil to him now. Because he thought Marc had killed Annabel? Or because of his own fear and guilt because he'd done it?

His stomach churned, his hands tightening on the wheel. Dinah had said that James cared for Annabel. He'd never realized that. How was it that the naive teenager had seen what he hadn't? Could Annabel have come to return those feelings? Had a lovers' quarrel turned deadly?

His instinct was to rush to James's office and confront him, but what good would that do? He had no evidence, nothing that would remotely convince Draydon, for instance. Just Dinah's drawing and a barely realized memory. And Draydon would be far more likely to consider that he now had motive, means, and opportunity against Marc.

Phillips wore a Citadel ring. The thought drifted through his mind and then clung like a burr. Not Phillips. It couldn't have been. Phillips was one person who could have had no possible reason to harm Annabel. He hadn't been attracted to her—just the opposite, in fact. He'd been polite to her, but made it clear in his subtle way that he thought her an idle debutante with nothing more serious in her head than the next cotillion.

And Annabel had dismissed Phillips as stuffy, stuck in the past, unable to talk about anything but his beloved history.

He shook his head, trying to clear it. He was groping in a fog, trying to come up with scenarios that would explain the inexplicable. There was only one reasonable next step. He had to go back to Dinah, apologize, and convince her to probe more deeply.

Something had put the image of the crest into her mind, projected it through her clever fingers. The memory had to be there, if only she could access it.

He pulled out his cell phone. Apologize. He'd treated Dinah badly, raging out at her that way. He had to make up for that. He was forming the phrases in his mind when he realized the phone had gone straight to Dinah's voice mail.

He clicked off. This was not a message that could be delivered via voice mail. He had to talk to her in person.

She'd be at Kate's, of course. It was dinnertime. He'd go there, he'd apologize, and Dinah would forgive him. He couldn't let himself envision any other possibility.

The door to the parlor stood ajar. She'd taken a long time to cross the hallway, step by cautious step, holding her shoes in one hand. She stopped a few inches from the door, barely breathing.

It wasn't too late. She could back away as quietly as she'd come. Go out the back door, run for help. Call the police, call Marc—

If she hadn't rushed out of the house that way, with nothing in her hand but that drawing, she'd have her cell phone. But she'd been acting on instinct, knowing she had to get to Marc.

That in itself showed that she'd known he couldn't have killed Annabel. She hadn't taken the time to see that, and Marc had been so shocked that he'd jumped to the worst possible conclusion. He'd recognize that, as soon as he calmed down enough to think. He'd put that analytical mind of his to work figuring out what the crest meant.

But she would know. Because she wasn't going to back away. She was going to find out who was in that room.

She leaned close to the crack of the door. She could see a sliver of the room—the fireplace, with its ornate mantel and gilt-framed mirror. The tall secretary desk that had once stood in Annabel's bedroom, brought down from the attic to make the room look furnished.

The front flap of the desk lay open. Someone stood in front of it. She could see part of a dark-jacketed shoulder, an arm.

Not Marc, then. He'd gone rushing out without a coat, and his sweater had been a cream fisherman's knit. But she'd known that all along, at some level.

She had to see who it was. Palm resting gently on the panel, she pushed the door wide enough to see the curve of neck, the fair, slightly graying hair. He was bent over the desk, looking at something she couldn't see.

She must have made some sound, perhaps the faintest gasp. He swung toward her.

"Dinah!" Phillips tried to smile, but it was an awkward twitch of the lips. "Goodness, you startled me. I thought there was no one home."

Too late now to run away. But Phillips—Annabel's killer couldn't be Phillips, could it?

"I was in the study." She got the words out through stiff lips and forced herself to step inside the room. To do anything else would look unnatural. If she bolted toward the door, he could be on her in an instant.

Act. Pretend. Make him believe you don't suspect a thing.

He gestured toward the desk. "I wanted to find a pen and paper, so I could leave a note for Marc. Do you know when he'll be back?"

Her mind raced. Was it better for him to believe Marc would show up at any moment? Or might that precipitate the very action she wanted to avoid?

"I don't know." She attempted a smile. "Court is over at Aunt Kate's, and dinner is almost ready. I'm sure Marc will show up soon."

Better. She sounded almost normal, didn't she? She turned, oh so casually, toward the door.

"I'd best get back to the house before Aunt Kate sends Court over to fetch me. I think you'll find a pen and paper on Marc's desk."

Her gaze hit the gilt-framed mirror over the mantel. The mirror reflected her face, chalk-white. Phillips standing by the desk, straightening his glasses in a characteristic gesture, the glint of the ring on his hand.

She froze, unable to speak, to move. She knew. Beyond all doubt, she knew.

"Oh, Dinah." He sounded grieved. "I can't let you go anywhere now."

Please, Lord, let me get out of here.

"Phillips, I don't know…" She swung her head to look at him, and the words died in her throat.

Still smiling that vague, scholarly smile, Phillips pulled a gun out of his pocket and pointed it at her.

Chapter Sixteen

"She's not here?" Marc stared blankly at Court, who'd opened the door. Behind him, in the hallway, Kate peered nervously over his shoulder.

"I haven't seen her all afternoon," Court said. "Dad? Is something wrong?"

"She didn't come back here?" Where was Dinah? She should be here. "She didn't come back about an hour ago?"

Court shook his head. "I told you. We haven't seen her since she went out ages ago."

Kate's lips began to tremble. She put her hand on Court's arm, and he turned instantly to support her. Even in the grasp of blinding fear for Dinah, Marc was glad to see the bond between them.

"What's happened?" Kate's voice wavered, sounding as old as her years. "Has something happened to Dinah?"

No point in lying now, even to spare her feelings.

The fear had turned into a drumbeat, thundering in his head.

Dinah hadn't come back. She hadn't come back from the house. Something had happened.

He grasped Court's arm. "Call the police. Send them to the house. Hurry!"

He spun, racing across the veranda, taking the path in a few quick strides. *Please, God, please, God, please, God.* The prayer echoed in rhythm with his feet.

He shoved the gate open and raced into the street, blood pounding in his head. A nightmare. It was a nightmare. He'd dreamed a thousand times of reaching the house in time to save Annabel. He never had.

Father, let me be in time to save Dinah. I have to. Please. Please.

Through the gate, up the walk, hurry, hurry. He pounded across the veranda, reached for the door. No time to slip in undetected—he didn't dare take the time for that. He might already be too late.

His momentum took him through the door, into the hall, toward the study where he'd left her—

He skidded to a stop.

Lights in the parlor. Voices, apparently undeterred by his noisy entrance.

Voices. Dinah's voice. Relief left him weak for an instant. *Thank You, God. Thank You.* She was alive. He wouldn't rush in and find her lying cold and still, as he'd found Annabel.

Two strides took him to the door, standing half-open. He thrust it the rest of the way, took a step into the room and stopped. Stared.

Dinah stood a few feet away from him, stiff with tension. She didn't turn to look at him, because her eyes were focused on the person who stood across the room.

Phillips smiled at him, the same grave, gentle smile that had been part of his life for years and years. The only thing out of place was the gun in his hand, pointing directly at Dinah.

"Marc. I didn't want you to come. I wanted to be finished with this, but it's all gone wrong." The smile wavered. "I never meant for this to happen."

Marc took a step closer to Dinah. He had to get her behind him, give her a few precious seconds to get out the door if Phillips used the gun.

"What didn't you want to happen, Phil?" He kept his voice calm, unthreatening. "Why don't you let me take that gun, and then we can sit down and talk about this?"

Phillips glanced down at the gun as if he'd forgotten he held it. He looked back up again at Marc's unwary step toward him.

"No, Marc. I can't. I can't put it down. There isn't any other way out. I've gone too far." He shook his head again, and tears shone in his eyes behind the glasses.

"He killed Annabel." Dinah's voice was hardly more than a whisper. "I heard them arguing. I stood on the steps, but I wasn't sure who it was."

For the moment he almost forgot Phil and the gun. All he could see was Dinah's pale face and huge eyes.

"It's all right, sugar." He closed the space between them, heedless of the gun, and clasped her cold hands in his. "You don't have to remember."

"I remember. I know what I saw." Her eyes flickered toward the mirror over the mantel. "I saw the re-flection of his hand, reflected again in the hall mirror. I saw the ring he wore."

"You didn't remember. No one knew. You shouldn't have remembered."

Phil's voice had gone shrill. He was losing control. How much longer before he fired the gun?

"What about Jasper Carr?" He had to divert Phil's attention from Dinah. "The way he was acting, he must have seen something." And now Carr was dead. This was unreal. Phil, Phil of all people, couldn't be a mur-derer.

The gun wavered slightly, as if Phil's hand was growing tired. "He saw me near the house. He didn't know anything, not really. I paid him to go away."

"Carr came back, though, didn't he? And you had to deal with him."

"Only because you came to Charleston."

His voice shook, and so did the gun. Fear jerked tighter. They could be just as dead if Phil fired acci-dentally.

"You're getting tired, Phil. Let's put the gun down and talk."

He shook his head, tears beginning to flow down his cheeks. "Why did you come back? I was so happy to see you, to be with my best friend again, but then it all started to unravel."

"It's too late. We both know that. The truth has to come out." He was taking a risk, but what choice did he have? He stepped in front of Dinah, pushing her back a step, putting his body between her and the gun.

"No! No, I can't face it. What will Margo say? What will everyone say? How can I live with the shame?"

"You're already living with the shame. You know that. You're tired of it." He took a step toward Phillips, holding out his hand. "Give me the gun now."

"I can't!" He sounded like that boy they'd dragged through the obstacle course.

He reached for the gun. "Come on, now, Phil. The only way out would be to shoot both of us, and you know you can't do that."

He held his breath, his mind a wordless prayer. If Phil turned the gun toward Dinah, he was close enough to jump him. Dinah would take care of Court, if it came to that.

The gun steadied, the barrel pointed directly at him. He didn't move, didn't breathe, just stared into the face of his old friend.

Slowly, very slowly, the gun lowered.

"No." Phillips managed a smile. "You're right. You were always right, Marc. I can't." He slid to the floor, curling his arms around his knees.

When the police burst through the door a few minutes later, he didn't even look up.

Dinah waited in Aunt Kate's parlor, fingers clasped around a cup of tea. Court was upstairs in bed, asleep, she hoped. Aunt Kate had tried to persuade her to take a sedative and go to bed, but she'd refused and kept on refusing, as gently as possible.

She didn't want to sleep, or be cosseted, or treated like a child. Marc would come as soon as he'd finished with the police and with Margo. Margo might not want his help, but she'd have it, because she was Phillips's wife.

She shoved her hair back wearily. Odd, how very odd it all was. She'd wanted to hate the person who robbed them of Annabel, but all she could feel for Phillips was pity. He was like a sick child.

The door clicked, and Marc came in. He hesitated on the threshold for a moment. He looked as if he'd been through agony. He had.

He came to sit next to her. His very presence seemed to bring warmth to the room.

"I thought you might have gone to bed."

"No. I needed to know."

Marc took her hand in his, holding it lightly, seeming hardly aware that he'd done so. "He's talking. As an attorney, I advised him not to say anything, but he wouldn't stop talking. I think he was just so tired of trying to hide it all these years."

"It takes a lot of energy to hide the truth." She should know that, even though her efforts had been beyond her conscious control. "He and Annabel—did they really have an affair?"

Let it all come out. Let the truth be said between them, even if the rest of the world never knew.

Marc nodded. "Funny." He gave the breath of a laugh. "I thought it was James. Once I started to think about the crest, I was convinced it was James."

He was still hurting, so much. She wanted to soothe the pain away, but this was beyond comfort. They'd just have to endure it.

"James cared about her, I think." Carefully. Don't make matters any worse. "He thought you'd killed her. That's why he was so hateful to you."

"I didn't even think Phil and Annabel liked each other. He and Margo had been having problems, and Annabel—well, I think mostly Annabel was bored and angry." He gave her a sideways glance. "Does my saying that upset you?"

"No."

At some point, she'd realized how it must have been. Maybe she'd always known, but she hadn't been able to admit it.

"I loved her. I love her still." She struggled to understand and put the feelings into words. "But I don't have to think her perfect any longer. She was just a fallible human being, like the rest of us."

His fingers tightened on hers. "I'm glad you can see that. It will make it easier, eventually."

"There's a lot to go through before that happens. The papers will have a field day." More to endure. Somehow Aunt Kate had to be protected from the worst of it.

"Poor Phil. I think he was telling the truth when he said he never meant any of it to happen. He wanted to end it, but Annabel threatened to tell me. She was in that kind of mood—ready to smash something, even if it hurt her, too."

"Yes." She could see it so clearly now, in everything Annabel had said and done that long, hot summer. "I imagine he panicked. He struck out at her and realized too late what he'd done."

Marc's fingers clenched, then relaxed. "He thought

he was in the clear when you didn't speak and Carr went away, but he worried about the letters."

"Letters?"

He nodded. "Apparently he wrote love letters to Annabel. How like Phillips that was, wasn't it? Indulging in some romantic dream, as if he and Annabel were Lancelot and Guinevere."

They hadn't been. They'd just been a willful, spoiled young woman and a weak man. She felt an eternity older than Annabel had been.

"So that's what he was looking for in the secretary. His letters."

"Apparently he never thought he could risk searching for them when the house was rented. But when I came back and Carr reappeared, he got desperate."

"He killed Carr." Her voice choked a little. "I'm the one who told him Carr was back in town. He was there when I asked James if he remembered Carr. If I hadn't mentioned it, Carr might still be alive."

Marc shook his head, frowning. "Don't think that. Carr had blackmailed him once and was apparently trying it again. It wasn't your fault."

"I still can't believe he killed Carr in cold blood." An impulsive crime of passion, maybe, but not this ugly premeditation.

"He provided the drugs and alcohol. Carr did the rest himself." His voice was dry. "He never intended that I should be blamed. That was pure accident, apparently."

A tiny spurt of fresh anger went through her. "He should have realized they'd suspect you." Her sympathy for Phillips was evaporating. He hadn't thought of anyone but himself from first to last, and too many people had paid for that.

Marc's fingers tightened on hers, as if he guessed her thoughts. "Anyway, he was still afraid I'd stumble across the letters in getting the house ready for sale. That was what he was doing. He thought the house was empty, and he was looking for his letters."

"Were there any letters?"

"No." His shoulders moved slightly. "She probably destroyed them ten years ago."

"The guilty flee where no man pursues," she murmured.

"Exactly." Fresh pain crossed his face. "I'd like to keep their affair from Court, but I don't suppose I'll be able to."

"Court is a very strong young man. He'll be fine."

"Yes." He glanced at the mantel clock and then got to his feet. "It's late. I'd better go home and let you get to bed."

"You're not going back there to sleep. We have a room ready for you here."

Don't go, Marc. Stay with me.

He shook his head. "I'll be fine. I'll come back for breakfast, if Aunt Kate wants me."

"Of course." She fixed a smile on her face. That was it, then. They were to go back to being cousins, apparently.

Ironic. She finally felt free of the past and ready to move on, but all Marc wanted to do was walk away.

She went with him to the door. They might never be alone together again. "Good night, Marc."

The mantel clock chimed the hour. Marc looked into her face.

"It's midnight. It's officially Christmas Eve, Dinah. Merry Christmas." He bent and kissed her quickly, lightly, and then walked away, taking her heart with him.

"It's beautiful, Court." Dinah folded the tissue paper over the lacy sweater and leaned across to kiss Court's cheek. He grinned and reddened but didn't dodge away.

"I couldn't ask for a lovelier Christmas morning than this." Aunt Kate beamed at all of them impartially, as if Marc and Court had been part of their Christmases forever. They were celebrating in Marc's family room, since Court insisted on unwrapping presents beneath the tree.

And, as Aunt Kate said, they may as well get over whatever uncomfortable feelings they had about the house. Celebrating Christmas there would go a long way toward doing that.

They'd gone to the early worship service together. She'd stood next to Marc, singing the joyful Christmas songs, and forced herself to keep smiling, in spite of the pain.

When the legalities were finished, Marc and Court would go back to Boston. They'd come back for visits, of course, but it wouldn't be the same. They wouldn't really be part of one another's lives.

And to Marc she'd go on being what she'd always been—Annabel's little cousin.

"This one's from both Dad and me." Court thrust a long envelope, adorned with a slightly lopsided red bow, into her lap. "Open it next, okay?"

She nodded, slipping her finger under the flap. She looked up at them questioning. "A plane ticket?"

"Not just a ticket." Court beamed. "It's a ticket to Boston that you can use anytime. You have to come and visit us."

She managed not to let the smile slip. "That is so nice. I've always wanted to see Boston in the springtime. You can show me all the sights." She stood quickly. "Now I'm going to bring in some coffee and hot chocolate. Opening gifts is thirsty work."

Nobody would know how hard it was to keep smiling as she hurried out of the room. She'd reached the kitchen before she heard him behind her.

"I can manage this." She clinked cups onto a tray. "You don't have to help me."

"I didn't come to help." Marc took her hands in his, turning her to face him. "I came to talk."

She couldn't look at him, for fear he'd see the hopeless love in her eyes. "I should take this tray in. They'll want to finish opening gifts."

"They'll wait. We've spent the past thirty-six hours surrounded by either family or police. I thought I'd never get you alone again, and I'm not giving that up too easily."

Her heart was thudding so loudly she could barely

speak over it. She focused on the top button of his shirt. "We were alone the other night."

"We were both still shaking the other night. I couldn't tell you what I need to say until you'd had a chance to recover a little. Dinah, will you please look at me?"

She lifted her gaze to his, and the warmth in his eyes set an answering warmth flooding through her. "I don't need recovery time. I've spent my life recovering. Now I want to spend it living."

Aunt Kate would be shocked if she heard her. A lady should always wait to be asked.

"That's what I want, too." He lifted her hands to his lips and kissed them. "You must know that I love you. And not as a cousin. As a woman." He took a breath, his face rueful. "If you don't feel the same, I'm risking losing you altogether. But I figure it's worth it. We've both already wasted too much time."

The joy that bubbled through her felt as if it would lift her right off the floor. "You're sure you don't still think of me as Annabel's little cousin?"

He pulled her into his arms, and the way he held her wiped any doubt from her mind. "I love you, Dinah Westlake. I want to spend the rest of my life with you. I know it's not going to be easy. But things that are worthwhile never are."

They had Aunt Kate to consider, and Court. More than two lives to blend together, gossip to overcome, decisions to be made.

But she was seeing clearly now, not darkly. God

had brought them both through the darkness and into the light.

"We can do it. If we've gotten through all this, we can do anything. Together." She lifted her face for his kiss, ready to step into the future.

* * * * *

Dear Reader,

I loved writing about Dinah and Marcus, and I've begun to feel as if the next time I'm in Charleston, I'll probably see them!

It's always a joy to go back to the Lowcountry of the Georgia and South Carolina coast, the setting for my earlier Caldwell Clan series. It's a beautiful area, filled with mystery and romance as well as with friendly people who love to make you feel at home.

This story is set in Charleston, South Carolina, and I hope you'll enjoy this armchair visit. I fell in love with Charleston when one of my daughters was in graduate school there, and now that she and her family live there, we have a chance to visit more often.

I hope you'll write and let me know how you liked this story. Address your letter to me at Love Inspired Books, 233 Broadway, Suite 1001, New York, NY 10279, and I'll be happy to send you a signed bookplate or bookmark. You can visit me online at martaperry.com or email me at marta@martaperry.com.

Blessings,

Marta Perry

Questions for Discussion

1. Grief over the loss of a loved one can take many forms. Aunt Kate doesn't talk about Annabel, while Dinah has nightmares. How else might they have dealt with their grief?

2. Court's attempts to protect her both amuse and touch Dinah. Have you seen a young teen act in an unusually mature way in an emergency? What do you think gives a young person that ability?

3. Dinah prays that God will keep her from remembering Annabel's death. Her prayer isn't answered in the way she wants, but God gives her the strength to cope with the results. Has God denied a prayer of yours? Have you later seen God's wisdom in that?

4. In the scriptural theme, Paul tells us that now we see in a glass dimly, but one day we'll see face-to-face. What do you think he means? Have you ever felt you were seeing dimly when you tried to understand God's working in your life?

5. How is the scriptural theme shown in the story? Through which characters and situations?

6. When Marc comes home to Charleston, he realizes how much he's missed it, even while seeing

things differently. Have you experienced going back to a place you loved after a long absence? How did it make you feel?

7. Some of Charleston's unique Christmas traditions are mentioned in the story. If a stranger came to your town, what interesting Christmas traditions would she find?

8. Christmas food means cheese bennes and pecan tassies in Charleston. What are some of your traditional Christmas recipes? Do they have special meaning to you because of the person who gave them to you or because you remember them from childhood?

9. Marc blames himself for the problems he and Annabel had. Is this common in your experience? How does one get past this?

10. In the end, Marc and Dinah both have to accept the betrayal of a friend and plan for a life together that will be complex because of their responsibilities. How do you think they can work that out?

The salvation of the righteous comes from the Lord;
He is their stronghold in time of trouble. The Lord
helps them and delivers them; He delivers them
from the wicked and saves them, because
they take refuge in Him.
—*Psalms* 37:39–40

A CHRISTMAS TO DIE FOR

This story is dedicated to my supportive
and patient husband, Brian, with much love.

Chapter One

Rachel Hampton stood on the dark country road where, seven months ago, she'd nearly died. The dog pressed against her leg, shivering a little, either from the cold of the December evening or because he sensed her fear.

No, not fear. That would be ridiculous. It had been an accident, at least partially her fault for jogging along remote Crossings Road in the dark. She'd thought herself safe enough on the berm of the little-used gravel road, wearing a pale jacket with reflective stripes that should have been apparent to any driver.

Obviously it hadn't been. He'd come around the bend too fast, his lights blinding her when she'd glanced over her shoulder. But now she was over it, she—

Her heart pumped into overdrive. The roar of a motor, lights reflected from the trees. A car was coming. He wouldn't see her. She'd be hit again, thrown into the air, helpless—

She grabbed Barney's collar and stumbled back into

the pines, pulse pounding, a sob catching in her throat as she fought to control the panic.

But the car was slowing, stopping. The driver's-side window slid smoothly down.

"Excuse me." A male voice, deep and assured. "Can you tell me how to get to Three Sisters Inn?"

How nice of him to ignore the fact that she'd leaped into the bushes when she heard him coming. She disentangled her hair from the long needles of a white pine and moved toward him.

"You've missed the driveway," she said. "This is a back road that just leads to a few isolated farms." She approached the car with Barney, Grams's sheltie, close by her side. "If you back up a bit, you can turn into a farm lane that will take you to the inn parking lot."

He switched on the dome light, probably to reassure her. Black hair and frowning brows over eyes that were a deep, deep blue, a pale-gray sweater over a dress shirt and dark tie, a glint of gold from the watch on his wrist, just visible where his hand rested on the steering wheel. He didn't look like a tourist, come to gawk at the Amish farmers or buy a handmade quilt. The briefcase and laptop that rested on the passenger seat indicated that.

"You're sure the proprietor won't mind my coming in that way?"

She smiled. "The proprietor would be me, and I don't mind at all. I'm Rachel Hampton. You must be Mr. Dunn." Since she and Grams expected only one visitor, that wasn't hard to figure out.

"Tyler Dunn. Do you want a lift?"

"Thanks, but it's not far. Besides, I have the dog."
And I don't get into a car with a stranger, even if he does have a reservation at the inn.

Maybe it was her having come so close to death that had blunted her carefree ways. Either that or the responsibility of starting the bed-and-breakfast on a shoestring had forced her to grow up. No more drifting from job to job, taking on a new restaurant each time she became bored. She was settled now, and it was up to her to make a success of this.

She stepped back, still holding Barney's collar despite his wiggling, and waited until the car pulled into the lane before following it to the shortcut. She'd walked down the main road, the way the car had come, but this was faster. She gestured Dunn to a parking space in the gravel pull-off near the side door to the inn.

He stepped out, shrugging into a leather jacket, and stood looking up at the inn. It was well worth looking at, even on a cold December night. Yellow light gleamed from the candles they'd placed in every one of the many nine-paned windows. Security lights posted on the outbuildings cast a pale-golden glow over the historic Federal-style sandstone mansion. It had been home to generations of the Unger family before necessity had turned it into the Three Sisters Inn.

Rachel glanced at the man, expecting him to say something. Guests usually sounded awed or at least admiring, at first sight. Dunn just turned to haul his briefcase and computer from the front seat.

Definitely not the typical tourist. What had brought

him to the heart of Pennsylvania Dutch country at this time of year? Visiting businessmen, especially those who traveled alone, were more likely to seek out a hotel with wireless connection and fax machines rather than a bed-and-breakfast, no matter how charming.

"May I carry something for you?"

He handed her the computer case. "If you'll take this, I can manage the rest."

The case was heavier than she'd expected, and she straightened, determined not to give in to the limp that sometimes plagued her when she was tired—the only remaining souvenir of the accident.

Or at least she'd thought that was the only aftereffect, until she'd felt that surge of terror when she'd seen the car. She'd have to work on that.

"This way. We'll go in the side door instead of around to the front, if you don't mind."

"Fine."

A man of few words, apparently. Dog at her heels, she headed for the door, hearing his footsteps behind her. She glanced back. He was taller than she'd realized when he sat in the car—he probably had a good foot on her measly five two, and he moved with a long stride that had him practically on her heels.

She went into the hallway, welcoming the flow of warm air, and on into the library. She didn't usually bring guests in through the family quarters, but it seemed silly to walk around the building just to give him the effect of the imposing front entrance into the high-ceiled center hall. The usual visitor ohhed and ahhed over that. She had a feeling Tyler Dunn wouldn't.

"My grandmother has already gone up to bed." She led the way to the desk. "You'll meet her in the morning at breakfast. We serve from seven-thirty to nine-thirty, but you can make arrangements to have it earlier, if you wish."

He shook his head, glancing toward the glowing embers of the fire she'd started earlier. Grams's favorite chair was drawn up next to the fireplace, and her knitting lay on its arm.

"That's fine. If I can just get signed in now and see my room—"

"Of course." Smile, she reminded herself. The customer is always right. She handed him a registration card and a pen, stepping back so that he had room to fill it out.

He bent over, printing the information in quick, black strokes, frowning a little. He looked tired and drawn, she realized, her quick sympathy stirring.

"That's great, thanks." She imprinted the credit card and handed it back to him. "You indicated in your reservation that you weren't sure how long you'd want the room?"

She made it a question, hoping for something a little more definite. With all the work she'd been doing to lure guests for the holiday season, the inn still wasn't booked fully. January and February were bound to be quiet. In order to come out ahead financially, they needed a good holiday season. Her money worries seemed to pop up automatically several times a day.

"I don't know." He almost snapped the words. She must have shown a reaction, because almost immediately he gave her a slightly rueful smile. "Sorry. I hope that doesn't inconvenience you, but I have business in the area, and I don't know how long it will take."

"Not at all." The longer she could rent him the room, the better. "Perhaps while you're here, you'll have time to enjoy some of the Christmas festivities. The village is planning a number of events, and of course we're not far from Bethlehem—"

"I'm not here for sightseeing." His gaze was on the dying fire, not her, but she seemed to sense him weighing a decision to say more. "That business I spoke of— there's no reason you'd recognize my name, but I own the property that adjoins yours on one side. The old Hostetler farm."

She blinked. "I didn't realize—" She stopped, not sure how to phrase the question. "I thought the property belonged to John Hostetler's daughter."

Who had annoyed the neighbors by refusing to sell the property and neglecting to take proper care of it. The farmhouse and barn had been invaded by vandals more than once, and the thrifty Amish farmers who owned the adjoining land been offended at the sight of a good farm going to ruin.

"My mother," he said shortly. His face drew a bit tighter. "She died recently."

That went a long way toward explaining the tension she felt from him. It didn't excuse his curtness, but made it more understandable. He was still grieving his mother's death and was now forced to deal with the unfinished business she'd left behind.

"I'm so sorry." She reached out impulsively to touch his arm. "You have my sympathy."

He jerked a nod. "I'm here to do something about my grandfather's property. My mother let that slide for too long."

It would be impolite to agree. "I'm sure the neighbors will be glad to help in any way they can. Are you planning to stay?"

"Live there, you mean?" His eyes narrowed. "Certainly not. I expect to sell as soon as possible."

Something new to worry about, as if she didn't have enough already. The best offer for the Hostetler farm might easily come from someone who wanted to put up some obnoxious faux Amish atrocity within sight of the inn.

"That's too bad. It would have been nice to hear that family would be living there again."

She'd made the comment almost at random, but Tyler Dunn's expression suggested that she'd lost her mind.

"I don't know why you'd think that." He bit off the words. "I'm hardly likely to want to live in the house where my grandfather was murdered."

Tyler closed his laptop and glanced at his watch. A little after eight—time for breakfast and another encounter with the Unger family.

He stood, pushing the ladder-back chair away from the small table, which was the only spot in the bedroom where one could possibly use a computer. He must be the first person who'd checked into the Three Sisters

Inn for business purposes. Most of the guests would be here to enjoy staying in the elegant mansion, maybe pretending they were living a century ago.

The place looked as if it belonged in a magazine devoted to historic homes. The bedroom, with its canopy bed covered by what was probably an Amish quilt, its antique furniture and deep casement windows, would look right on the cover.

From the window in his room, he had a good view of Churchville's Main Street, which was actually a country route along which the village had been built. The inn anchored the eastern edge of the community, along with the stone church which stood enclosed in its walled churchyard across the street. Beyond, there was nothing but hedgerows and the patchwork pattern of plowed fields and pasture, with barns and silos in the distance.

Looking to the left, he could see the shops and restaurants along Main Street, more than he'd expect given the few blocks of residential properties, but probably the flood of tourism going through town accounted for that. The inn had a desirable position, almost in the country but within easy walking distance of Main Street attractions. It was surprising they weren't busier.

He opened the door. The upstairs landing was quiet, the doors to the other rooms standing open. Obviously, he was the only guest at the moment. Maybe that would make things easier.

Had it been a mistake to come out so bluntly with the fact of his grandfather's murder last night? He wasn't sure, and he didn't like not being sure. He was used to dealing with facts, figures, formulas—not something as amorphous as this.

At least he'd had an opportunity to see Rachel Hampton's reaction. He frowned. Her name might be Hampton, but she was one of the Unger family.

If his mother had been right—but he couldn't count on that. In any event, he'd understood what she'd wanted of him. The impossible.

He started down the staircase, running his hand along the delicately carved railing. The downstairs hall stretched from front to back of the house. To his right, the door into the library where he'd registered last night was now closed. On his left, a handsome front parlor opened into another parlor, slightly smaller, behind it, both decorated with period furniture.

He headed toward the rear of the building, where Rachel had indicated he'd find the breakfast room. He'd cleared his calendar until the first of the year. If he couldn't accomplish what he planned by then, he'd put his grandfather's farm on the market, go back to his own life and try to forget.

The hallway opened out into a large, rectangular sunroom, obviously an addition to the original house. A wall of windows looked onto a patio and garden, bare of flowers now, but still worth looking at in the shapes of the trees and the bright berries of the shrubs. The long table was set for one.

Voices came from the doorway to the left, obviously the kitchen. He moved quietly toward them.

"…if I'd known, maybe I wouldn't have opened my

mouth and put my foot in it." Rachel, obviously talking to someone about his arrival.

"There was no reason for you to know. You were just a child." An older voice, cultured, restrained. If this woman was hiding something, he couldn't tell.

A pan clattered. "You'd best see if he's coming down, before these sticky buns are cold."

That was his cue, obviously. He moved to the doorway before someone could come out and find him. "I'm here. I wouldn't want to cause a crisis in the kitchen."

"Good morning." The woman who rose from the kitchen table, extending her hand to him, must be Rachel's grandmother. Every bit the grande dame, she didn't look in the least bothered by what he might or might not have overheard. "Welcome to the inn, Mr. Dunn. I'm Katherine Unger."

"Thank you." He shook her hand gently, aware of bones as fine as delicate crystal. The high cheekbones, brilliant blue eyes, and assured carriage might have belonged to a duchess.

Rachel, holding a casserole dish between two oversize oven mitts, had more color in her cheeks than he'd seen the night before, but maybe that was from the heat of the stove.

The third person in the kitchen wore the full-skirted dark dress and apron and white cap of the Amish. She turned away, evading his gaze, perhaps shy of a stranger.

"It's a pleasure to meet you, Mrs. Unger. I suppose your granddaughter told you who I am."

"Yes. I was very sorry to hear of your mother's

death. I knew her when she was a girl, although I don't suppose she remembered me. I don't remember seeing her again after she graduated from high school."

"Actually, she spoke of you when she talked about her childhood." Which hadn't been often, for the most part, until her final days. He'd always thought she'd been eager to forget.

"I'm sure you'd like to have your breakfast. Rachel has fixed her wild-mushroom and sausage quiche for you."

"You can have something else, if you prefer," Rachel said quickly. "I didn't have a chance to ask—"

"It sounds great," he said. "And I'm looking forward to the sticky buns, too." He smiled in the direction of the Amish woman, but she stared down at the stovetop as if it might speak to her.

Rachel, carrying the steaming casserole dish, led the way to the table in the breakfast room. He sat down, but before he had a chance to say anything, she'd whisked off to the kitchen, to reappear in a moment with a basket of rolls.

He helped himself to a fresh fruit cup and smiled at her as she poured coffee. "Any chance you'd pour a cup and join me? It's a little strange sitting here by myself."

This time there was no mistaking the flush that colored her cheeks. That fair skin must make it hard to camouflage her feelings. "I'm sorry there aren't any other guests at the moment, but—"

"Please. I need to apologize, and it would be easier over coffee."

She gave him a startled look, then turned without

a word and took a mug from a mammoth china cup-
board that bore faded stenciling—apples, tulips, stars.
It stood against the stone wall that must once have been
the exterior of the house.

Her mug filled, she sat down opposite him. "There's
really no reason for you to apologize to me."

Green eyes serious in a heart-shaped face, brown
hair curling to the shoulders of the white shirt she wore
with jeans, her hands clasped around the mug—she
looked about sixteen instead of the twenty-nine he
knew her to be. He'd done his homework on the resi-
dents of Three Sisters Inn before he'd come.

"I think I do. You were being friendly, and I
shouldn't have thrown the fact of my grandfather's
death at you."

"I didn't know." Her eyes were troubled, he'd guess
because she was someone who hated hurting another's
feelings. "We left here when I was about eight, and I
didn't come back until less than a year ago, so I'm not
up on local history."

"I guess that's what it seems like." He tried to pull
up his own images of his grandfather, but it was too
long ago. "Ancient history. I remember coming for the
funeral and having the odd sense that conversations
broke off when I came in the room. It must have been
years before I knew my grandfather had been killed
in the course of a robbery."

She leaned toward him, sympathy in every line of
her body. "I'm sure it's hard to deal with things so soon
after your mother's death. Is there any other family to
help you?"

"I'm afraid not." He found himself responding to her warmth even while the analytical part of his mind registered that the way to gain her cooperation was to need her help. "I hate the thought of seeing the farm again after all this time. It's down that road I was on last night, isn't it?"

He paused, waiting for the offer he was sure she'd feel compelled to make.

Rachel's fingers clenched around the mug, and he could sense the reluctance in her. And see her overcome it.

"Would you like me to go over there with you?"

"You'd do that?"

She smiled, seeming to overcome whatever reservation she had. "Of course. We're neighbors, after all."

It took a second to adjust to the warmth of that smile. "Thanks. I'd appreciate it."

Careful. He took a mental step back. Rachel Hampton was a very attractive woman, but he couldn't afford to be distracted from the task that had brought him here. And if she knew, there might very well be no more offers of help.

The dog danced at Rachel's heels as she walked down Crossings Road beside Tyler that afternoon. At least Barney was excited about this outing. She was beginning to regret that impulsive offer to accompany Tyler. And as for him—well, he looked as if every step brought him closer to something he didn't want to face.

Fanciful, she scolded herself, shoving her hands into the pockets of her corduroy jacket. The sun was bright enough to make her wish she'd brought sunglasses, but the air was crisp and cold.

"There's the lane to the farmhouse." She pointed ahead to the wooden gate that sagged between two posts. If there'd ever been a fence along the neglected pasture, it was long gone. "Is it coming back to you at all?"

Tyler shook his head. "I only visited my grandfather once before the time I came for the funeral. Apparently, he and my mother didn't get along well."

From what Grams had told her this morning, John Hostetler hadn't been on friendly terms with anybody, but it would hardly be polite to tell Tyler that. "That's a shame. This was a great place to be a kid."

Her gesture took in the gently rolling farmland that stretched in every direction, marked into neat fields, some sere and brown after the harvest, others showing the green haze of winter wheat.

He followed her movement, narrowing his eyes against the sun. "Are those farms Amish?"

"All the ones you see from here are. The Zook farm is the closest—we share a boundary with them, and you must, as well." She pointed. "Over there are the Stolzfuses, then the Bredbenners, and that farthest one belongs to Jacob Stoker. Amish farms may be different in other places, but around here you'll usually see a white bank barn and two silos. You won't see electric lines."

He gave her an amused look. "You sound like the local tour guide."

"Sorry. I guess it comes with running a B&B."

He looked down the lane at the farmhouse, just coming into view. "There it is. I can't say it brings any nostalgic feeling. My grandfather didn't seem welcoming when we came here. If my mother ever wanted to change things with him—well, I guess she left it too late."

Was he thinking again about his grandfather's funeral? Or maybe regretting the relationship they'd never had? She knew a bit about that feeling. Her father had never spent enough time in her life to do anything but leave a hole.

"You said something this morning about conversations breaking off when you came in the room—people wanting to protect you, I suppose, from knowing how your grandfather died."

He nodded, a question in his eyes.

"I know how that feels. When my father walked out, no one would tell us anything." She shook her head, almost wishing she hadn't spoken. After all these years, she still didn't like thinking about it. But that was what made her understand how Tyler felt. "Maybe they figured because he'd never been around much anyway, we wouldn't realize that this time was for good, but the truth would have been better than what we imagined."

His deep-blue eyes were so intent on her face that it was almost as if he touched her. "That must have been rough on you and your sisters."

She registered his words with a faint sense of unease. "I don't believe I mentioned my sisters to you."

"Didn't you?" He smiled, but there was something guarded in the look. "I suppose I was making an assumption, because of the inn's name."

That was logical, although it didn't entirely take away her startled sense that he knew more about them than she'd expect from a casual visitor.

"The name may be wishful thinking on my part, but yes, I have two sisters. Andrea is the oldest. She was married at Thanksgiving, and she and her husband are still on a honeymoon trip. And Caroline, the youngest, is an artist, living out in Santa Fe." She touched the turquoise and silver pin on her shirt collar. "She made this."

Tyler stopped, bending to look at the delicate hummingbird. He was so close his fingers almost touched her neck as he straightened the collar, and she was suddenly warm in spite of the chill breeze.

He drew back, and the momentary awareness was gone. "It's lovely. Your sister is talented."

"Yes." The worry over Caro that lurked at the back of her mind surfaced. Something had been wrong when Caro came home for the wedding, hidden behind her too-brittle laugh and almost frantic energy. But Caroline didn't seem to need her sisters any longer.

"The place looks even worse than I expected." Tyler's words brought her back to the present. The farmhouse, a simple frame building with a stone chimney at either end, seemed to sag as if tired of trying to stand upright. The porch that extended across the front sported broken railings and crumbling steps, and several windows had been boarded up.

"Grams told me the house had been broken into several times. Some of the neighbors came and boarded up the windows after the last incident. The barn looks in fairly good shape, though."

That was a small consolation to hold out to him if he really hadn't known that his mother let the place fall to bits. Still, a good solid Pennsylvania Dutch bank barn could withstand almost anything except fire.

"If those hex signs were meant to protect the place, they're not doing a very good job." He was looking up at the peak of the roof, where a round hex sign with the familiar star pattern hung.

"I don't think you'd find anyone to admit they believe that. Most people just say they're a tradition. There are as many theories as there are scholars who study them."

Tyler went cautiously up the porch steps and then turned toward her. "You'll have to climb over the broken tread."

She grasped the hand he held out, and he almost lifted her to the porch. She whistled to the dog, nosing around the base of the porch. "Come, Barney. The last thing we need is for you to unearth a hibernating skunk."

"That would be messy." Tyler turned a key in the lock, and the door creaked open. He hesitated for an instant and then stepped inside. She followed, switching on the flashlight that Grams had reminded her to bring.

"Dusty." A little light filtered through the boards on the windows, and the beam of her flashlight danced around the room, showing a few remaining pieces of furniture, a massive stone fireplace on the end wall, and a thick layer of dust on everything.

Tyler stood in the middle of the room, very still. His face seemed stiff, almost frozen.

"I'm sorry if it's a disappointment. It was a good, sturdy farmhouse once, and it could be again, with some money and effort."

"I doubt I'd find anyone interested in doing that." He walked through the dining room toward the kitchen, and she followed him, trying to think of something encouraging to say. This had to be a sad homecoming for him.

"There's an old stone sink. You don't often see those in their original state anymore."

He sent her the ghost of a smile. "You want to try out the pump?"

"No, thanks. That looks beyond repair. But I can imagine some antique dealer drooling over the stone sink. Those are quite popular now."

"I suppose I should get a dealer out to see if there's anything worth selling. I remember the house as being crowded with furniture, but there's not too much left now."

"My grandmother could steer you to some reputable dealers. Didn't your mother take anything back with her after your grandfather died?"

She couldn't help being curious. Anyone would be. Why had the woman let the place fall apart after her father died? Grief, maybe, but it still seemed odd. Surely she knew how valuable a good farm was in Lancaster County.

"Not that I remember." He turned from a contemplation of the cobwebby ice box to focus on her. "You spoke of break-ins. Was anything stolen?"

"I don't know. My grandmother might remember. Or Emma Zook, since they're such close neighbors. She's our housekeeper."

"The Amish woman who was in the kitchen this morning? According to the lawyer who handled my grandfather's will, the Zooks leased some of the farmland from his estate. I need to get that straightened out before I put the place on the market. I should talk to them. And to your grandmother."

Something about his intent look made her uneasy. "I doubt that she knows anything about their leases."

"According to my mother, Fredrick Unger offered to buy the property. That would make me think your family had an interest."

There was something—an edgy, almost antagonistic tone to his voice, that set her back up instantly. What was he driving at?

"I'm sure my grandfather's only interest would have been to keep a valuable farm from falling to pieces. Since he died nearly five years ago, I don't imagine you'll ever know."

"Your grandmother—"

"My grandmother was never involved in his business interests." And she wasn't going to allow him to badger her with questions. "I can't see that it matters, since your mother obviously didn't want to sell. Maybe what you need to do is talk to the attorney."

Her own tone was as sharp as his had been. She wasn't sure where the sudden tension had come from, but it was there between them. She could feel it, fierce and insistent.

Tyler's frown darkened, but before he could speak, there was a noisy creak from the living room.

"Hello? Anybody here?"

"Be right there," she called. She'd never been quite so pleased to hear Phillip Longstreet's voice. She didn't know where Tyler had been going with his questions and his attitude, and she didn't think she wanted to.

Chapter Two

Tyler didn't miss the relief on Rachel's face at the interruption. The speed with which she went into the living room was another giveaway. She might not know what drove him, but she'd picked up on something.

Or else he'd been careless, pushing too hard in his drive to get this situation resolved.

He followed her and found her greeting the newcomer with some surprise. "Phillip. What are you doing here?"

The man raised his eyebrows as she evaded his attempt to hug her. "Aren't you going to introduce me?" He held out his hand to Tyler. "Phillip Longstreet. You may have noticed Longstreet Antiques on Main Street in the village."

He was in his late forties or early fifties at a guess, but he wore his age well—fit-looking, with fair hair that showed signs of gray at the temples and shrewd hazel eyes behind the latest style in glasses.

"This is Tyler Dunn." She glanced at him, and he thought he read a warning in her eyes.

"Nice to meet you. Were you looking for Ms. Hampton?"

"It's always pleasant to see Rachel, but no, I wanted to meet the new owner." Longstreet shrugged, smiling. "I like to get in before the other dealers when I can."

"How did you know?" Rachel sounded exasperated. "If we had a party line, Phillip, I'd suspect you of eavesdropping."

"I have to be far more creative than that to stay ahead of the competition. If you want to keep secrets, don't come to a village. Emma's son, Levi, delivered the news along with my eggs this morning."

It was an insight into how this place worked. "Are you interested in the contents of the house, Mr. Longstreet?"

A local dealer might be the best choice before putting the house on the market, but Longstreet was obviously trolling for antiques, probably hoping to get an offer in on anything of value before his competition did. Or possibly before Tyler realized what he had.

"Phil, please. I'd like to look around." Longstreet's gaze was already scoping out the few pieces left in the living room. "Sometimes there are attractive pieces in these old farmhouses, although more often it's a waste of time."

"I'm afraid your time was definitely wasted this afternoon." He gestured toward the door. "I'm not ready to make a decision about selling anything yet."

"If I could just take a look around, I might be able to give you an idea of values." Longstreet craned his neck toward the dining room.

Tyler swung the door open and stepped out onto the porch, so that the man had no choice but to follow. "I'll be in touch when I'm ready to make a decision. Thank you for stopping by."

"Yes, well, thanks for your time." Longstreet stepped gingerly over the broken step. "Rachel, I'll see you at the meeting tonight."

Rachel, coming out behind him, bent to snap a leash onto the dog's collar. "Fine."

Tyler waited until Longstreet had backed out of the driveway to turn to her. "Is that one of the reputable dealers your grandmother might recommend?"

"Grams probably *would* suggest him. His uncle was an old crony of my grandfather."

"But…?"

Her nose crinkled. "Phil's nice enough, in his way. It's just that every time he comes to the inn, I get the feeling he's putting a price on the furniture."

"I'm not bad at showing people the door, if you'd like some help."

"I run an inn, remember?" She smiled, her earlier antagonism apparently gone. "The idea is to get people in, not send them away. Are you a bouncer in your real life?"

"Architect. Showing people the way out is just a sideline."

She looked interested. "Do you work on your own?"

He shook his head. "I'm with a partner in Baltimore, primarily designing churches and public buildings. Luckily I'm between projects right now, so I can take some time off to deal with this." Which brought him back to the problem at hand. "Well, if your grand-mother recommends Longstreet, I'll still be sure to get offers from more than one dealer."

"That should keep him in line. He's probably easier to cope with when he wants to buy something from you. I'm on the Christmas in Churchville committee with him, and he can be a real pain there."

He pulled the door shut and turned the key in the lock.

"Are you sure you're finished? You didn't look around upstairs."

"I've had enough for the moment." He tried to dismiss the negative feelings that had come with seeing the place again. This was a fool's errand. There was no truth left to find here—just a moldering ruin that had never, as far as he could tell, been a happy home.

The dog leaped down from the porch, nearly pulling Rachel off balance, and he caught her arm to steady her.

"Easy. Does he really need to be on the leash?"

"I wanted to discourage any more digging around the porch. I'm afraid you may have something holed up in there for the winter."

"Whatever it is, let it stay." He took the leash from her hand and helped her over the broken step to the ground. "I won't bother it."

She glanced at him as they walked away. "You must be saddened to see the place in such a state."

He shrugged. "I only saw it twice that I recall. It would have been worse for my mother than for me. She grew up here."

"Do you think—" She stopped, as if censoring what she'd been about to say.

"That's why she let it fall to pieces?" He finished the thought for her. "I have no idea. I'd have expected my dad to intercede, but—" he shrugged "—I didn't know she still owned the place until a few weeks ago, and by then she was in no shape to explain much. Maybe she just wanted to forget, after the way her father died."

Rachel scuffed through frost-tipped dead leaves that the wind had scattered over the road. "I don't think I've ever actually heard how it happened."

"From what my mother told me, he apparently confronted someone breaking into the house. There was a struggle, and he had a heart attack. He wasn't found until the next day."

She shivered, shoving her hands into her pockets. "It's hard to think about something like that happening here when I was a child. It always seemed such an idyllic place."

They walked for a few moments in silence, their footsteps muted on the macadam road. He glanced at her, confirming what he heard. "You're limping. Did you twist your ankle getting off that porch?"

"It wasn't that." She nodded toward the bend in the road ahead of them, the wind ruffling her hair across her face so that she pushed it back with an impatient movement. "I had an accident just up the road back in the spring."

He frowned down at her. "It must have been a bad one. Did you hit a tree?"

She shook her head. "I was jogging, too late in the

evening, I guess. A car came around the bend—" She stopped, probably reliving it too acutely.

That explained why she'd stepped back into the trees when he'd come down the lane last night. "How badly were you hurt?"

"Two broken legs." She shrugged. "Could have been worse, I guess. It only bothers me when I'm on my feet too long."

"I hope the driver ended up in jail."

"Hit and run," she said briefly.

Obviously she didn't want to talk about it any further. He couldn't blame her. She didn't want to remember, any more than he wanted to think about the way his grandfather died, or the burden his mother had laid on him to find out why.

"I guess this place isn't so idyllic after all."

"Bad things happen anywhere, people being people."

"Yes, I guess they do." Of course she was right about that. It was only the beauty that surrounded them that made violence seem so out of place here.

Rachel was thankful when the business part of the "Christmas in Churchville" meeting was over. The strain of mediating all those clashing egos had begun to tell on her after the first hour.

Now the battling committee members wandered around the public rooms of the inn, helping themselves to punch and the variety of goodies placed on tables in both the back parlor and the breakfast room. She'd figured out a long time ago that if you wanted to keep people circulating, you should space out the food and drink.

She and Grams had put cranberry punch on the round table next to the fireplace in the back parlor, accompanied by an assortment of cheeses, grapes and crackers. The breakfast room had coffee, tea and hot chocolate on the sideboard, along with mini éclairs and pfeffernüsse, the tiny clove and cardamom delicacies that were her grandmother's special holiday recipe.

Would Tyler come down? Thinking of him alone in his room, she'd suggested he join them for refreshments. He'd know when the business meeting was over, she'd told him, when the shouting stopped.

Her committee members weren't quite that bad, but they did have strong opinions on what would draw the holiday tourists to spend their money in Churchville.

She checked on the service in the parlor and walked back toward the breakfast room. Tyler was in an odd position here—part of the community by heritage and yet a stranger. He probably wouldn't be around long enough to change that. He'd sell the property and go back to his life in Baltimore.

Hopefully he wouldn't leave problems behind in the form of whoever bought his grandfather's farm. The neighbors disliked seeing it derelict, but there were certainly things they'd hate even more.

"Rachel, there you are." Phillip intercepted her in the doorway, punch cup in hand. Fortunately the cup made it easier to escape the arm he tried to put around her. "I wanted to speak with you about the Hostetler place."

"So does everyone else, but I don't know anything. Tyler hasn't told me what his plans are for the property."

"You know I'm all about the furniture, my dear. I remember a dough box that my uncle tried to buy once from old Hostetler. If there's anything like that left—"

"You saw the living room. Most of the furniture is already gone."

"I didn't see the rest of the house." His voice turned wheedling. "Come on, Rachel, at least give me a hint what's there."

"Sorry, I didn't see anything else." She slipped past him. "Excuse me, but I have to refill the coffeepot."

Phillip was nothing if not persistent. That probably explained how he managed to make such a success of the shop. His uncle had been a sweet old man, but he'd never had much of a head for business, from what Grams said.

She snagged a mug of hot chocolate and a pfeffernüsse for herself, turning from the table to find Sandra Whitmoyer bearing down on her. As wife of Churchville's most dedicated, as well as only, physician, Sandra seemed to feel the chairmanship of the decorating subcommittee was hers by right. Luckily no one else had put up a fight for it.

"Rachel, we really must keep our eyes on the rest of the shop owners along Main Street. It would be fatal to allow anyone to put up a garish display."

"I'm sure you'll do a wonderful job of that, Sandra." She had no desire to turn herself into the decorating police. "I have my hands full already, preparing the inn and organizing the open house tour." Maybe a little flattery was in order. "You have such wonderful taste. I know everyone will be seeking your advice. And they've all agreed to go along with the committee's decisions."

"Well, I suppose." Sandra ran a manicured hand over sleek waves of blond hair. She was dressed to perfection tonight as always, this time in a pair of gray wool slacks that made her legs look a mile long, paired with a silk shirt that had probably cost the earth.

Glancing past Sandra, she spotted Tyler standing in the doorway. So he had come down. He looked perfectly composed in the crowd of strangers—self-possessed, as if he carried his confidence with him no matter where he was.

She'd seen him ruffled at moments that afternoon, though, and she'd guess he didn't often show that side to people. The derelict house had affected him more than she'd expected.

And there had been an undercurrent when he talked about his mother, something more than grief, she thought.

Sandra had moved to the window, peering out at the patio and garden. "I suppose you'll be decorating the garden for the open house."

"White lights on the trees, and possibly colored ones on the big spruce."

"It would be more effective without the security lights," Sandra said. "You could turn them off during the house tour hours. And maybe put a spotlight on the gazebo."

"I don't want to draw attention to the gazebo. I'd be happy to demolish it completely."

"You wouldn't have to do something that drastic."

She turned at the sound of Tyler's voice, smiling her welcome. "What would you suggest, other than a stick of dynamite? Sandra Whitmoyer, I'd like to introduce Tyler Dunn. He owns the Hostetler place, down the road from us."

Sandra extended her hand. "Welcome to Churchville. Everyone is curious about what you intend for the property. Well, not my husband, of course. As a busy physician, he doesn't have time for many outside interests."

Bradley Whitmoyer was as self-effacing a man as she'd ever met, but his wife had appointed herself his one-woman press agency.

Tyler responded, politely noncommittal, and turned back to Rachel. "I wouldn't recommend high explosives for the gazebo. You wouldn't like the results."

"I don't like it the way it is."

He smiled down at her. "That's because it's in the wrong place. If you moved it to the other side of the pond, it would be far enough away to create a view."

"Well, I still think you should decorate it for the house tour." Sandra put down her cup. "I have to go. There's Jeff looking for me. It was nice meeting you, Mr. Dunn." She nodded to Rachel and crossed the room toward the hallway.

"Is that her husband, the physician?" Tyler's tone was faintly mocking.

"No, his brother. Jeff Whitmoyer. He has a small

construction company. It looks as if he didn't find it necessary to change before coming by for Sandra."

Jeff's blue jeans, flannel shirt and work boots were a sharp contrast to Sandra's elegance. There was a quick exchange between them before Sandra swept out the hallway.

Rachel dismissed them from her mind and turned back to Tyler. "About the gazebo—"

"Single-minded, aren't you?" His smile took any edge off the comment. "It might be possible to move it, rather than destroy it. If you like, I'll take a look while I'm here."

"I'd love to find a solution that makes everyone happy. Grams never liked the gazebo at all—she feels it doesn't go with the style of the house. But Andrea thinks it should stay because Grandfather had it put up as a surprise for Grams."

"And it's your job to keep everyone happy?" The corners of his mouth quirked.

"Not my job, exactly." Every family had a peacemaker, didn't they? She was the middle one, so it fell to her. "My sister says I let my nurturing instincts run amok, always trying to help people whether they want it or not."

"It's a nice quality." Those deep-blue eyes seemed to warm when they rested on her. "I wouldn't change if I were you."

"Thank you." Ridiculous, to be suddenly breathless because a man was looking at her with approval. "And thank you for the offer."

He shrugged. "It's nothing. We're neighbors, remember?"

It was what she'd said to him, but he seemed to invest the words with a warmth that startled her.

Careful, she warned herself. It wouldn't be a good idea to start getting too interested in a man who'd disappear as soon as his business here was wound up.

Rachel did not like climbing ladders. Any ladder, let alone this mammoth thing that allowed her to reach the top of the house. Unfortunately, there didn't seem to be another way of putting up the outside lights anytime soon.

Grams had suggested hiring someone to do the decorating, but Grams didn't have a grasp on how tight money was right now. Rachel could ask a neighbor for help, of course, but this was a business. It didn't seem right if she couldn't pay.

But she really didn't like being up on a ladder.

She leaned out, bracing herself with one hand on the shutter, and slipped the strand of lights over the final hook. Breathing a sigh of relief, she went down the ladder. In comparison to that, doing the windows should be a breeze.

Reaching the ground, she took a step back, reminding herself of just how many windows there were. Well, maybe not a breeze, but she could do it.

And what difference would it make, the voice of doubt asked. *You have one whole guest at the moment.*

Tyler had gone off to Lancaster this morning to see the attorney who'd handled his grandfather's estate.

He'd seemed eager to resolve the situation with the farm. Well, why not? He probably had plans for Christmas in Baltimore.

Once he left, she'd have zero guests. There were a few people scheduled for the coming weekends, but not nearly enough. They'd hoped for a good holiday season to get them through the rest of the winter, but that wasn't happening.

If she could get some holiday publicity up on the inn's website, it might make all the difference. Andrea had intended to do that, but the rush to get ready for the wedding had swamped those plans. And she could hardly call her big sister on her honeymoon to ask for help. They had already invested all they could afford in print ads in the tourist guides, and the website was the only option left.

She fastened a spray of pine in place, taking satisfaction in the way the dark green contrasted with the pale stone walls. This she could do. Decorate, cook gourmet breakfasts, work twenty-four/seven when it was necessary—those were her gifts.

Her gaze rested absently on the church across the street, its stone walls as gold as the inn. Someone had put evergreen wreaths on the double doors, and the church glowed with welcome. That was what she'd sensed when she'd come back to Churchville. Welcome. Home. Family. Community. She'd lost that when Daddy left and their mother had taken them away from here.

She paused with her hand on the burgundy ribbon she was tying. *Lord, this venture can't be wrong, can it? It seems right. Surely You wouldn't let me have a need so strong if it weren't meant to be satisfied.*

"Rachel, you look as if you've turned to stone up there. Are you all right?"

She glanced down from the window to see Bradley Whitmoyer standing on the walk, eyeing her quizzically. She scrambled down from the stepladder.

"I guess that's what they mean by being lost in thought, Dr. Whitmoyer. What can I do for you?"

She saw him occasionally, of course, when she took Grams for a check-up, at church, at a social event, but he'd never come to the inn.

"Bradley," he corrected. "I'm on an errand." He gave her his gentle smile, pulling an envelope from the pocket of his overcoat. "My wife asked me to drop this off on my way to the office. Something to do with this Christmas celebration you're working on, I think."

She took the envelope. "You shouldn't have gone out of your way. I could have picked it up." She knew how busy he was. Everyone in the township knew that.

"No problem." He drew his coat a little more tightly around him, as if feeling the cold. "I've been meaning to see how you're getting along. This is an ambitious project you and your grandmother have launched."

"Yes, it is." He didn't know how ambitious. "But Grams is enjoying it."

"That's good." His eyes seemed distracted behind the wire-rimmed glasses he wore, his face lined and tired.

He wore himself out for everyone else. People said he'd turned down prestigious offers to come back to

Churchville and become a family doctor, because the village and the surrounding area needed him.

"I understand you have old Mr. Hostetler's grandson staying here." He rocked back and forth on his heels. "I suppose he's come to put the farm on the market."

"I don't know what his plans are. Probably he'll sell the land. The house is in such bad shape, I'm not sure anyone would want it."

"He should just tear it down. Every old house isn't worth saving, like this one. You're doing a fine job with it."

"Thank you." She resisted the urge to confide how uncertain she was about her course. She wasn't his patient, and her problems weren't medical. She waved the envelope—no doubt Sandra's notes on the town brochure. "Please tell your wife I'll get right on this."

"I'll do that." He turned, heading for his car quickly, as if eager to turn on the heater.

Even as he got into his sedan, she saw Tyler's car pulling into the driveway. If he'd arrived a few minutes earlier, she could have introduced them.

"Was that a new guest?" Tyler came toward her across the crisp grass.

"Unfortunately not. That was Dr. Whitmoyer. You met his wife last night."

"So that's the good doctor."

"He really is. Good, I mean. He's the only doctor in the village, and in addition to carrying a huge patient load, he's doing valuable research on genetic diseases among the Amish."

"I'll agree that he's a paragon if you'll come inside

for a few minutes." He was frowning. "I need to talk to you."

Now that she focused on him, she could sense his tension. Something was wrong.

She put down the ribbon she'd been holding. "Of course."

The warm air that greeted her when she walked inside made her fingers tingle. She led the way to the library, shrugging out of her jacket, and turned to face him. "What is it? Can I help you with something?"

He shoved his hands into his pockets, frowning, and ignored the invitation to sit. "I saw the attorney who's been handling things since my grandfather died. According to him, your grandfather tried to buy the farm at least six times since then."

She didn't understand the tone of accusation in his voice. "I suppose that's true. The neighbors weren't happy to see the place falling to pieces. It would be natural for my grandfather to make an offer for it."

"It sounds to me as if he was eager to snap up the property once my grandfather was out of the way. According to my mother, he and my grandfather had been feuding for years."

She planted her hands on her hips. There weren't many things that made her fighting mad, but innuendos about her family certainly did. "I'm not sure what you're driving at, Tyler. I don't know anything about any feud, but if it did exist, it's been over for twenty years or so. What does that matter now?"

His eyes seemed to darken. "It mattered to my mother. She talked to me about it before she died. She said her father told her someone was trying to cheat him out of what was his. That she didn't believe his death was as a result of a simple robbery. And that she believed the Unger family was involved."

Chapter Three

Rachel's reaction to his statement was obvious. Shock battled anger for control.

That was what he'd felt, too, since the attorney told him about old Mr. Unger's attempt to buy the place. He'd hoped the lawyer would say his mother had been imagining things. Instead, his words seemed to confirm her suspicions.

Rachel took a breath, obviously trying to control her anger. She held both hands out, palms pushing away, her expression that of one who tries to calm a maniac. "I think you should leave now."

"And give you time to come up with a reasonable explanation? I'd rather have the truth."

Her green eyes sparked fire. "I don't need to come up with anything. You're the one making ridiculous accusations."

"Is it ridiculous? My grandfather claimed someone was trying to cheat him. Your grandfather tried repeatedly to buy his property. How else do you add those things up?"

"Not the way you do, obviously. There's a difference between buying and cheating someone. If your grandfather thought the offer low, he didn't have to sell." She flung out a hand toward the portrait that hung over the fireplace mantel. "Look at my grandfather. Does he look like someone who'd try to cheat a neighbor?"

"Appearances can be deceiving." Still, he had to admit that the face staring out from the frame had a quality of judicious fairness that made the idea seem remote.

She gave a quick shake of her head, as if giving up on him. "This is getting us nowhere. I'm sorry for your problems, but I can't help you. I'll be glad to refund your money if you want to check out." She stood very stiffly, her face pale and set.

He'd blown it. He'd acted on impulse, blurting out his suspicions, and now he wouldn't get a thing from her. Time to regroup.

"Look, I'm sorry for coming out with it that way. Can we sit down and talk this over rationally?"

Anger flashed in those green eyes. "Now you want to be rational? You're the one who started this with your ridiculous accusations."

He took a breath. He needed cooperation from Rachel if he were going to get anywhere. "Believe it or not, I felt as if I'd been hit by a two-by-four when I heard what Grassley, the attorney, had to say. Just hear me out. Then I'll leave if you want."

Rachel looked as if she were counting to ten. Finally

she nodded. She waved him to the sofa and pulled the desk chair over for herself. She sat, planting her hands on its arms and looking ready to launch herself out of the chair at the slightest wrong word.

He sat on the edge of the sofa, trying to pull his thoughts into some sort of order. He was a logical person, so why couldn't he approach this situation logically?

Maybe he knew the answer to that one. Grief and guilt could be a powerful combination. He'd never realized how strong until the past few weeks.

"You have to understand—I had no idea all this was festering in my mother's mind. She didn't talk about her childhood, and I barely knew her father. I'd been here once, before I came for my grandfather's funeral."

She nodded. "You told me that. I thought then that there must have been some breach between your mother and your grandfather."

So she'd seen immediately what he'd have recognized if he weren't so used to the situation. "I never knew anything about it. My father may have known, but he died when I was in high school."

"I'm sorry." Her eyes darkened with sympathy, in spite of the fact that she must still be angry with him.

"My mother had always been—" He struggled to find the right word. "Secretive, I guess you'd say. After my father died, she started turning to me more. Change the lightbulbs, have the car serviced, talk to the neighbors about their barking dog. But she never shared anything about her finances or business matters. I knew my father had left her well off, so I didn't pry. That's why I didn't have any idea she still owned the property here."

"I suppose she let the attorney take care of anything that had to be done. I'm surprised he didn't urge her to sell—to my grandfather or anyone else." Her voice was tart.

"He did, apparently, but he said she'd never even discuss it. She didn't with me until her illness." It had been hard to see her go downhill so quickly, hard to believe that none of the treatments were doing any good.

"What was it?"

"Cancer. When she realized she wasn't recovering, that's when she started to talk." He paused. "She'd left it late. She was on pain medication, not making much sense. But she said what I told you—that her father had insisted he was being cheated, that everyone was out to take advantage of him."

"That sounds as if he felt—well, that he thought he was being persecuted. How can you know that any of what he told her was true?"

"I can't. But she thought there were things about his death that had never been explained. She regretted that she'd never attempted to find out. She demanded my promise that I'd try to learn the truth."

His hands clenched. He'd told Rachel more than he'd intended. If she knew about what had happened then—but that was ridiculous. She'd been a child twenty-two years ago. At most, she'd oppose him now out of a need to protect her grandfather's reputation.

"I can understand why you feel you have to honor her wishes," she said, looking as if she chose her words carefully. "But after all this time, how can you possibly hope to learn anything?"

"I thought I might talk to your grandmother—"

"No!" She flared up instantly at that. "I won't have my grandmother upset by this."

A step sounded from the hallway, and they both turned. "That is not your decision to make, Rachel." Rachel's grandmother stood in the doorway, her bearing regal, her face set and stern.

Rachel's throat tightened. Grams, standing there, hearing the suspicions Tyler was voicing. She'd like to throw something at him for causing all this trouble, but that wouldn't help.

"Now, Grams…" She had to think of something that would repair this situation. Protecting Grams was her responsibility.

She stood and went to her, the desk chair rolling backward from the pressure of her hands. She put her arm around her grandmother's waist.

Grams didn't seem to need her support. She had pride and dignity to keep her upright.

"Don't 'now, Grams,' me, Rachel Elizabeth. I know what I heard, and I don't require any soothing platitudes."

Rachel shot a fulminating glance at Tyler. At least he had the grace to look unhappy at this turn of events. He'd look worse when she finished telling him what she thought.

"Grams, I'm sure you misunderstood." She tried for

a light tone. "You always told us that eavesdroppers never hear anything good, remember?"

Grams ignored her, staring steadily at Tyler. "I must apologize. I'm not in the habit of listening in on other people's conversations, but you were both too busy arguing to realize I was there."

"I just want to protect you—" Rachel began.

Her grandmother cut her short with a look. "I don't require protection. I knew my husband well enough to be quite confident that he'd never have been involved in anything underhanded. I have nothing to fear from Mr. Dunn's inquiry."

"Of course not, but it's still upsetting. Please, Grams, let me handle this."

Her only response was to move to her armchair and be seated, folding her hands in her lap. "I'll answer any question you wish to ask." She glanced up at the portrait. "The truth can't harm my husband."

Grams might want to believe that, but Rachel wasn't so sure. Of course she knew Grandfather had been perfectly honest, but rumors, once started, could be difficult to stop.

She glanced at Tyler. He looked as if getting what he wanted had taken him by surprise.

"It's very good of you to agree to talk with me about this." He'd apparently decided on a formal approach. Good. If she caught the slightest whiff of disrespect, he'd be out of here before he knew what hit him.

Grams inclined her head graciously. "I don't know that I have much to offer. My husband only discussed business with me in very general terms."

Tyler's mouth tightened fractionally. "Start by telling me what you remember about John Hostetler. You must have known him, since you were such close neighbors."

"I knew him. Knew of him, certainly. He was a rather difficult person, from everything I recall. After his wife died, he became bitter, cutting himself off from the community."

"Do you know if your husband had any business dealings with him? Did he talk to you about wanting to buy the place?"

She frowned. "I don't remember, but if he did, it would be in his ledgers. Rachel will make them available to you."

She swallowed the protest that sprang to her lips. Tyler could strain his eyes looking through decades of her grandfather's fine black script, and he wouldn't find anything wrong.

"That's kind of you." Tyler seemed taken aback by that kindness, but that was her grandmother. "Do you know of anyone he was on bad terms with?"

A faint smile rippled on Grams's expression. "It might be easier to ask with whom he didn't quarrel. I don't mean to speak ill of him, but it's fairly well known that he argued with just about everyone."

"I remember a visit we made when I was about six. Certainly he and my mother seemed to battle most of the time."

"I'm afraid that was his nature." Grams spread her hands. "I don't know what else I can say. After his death, the neighbors were concerned about the condition of the farm. Several of them came to Fredrick about it, I remember that." She glanced up at the portrait again. "If he did try to buy it, I'm sure that's why."

He nodded, not offering any comment. It was what Rachel had told him, too, but she didn't think he was convinced. He wouldn't understand her grandfather's almost-feudal-lord position in the community. Everyone, Amish and English alike, had come to him with their concerns.

"Do you remember anything about the robbery and his death?"

Grams moved slightly, and Rachel was instantly on the alert. This questioning bothered her grandmother more than she'd want to admit.

"I know we were shocked. Everyone was."

She put her arm around her grandmother. "Of course they were." She darted him a look. "I think my grandmother has told you everything she can."

Grams gave Tyler a level look. "I have, but if there's anything else…"

"Not right now." Tyler seemed to know he'd pushed enough.

Grams rose. "We'll cooperate in any way we can. It's what my husband would wish." She turned toward the kitchen and walked away steadily.

Rachel hesitated. She wanted his promise that this wasn't going to be all over the township by sunset, but she didn't want to say that where Grams could hear.

She'd better make sure Grams was safely in the kitchen with Emma.

"Would you mind sticking around for a minute or two while I speak to Emma? I could use some help moving that ladder."

He nodded, his expression telling her he understood what she wasn't saying. "I'll wait for you outside."

By the time she went out the front door a few minutes later, Rachel knew exactly how she should behave. She'd talk with Tyler very calmly, explaining the harm that could be done to her grandmother by careless talk. She'd make it clear that they'd already done everything he'd asked of them and that there really was nothing else they could contribute.

She would not express the anger she felt. She'd extended friendship to the man, and all the time he'd been using her to pry into her family.

He waited by the ladder she'd left propped against the house, his leather jacket hanging open in the warmth of the afternoon sunshine. He straightened when he saw her. "Is your grandmother all right?"

"She didn't like being cross-examined," she said sharply, and then snapped her mouth shut on the words. If she wanted discretion from Tyler, she'd better try a little tact of her own. "She was telling you the truth." Katherine Unger was not someone who'd lie to cover up her own or anyone else's misdeeds.

He gave her a slight smile. "I know. Do you think I don't recognize integrity when I see it?"

"I was afraid your judgment might be skewed by your need to find out about your grandfather."

"Look, I said I was sorry for jumping on you with it. I want to be fair about it."

Did he mean that? She hoped so. "There's one thing you said to me that you didn't mention to my grandmother."

He frowned. "What's that?"

He knew. He had to. "You said your mother didn't think her father's death had been adequately explained. You called it murder."

The word seemed to stand there between them, stark and ugly.

He was silent for a long moment, and then he shook his head. "I don't know, Rachel. That's the truth. I can tell you what my mother said. What she seemed to believe. As to whether it had any basis in fact—" he shrugged "—I guess that's what I have to find out."

"I hope—" She stopped. Would he think she was trying to control his actions? Well, in a way, she was.

"What do you hope?" He focused on her, eyes intent.

"I hope you'll be discreet with the questions you ask people around here, especially anything to do with my grandparents. It doesn't take much to set rumors flying in a small community like this."

"Your grandmother didn't seem to be worried about that."

No, she wouldn't worry about people talking when she felt she was doing what was right.

"Grams can be naive about some things. If the

rumor mill starts churning, the situation will be difficult for her. So be tactful, will you please?"

"I'll try." He took a step back from the wooden stepladder as she approached it. "I'm not here to stir up trouble for innocent people."

"Sometimes innocent people get hurt by the backlash." She bent to plug the end of the string of lights into the outlet.

"I can't let that stop me from looking for the truth." His jaw set like a stone.

"And I won't let anything stop me from protecting my family," she said. "Just so we're clear."

"We're clear. Does that mean you want me to move out?"

It was tempting to say yes, but it was safer to have Tyler where she could keep track of him. "You're welcome to stay as long as you want." She started up the ladder, the loop of lights in her hand.

"Thank you. And since I'm staying, I'd be glad to climb up and do that for you. I wouldn't have to stretch as far."

"I can reach." If she stood on the top step on her tiptoes, she could.

She looped the string of lights over the small metal hook that was left in the window frame from year to year. Pulling the string taut, she grasped it and leaned toward the other side.

She stretched, aware of him watching her, and pushed the wire toward the hook—

"Wait!" Tyler barked.

The wire touched the hook—a sharp snap, a scent of burning, a jolt that knocked her backward off the ladder and sent her flying toward the ground, stunned.

Chapter Four

"**I**'m fine. Really." Rachel tried to muster a convincing tone, but if she looked half as shaken as she felt, it was hardly surprising that Tyler wanted to rush her to the hospital.

"You don't look fine." He had a firm hold on her arm, and he didn't seem inclined to let go any time soon. "My car's right there. If you won't go to the E.R., at least let that local doctor you were talking to have a look."

"I don't need Dr. Whitmoyer to look at me." She rubbed her hands together, trying to get rid of the tingling sensation. "It just knocked the wind out of me, that's all."

He still seemed doubtful, but finally he gave a reluctant nod. "I'll help you inside."

"No." She tried to pull her arm free, but he continued to propel her toward the door. "Look, I don't want my grandmother upset, okay? She's been worried enough about me since the accident, and the last thing she needs is any fresh reason to fear. Besides, she's already had her quota of crises today."

Tyler's face settled in a frown, but at least he stopped pulling her toward the door. "That's dirty pool, you know that?"

"I'll do whatever works where Grams is concerned. She may think she's still as tough as she always was, but that's not true."

After her accident and then Andrea's brush with death in the early summer, Grams had shown a fragility that had hit both of them hard. She was doing much better now—confident that the inn would succeed, happy about Andrea's wedding. Nothing must disrupt that.

Tyler urged her toward the step. "Sit down and get your breath back, at least. When I saw the power arc and you fly backward, I thought my heart would stop."

"Sorry about that." She managed a smile as she sank down on the low stone step. It was nice of him to be so concerned about her. "I felt a bit scared myself, not that I had time to think about it. Is it my imagination, or did you tell me to stop just before I touched the hook?"

He nodded, putting one foot on the step and leaning his elbow on his knee as he bent toward her. "A second too late. I caught a glimpse of bare wire where the sun glinted on it. Sorry I didn't see it sooner. And sorry you didn't think to check those lights before you plugged them in."

"I'll admit that wasn't the smartest thing I ever did, but I did look over them when I got the box out of the attic. At least—" She stopped, thinking about it.

"Well?"

She glared at him. "I think I checked them, but I was in a rush to get ready for last night's meeting." She'd shoved the box in the downstairs restroom when she'd realized how late it was. Maybe she had missed some of the strings.

Tyler, apparently feeling it wiser not to pursue the conversation, walked over to the stepladder and cautiously detached the string of lights. He frowned down at it for a moment before carrying it back to her.

"There's the culprit." He held the strand between his hands. Green plastic coating had melted away from a foot-long stretch of cord, and the wire between was blackened and mangled, shreds of metal twisting up like frizzled hair. The acrid smell of it turned her stomach.

"Guess I won't be using that string of lights anytime soon." It took an effort to speak lightly.

"Or ever." He was still frowning, the cord stretched taut between his hands. "That's a lot of bare wire."

She shrugged, trying to push away the creeping sensation on the back of her neck. "All's well that ends well. I'm relatively unscathed, and I'd better get back to work."

"Sit still." He softened the command with a half smile. "Sorry, but you look washed out."

"Gee, thanks."

Now he grinned, his face relaxing. "Just let me see if this blew a fuse before you do anything else."

She hadn't even thought of that, so she leaned back

against the step, watching him test the heavy-duty extension cord on a fresh strip of lights.

"Looks okay. Actually that's surprising. Usually the wiring in these old places isn't in great shape."

"You should see the maze of wires in the cellar. It's an electrician's nightmare, but it all seems to work. We did have to have the wiring checked out before we could open the inn, of course."

He gazed up at the house. "It's early eighteenth century, isn't it?"

"I guess an architect would know. The oldest part dates to 1725, according to the records."

"It's been in your family ever since?"

"Pretty much. My maternal grandfather's family, the Ungers, that is."

He was probably making conversation to distract her from the fact that he was going over each strand of lights in the box, checking all of them methodically with eyes and hands.

Well, she wouldn't object to that. She was happy enough just to sit here, feeling the sun's warmth chase the winter chill away.

"Satisfied?" she asked when he'd put gone through every one.

"They're in better shape than I expected." He frowned a little. "You'd think if one was that bad, some of the others would show similar signs."

"Maybe a squirrel tried to make a meal of it, didn't like the taste, and left the rest alone."

"Could be." He picked up a strand of lights and mounted the stepladder.

"What are you doing?" She stood, fighting a wave of dizziness at the sudden movement. "I'll take care of that."

"I've got it."

She'd keep arguing, but he really was getting the job accomplished more easily than she could, given his height. She watched, liking the neat efficiency of his movements, the capability of his strong hands. She was used to doing for herself, and in the months of running the inn she'd learned how to do all kinds of things she'd never dreamed of before, but it was nice to have some help.

She couldn't rely on him. Not Tyler, of all people, given what brought him here. That galvanized her, and she went quickly to the stepladder.

"I'm sure you have work of your own to do." Such as investigating his grandfather's death.

"This is the least I can do, since your grandmother offered your cooperation in dealing with my problem."

"That's not exactly what she said."

He smiled faintly but continued to thread the cord through the hooks.

And if she did help him, what then? She was as convinced as Grams that Grandfather hadn't done anything wrong.

She watched Tyler, frowning a little, trying to pinpoint the cause of her uneasiness. No matter how irrational it was, she couldn't help feeling that Tyler's determination to look into his grandfather's death was similar to poking a stick into a hornet's nest.

* * *

Rachel searched through the changes she was attempting to make to the inn's Web site. Did she have everything right? Andrea could probably have done this in half an hour, but she'd been working for what seemed like hours.

She glanced at the ornate German mantel clock that stood on one side of her grandfather's portrait above the fireplace. Nearly ten. It *had* been hours. Grams had gone up to bed some time ago, but Barney still dozed on the hearth rug, keeping her company.

She smiled at the sheltie, and he lifted his head and looked at her as if he'd sensed her movement. "Just a little longer, Barney. I'm almost finished."

He put his head back on his front paws, as if he'd understood every word.

Tyler had gone out earlier and hadn't come back yet. She certainly wouldn't wait up for him, although she'd had difficulty all summer going to bed when guests were still out. He had a key—he'd let himself in.

Thinking about that opened the door to thoughts of him, just when she'd succeeded in submerging her concerns about Tyler in her more prosaic worries.

If she could stay angry with him, dealing with the situation might be easier. Unfortunately, each time he had her thoroughly riled, he managed to show her some side of himself that roused her sympathy.

Tyler was determined to give this quest his best effort, and she'd guess he brought that same single-minded attention to every project he undertook. That would be an asset in his profession, but at the moment she wished he were more easily distracted.

He'd had a difficult relationship with his mother— that much was clear. She sympathized, given her own mother, who was as careless with people as she was with things. She'd always had the sense that her mother could have left her behind on one of their frequent moves and not even noticed she was gone. Not that Andrea would have let that happen.

She rubbed her temples, trying to ease away the tightness there.

I'm spinning in circles, Lord, and I don't know how to stop. Please help me see Tyler through Your eyes and understand how to deal with him in the way You want.

Even as she finished the prayer, she heard the sound of the door opening and closing, followed by Tyler's step in the hallway. She paused, fingers on the keyboard, listening for him to go up the stairs.

Instead he swung the library door a bit farther open and looked around it. "Still working? I didn't realize bed-and-breakfast proprietors kept such late hours."

"It's pretty much a twenty-four-hour-a-day job, but at the moment I'm just trying to finish up some changes to the webpage. Not my strong suit, I'm afraid."

"Mind if I have a look?" He hesitated, seeming to wait for an invitation.

"Please. I think I have it right, but I'm almost afraid to try and upload it."

He smiled, putting one hand on the back of her chair and leaning over to stare at the screen.

"Never let the computer know you're afraid of it. That's when it will do something totally unexpected."

"Just about anything to do with it is unexpected as far as I'm concerned. I'd still be keeping reservations in a handwritten log if Andrea hadn't intervened."

"Andrea. That's the older sister, right?" He reached around her to touch the keyboard, correcting a typo she hadn't noticed.

"Two years older." She tried not to think about how close he was. "She and her new husband are on their honeymoon. Somehow I don't think I can call and ask her computer questions at the moment."

"Probably wouldn't be diplomatic," he agreed. "As far as I can see, this looks ready. All you have to do is upload."

She hesitated, cursor poised. "That's it?"

"Just click." He smiled down at her, giving her a slightly inverted view of his face, exposing a tiny scar on his square chin that she hadn't noticed before.

And shouldn't be noticing now. She was entirely too aware of him for her own peace of mind.

She forced her attention back to the computer and pressed the button, starting the upload. "I can see you're a fixer, just like my big sister. She's always willing to take over and do something for the inept."

As soon as the words were out of her mouth, she heard how they sounded and was embarrassed. She thought she'd gotten over the feeling that she would never measure up to Andrea. And if she hadn't, she certainly didn't want to sound insecure to Tyler.

"There's nothing wrong with admitting you don't

know how to do something. I couldn't make a quiche if someone offered me a million bucks."

"It's nice of you to put it that way." She leaned back, looking with faint surprise at the updated website. "It actually worked."

"You sound impressed. The program you're using is pretty much 'what you see is what you get.'"

"I seem to remember Andrea saying that. She actually told me how to do it, but my brain doesn't retain things like that."

Tyler's smile flickered. "Maybe you should write it up as if it's a recipe."

"Just might work." She smiled up at him, relaxing now that the work was done. For a moment time seemed to halt. She was lost in the deep blue of his eyes, the room so quiet she could hear his breathing.

She drew in a strangled breath of her own and broke the eye contact, grateful he couldn't know how her pulse was pounding.

That was unexpected. Or was it? Hadn't the attraction been there, underlying the tension, each time they were together?

Tyler cleared his throat. "You know, you could hire someone to run the website for you." He seemed to be talking at random, as much at a loss as she was.

Oddly enough, that helped her regain her poise. "Can't afford it," she said bluntly. "We're operating on a shoestring as it is, and it's getting a bit frayed at the moment."

He blinked. "I didn't realize. I mean—" His gesture took in the room, but she understood that he meant the house and grounds, too. "People who live in places like this often don't have to count their pennies."

"That's why it's a bed-and-breakfast." She wasn't usually so forthcoming, but it wasn't anything that everyone in the township didn't already know. And probably would be happy to gossip about. "If Grams is going to keep the place, this seems her only option. Luckily, she's a born hostess, and she's enjoying it. Otherwise, she'd have to sell."

"She doesn't want to do that, so you feel you have to help her."

"Not exactly. I mean, I love it, too." Was it possible he'd understand her feelings? "But even if I didn't, Grams was always there for us when our parents weren't. I owe her."

"I take it your folks had a rocky marriage."

"You could say that. My father left more times than I can count, until finally he just didn't come back."

"That's when you lived with your grandparents?"

She nodded. "They were our rock. Now it's our turn. I'll do whatever is necessary to make this work for Grams."

His face seemed to become guarded, although his voice, when he spoke, was light. "Even if it means learning how to do the website."

"Only until Andrea comes back." She frowned, thinking of yet another chore. "I guess I really should put some Christmas photos up, too. She and Cal won't be home in time to do that."

"If you get stuck, just give me a shout." He turned away, his expression still somehow distant.

Some barrier had gone up between them, and she wasn't sure why. Because of her determination to take care of her grandmother, and he equated that with interference in what he planned? If so, he was right.

He paused at the door, glancing back at her. "Good night, Rachel. Don't work too hard."

"Thanks again for the help."

He vanished behind the partially open door, and she heard his steady footsteps mounting the stairs.

If she let herself start thinking about Tyler's situation, she'd never sleep tonight. "Come on, Barney." She clicked her fingers at the dog. "Let's go to bed. We'll worry about it tomorrow."

It was unusual to be unable to concentrate on work. Tyler had always prided himself on his ability to shut out everything in order to focus on the job at hand, but not this time.

He closed the computer file and shut down his laptop. No, not this time. Before he came to Churchville, he'd thought the task he'd set himself, although probably impossible, was at least fairly straightforward. Find out what he could about his grandfather's death, deal with the property, go back to his normal life with his conscience intact.

He hadn't counted on the human element. Everyone he'd met since he arrived seemed to have a stake in his actions—or at least an opinion as to his choices.

Restless, he moved to the window that overlooked the street, folding back the shutters, and leaned on the deep windowsill. The innkeeper, the antique dealer, the doctor's wife—it sounded like a ridiculous version of doctor, lawyer, Indian chief.

He glanced down the road in the direction of the antique shop, but there was nothing to be seen. Churchville slept. Not even a car went by to disturb the night. He'd heard of places so small they rolled up the sidewalks at night. Churchville was apparently one of them.

Presumably Rachel and her grandmother were asleep as well, off in the other wing of the building.

He couldn't help wondering how she'd adjusted from the pressure-cooker atmosphere of a trendy restaurant kitchen to the grueling work but slower pace of running a B&B in the Pennsylvania Dutch countryside. Still, she'd shown him how dedicated she was.

Dedicated to her family, most of all. And yet, from what she'd said, her relationship with her father had been as strained as his with his mother. Maybe that made her other relatives more precious to her.

At least he'd eventually grown up enough to pity his mother for resorting to emotional blackmail with the people she loved. He'd learned to look at her demands in a more objective way. But now he was back in the same trap, trying to fulfill her impossible dying request. No, not request. Demand.

Looked at rationally, the proposal was ridiculous. He'd known that from the start, even colored as the moment had been by shock and grief.

Still, he'd had to deal with the property, and he'd told himself he'd find out what he could about the circumstances of his grandfather's death and then close the book on the whole sad story.

Now that he was here, he realized how much more difficult the situation was than he'd dreamed. Rachel's grandmother's integrity was obvious, and he couldn't imagine her covering up a crime, any more than he could imagine the personality that dominated the portrait over the mantel committing one.

This was a wild-goose chase. A sad one, but nothing more. Moreover, it could hurt innocent people, if Rachel's opinion was true, and he saw no reason to doubt that.

He closed the shutters again, feeling as if he were closing his mind to the whole uncomfortable business. He'd make a few inquiries, maybe talk to the local police and check the newspaper files. And at the end of it he'd be no wiser than he was now.

The shutters still stood open on the window that looked out the side of the house, so he went to close them. And stopped, hand arrested on the louvered wood.

Where was that light coming from?

Below him was the gravel sweep of the drive, well-lit by the security lighting, his car a dark bulk. There was the garage, beyond it the lane that led onto Crossings Road.

The pale ribbon of road dipped down into the trees. From ground level, he wouldn't have seen any farther, but from this height the shallow bowl of the valley stretched out. As his eyes grew accustomed to the dimness, he could make out the paler patches of fields, darker shadows of woods. That had to be the farmhouse—there was nothing else down on that stretch of road.

A faint light flickered, was gone, reappeared again. Not at ground level. Someone was in the house, moving around the second floor with a flashlight.

He spun, grabbing his car keys, and rushed into the hall. He pounded down the stairs, relieved there were no other guests to be disturbed by him.

In the downstairs hall he paused briefly. He should call the police before heading out, should tell Rachel what was going on before she heard him and thought someone was breaking in.

He tried the library door, found it unlocked, and hurried through to the separate staircase that must lead to the family bedrooms. If she was still awake—

A light shone down from an upstairs hall.

"Rachel?"

Soft footsteps, and she appeared at the top of the stairs, clutching a cell phone in one hand. At least she was still dressed, so he hadn't gotten her out of bed.

"What's wrong?" Her eyes were wide with apprehension.

"Someone's in my grandfather's house. I could see the light from my window."

She didn't try to argue about it, but hurried down the steps, dialing the phone as she did. "I'll call the police."

"Good. I'm going down there."

She grabbed his arm. "Wait. You don't know what you might be rushing into."

"That's what I'm going to find out." He shook off

her hand. "Just tell the cops I'm there, so they don't think I'm the burglar."

He strode toward the back door, hearing her speaking, presumably to the 911 operator, as he let the door close behind him.

He jogged toward the car, a chill wind speeding his steps. This could be nothing more than some teenage vandals.

And if it was someone else?

Well then, he'd know he'd been wrong. He'd know there was something to investigate after all.

He took off down the lane, gravel spurting under his tires. A clump of bushes came rushing at him as the lane turned, and he forced himself to ease off the gas. Wouldn't do any good for him to smash into a tree.

Rachel's accident slid into his mind, displacing his concentration on the prowler. An image of her, standing in the road, whirling, face white, to stare in horror at the oncoming car—

He shook his head, taking a firm control on both thoughts and reactions. Get to the farm in one piece. Find out what was happening. Hope the cops got there in time to back him up.

The car rounded the final bend, and the dilapidated gateposts came into view. He stepped on the brake, took the turn cautiously and then snapped off his headlights. He couldn't have done it earlier, not without smashing up, but he could probably get up the lane without lights. He didn't want to alert the prowlers to his presence too soon. They could hear the motor, of course, but they might attribute that to a car going past on the lane. Headlights glaring at them would be a dead giveaway.

If they were still there. He frowned, squinting in the dim light of a waning moon. He could make out the rectangular bulk of the house, gray in the faint light, and the darker bulk behind it that was the barn. No sign of a vehicle—no glimmer of metal to give it away. It looked as if he was too late.

He drew to a stop next to the porch, cut the motor, opened the door and listened. No sound broke the night silence, not even a bird. He got out, moving cautiously, alert for any sign of the intruder.

Still nothing. He walked toward the steps. Stupid, to have come without a decent torch. He had only the small penlight on his keychain to show him the broken stair. He stepped over it, mounting the porch, the wooden planks creaking beneath his feet.

He focused the thin stream of light on the door, senses alert. It seemed to be as securely closed as it had been on his first visit. A flick of the light showed him boards secure over the windows.

The urgency that had driven him this far ebbed, leaving him feeling cold and maybe a little foolish. Could the light he'd seen have been some sort of reflection? He wouldn't think so.

Well, assuming someone had been here, they were gone now. Maybe he could at least figure out how they'd gotten in.

He bent, aiming the feeble light at the lock. Had those scratches—

A board creaked behind him. Muscles tightening, he started to swing around. A shadowy glimpse of a dark figure, an upraised arm, and then something crashed into his head and the floor came up to meet him.

Chapter Five

Given the small size of the township police force, Rachel knew her call would go straight through to whoever was on duty. Thankfulness swept her at the sound of Chief Burkhalter's competent voice.

It took only seconds to explain, but even so she was aware of how quickly Tyler would reach the farm. And put himself in danger.

"My guest, Tyler Dunn, the one who saw the lights—"

"Owns the farm. Right, I know."

Of course he would. Zachary Burkhalter made it his business to know what went on in the township.

"He's gone down there. Don't—"

"I'm not going to shoot him, Ms. Hampton, but he's an idiot. I'll be there in a few minutes."

And she could hear the wail of the siren now, through the air as well as the telephone. She could also hear Grams coming out of her bedroom.

"I could go down—" Rachel began, with some incoherent thought of identifying Tyler to the chief.

"No." The snapped word left no doubt in her mind. "I'll call you back on this line when we've cleared the place. Then you can come pick up your straying guest, but not until then."

She had no choice but to disconnect. The change in tone of the siren's wail as it turned down Crossings Road was reassuring. They'd be there soon. Tyler would be all right.

Grams reached her. "What is it, Rachel? What's happening?"

Rachel put her arm around Grams, as much for her comfort as her grandmother's. "Tyler saw a light moving around in the farmhouse. He insisted on going down there by himself, but the police are on their way."

Grams shook her head. "Foolish, but I suppose he wouldn't be one to sit back when there's trouble."

No, he probably wouldn't. It didn't take a long acquaint with Tyler to know that much about him.

"I still wish he hadn't. If he runs right into whoever's there—"

"I'm sure he'll be sensible about it." Grams's voice was matter-of-fact. "The police are probably there by now."

She'd thought she'd have to comfort her grandmother, but it seemed to be working the other way around. Grams patted her shoulder.

"I'll start some hot chocolate. He'll be chilled to the bone, I shouldn't wonder, running out on a cold night like this."

She followed Grams to the kitchen, phone still in her hand, watching as her grandmother paused for a moment, head bowed.

Dear Lord, I should be turning to You, too, instead of letting worry eat at me. Please, be with Tyler and protect him from harm.

Even as she finished the prayer, the telephone rang. Exchanging glances with Grams, she answered.

"You can come on down here now, if you want." The chief sounded exasperated, which probably meant they hadn't been in time to catch anyone. "Maybe help Mr. Dunn figure out what's missing."

Questions hovered on her tongue, but better to wait until she saw what was going on. "I'll be right there."

It took a moment to reassure Grams that she'd be perfectly safe, another to grab her jacket and shove Barney back from the door, and she ran out and slid into the car, shivering a little.

She shot out the drive and turned onto Crossings Road with only a slight qualm as she passed the place where she'd been hit.

Why? The question beat in her brain as she drove down the road as quickly as the rough surface would allow. If someone was in the house, why? More specifically, why now? It had stood empty all these years and been broken into more than once. Why would someone break in now, when surely most people knew that the new owner was here?

Lots of questions. No answers.

She turned into the rutted lane that led to the farmhouse, slowing of necessity. The police car, its roof light still rotating, sat next to Tyler's car. Its headlights showed her Chief Burkhalter's tall figure, standing next to the porch.

Tyler sat on the edge of the porch, head bent, one hand massaging the back of his neck.

She pulled to a stop and slid out, hurrying toward them. "Are you all right?"

"I'm fine." Tyler frowned at the chief. "There was no need for him to call you."

"There was every need." She hoped her tone was brisk enough to disguise the wobble in her tummy. "You're hurt. Let me see."

Ignoring his protests, she ran her hand through the thick hair, feeling the lump gingerly.

He winced. "Are you a nurse as well as a chef?"

"No, but I know enough to be sure you should have some ice on that."

"I offered to take him to the E.R. or call paramedics," the chief said. "He turned me down."

"I don't need a doctor. I've had harder knocks than that on the football field. And the ice can wait until we've finished here."

"Just go over it once more for me," Burkhalter said, apparently accepting him at his word. "You saw the lights from your window at the inn, you said."

Tyler started to nod, then seemed to think better of it. "The side window of my room looks out over Crossings Road. I can see the house—or at least, the upper floor of it. I spotted what looked like a flashlight moving around on the second floor."

"So you decided to investigate for yourself." Burkhalter sounded resigned, as if he'd taken Tyler's measure already.

"I figured I could get here faster than you could."

She wanted to tell Tyler how foolish that had been, but his aching head was probably doing that well enough. Besides, she had no standing—they were nothing more than acquaintances. The reminder gave her a sense of surprise. She'd begun to feel as if she'd known him for years.

"What did you see when you got here?"

"No vehicle, so I thought maybe they'd gone already. My mistake." Tyler grimaced. "I went to look at the front door, to see if it had been broken into, and while I was bending over, somebody hit me from behind."

"You didn't get a look, I suppose."

"Only at the floorboards." Tyler massaged the back of his neck again. "I heard the car come round the house then. They must have parked it in the back. The guy who slugged me jumped in, and off they went. I managed to turn my head at some point, but all I could see were red taillights disappearing down the lane."

"Vehicle was parked by the kitchen door." The patrolman who joined them gave Rachel a shy smile. "Looks like a big SUV, maybe, by the size of the tires. They broke in the back."

"I should have gone around the house first." Tyler sounded annoyed with himself. "I didn't think."

"Wait for us next time," the chief said. "Not that I expect there to be a next time. If these were the same thieves who have broken into other empty houses, they won't be careless enough to come back again, now that they know someone's watching."

"This has happened before?" Tyler's gaze sharpened. "What are they after?"

"Anything they find of value. Old-timers in country places often don't think much of banks, so sometimes it's been strong boxes broken open. Other times silver or antiques."

Burkhalter's lean face tightened. At a guess, he didn't like the fact that someone had been getting away with burglaries in his territory. Nobody blamed him, surely. The township was far-flung, the police force spread too thin.

"If there's nothing else Mr. Dunn can tell you, maybe he ought to get in out of the cold." She was shivering a little, whether from the cold or the tension, and Tyler had rushed out in just a shirt and sweater.

"If you wouldn't mind taking a look around inside first, I'd appreciate it. See if anything's missing."

Tyler stood, holding on to the porch post for a moment. "Ms. Hampton and I were here yesterday, but we didn't go upstairs. And Philip Longstreet stopped while we were here, wanting to have a look around. I told him I'd let him know if I decided to sell anything."

Philip wouldn't be delighted to have his name brought up in the middle of a police investigation. Still, there was no reason for Tyler to hold the information back.

The chief's expression didn't betray whether that interested him or not. He ushered them inside and swung his light around, letting them see the contents of the living room.

In the daylight the place had looked bad enough. In the cold and dark it was desolate, but as far as she could tell, nothing had been moved.

"I think this is pretty much the way it was. Tyler?"

He seemed tenser inside the house than he had sitting on the porch. He gave a short nod. "I don't think they were in this room."

They walked through the dining room, then into the kitchen. Everything seemed untouched, other than the fact that the kitchen door had been broken in.

The chief's strong flashlight beam touched the stairway that opened into the kitchen. "Let's have a look upstairs."

"I haven't been up there yet," Tyler warned. "I can't say I know everything that should be there."

"Anything you remember could help." The chief was polite but determined.

Tyler nodded and started up the stairs. She couldn't assist in the least, since she'd never been in that part of the house, but she didn't like the idea of staying downstairs alone. She followed them, watching her footing on the creaking stairs.

The flight of steps led into a small, square hallway with bedrooms leading off it. Tyler stopped, gripping the railing. "There used to be a slant-top desk there, I remember."

"Not recently." The chief swung his flashlight over the thick layer of dust that lay, undisturbed, where Tyler indicated.

They peered into one bedroom after another. There was more furniture up here, sturdy country pieces, most of it, some probably of interest to collectors. Tyler really should have it properly valued.

The thieves had evidently started in the master bedroom, where the dresser drawers gaped open and empty. A small marble-topped stand had been pulled away from the faded wallpaper, and a basin and ewer set lay smashed on the floor.

Rachel bent, touching a piece gingerly. "Too bad they broke this. There's been quite a demand recently for sets of this vintage."

"Maybe they weren't educated thieves," Tyler said.

"Or they just don't know about china."

Tyler stepped carefully over the pieces. "Seems like a stupid place for them to hit. Obviously there's no money or small valuables left. My impression is that the rooms used to be fairly crowded with furniture, but that's hardly going to let you trace anything."

"I don't suppose there's such a thing as an inventory," the chief asked.

"My grandfather's attorney did give me a list, but I don't know how complete it is." Tyler's smile flickered. "And given how little I know about Pennsylvania Dutch furniture, I doubt I could even figure out what's being described on the list."

"I can probably help you with that. Furnishing the inn made me something of an instant expert on the subject." She was faintly surprised to hear the offer coming out of her mouth. Didn't she already have enough to keep her busy?

"Sounds like a good idea," Chief Burkhalter said. "Let me have a copy of the list, and mark anything you and Ms. Hampton think has gone missing. At least that gives us a start."

His light illumined Tyler's face briefly. Was Tyler really that pale and strained, or was it just the effect of the glaring white light?

"You folks might as well get home." Burkhalter swung his torch to show them the way out. "We'll be a bit longer. Ms. Hampton, if you wouldn't mind taking Mr. Dunn, I'll have my officer drop his car off later. I don't think he should be driving."

"That's fine," she said, grabbing Tyler's arm before he could protest. "Let's go."

He must have been feeling fairly rocky, since he let her tug him down the stairs. When they reached the front porch, she took a deep breath of cold air. Even its bite was preferable to the stale, musty scent of decay inside.

No wonder Tyler disliked the place. His grandfather had been an unhappy, miserable man, by all accounts, and that unhappiness seemed to permeate the very walls of the house.

They stepped off the porch, and Tyler shivered a little when the wind hit him. He shoved his hands into his pockets. "So that's it. Minor-league housebreakers." He sounded— She wasn't sure what. Dissatisfied, maybe?

"I suppose so." She led the way to the car.

Maybe Tyler was thinking the same thing she was. Thieves, yes. That seemed logical.

But why now? That was the thing that bothered her the most. Why now?

"Are you sure you want to do this?" Tyler glanced at Rachel as they walked down Churchville's Main Street the next morning, headed for the antique shop.

She looked up at him, eyebrows lifting. "Why not? It'll be much easier for you to understand the look and value of the furniture on that list if you actually see some examples of Pennsylvania Dutch furniture. And the inn's furnishings aren't really the plain country pieces your grandfather had, for the most part. I have to pick up the final draft of the house tour brochure from Phillip, anyway."

"You're forgetting that I gave Phil Longstreet's name to the police last night. If they've come to call, he may not appreciate the sight of me."

"I'm sure Phil realizes that after the break-in, you had to mention anyone who'd been there. You certainly didn't accuse him of anything."

But he thought he read a certain reservation in her green eyes. She needed the goodwill of her fellow business people in the village. He'd been so focused on getting what he wanted that he hadn't considered how her efforts to help him might rebound against her.

"I don't want you to get involved in my troubles if it's going to make things sticky for you with people like Longstreet. And I sure don't want you involved if it means putting you at any risk."

They were on the opposite side of the road from the inn, because Rachel had wanted to take a digital photo of the inn's exterior decorations. He paused, turning to face her and leaning against the low stone wall that surrounded the church and cemetery.

"Because of what happened last night?" A frown puckered her smooth forehead. "But that was just—" She paused, shook her head. "I was going to say an accident, but it certainly wasn't that. Still, anyone who goes charging into a deserted house at night to investigate a prowler—"

"Deserves a lump on the head?" He touched the tender spot and smiled wryly. "You may have a point there. I just can't help but wonder if last night's episode had anything to do with my reason for being here."

She leaned against the wall next to him, her green corduroy jacket bright against the cream stone. Two cars went by before she spoke.

"Why now, that's what you mean. After all this time of sitting empty, why would someone choose to burglarize the place just when you've returned? I've been wondering about that myself."

She had a sharp mind behind that sensitive, heart-shaped face.

"Right. Assuming it had something to do with my return, or my reason for being here—"

She shook her head decisively. "Not that, surely. No one knows except Grams and me, and I assure you, neither of us goes in for late-night prowling. Everyone else thinks you're here just to sell the property."

He found he wanted to speak the thought that had

been hovering at the back of his mind. "If someone had guilty knowledge of my grandfather's death, my coming to dispose of the property might still be alarming." He planted his hands against the top of the wall. "If there's even a chance of that, I shouldn't involve you."

"First of all, I think the chance that last night's thieves were in any way related to your grandfather's death twenty-some years ago is infinitesimal. And second, I'm not offering to mount guard on the farm at midnight. Helping you identify the furniture hardly seems like a threatening activity, does it?"

"Not when you put it that way. You're determined to help, aren't you?"

She nodded, but her mouth seemed to tighten. "Andrea is the superstar. Caro is the dreamer. I'm the one who helps."

"I didn't mean that negatively," he said mildly. "It's a quality I admire."

Her face relaxed in a genuine smile. "Then you're an unusual man." She pushed herself away from the wall. "Come on, let's put my helpfulness to use and check out some Pennsylvania Dutch antiques."

"Rachel?"

She glanced back at the query in his tone.

"Thanks. For the help."

"Anytime."

She started briskly down the street. He caught up with her in a few strides, and they walked in a companionable silence for a few minutes. Rachel was obviously taking note of the decorations on the shops, and twice she stopped to take photos.

"They've done a good job of making the place look like an old-fashioned Christmas," he commented. "I like the streetlights."

Churchville's Main Street had gas streetlamps that reminded him of the illustration for a Dickens novel. Each one had been surrounded with a wreath of live greens and holly, tied with a burgundy ribbon.

"You're just lucky you weren't here for the arguments when we made that decision," she said. "I thought Sandra Whitmoyer and Phillip Longstreet would come to blows."

"I couldn't imagine people would get so excited about it."

She raised her eyebrows. "You mentioned that you sometimes design churches. Don't you get into some passionate debates on that subject?"

He thought of one committee that had nearly canceled the entire project because they couldn't agree on the shape of the education wing. "You have a point there. People do feel passionate about things that affect their church or their home. I suppose the same applies when you're talking about a village the size of Churchville. They all feel they have a stake in the outcome."

She nodded. "It surprised me a little, when I came back after spending a lot of time in an urban setting. At first it bothered me that everyone seemed to know everyone else's business, but then I realized it's not just about wanting to know. It's about caring."

He was unaccountably touched. "That's a nice tribute to your community."

"I like belonging."

The words were said quietly, but there was a depth of feeling behind them that startled him. He would like to pursue it, but they'd come to a stop in front of Longstreet's Antiques, and Rachel's focus had obviously shifted to the job at hand.

"Don't show too much interest in any one thing," she warned as he opened the door, setting a bell jingling. "Unless you want to walk out the door with it."

He nodded, amused that she thought the warning necessary, and followed her into the shop.

Chapter Six

Longstreet's Antiques always looked so crowded that Rachel thought Phil must use a shoehorn to fit everything in. When she'd said that to him, he'd laughed and told her that was one of the secrets of his business. When people saw the overwhelming display, they became convinced that they were going to find a hidden treasure and walk away with it for a pittance.

Even though she knew the motive behind it, the place exerted exactly that sort of appeal over her. She'd like to start burrowing through that box of odds and ends, just to see what was there. But she doubted that anyone ever got the better of Phil Longstreet on a deal. He was far too shrewd for that.

Thinking about bargains was certainly safer than letting her thoughts stray toward Tyler. She watched as he squatted beside a wooden box filled with old tools, face intent as he sifted through them. They'd gone so quickly to a level where she felt as if she'd known him for years instead of days.

But there was nothing normal about their friendship, if you could call it that. He'd come here for a purpose that involved her family, and she couldn't forget that. If anything he learned threatened her people—

He glanced up, catching her gaze, and smiled. A wave of warmth went through her. Maybe just for the moment she could shove other issues to the back of her mind and enjoy being with him.

"I'm ready for my lesson whenever you are, teacher." He stood, taking a step toward her.

Pennsylvania Dutch furniture, she reminded herself.

"Well, here's a good example of what's called a Dutch bench, which was on your list." She pointed to the black wooden bench with its decorative painting of hearts and tulips. "It's basically a love-seat-size bench with a back. It's a nice piece to use in a hallway."

He nodded, touching the smooth lacquer of the arm. "Now that I see it, I remember one like this. It was in the back hall. My grandfather used to sit there to pull his boots on before he went to the barn."

"It's not there now. I'd have noticed it when we were in the kitchen."

"No." He frowned. "Of course, it could have gone anytime in the past twenty years, and I wouldn't know the difference."

"A lot of small things might have disappeared without being noticed, even if the attorney visited the place occasionally. You should check on the dishes. According to the inventory, your grandfather had a set of spatterware."

His eyebrows lifted. "And I would recognize spatterware how?"

She glanced around, found a shelf filled with china, and lifted a plate down. "This is it. Fairly heavy, brightly painted tableware. Very typical of Pennsylvania Dutch ware."

Tyler bent over the plate, his hand brushing hers as he touched it. "So I'm looking for gaudy plates with chickens on them."

Laughter bubbled up. "I'll have you know that's not a chicken, it's a peafowl."

"I doubt any real bird would agree with that."

The amusement that filled his eyes sent another ripple of warmth through her. For a moment she didn't want to move. She just wanted to stand there with their hands touching and their gazes locked. His deep-blue eyes seemed to darken, and his fingers moved on hers.

She took a step back, her breathing uneven. It was some consolation that the breath he took was a bit ragged, as well.

"I...I should see where Phil has gotten to. Usually he comes right out when the bell rings." She walked quickly to the office door, gave a cursory knock and opened it. "Phil, are you in here?"

A quick glance told her he wasn't, but the door that led to the alley stood open, letting in a stream of cold air. She crossed to the door, hearing Tyler's footsteps behind her.

"Phil?"

A panel truck sat at the shop door, and two men were loading a piece of furniture, carefully padded with quilted covers. Phil stood by, apparently to be sure they did it right. He looked toward her at the sound of her voice.

"Rachel, hello. I didn't hear you. And Mr. Dunn."

"Tyler, please." He was so close behind her that his breath stirred her hair when he spoke. And she shouldn't be so aware of that.

"I wanted to let you know we're here. I can see you're busy, so we'll look around." She glanced at the man lifting the furniture into the van, but his head was turned away as he concentrated on his work. Youngish, long hair—not anyone she recognized.

"Fine." Phil made shooing motions with his hands. "Go back in where it's warm. I'll be with you in a few minutes."

"Okay." Shivering a little, she hurried back to the showroom, relieved when Tyler closed the office door on the draft. "It's good that he's occupied. We can look at a few more things without listening to a sales pitch." She took the inventory from Tyler's hand. "Let's see what we can find."

By concentrating firmly on furniture, she filled the next few minutes with talk of dower chests, linen presses and pie cupboards, because if she didn't, she'd be too aware of the fact that Tyler stood next to her, looking at her as often as at the pieces of furniture she pointed out.

Finally the office door opened and Phil came in, rubbing his hands together briskly. "There, all finished at last. That lot is headed to a dealer in Pittsburgh."

"Do you have some new help?" she asked.

Phil shook his head. "Just a couple of guys I use sometimes for deliveries. Now, what can I show you today?"

"How about showing me the brochure for the Christmas House Tour?"

"Now, Rachel, didn't I tell you I'd bring it over?"

"You did. You also said I'd have it yesterday."

She was vaguely aware of Tyler taking the inventory from her and sliding it into his pocket. Well, fair enough. She could understand his not wanting to share that information with anyone.

Phil threw his hands up in an exaggerated gesture. "Mea culpa. You're right, you're right, it's not finished yet."

"Phil, that's not fair." She didn't mind letting the exasperation show in her voice. This house tour had turned into a much bigger headache than she'd imagined. "You know that has to go to the printer, and the tour is coming up fast."

He stepped closer, reaching out as if he'd put his hand on her shoulder and then seeming to think better of it. "Forgive me, please? I know I promised, but you wouldn't believe how busy the shop has been lately."

"I'm happy for you. But the house tour is designed to help everyone's business, remember?"

"I'll finish it tonight and bring it to the inn first thing tomorrow morning. I promise. Forgive me?" He made a crossing-his-heart gesture, giving her the winsome smile that had persuaded too many elderly ladies to pay more than they'd intended.

She was immune. "Only if you don't let me down.

Tomorrow. By nine, so I can proof it and get it to the printer."

He sighed. "You're a hard woman. I'll do it, I promise. Now, did you come to buy or sell?" He looked expectantly at Tyler.

"Neither, I'm afraid. I just walked down with Rachel so I could have a look at your shop." Tyler smiled pleasantly. "Very impressive collection."

"Thank you, thank you. I'm always looking, you know. Any chance I might see what you have at the farmhouse soon?"

The police must not have been around. Surely he'd mention the break-in if he knew about it. She was relieved. Knowing Phil, an encounter with the police would probably throw him off his game so much that he'd be another week getting around to the brochure.

"I'll let you know." Tyler took a step toward the door.

"I'd be happy to do a free appraisal. Anytime." Phil retreated toward the counter. "I'll get right on the brochure, Rachel. You're going to love it."

"I'm sure I will." Aside from his propensity to put things off, Phil had a genuine artistic gift. Once he actually produced the brochure, it would be worth the wait.

She pulled the door open and nearly walked into Jeff Whitmoyer. They each stepped back at the same time, surprising her into a smile. "Come in, please. We were just on our way out."

"Morning, Rachel." His gaze went past her. "You must be Tyler Dunn. I've been wanting to talk to you."

Apparently they weren't getting out so quickly, after all. "Tyler, I'd like to introduce Jeff Whitmoyer. Jeff, Tyler Dunn."

Reminded of his manners, Jeff stuck his hand out, and Tyler shook it.

It was hard to believe Jeff and Bradley Whitmoyer were brothers—she thought that each time she saw one of them. Bradley was a lean, finely drawn intellectual with a social conscience that kept him serving his patients in this small community in spite of other, some would say better, opportunities.

Jeff was big, bluff, with a once-athletic frame now bulging out of the flannel shirt and frayed denim jacket he wore—certainly not because he couldn't afford better. He might not be the brightest bulb in the pack, as she'd heard Phil comment, but he made a good living with his construction company and was probably a lot smarter than people gave him credit for.

"Well, shut the door if you're going to talk." Phil's tone was waspish. "I'm paying the heating bill, remember?"

Jeff slammed the door, making the bell jingle so hard it threatened to pop off its bracket. "Wouldn't want you to spend an extra buck." He focused on Tyler. "I'd like to talk to you about the property of yours. I hear you're going to sell."

Tyler seemed to withdraw slightly. "Where did you hear that?"

Jeff shrugged massive shoulders. "Around. Anyway, I've had my eye on that place. I have some plans to develop that land, so how about we sit down and talk?"

Tact certainly wasn't Jeff's strong suit, but she supposed he'd think it a waste of time where business was concerned.

"I haven't reached that point yet, but thanks for your interest." Tyler reached for the door.

"Don't wait too long. I'll find something else if your place isn't for sale."

"Will you?" Phil's voice was soft, but Rachel thought she detected a malicious gleam in his eyes. "Given the scarcity of prime building land, I wonder where."

"Call me anytime. I'm in the book. Whitmoyer Construction." Jeff shook off Phil's needling like a bull shaking off a fly. "Talk to you soon."

Rachel waited until the door had closed behind them. Once they were well away from the shop, she spoke the thought in her mind. "You aren't seriously considering his offer, are you?"

"He didn't make an offer. But what's wrong with him? I thought those people were friends of yours."

"Nothing's wrong with him, except that I don't trust his taste. If he's talking about developing the land, he might have in mind a faux-Amish miniature golf course, for all I know."

His eyebrows lifted. "I should think a new attraction would draw more people. Isn't that what you want as a business owner?"

"Not something that turns the Amish into a freak show. Besides, our guests come to the inn for the peace and quiet of the countryside. How would you like your window to overlook a putting green or shooting range?"

"If and when I sell, I probably won't have much

choice about what use the new owners make of the property. Any more than your neighbors could control your turning the mansion into a bed-and-breakfast."

He was being annoyingly rational, turning her argument against her in that way. She'd like to argue that at least her bed-and-breakfast, even if it benefited from its proximity to Amish farms, didn't make fun of them.

Maybe she shouldn't borrow trouble, but she couldn't help worrying how much Tyler's plans for the property were going to affect her future.

The strains of "Joy to the World" poured from the speakers of the CD player the next morning, filling the downstairs of the inn with anticipation. Rachel took a step back from the side table in the center hall to admire the arrangement of holly and evergreens she'd put in a pewter pitcher. The antique wooden horse toy next to it sported a red velvet bow around its neck.

"What do you think?" She turned to Grams and Emma, who were winding a string of greens on the newel post. "Should I add some bittersweet, too?"

"It looks perfect the way it is," Grams said. "I wouldn't change a thing."

Nodding, Rachel looked up at the molding along the ceiling, finding the eyehooks from which something could be hung. "Where's the Star of Bethlehem quilt? I'm ready to hang it now."

"The Star of Bethlehem quilt," Grams echoed. "I haven't seen it in ages."

Rachel blinked. "But we always hang it here. It's part of my earliest Christmas memories. We can't not have it." Absurd. She actually felt like bursting into tears.

Grams exchanged glances with Emma.

"I know chust where it is, *ja,*" Emma said quickly. "I will get it."

How silly she was, to be that obsessed with recreating the Christmases of her childhood. "You don't have to. If you'd rather put something else here—"

"Of course not," Grams said quickly.

"Well, let *me* get it, at least."

But Emma was already halfway up the stairs, her sturdy, dark-clad figure moving steadily. "It makes no trouble." She disappeared around the bend in the stairs.

Grams smiled. "Don't worry about Emma. She enjoys the decorating as much as we do, even though it's not much of a tradition among the Amish."

"Not like you Moravians." Rachel smiled. "You're Christmas-decorating fanatics."

Grams's face went soft with reminiscence. "That's what it is when you grow up in Bethlehem. Every aspect of Christmas has its own tradition."

Grams had brought those traditions with her when she married. The Moravian star, the peppernuts, the *putz*, an elaborate crèche beneath the Christmas tree— those were part of the lovely Christmas lore she'd passed on to her granddaughters.

All Rachel's memories of Christmas had to do with Grams and Grandfather, not her parents. Hardly surprising, she supposed. Her parents had been separated so much of the time, with her father always off pursuing some get-rich-quick scheme or another. And her mom—well, Lily Unger Hampton had used the holidays as an excuse for extended visits to friends in the city. It had been Grams and Grandfather who made up Christmas lists, baked cookies, filled stockings.

Then Daddy had left for good and Mom had fought with Grandfather and taken the girls away. And their childhood ended.

She smiled at her grandmother, heart full. "We should go over to Bethlehem some evening while the decorations are still up. You know you'd love it."

"If we have time," Grams said, avoiding an answer. "We still have a lot to do before Christmas. I hope this weekend's guests don't mind our decorating around them."

"I'm sure they'll want to pitch right in." She hoped. Two couples would be arriving tomorrow, and there was no possibility she'd have everything finished by then. So her idea was to turn necessity into opportunity and invite the guests to join in.

"I hope so. They might be more enthusiastic than Tyler is, anyway." Grams looked a little miffed. She had suggested that Tyler might want to help them today, but he'd left the house early.

"Tyler's not in Churchville to enjoy himself, is he?"

Grams must have read something in her tone, because she gave her an inquiring look. "You're worried about that young man. I've told you—there's nothing he can find about your grandfather that will hurt us."

"I'm not worried so much about that as about what he's going to do with the property. Jeff Whitmoyer approached him about buying it. Says he has plans to develop it."

"And you don't want that to happen?"

Rachel stared. "Grams, surely you don't want that either. He could put up something awful in full view of our upstairs windows. Fake Amish at its worst, if his other businesses are any indication."

"Oh, well, it won't bother us, and the Amish will ignore it as they do every other ridiculous thing that uses their name." Grams tweaked the ribbon on the newel post as Emma came down the stairs, the quilt folded over her arm.

Grams didn't seem too concerned, maybe because she didn't understand the possible effects. Their peaceful, pastoral setting was one of their biggest assets.

Emma unfurled the Star of Bethlehem quilt, and every other thought went right out of her mind. Here was the warmth of Christmas for her, stitched up in the handwork of some unknown ancestor.

Together she and Emma fastened the quilt to its dowel and climbed up to hang it in place. Once it was secure, she climbed back down and moved the stepstool away, then turned to look.

The star seemed to burst from the fabric, shouting its message of good news. Warmth blossomed through her. It was just as she remembered. After all those years of trekking around the country with her mother, with Christmas forgotten more often than not, the years when she'd been on her own, working on the holiday out of necessity, she'd longed for Christmas here.

Now she finally had it, and she wouldn't let it slip away. She had come home for Christmas.

"Ah, that looks lovely. I don't know why we ever stopped putting it up." Grams smiled. "This will be a Christmas to remember. You here to stay, Cal and Andrea coming home soon—if we could get Caroline to come back, it would be perfect."

Rachel hugged her. "We'll make it perfect, even if Caro doesn't come."

Grams patted her shoulder. "It's just too bad Tyler doesn't have any sense of belonging here. I'm afraid his grandfather and mother took that away from him a long time ago."

As was so often the case when it came to people, Grams had it right. Thanks to a family quarrel, Tyler had been robbed of that. Small wonder he didn't care who bought the land.

"His grandfather was a bitter man." Emma entered the conversation, planting her hands on her hips. "Turned against God and his neighbors when his wife died, left the church as if we were all to blame."

Rachel blinked. We? "Are you saying John Hostetler, Tyler's grandfather, was Amish?"

"*Ja,* of course." Emma's eyes widened. "Until he came under the *meidung* for his actions. You mean you didn't know that?"

The *meidung*—the shunning. The ultimate act for the Amish, to cut off the person completely unless and until the rebel repented. "How would I?" She turned to Grams. "You knew? But you didn't mention it to Tyler."

"Well, I just assumed he knew. Everyone in the area knew about it, of course. Do you mean he doesn't?"

She thought about their conversations and shook her head slowly. "I don't think so." Would it make a difference to him? To what he decided to do with the property?

She wasn't sure, but he should be told. And probably she was the one to tell him.

Chapter Seven

The office of the township police chief was tiny, with a detailed map of the township taking up most of one wall. Tyler sat in the sole visitor's chair, taking stock of his surroundings while he waited for Chief Burkhalter to return.

At a guess, the faded, framed photographs of past township events and the signed image of a former president were relics of the previous chief. He'd credit Zach Burkhalter with the up-to-date computer system and what seemed, looking at it upside down, to be a paperweight on the desk bearing the insignia of a military unit.

The door opened before he could follow the impulse to turn it around and take a closer look. Burkhalter came in, carrying a manila file folder and looking slightly apologetic.

"Sorry it took me so long to come up with this. My predecessor had his own method of filing that I still haven't quite figured out."

Tyler grasped the file, unable to suppress a sense of optimism. If there was anything to learn about his grandfather's death, surely it would be here, in the police report.

He opened it to a discouragingly small sheaf of papers. "It looks as if he also didn't care to keep very complete records."

Burkhalter sat down behind his desk. "Things were pretty quiet around here twenty years ago. I don't suppose he'd ever had occasion before to investigate a case of murder."

Tyler shot him a glance. Burkhalter's lean, weathered face didn't give anything away. He couldn't be much older than Tyler himself, but he had the look of a man who'd spent most of those years dealing with human frailty in all its forms.

"Murder? I was afraid you wouldn't see it that way, since the death certificate says it was a heart attack that actually killed him."

The chief's eyes narrowed. "Heart attack or not, he died in the course of a crime, so that makes it murder in the eyes of the law. Since no one was ever charged, we don't know what a jury would have thought."

"That bothers you?"

"I don't like the fact that it was never solved." He looked, in fact, as if the case would have been worked considerably more thoroughly had he been the man in charge then.

Tyler flipped through the papers, seeing little that he hadn't already known. Apparently the crime had been discovered the next morning when a neighboring farmer noticed that the cows weren't out in their usual field. His interest sharpened at the name of the farmer. Elias Zook. A relative of the current Zook family, probably. He'd have to ask Rachel.

"The state police were called in," Burkhalter said. "I'll get in touch, see if they've kept the files."

"I'd appreciate it." He frowned down at a handwritten sheet of notes. "Apparently there were indications that more than one person was involved."

The chief nodded. "Hardly surprising, if they intended to rob him. Since I talked with you, I've looked through the records for that year. There were a number of robberies reported, isolated farms, owners elderly folks who sometimes couldn't even be sure when things went missing. Sort of like what's been happening recently."

"There've been other incidents of break-ins, then?"

Burkhalter's gray eyes looked bleak. "Several. Always isolated farmhouses, usually when no one was home. They're slick enough not to overdo it—might be a couple in a month, and then nothing for several months." His hand, resting on the desktop, tightened into a fist. "I'd like to lay my hands on them. Surprising, in a way, that they'd strike your place after you'd come back."

"Yes." He frowned. "I can't help but wonder if it had anything to do with the earlier crime, although I guess that's not very likely."

"No." But he detected a spark of interest in the chief's eyes. "If they thought they'd left any hint to their identity, they've had twenty years to take care of it."

"You think it's a coincidence, then."

Burkhalter considered for a moment. "Let's say I think it's a coincidence. But that I don't like coincidences."

It would not be a good idea to get on this man's bad side. Well, they both wanted the same thing, so that shouldn't be an issue.

He looked back down at the file. It contained a list of items that were presumed to have gone missing, the phrases so generic as to be useless. One side table. One rocking chair. He read a little farther. "There's mention here of a strong box that was found broken open and taken in for examination. No indication that it was ever returned to my mother. Any idea where that might be?"

Burkhalter held out his hand for the file, scanning it quickly. "If it didn't go back to the family, it's hard to tell. There are a few more files I can check. And the basement of this building is filled with all kinds of stuff that no one has ever properly documented. I'll have someone take a look around, but there's no guarantee we'll find it."

"I'd appreciate that." He rose. He'd been here long enough and found out very little. There wasn't much left to find after all this time. The sense of frustration was becoming familiar.

Burkhalter rose, too. "I'll let you know if we come up with anything. You're still at the inn?"

"Yes. I'm not leaving until I've disposed of the property. That's been left hanging for too long." Because his mother hadn't been able to forget how her father died, but she also hadn't known how to deal with it. Or hadn't wanted to.

"Folks will be glad to see that place taken care of." Burkhalter's eyes narrowed. "I just hope you're not planning to do any more police work on your own. If you know anything that might be helpful, even on a crime this old, you have a responsibility to divulge it."

Information? His mother's suspicions hardly fell into that category, and revealing them could harm innocent people.

"There's nothing, I'm afraid."

He had a feeling that Chief Burkhalter didn't entirely buy that, but he seemed to accept it for the moment.

"You'll let me know if anything occurs to you." It was more of an order than a request. "I'll be in touch if I find any reference to that strong box."

Tyler shook hands, thanking him, but without any degree of confidence that the strong box, or anything else, would appear. Everywhere he turned, it seemed all he found was another dead end.

Rachel tugged at the blue spruce she was trying to maneuver through the front door. Even with gloves on, the sharp needles pricked her, and as wide as the doorway was, it didn't seem—

"Having a problem?"

She'd seen Tyler pull in and had hoped she'd have the tree inside before he felt he had to come to the rescue. With the knowledge of his grandfather's Amish roots fresh in her mind, she'd have liked a little more time to decide how to approach the subject.

She managed a smile. "Large doorway, larger tree. It didn't look this big in the field."

"They never do." He replied easily enough, but she had the sense that some concern lurked.

Where had he been? She'd love to ask, but that would be prying.

"I seem to be stuck for the moment." She eyed the tree, halfway through the door. "I'm afraid you'll have to go around to the side."

"We can do better than that." He brushed past her, grasping the tree before she could caution him. "Ouch. You have one sharp Christmas tree."

She held up her hands, showing him the oversize gardening gloves she wore. "Blue spruce is my grandmother's favorite, and that's what I always remember being in the parlor when I was a child."

He paused in the act of pushing the tree through the door, turning to regard her gravely. "That's important to you, isn't it? Preserving the family traditions, that is."

Her throat tightened. If he knew a little more about her parents, he'd understand her longing to have the Christmas she remembered from her early childhood.

"I like family traditions." She could only hope she didn't sound defensive. "I just hope our guests will appreciate ours."

"It sounds as if you have plenty to choose from." With a final lift, he shoved the tree through into the entrance hall. Rachel followed quickly, closing the door against the chill air.

"True enough. Grams is of Moravian ancestry, and to them, celebrating Christmas properly is one of the most important parts of their heritage."

"What about the Amish?" He lifted the tree at the bottom, seeming to assume he'd help her put it up. "Don't they have a lot of Christmas customs?"

The casual way he asked the question affirmed her belief that he didn't know about his grandfather's background. The need to tell him warred with her natural caution. What if she told him, and that knowledge influenced his decisions about the property in a negative way?

She grasped the upper part of the trunk and nodded toward the parlor, where the tree stand was ready. "The Amish, along with the other plain sects, don't do the type of decorating that the rest of the Pennsylvania Dutch do. Their celebration is focused on home and school. The children do a Christmas play that's a huge event for the Amish community."

He nodded, but again she had the sense that he was really thinking of something else.

"If I lift it into the stand, do you think you can steady it while I tighten the clamps?"

"You don't need to help, really." She shouldn't be relying on him, even for something as minor as this.

"I'm a better bet than enlisting your grandmother or the housekeeper." He hoisted the tree, lifting it into the stand.

"I'm sure you have other things to do." But she

reached carefully through the branches to grasp the trunk where he indicated.

Tyler shed his jacket and got down on the floor, lying on his back to slide under the tree. The branches hid his face to some extent, and his voice sounded muffled.

"I've done all I can today, in any event. I had a talk with your police chief."

She wasn't sure how she felt about that, especially if he'd seen fit to tell Zach Burkhalter about his mother's suspicions.

"Was he helpful?" She hoped she sounded neutral.

She must not have succeeded, because Tyler slid out far enough to see her face.

"I didn't say anything about your family." He frowned. "He seems pretty shrewd. He probably knew I was holding something back."

"Yes, he is." Her thoughts flickered back to the problems they'd gone through in the spring. Burkhalter had suspected, correctly, that they'd been withholding information then. "Did he have anything you didn't already know?"

"He was open about sharing the files." Tyler's hands moved quickly, tightening the tree stand's clamps around the base of the spruce. It was a good thing. Her leg ached from the effort of holding the heavy tree upright.

"But…?"

"But apparently his predecessor wasn't very efficient. It looked to me as if he'd just gone through the motions of investigating."

"I'm sorry. I know how much that must frustrate you."

Tyler slid back out from under the tree, giving it a critical look. "Seems fairly straight to me. What do you think?"

She let go and stepped back. "Wonderful. Thank you so much." Her gaze met his. "Really, I'm sorry the chief wasn't able to help you."

He shrugged. "I didn't expect much, to be honest. If there'd been anything obvious, the case would have been resolved a long time ago."

"I suppose so." But she knew he wasn't as resigned as he'd like to appear. He struck her as a man who succeeded at things that were important to him, and fulfilling a promise to his dying mother must be one of those.

The fact that his grandfather had been Amish didn't seem to relate at all, but how could she judge what might be important to him? She had to tell him, and now was as good a time as any.

She took a breath, inhaling the fresh aroma of the tree that already seemed to fill every corner of the room. "There is something that Grams mentioned to me. Something I think you ought to know, if you don't already."

He shot her a steely look, and she shook her head in response.

"I don't think it can have anything to do with his death. But did you know that your grandfather had been Amish?"

His blank stare answered that. "Amish? No. Are you sure? I don't remember seeing any Amish people at the funeral, and I'd have noticed something like that at that age."

"He'd left the church by then." She suspected he wouldn't be content with that.

"Left the church? You mean they shunned him?" His voice showed distaste. "They wouldn't even come to his funeral?"

She was probably doing this all wrong. "From what Grams said, the choice was his, not theirs. Please don't think the Amish—"

"I don't think anything about them, one way or the other. Why should it matter to me? It's not as if my grandfather ever wanted a relationship with me. I'm doing this for my mother."

How much of his mother's personality had been determined by that bitter old man? Instinct told her Tyler needed to deal with those feelings, but she felt unable to reach him without crossing some barrier that would turn them into more than casual acquaintances.

"Families can be wonderful, but they can be hurtful, too." Like Daddy, leaving them without a goodbye. Or Mom, taking them away from the only security they'd ever known.

His hand came out and caught hers, holding it in a firm, warm grasp. "I guess you know something about it, don't you?"

"A bit. For me, my grandparents were the saving grace. I don't know who I'd be without them."

"My dad was the rock in our family. Anything I know about how to be a decent Christian man, I learned from him."

"You still miss him," she said softly, warmed by the grasp of his hand and the sense that he was willing to confide in her.

They had crossed that barrier, and it was a little scary on the other side.

He nodded. "He died when I was in my last year of high school, but I measure every decision against what I think he'd expect of me."

"If he knows, he must be glad that he had such an influence on your life."

"I hope he does." His voice had gone a little husky. He cleared his throat, probably embarrassed at showing so much emotion.

"You know," she said tentatively, "maybe knowing a little more about why your grandfather was the way he was would help you understand your mother, as well." She gave a rueful smile. "Believe me, if I could figure out what made my parents tick, I'd jump at the chance."

He seemed to become aware that he was still holding her hand, and he let go slowly. "I'll think about it. But there is something else you can do for me."

"Of course. What?"

"Your grandmother said you'd let me see your grandfather's ledgers. I'd appreciate that."

She felt as if someone had dropped an ice cube down her back. It took a moment to find her voice.

"Of course. I'll get them out for you." She turned away. She'd been wrong. They hadn't moved to a new relationship after all. Tyler still suspected her grandfather, and to him she was nothing but a source of information.

* * *

She had told Tyler she'd have the ledgers ready for him this evening, but that was beginning to look doubtful. Rachel looked up toward the ceiling of the church sanctuary, where a teenager perched at the top of a ladder, the end of a string of greenery in his hand. She was almost afraid to say something to him, for fear it would throw off his balance.

"That's fine, Jon. Just slip it over the hook and come back down."

He grinned, apparently perfectly at ease on his lofty perch. "Am I making you nervous, Ms. Rachel?"

"Definitely," she replied. "So get down here or I'll tell Pastor Greg on you."

Still grinning, he hooked the garland in place and started down, nimble as a monkey. She could breathe again.

She wasn't quite sure how she'd allowed herself to be talked into helping with the youth group's efforts to decorate the sanctuary for Advent. Supervising the teenagers' efforts might be harder than doing it herself, except that she'd never have gotten up on that ladder. The memory of flying off that stepladder when she'd put up the inn's Christmas lights was too fresh in her mind. She still didn't understand how that could have happened. How could she have missed something so obvious?

She moved back the center aisle, assessing their progress. In spite of a lot of horseplay and goofing off, the job was actually getting done. Swags of greenery cascaded down the cream-colored pillars that supported the roof, huge wreaths hung on either side of the chancel, and candleholders in each window had been trimmed with greenery. All that was left to do was to put new candles in all the holders.

She glanced at her watch. That was a good thing, since it was nearly nine, and she'd been told to send the kids off home promptly at nine.

"Okay, everyone, that's about it," she called above the clatter of voices. "You've done a fantastic job. Just put the ladders away, please, and you'd better cut along home."

Jon Everhart paused, holding one end of the ladder. "Do you want me to stay and turn off the lights for you?"

"Thanks anyway, Jon. I'll do it. After all, I just have to walk across the street to get home."

Of course the kids didn't leave that promptly, but by ten after nine the last of them had gone out the walk through the cemetery to the street.

She picked up the box of new candles and started along the side of the sanctuary, setting them carefully in the holders. Maybe it was best that she do them herself in any event. Not that the kids hadn't done their best, but she'd feel better if she made sure the tapers were secure in the holders. On Christmas Eve every candle would be aflame, filling the sanctuary with light and warmth.

The sanctuary was quiet—quieter than she'd ever experienced. She seemed to feel that stillness seeping into her, gentling the worry that ate at her over the problem presented by Tyler and her continuing anxiety about the financial state of the inn.

She looked at the window above her, showing Jesus talking with the woman at the well. His face, even represented in stained glass, showed so much love and acceptance. In spite of her tiredness, she felt that caring touch her, renewing her.

I've come so close to You since the accident. Maybe the person who hit me actually did me a favor. He couldn't have intended it, but the accident forced me to stop running away spiritually.

She knew why she'd done that, of course. She spent years unable to refer to God as Father, until she'd finally realized that it made her think of her own father, absent most of the time and fighting with Mom when he was around.

Tyler had his own issues with his parents, but at least he'd had a positive relationship with his father for most of his young life. Did he realize how fortunate he was in that? Or was he too wrapped up in his inability to satisfy his mother's demands?

She started down the opposite side of the sanctuary, securing candles in holders. She should finish this up and get back to the inn. It wasn't really all that late. She could still locate the pertinent ledgers and turn them over to Tyler. Let him strain his vision all he wanted, reading through her grandfather's meticulous notes. He wouldn't find anything to reflect badly on Grandfather, no matter how hard he looked.

She was putting the last candle in place when the

lights went out. A startled gasp escaped her. She froze, feeling as if she'd suddenly gone blind.

Slowly her vision adjusted. The faintest light filtered through the windows, probably from the streetlamp at the gate to the churchyard. Dark shadows fell across the sanctuary, though, and if she tried to cut across to where she knew the light switches were, she'd probably crash right into a pew.

Here she stood with a box full of candles and not a single match to light one. The sensible thing was to feel her way along the wall until she got to the front pew where she'd left her handbag. The small flashlight she kept in her bag would help her reach the light switches.

Running her left hand along the cool plaster, reaching out with her right hand to touch the pews, she worked her way toward the front of the sanctuary. Why would the lights go out, anyway? It wasn't as if they were in the midst of a lightning storm.

Still, Grams had often said that the church building, just about as old as the inn, had similar problems. Maybe the overloaded circuits had chosen this moment to break down.

Or the explanation might be simpler. Mose Stetler, the custodian, could have come in, thinking they'd all left, and switched the lights off.

She paused, one hand resting on the curved back of a pew, its worn wood satiny to the touch. "Mose? Is that you? I'm still in the sanctuary."

Really, he should have checked to see if anyone was here before going around switching off lights.

No one answered. If it was Mose, he apparently couldn't hear her.

She took another step and stopped, her heart lurching into overdrive. Someone was in the sanctuary with her.

Ridiculous. She was being foolish, imagining things because she was alone in the dark. She took another step. And heard it. A step that echoed her own and then stopped.

She should call out. It must be someone on a perfectly innocent errand—Mose, or even the pastor, come to see that the church had been properly locked up. She should call out, let them know she was there.

But some instinct held her throat in a vise. She couldn't—she really couldn't speak. Stupid as it seemed, she was unable to make a sound.

Or was it so stupid? She'd already called out, and no one had answered. Whoever was there, he or she seemed anxious not to be heard or identified.

She drew in a cautious breath, trying to keep it silent. Think. A chill of fear trickled down her spine. She'd become disoriented in the dark. How far was she from the double doors at the rear of the sanctuary? How far from the chancel door that led out past the organ to the vestry?

Her fingers tightened on the pew back, and she strained to see. Directly opposite her there was a faint gleam coming through the stained glass. Surely that was the image of Jesus with the woman at the well, wasn't it? She could just make out the shape of the figure.

All right. Be calm. If that window was opposite, then she was nearer to the chancel door, wasn't she?

She took a cautious step in that direction, then another, gaining a little confidence. She didn't know where the other person was in the dark, but if she could make it to the door and get through, she could close it. Lock it. She tried to form an image of the door. Lots of the sturdy old wooden doors in the church had dead bolts. Did that one?

She wasn't sure. But she'd still feel a lot better with a closed door between her and the unknown person. She could move quickly through the small vestry, and beyond it was the door that led out to the ramp. It had a clear glass window, so she'd be able to see to get out.

She took another step, groping for the next pew, and froze, her breath catching. A footstep, nearer to her than she'd thought. He was between her and the chancel door—a thicker blackness than the dark around him. Did he realize how close they were? Surely he couldn't see her any better than she could him. If he did, a few steps would close the gap between them.

Not daring to breathe, she inched her way backward, moving toward the outer wall this time. Follow the wall back to the rear of the sanctuary, work her way to the door.

Please, Lord, please. Maybe I'm being silly, but I don't think so. I think there's danger in this place. Help me.

A few silent steps, and her hand brushed the wall. Holding her breath, she moved along it. She'd be okay, she'd reach the back of the church—and then she realized that the footsteps were moving toward her, deliberately, no longer trying to hide.

How did he know—stupid, she was silhouetted against the faint light coming through the stained glass. Moving to the outer wall was the worst thing she could have done. Heedless of the noise, she dove into the sheltering blackness of the nearest pew, sensing the movement toward her of that other, hearing the indrawn breath of annoyance.

Her heart thudded so loudly she could hear it, and terror clutched her throat. She couldn't stay here, helpless in the dark, waiting for him to find her. Even as she formed the thought she heard him move, heard a hand brushing against the pew back, groping.

She scuttled toward the center aisle, praying he couldn't tell exactly which row she was in. If he came after her—yes, he was coming, she couldn't stop, she didn't dare hesitate—

She bolted along the row, giving up any idea of silence. Her knee banged painfully against the pew and then she was out, into the aisle, sensing the clear space around her.

No time to feel her way. She ran toward the back, a breathless prayer crying from her very soul. *Help me, help me.*

Running full tilt, she hit the door at the rear of the sanctuary. It exploded open, and she bolted out into the cold night, less black than the sanctuary had been. She flew down the few stairs and ran into a solid shape, heard a gasp and felt hard hands grab her painfully tight.

Chapter Eight

Tyler wrapped his arms around Rachel, feeling her slender body shake against him. The grip of her hands was frantic, her breath ragged.

"Rachel, what's wrong?" He drew her close, all the exasperation he'd been feeling gone in an instant. "Are you hurt?"

She shook her head, but her grip didn't loosen, and he found her tension driving his own.

"Come on, Rachel. You're scaring me. Tell me what's wrong." He tried to say it lightly, but the depth of concern he felt startled and dismayed him. When had he started caring so much about Rachel?

She took a deep breath, and he felt her drawing on some reserve of strength to compose herself. "Sorry. I'm sorry." She drew back a little. "I'm not hurt. Just scared."

"Why? What scared you?" Fear spiked, making his voice sharp.

She pushed soft brown curls away from her face with a hand that wasn't entirely steady.

"The lights went out. I was in the sanctuary, finishing up the decorating by myself, when the lights suddenly went out."

"There's more to it than that." He gripped her shoulders. "You wouldn't panic just because you were alone in the dark."

She shook her head. "That's just it. I wasn't alone." She drew in a ragged breath. "Someone was there. I know how stupid that sounds, but someone was in there with me."

The fear in her voice made him take it seriously. "Did someone touch you—say something to you?" His mind jumped to the dark figure who'd struck him down at the old farmhouse. But the two things couldn't be related, could they?

She seemed to be steadying herself, as if talking about it was relieving her fear. "I heard him. Or her. I couldn't be sure. And I saw—well, just a shadow."

He studied her face, frowning a little. He didn't doubt what she was saying, but it was hard to imagine a threat against her in the church.

"You don't believe me." Her chin came up.

"I believe you." He ran his hands down her arms. "I'll go in and have a look around." He hefted the torch Rachel's grandmother had given him when he'd said he'd come over to the church and walk her back.

"Not without me." Her fingers closed around his wrist. "Come around to the side. We can go through the education wing door and get to the light switches from there."

If someone was hiding in the sanctuary, that would give the person a chance to escape while they were going around the building. "Maybe we should call the police."

She hesitated, and he could almost see her weighing the possibilities. Finally she shook her head. "I guess it's not a crime to turn off the lights, is it? Let's see what we can find."

He nodded and let her lead him along the walk. Once they'd rounded the corner, they could see the lamp above the side door shining. "Looks like the power's still on in this wing. Could be only one circuit was shut off."

Rachel marched to the door and turned the knob. It wasn't locked. "This is the way we came in. I was supposed to lock it with the key when I left. The sanctuary doors are locked, but they open from the inside."

A good thing, given the way she'd erupted through them. He followed her inside. She reached out, flipping a switch, and lights came on down a hallway with what were probably classrooms on either side.

"Everything seems okay here."

She nodded. "The door to the vestry is around the corner at the end of the hall."

He started down the hallway, not attempting to be quiet. His footsteps would echo on the tile floor, in any event.

Rachel walked in step with him, her face intent but pale, her hands clenched. Obviously she was convinced that something malicious had been intended in the incident. He still wasn't so sure, but—

Footsteps. Someone was coming toward them, around the corner. He heard the quick intake of Rachel's breath. His hand tightened on the flashlight. He grasped Rachel's arm, pushing her behind him.

A figure came around the corner, and all of his tension fell flat. The man had to be eighty at least, and he peered at them through the thick lenses of his glasses.

"Rachel?" His voice quavered. "That you?"

"Mose." Relief flooded Rachel's voice. "I'm glad to see you."

He grunted. "Pastor told me you'd be hanging the greens in the sanctuary tonight. You all finished?"

"Yes, we're done. Why didn't you answer me when I called to you in the sanctuary?"

The old man blinked several times before replying. "In the sanctuary? Haven't been in the sanctuary yet. Just came in the side door and was on my way here when I heard you folks come in." He glanced at Tyler suspiciously.

The color she'd regained melted from Rachel's face. "You weren't? But someone was. The lights went off."

"Lights off?" He sniffed. "We'll just see about that." He turned and shuffled off the way he'd come.

They followed him, and Tyler realized that at some point he'd grasped Rachel's hand. Well, she was scared. Giving her a little support was the least he could do.

Around the corner, through a set of double fire doors, and they were abruptly in the old part of the building again. In the dark. He switched on his flashlight, and the old man's face looked white and startled in its glare.

"Must be a circuit. Just shine your light over to the right, so's I can see what's what."

Tyler did as he was told and the flashlight's beam picked out the gray metal circuit box, looking incongruous against a carved oak cabinet that must be at least a hundred years old.

The custodian flipped it open. "There's the problem, all right. Breaker's thrown." He clicked it, and lights came on immediately, gleaming through an open door that led into the sanctuary.

"Let's have a look inside." Tyler moved to the door. "Rachel heard someone in there."

The elderly man followed them into the sanctuary. The lights showed evergreen branches looping around the columns and flowing around the windows. Everything looked perfectly normal.

Rachel stood close to him. "I'd like to walk back through, just to be sure."

He nodded, sensing that she didn't want to say anything else within earshot of the custodian.

Halfway back along the outside wall, she stopped. "This is where I was," she murmured. "When I realized he was coming toward me. I ducked into that pew, ran along it and out the center aisle to the doors."

"He didn't follow you then?"

"I'm not sure. I was pretty panicked by then. All I wanted was to get out."

Hearing a faint tremor in her voice, he found her hand and squeezed it. "You're okay now."

She nodded, sending him a cautioning look as the custodian came toward them.

"Well, if someone was here, they're gone now." He patted Rachel's arm. "Don't like to say it, but most likely it was one of them kids. Their idea of a joke."

"I guess it could have been." Rachel sounded unconvinced. "Thanks, Mose. Do you want me to go back through and turn off the lights?"

"No, no, you folks go on. I'm going that way anyhow."

Touching Rachel's arm, Tyler guided her toward the door, still not sure what he thought of all this. That Rachel had been frightened by someone, he had no doubt. But was it anything more than that?

They walked side by side out into the chilly night and along the walk. He waited for Rachel to speak first. Their relationship was fragile at best, and he wasn't sure what he could say to make this better.

They reached the street before she spoke. She glanced at him, her face pale in the gleam of the streetlamp. "I suppose Mose could be right about the kids. Though I hate to think they'd be so mean."

He took her hand as they crossed the street toward the inn. "Kids don't always think through the results of their actions. I can remember a couple of really stupid things I did at that age."

She smiled faintly. "I suppose I can, too. Well, thank you for coming to the rescue. I hope I didn't look like too much of an idiot."

"You didn't look like an idiot at all." His fingers tightened on hers. "It was a scary experience, even if

Mose is right and it was just intended as a joke. I'm just not sure—" He hesitated. Maybe he shouldn't voice the thought in his mind.

"What?" They neared the side door, and she stopped just short of the circle of illumination from the overhead light.

"I've only known you…what? A week? In that time you've been nearly electrocuted by Christmas lights and—well, call it harassed in the church."

Her face was a pale oval in the dim light. "And you've been hit on the head."

"Seems like we're both having a run of bad luck." He waited for her response.

She frowned, looking troubled. "It does seem odd. But the Christmas lights—surely no one could have done that deliberately."

"Not if they didn't have access to them. If they were safely up in your attic until the moment you brought them down to hang—"

"They weren't," she said shortly. "I brought them down the day before. I was checking on them when I realized it was time for the committee meeting."

He didn't think he liked that. "Where were they during the meeting?"

"In the downstairs rest room."

"Where someone could tamper with them," he said.

"Why would anyone do that? They're all my friends. Anyway, how could they have known I'd be the one to put them up?"

"Anyone who's been around the inn would know that."

She took a quick step away from him, into the pool of light. "I can't believe that someone I know would try to hurt me." But her voice seemed to wobble on the words.

"I'm not trying to upset you." An unexpected, and unwelcome, flood of protectiveness swept through him. "I'm just concerned."

"Thank you. But please, I don't want Grams to know anything happened. She worries about me."

"She loves you," he said quietly, prompted by some instinct he wasn't sure he understood. "That's a good thing."

She tilted her face back, a smile lifting the corners of her lips. "Most of the time," she agreed.

"All of the time." Without thinking it through, he brushed a strand of hair back from her face. It flowed through his fingers like silk.

Her eyes widened. Darkened. He heard the faint catch of her breath. Knew that his own breathing was suddenly ragged.

He took her shoulders, drawing her toward him. She came willingly, lifting her face. The faintest shadow of caution touched his mind, and he censored it. His lips found hers.

Astonishing, the flood of warmth and tenderness that went through him. The kiss was gentle, tentative, as if Rachel were asking silently, Is this right? Do we want to do this? Who are you, deep inside where it's important?

She drew back a little at last, a smile lingering on her lips. "Maybe we'd better go in."

He dropped a light kiss on her nose. "Maybe we'd better. Your grandmother will be worrying."

But he didn't want to. He wanted to stay out here in the moonlight with her as long as he could. And he didn't care to explore what that meant about the state of his feelings.

Barney trotted along Crossings Road next to Rachel, darting away from her from time to time to investigate an interesting clump of dried weeds or the trunk of a hemlock. She smiled at his enthusiasm, aware that they were coming closer to the farm with every step.

And that Tyler was there. She'd really had no intention of coming back here or seeing Tyler this afternoon. But Grams had said Rachel was driving them crazy tinkering with the Christmas decorations, and that everything was as ready as it could be for the guests who'd be arriving late this afternoon. Why didn't she take Barney for a walk and get rid of her fidgets?

The dog, apparently remembering their last excursion, had promptly led her down Crossings Road to the Hostetler farm. They reached the lane, and Barney darted ahead of her. She could see Tyler's car, pulled up next to the porch. He'd told Grams he was trying to identify the rest of the furniture today.

To say that she had mixed feelings about seeing Tyler was putting it mildly. She'd appreciated his help the previous night. He'd managed to submerge whatever doubts he had about her story and given her the help she needed.

As for what had happened—she stared absently at

the clumps of dried Queen Anne's lace in what had once been a pasture.

Surely she could think about it rationally now. Little though she wanted to believe it, Mose's suggestion was the only sensible one. One or more of the teenagers, motivated by who knew what, could easily have flipped the switch to turn the lights off. Maybe they'd thought it would be funny to give her a scare in the dark.

Well, if so, she'd certainly gratified them by bolting out the way she had. She should have turned the tables on them and grabbed that person in the sanctuary.

She couldn't have. Cold seemed to settle into her. Even now, in the clear light of day with the thin winter sun on her face, she couldn't imagine reaching out toward that faceless figure.

Her steps slowed, and Barney scampered over to nose at her hand. She patted him absently.

Maybe it had been her imagination. She sincerely hoped it had been. But that sense of enmity she'd felt, there in the dark in what should have been the safest of places, had simply overpowered her. She'd reacted like any hunted animal. Run. Hide.

She forced her feet to move again. Just thinking about it was making her feel the fear again, and she wouldn't let fear control her.

Remembering what had happened afterward was disturbing in a different way. She couldn't stop the smile that curved her lips when she remembered that kiss. It had held a potential that warmed her and startled her. It certainly hadn't clarified things between them—if anything, she felt more confused.

And then what he'd suggested about the Christmas lights—well, it couldn't be, that was all. Except that his words had roused that niggling little doubt she'd felt every time she looked at the lights.

And he was right. Anyone who was there that night could have guessed she'd put them up. It would have been the work of a minute to strip the wires.

Not a surefire way of hurting her, but a quick and easy impulse.

Tyler had left someone out, though. Himself.

He'd had access to the lights, too. And he'd come here convinced that her family was guilty of something in relation to his grandfather's death.

Was he really just after the truth? Or did revenge figure in somewhere?

Ridiculous, she told herself firmly. He wasn't that sort of devious person.

But still—maybe that was all the more reason not to see Tyler alone today. She'd reached the house, but he wasn't inside. Instead she spotted him where the ground sloped up behind the barn.

For a moment she didn't know what he was doing, but then she realized. That tangle of brush and rusted fence was a small cemetery, of course. There were plenty of them, scattered throughout the township, most of them remnants of the earliest days of settlement. Some were well kept, others abandoned. This one fell into the abandoned category.

Tyler seemed totally absorbed. He hadn't noticed her. Good. She'd turn around and go back to the inn—

But before she could move, Barney spotted Tyler

and plunged toward him, tail waving, letting out a series of welcoming barks. Tyler looked up and waved. Nothing for it now but to go forward.

Tyler climbed over the remnants of the low wrought-iron fence and stood, waiting for her. Barney reached him first, and Tyler welcomed him, running his hand along the dog's back and sending Barney into excited whines.

"Hi." He surveyed her, as if measuring the amount of strain on her face. "How are you doing? I wondered when I didn't see you at breakfast."

"I'm fine," she said quickly. "Just fine. Grams thought I could use a sleep-in day before the weekend guests get here, that's all."

He nodded, as if accepting that implication that she didn't want to discuss the previous night.

"How did you make out with the furniture?" she asked quickly. "Grams said you were trying to get through the list today."

"I managed to do that, but I'm not sure how far ahead it gets me. There are certainly plenty of things missing, and I can make up a list to give the chief. But there's no way of knowing when anything disappeared. My grandfather could have sold some of it himself, for all I know."

She could understand his frustration. He was finding dead ends everywhere he turned.

"So you're investigating the family cemetery, instead."

"Not so much family, as far as I can tell. Most of

the people buried here seem to be Chadwicks, dating back to the 1700s."

"The land probably originally belonged to a family called Chadwick. Once it came into Amish hands, they'd have been buried in the Amish cemetery over toward Burkville."

He knelt, straightening a small stone that had been tipped over. "Miranda Chadwick. Looks as if she was only three when she died."

She squatted next to him, heart clenching, and shoved a clump of soil against the marker to hold it upright. "So many children didn't survive the first few years then. It's hardly surprising that people had big families." She touched the rough-cut cross on the marker, unaccountably hurt by the centuries-old loss. "They grieved for her."

He nodded, his face solemn, and then rose, holding out his hand to help her to her feet.

She stood, disentangling her hand quickly, afraid of what she might give away if she held on to him any longer.

He cleared his throat. "So you said the Amish are buried elsewhere?"

"The Amish have a church-district cemetery—at least, that's how it's done here. Just simple stones, most of them alike, I guess showing that even in death, everyone is equal."

"But my grandfather had left the church by the time he died." Something sharp and alert focused Tyler's gray eyes. "So where would he be buried?"

"I don't know. Maybe my grandmother—"

But Tyler was already moving purposely through the small graveyard, bending to pull the weeds away from each stone. Feeling helpless, she followed him.

Chadwicks and more Chadwicks. Surely he wasn't—

But Tyler had stopped before one stone, carefully clearing the debris from it, and she realized the marker looked newer than the others.

Why this sudden feeling of dismay? She struggled with her own emotions. It didn't really make a difference, did it, where Tyler's grandfather was buried?

She came to a stop next to him, looking at Tyler rather than the stone. His face had tightened, becoming all sharp planes and angles.

"Here it is. John Hostetler. Just his name and the dates. I guess my mother held to Amish tradition in that, at least."

She couldn't tell what he was feeling. She rested her hand lightly on his shoulder. Tension, that was all she could be sure of. She focused on the marker.

John Hostetler. As Tyler said, just date of birth. Date of death.

Date of death. For an instant her vision seemed to blur. She shook her head, forcing her gaze to the carved date. It was like being struck in the stomach. She actually stumbled back a step, gasping.

Tyler was on it in an instant, of course. He shot to his feet, grasping her hands in both of his. "What is it?"

She shook her head, trying to come up with something, anything other than the truth.

Tyler's grip tightened painfully. He couldn't have

known how hard he was holding her. "What, Rachel? What do you see when you look at the tombstone?"

She couldn't lie. Couldn't evade. Couldn't even understand it herself.

"The date. The date your grandfather died." She stopped, feeling as if the words choked her. "My father deserted us at just about the same time."

Chapter Nine

Tyler could only stare at Rachel for a moment, questions battering at his mind. He reached out, wanting to hold her so that she couldn't escape until he had all the answers. How could she land a blow like that and then stand looking at him as if it didn't matter?

Then he realized that it wasn't lack of caring that froze her face and darkened her eyes. Shock. Rachel was shocked by this, just as he was.

A cold breeze hit them, rustling the bare branches of the oak tree that sheltered the few tilted gravestones. Rachel shivered, her whole body seeming to tremble for a moment.

He grasped her arm. "Come on. Let's get back to the car and warm up."

She walked with him down the hill, stumbling a little once or twice as if not watching where she was going. Barney, darting around them in circles in the frostbitten field, seemed to sense that something was wrong. He rushed up to Rachel with small, reassuring yips.

They reached the car. He tucked her into the passenger seat and started the ignition, turning the heater on. Barney whined until he opened the back door so the dog could jump in.

Tyler slid into the driver's seat, holding out his hand to the vent, grateful for the power of the car's heater. Already warmth was coming out, and he turned the blower to full blast. He couldn't possibly get any answers until Rachel lost that frozen look.

For several minutes she didn't move. He should take her back to the inn, but he'd never have a better time than this to find answers.

She stretched her hands out toward the heater vent, rubbing them together, and the movement encouraged him. She seemed to have lost a little of that frozen look.

"Feeling better now?" He kept his voice low.

She nodded, darting a cautious, sideways glance at him. To his relief the color had returned to her cheeks.

"I'm sorry. I don't know what got into me."

"Shock," he suggested.

"I don't—" She stopped, shook her head, made an effort to start again. "I'm being stupid, letting the coincidence upset me so much."

He discovered his hand was gripping the steering wheel so hard the knuckles were white, and he forced his fingers to loosen.

"Do you really think it's a coincidence that your father deserted you about the time of my grandfather's death?"

"What else could it be?" Defiance colored the words.

Plenty of things, most notably a guilty conscience. But he suspected she would come to that conclusion on her own if he didn't push too hard.

She moved, as if the silence disturbed her. "I was only eight. I might be remembering incorrectly." Her voice was so defensive that he knew there was more to it than that.

"You must know around when it was. Didn't you tell me that your mother took you and your sisters away shortly after that?"

Her mouth was set, but she gave a short nod.

"Kids usually have their own ways of remembering when things happened. Connecting the experiences to being off school or holidays or—"

He stopped, because a tremor had shot through her, so fierce he could feel it. He reached out, capturing her cold hand in his. "What is it, Rachel? You may as well tell me, because you know I'm not going to give up."

She stared through the windshield at the bleak landscape. Barney whined from the backseat, seeming to sense her distress.

"My birthday would have been a week after your grandfather's death." The words came out slow. Reluctant. "I was excited because Daddy had promised to stay for my birthday and give me a gold cross necklace, like the one Andrea had." She seemed to be looking back over a dark, painful chasm. "But he was gone before then."

"Promised to stay? You mean he wasn't usually there?"

"Our parents were separated so much it's hard to keep track. Daddy would be gone for months at a time, and then show up. He and Mom might get along for a few weeks, then something would blow up between them and he'd leave." She threaded her fingers through her hair. "Not the most stable of parents. I sometimes wonder why they had us."

He willed himself to go slow, to think this through. Hampton had deserted his family at about the time of his grandfather's death; that was clear. But connecting the two incidents with any sureness was iffy, given what Rachel said about her father's absences.

"Had your dad been around much that summer?"

She frowned, shaking her head. "I'm not sure. It seems to me that he had, but—" She shrugged. "He could be so charming, although I don't think my grandparents saw it. Life seemed exciting when he was here."

She'd wanted to be loved, of course. Any child knows instinctively that a parent's love is crucial.

"Do you remember anything about when your dad left?" He tried to keep his voice gentle.

She stared down at her hands. He sensed that she was pulling her defenses up, figuring out how to cope with this situation.

"I don't know much." Her voice was calmer now, as if she were able to detach her grown-up self from the little girl who'd been looking forward to her birthday. "I'm sure the adults were all trying to protect us, but of course Andrea and I speculated. We crept out on the stairs at night. I remember sitting there, holding her hand, listening to my mother shouting at my grandparents, as if it was their fault he'd gone."

Her fingers twisted a little in remembered pain, and he smoothed them gently, hurting for her.

"Your mother must have explained things to you in some way."

A wry smile tugged at her lips. "You didn't know our mother if you think that. She just announced that Daddy was gone and that we were going away, too. She hauled us out of the house with half our belongings. For a while Drea and I thought we were going to join our father, but that didn't happen. Every time we asked, she'd tell us to be quiet." She shrugged. "So finally we stopped asking."

He struggled to piece it together. It sounded as if her family had been far more messed up than his. "So your parents never got back together?"

She shook her head. "Being taken away from our grandparents hurt the worst. Daddy had been in and out of our lives so much, always trying some great new job that was going to make all the difference. It never did."

"So your grandparents were the stable influence." And probably only her grandmother, or possibly Emma, could tell him the story from an adult perspective.

"They were. If Mom had let us see them more often—but she nursed her own grudge against them. It really wasn't until we were in college that we had much contact with them. Still, we always knew they were there." She brushed back a strand of silky hair, managing to give him something approaching a normal smile. "When I came back a year ago, just for a visit, I realized this place was what I'd been longing for all along. It's home, even though I left it when I was eight."

He nodded, understanding. Wanting to make it better for her, even at the same time that he knew he'd have to find out more about her father.

He touched the strand of hair she fiddled with, tucking it behind her ear. His fingers brushed her cheek, setting up a wave of longing that he had to fight.

"I'd have to say you turned out pretty well, in spite of your parents. What happened to them? Are you still in contact?"

She shook her head. "Mom died in a car accident three years ago in Nevada."

"I'm sorry." Although it didn't sound as if she'd been much of a loss as a mother. "What about your dad?" Casual. Keep it casual.

She blinked. "I thought you realized. We haven't heard a word from him from that day to this."

Maybe the worst thing about running an inn was the fact that no matter what was going on in her personal life, Rachel had to be smiling and welcoming for the guests. She could only be thankful that at the moment, Grams had their weekend guests corralled in the front parlor, serving them eggnog and cookies and regaling them with Pennsylvania Dutch Christmas legends, while Rachel had the back parlor to herself, getting the nativity scene ready to go beneath the Christmas tree.

If only she'd had a little more self-control, Tyler would never have known about the coincidence in dates between her father's leaving and his grandfather's death. That was all it had been. A coincidence. She'd never believe that her feckless, generous father could have been involved in that. Never.

She frowned at the low wooden platform that was meant to hold the *putz*. That end didn't seem to be sitting properly.

Keeping her hands busy unfortunately allowed her mind to wander too much.

I guess I couldn't have kept it from Tyler, could I? She had a wistful longing that God would come down on her side in this, but in her heart she knew it wouldn't happen. "Be ye wise as serpents and innocent as doves." Hiding the truth from Tyler was hardly an act of innocence.

Still, the fear existed. What would he do with the information he now had? She already knew part of that answer, didn't she? He'd want to talk to Grams. She hadn't remembered much about that time, but Grams would.

All her protective family instincts went into high gear at the thought, but there was nothing she could do. Tyler wouldn't be deflected, and Grams would do what was right.

Having arranged the molds to hold the hills and valleys on the wooden platform, she spread out the length of green cloth that was meant to cover them. The fabric fell in graceful folds, looking for all the world like real hills and valleys.

And then the end of the platform collapsed, sending her neat little world atilt. For a moment she felt like bursting into tears. Her world really was falling around her, and there seemed to be nothing she could do to stop it.

"Looks as if you need a carpenter."

Her heart jolted at the sound of Tyler's voice. She didn't look up. "My brother-in-law is a carpenter, but he moved his shop to the property he and Andrea bought in New Holland. And he's off on his honeymoon, anyway."

Tyler knelt beside her, his arm brushing hers as he righted the platform. She caught the tang of his aftershave and resisted the instinct to lean a little closer to him.

"I think I can manage to fix this. Will you hand me that hammer?"

She passed it over to him. With a few quick blows he firmed up the nails that had begun to work themselves loose.

She caught his sideways, questioning glance, as if he wanted to ask how she was but was afraid to start something.

"This is the foundation for the nativity scene, I take it."

"We call it the *putz*." She spread the cloth out again, aware of his hands helping her. "If you want to hear about it, you should go to the front parlor. Grams is giving the details to the other guests."

Was that ungracious? Grams would certainly think so.

"I'd rather hear it from you." Tyler's voice was low, pitched under the chatter from the other room.

"That's not what you want, and you know it." She couldn't seem to help the tartness in her tone.

Tyler nodded, blue eyes serious as he studied her face. "All right. That's true. You realize I have to talk to your grandmother, don't you?"

She paused in the act of removing one of the clay nativity figures from its nest of tissue paper. Even without seeing it, she could identify the shape of a camel through the paper.

She'd been anticipating this moment—getting out the familiar old figures, setting up the scene until it was just perfect. Irrational or not, she couldn't help but resent the fact that Tyler was spoiling it for her.

"I know you need to hear the story from Grams." Her words felt as fragile as the crystal ornaments on the tree. "I'd appreciate it if you'd wait until we've gotten through this evening."

"I'll wait, but later we have to talk." The implacability in his tone chilled her. He wouldn't be turned back, no matter what.

Even if what he was trying to do implicated her father.

"And now we're ready to set up the *putz*, or nativity scene." Grams came through the archway, shepherding the four new couples firmly. "We hope you'll enjoy doing this traditional Pennsylvania German tradition with us."

Both mother-daughter pairs looked enthusiastic. The other two couples were from Connecticut. The women seemed pleased, the men bored. How long before they made some excuse to get out of this? They looked slightly heartened at the sight of Tyler—another male to support them, she supposed.

But Tyler would want to get this over as quickly as possible, so he would corner Grams.

"You've already met my granddaughter Rachel when you checked in." Grams performed introductions. "And this is our friend, Tyler Dunn."

How did Tyler feel about being promoted from guest to friend? It wouldn't stop him from finding out all he could about her father.

While Grams explained the tradition of the *putz*, the elaborate Nativity scene that went under the tree, Rachel unwrapped the six-inch clay figures, setting them out on the folding table she'd brought in for the purpose.

"...not just a manger scene," Grams explained. "We start at the left and create little vignettes of the events leading up to the birth of Jesus—Joseph in his carpentry shop, Mary with the angel, the trip to Bethlehem. The stable scene goes front and center, of course, and then the shepherds with their flocks, the wise men following the star, even the flight to Egypt."

"These are beautiful figures." One of the women grabbed an angel, holding it up in one hand.

Rachel had to force herself not to take it back. That was the angel with the broken wing tip. She'd knocked it over the year she was six and been inconsolable until Daddy, there for once, had touched it up with gilt paint, assuring her that no one would ever notice.

"Antique," Tyler said smoothly, "and very fragile. Difficult to replace."

The woman seemed to take the hint, holding the angel carefully in both hands. "We actually get to help set this up? Well, if that isn't the sweetest thing."

She knelt by the platform. The others, seeming infected by her enthusiasm, gathered around to take the delicate figures or the stones and moss Rachel had brought in to add realism to the scene. In a few moments everyone was happily involved. Tyler even enlisted the two men to create a miniature mountain, and she thought she caught a serious discussion about how one might add a running stream.

She stood back a little, watching the scene take shape, handing out a figure where needed. Funny, how sharp the memory had been when she'd seen the angel with the chipped wing. She hadn't thought of that in years.

Maybe it had been so strong because it involved her father. Funny. You'd have expected the oldest daughter to be Daddy's girl, but instead it had been her. The whole time they'd lived here, everyone had known that Andrea was Grandfather's little helper and she was Daddy's girl.

Was it because Andrea was less guided by sentiment? A little more clear-sighted about their parents? The thought made her uncomfortable, and she tried to push it away.

"Rachel?"

She blinked, realizing that one of the guests must have said her name several times. "Yes? Peggy," she added, pleased to have pulled the woman's name from her memory banks.

"Will you show me how to put these Roman soldiers together? It looks as if the shield should hook on, but I don't quite see..."

"Let me." Tyler took it from the woman. She looked up at him, obviously flattered at his attention. "I think we can figure this out together, can't we?"

The woman fluttered after him in an instant, kneeling at the base of the tree next to him.

Rachel pinned a smile to her face. She couldn't let her private worries distract her from her duty to her guests. But Tyler—

Tyler had been watchful. Sensitive. Seeming to know what she was feeling, quick and subtle about helping out.

Even as she thought that, she caught him taking a clay donkey from Grams and handing her a star to be nestled in the branches instead, so that she didn't attempt to get down on the floor.

The simple gesture gripped her heart. Without warning, the thought came. This was a man she could love.

No. She couldn't. Because whether he wanted to or not, Tyler threatened everything that was important to her.

Rachel clearly didn't intend to let him talk to her grandmother tonight. The other guests had lingered long after the Nativity scene was finished. As it happened, one of the women was an accomplished pianist, and she'd entertained them with Christmas music while a fire roared in the fireplace and tree lights shone softly on the *putz*.

It was lovely. He'd had to admit that—admit, too, that he'd enjoyed watching the firelight play on Rachel's expressive face.

Too expressive. She probably didn't realize how clearly her protectiveness toward her grandmother came through. Once the last of the guests had wound down, she'd put her arm around the elderly woman's waist and urged her toward the stairs with a defiant look at him.

Well, much as he needed to talk to Katherine Unger, he had to agree with Rachel on this one. She had looked tired, and it was late. Tomorrow would have to do.

He put the book he'd been leafing through back on the shelf and headed for the stairs. As he did, the door into the private wing of the house opened. It wasn't Rachel who came through—it was her grandmother.

"Mrs. Unger." He stopped, foot on the bottom step. "I thought you'd already gone to bed."

"That's what my granddaughter thinks, too." She stepped into the hall, the dog padding softly behind her, and closed the door. "I think it's time we had a talk about whatever it is you and Rachel have been trying to keep from me all day."

"I'm not sure—"

She took his arm and steered him back down the hall toward the kitchen. "My granddaughter is too protective. Now, don't you start, too. Whatever it is won't be improved by making me wait and wonder about it until morning."

A low light had been left on in the kitchen, shining down on the sturdy wooden table that had undoubtedly served generations of the family, and a Black Forest clock ticked steadily on the mantelpiece. Mrs. Unger sat at the table and gestured him to the chair next to her.

"Now. Tell me." She folded thin, aristocratic hands in a gesture that was probably her way of armoring herself against bad news. "You and Rachel learned something today that upset her. What was it?"

He hesitated. "I don't think Rachel is going to like my talking with you alone."

"I'll deal with Rachel." She waited.

"All right." Actually, this might bother her less than it did Rachel. "I was in the small cemetery at the farm today. The one where my grandfather is buried. Rachel saw the date he died. I think you know why that upset her."

Her face tightened slightly at the implied challenge, but she nodded. "It reminded Rachel of when her father left."

"That's what she said." He frowned, trying to find the right way to ask questions that were certainly prying into her family's affairs. "She didn't remember the sequence of events exactly. Maybe she didn't even know, at the time."

"But you knew I would." She said the words he'd omitted, shaking her head as if she didn't want to remember. "That was a difficult time. Rachel's father had been around for nearly a month—long for him. The quarrels were starting up. We knew it was only a question of time until he left. The fact that it happened shortly after your grandfather's death doesn't mean they were related."

"Perhaps not. But you must know I won't be satisfied unless I get some answers."

She inclined her head, conceding the point. "You have that right, I suppose." A faint, wry smile flickered. "Oddly enough, I've waited for years for Rachel to ask the questions. Why did her father leave? Why did their mother take them away? She never has."

That was strange. He'd think the questions would burn in her. "I don't want to hurt her. Or you. But I need the truth."

"The truth always costs something. Probably pain." She held up her hand to stop his protest. "I'm not refusing to tell you. I'm just pointing out that you can't always protect people." She sighed, her fingers tightening against each other. "Maybe that was my mistake. Trying to protect everyone."

Yes, he could see that. She was someone who would always try to protect her family. Rachel was exactly the same. As much as it might annoy him at times, he had to admire it, too.

"We only had the one child, you know." Her voice was soft. "Perhaps things would have been different if we'd had more. As it was, Lily was the apple of her father's eye—spirited, willful and headstrong. My husband liked those qualities in her, until she met Donald Hampton."

"He didn't approve." He'd only had Rachel's child's-eye view of her father, but he hadn't been too impressed.

"No. Oh, Hampton was charming. Good-looking, polite. It was easy to see why she fell in love with him. But Frederick didn't think there was much character behind the charm."

His mind flickered to his own father. Maybe not long on charm, but he'd been a sound man and a good father. Odd, to be sitting in this quiet room with this elderly woman, pulled willy-nilly into a bond with her.

She sighed, the sound a soft counterpoint to the ticking of the clock. "Frederick would have stopped the marriage if he could have, but she was determined. And afterward there were the babies—" Her face bloomed with love. "He adored those girls. Hampton was just as unreliable as my husband predicted, but Frederick managed to keep his opinions to himself, for the most part. And we were happy when they moved in here. Then it didn't matter when Hampton took off, supposedly in search of some wonderful deal. We could take care of the children."

It seemed to him that their mother should have done that, but apparently she hadn't, from what Rachel said, been especially gifted as a mother.

"They were living here when my grandfather was attacked." Maybe best to move things along.

"Yes. As I said, Hampton had been back for about a month, supposedly trying to find a decent job around here, although Frederick always said he would run at the sight of one. Still, he was here, and Rachel adored him."

He'd seen that, in her eyes, when she spoke of him.

"Maybe that's why she's never asked. She wants to hold on to her image of him."

She nodded. "We thought he'd be here until Rachel's birthday, at least."

"How long after the attack on my grandfather did he leave?" That was the important point to him.

"Two days." Her face tightened until the skin seemed molded against the bone. "We woke up to find him gone. He left a note, telling Lily he'd heard of some wonderful job opportunity out west. He left, never even saying goodbye to the girls. I don't think they ever heard from him again."

The timing was certainly suspicious. "I understand your daughter left soon after that."

"There was a terrible quarrel between them—my daughter and my husband. Frederick was rash enough to say what he thought of her husband, never imagining she'd carry out her threat to leave." She shook her head, the grief she'd probably carried since that day seeming to weigh her down. "I tried to reason with them, but they were both too stubborn to listen. There was a time when I thought I'd never get my granddaughters back again."

"But you have," he said quickly. "They never stopped loving you." Love. Connections. They went together, didn't they? Binding people together for good or ill. Like it or not, his family and hers were bound, too.

"I do." She looked at him then, and he saw the pleading in her lined face. "I have Rachel, and through her Andrea came back, too. But Rachel is the vulnerable one. She always has been. Family is everything to her."

What could he say to that? She didn't seem to expect anything. She just leaned across the table, putting her hand over his.

"Please," she said. "Please don't do anything that will take family away from Rachel. Please."

Chapter Ten

Rachel charged up the stairs the next morning, fueled by a mix of rage and betrayal. Tyler had gone too far this time.

Imagine the nerve—he'd sat there at breakfast calmly eating her cream-cheese-filled French toast, listening to the other guests talk about their planned day in Bethlehem, and he hadn't shown her by word or look that he had talked to Grams last night.

Some latent, fair part of her mind suggested that he could hardly have brought up something so personal in the presence of strangers, but she slapped it down. She wasn't rational about this. She was furious.

She paused on the landing, catching her breath, calming her nerves. Her sensitivity where her father was concerned was probably getting in the way of her judgment, but she couldn't seem to help it.

If only Andrea were here. She knew her big sister well enough to know that if she called Andrea's cell phone and told her what was going on, she and Cal would be on their way home immediately. But that wasn't fair—not to Andrea, who deserved to have her honeymoon in peace, and not to herself. It was time she stopped depending on her big sister.

She went quickly up the rest of the flight, running her hand along the carved railing. The square, spacious upstairs hall looked odd with the bedroom doors closed. All of their guests had gone out for the day. Except Tyler.

She swung on her heel toward his door just as it opened.

"Rachel." His face changed at the sight of her.

Small wonder. She probably looked like an avenging fury. She certainly felt like one.

"We have to talk." She said the words with control, but her nails were biting into her palms.

He nodded, opening the door wide. "I know. Do you want to come in?"

Instinct told her not to have this conversation in the privacy of the bedroom. "Out here is fine. Everyone's left. We won't be overheard." No matter what she had to say to him.

"Right." He stepped out into the hallway, closing the door behind him, and just stood, waiting for her to say what she would.

All the insults she'd been practicing in her head seemed to fly away at the sight of his grave face. She could only find one thing to say.

"How could you? How could you talk to my grandmother without me?" Saying the words seemed to give her momentum. "You must have known how tired she was and how much that was bound to upset her. I can't believe you'd do that."

It was true, she realized. At some level, she couldn't believe that the Tyler she'd grown to know and care for would go behind her back that way.

"If you've talked with your grandmother, you know I didn't go to her," he said calmly. "She came to me."

"Yes. I know. I also know that you could have made some excuse. You could have waited until today at least. Why was it so important that you had to talk about it last night? Grams—" To her horror, she felt tears welling in her eyes. She blinked them back.

But he saw. He took a step toward her, closing the gap between them, his face gentling.

"Don't, Rachel. Please. I don't want to hurt you. I didn't want to hurt her. But your grandmother is one smart lady. She knew we were hiding something from her, and she wasn't going to rest until she knew what it was."

She drew in a breath, trying to ease the tension in her throat. "She is smart. And stubborn."

His fingers closed over hers for a brief moment. "Like her granddaughter."

Another breath, another effort to gain control of the situation that seemed to be slipping rapidly away from her. Or maybe there had never been anything she could do about this, but it had taken her this long to realize it.

"Grams told me what she'd told you. About my father leaving, the fight between my grandfather and mother." She shook her head slightly, not liking the pictures that had taken up residence there. "She's convinced that his leaving didn't have anything to do with what happened to your grandfather." She forced herself to meet his eyes. "So am I. Maybe he was just as charming as I remember and just as weak as my grandparents thought, but he wasn't a man who'd turn to violence."

"I hope you're right, Rachel." His fingers brushed hers again in mute sympathy. "I hope you're right about him."

She nodded, throat clogging so that she had to clear it. Unshed tears would do that to a person. "Well. I guess I'm not angry enough to slug you after all."

His smile was tentative, as if he were afraid of setting her off again. "I'm sure there are things for which I deserve it, anyway, so feel free."

Her tension drained away at the offer. "Not today. Grams said I should thank you for bringing it out in the open—about my father leaving, I mean. I'm not quite ready to do that."

"Not necessary," he said quickly. "I know things I have no right to about your family. And you about mine. Neither of us can do anything about it."

He was right about that. She didn't have to like it, but she had to accept it. He probably felt the same way.

"I am grateful for your help last night with the guests." She managed a smile that was a bit more genuine. "You really picked up the slack for me."

He shrugged, seeming to relax, as well. "My pleasure. I have to hand it to you and your grandmother. You certainly have a hit on your hands with the Pennsylvania Dutch Christmas traditions. Those people will tell their friends, and before you know it, every room will be full for the holidays."

"I just hope everything will go more easily once we've had a little practice." Realizing how close they were standing, she took a step back, bumping into the slant-top desk that stood between the doors.

"Easy." He reached out to steady her and then seemed to change his mind about touching her again and put his hand on the satiny old wood instead. "Don't want to harm either you or this beautiful thing."

"I'm not sure which is more valuable." She straightened the small vase of bittersweet that stood on the narrow top.

"You are," he said, and then nodded toward the desk. "But that is a nice piece. I remember something like it in my grandfather's house." He frowned, and she thought memory flickered in those deep-blue eyes.

"What is it?"

He shook his head. "Funny. I guess being here has brought back more memories. It's as if a door popped open in my mind. I can actually picture that desk now. It used to stand in the upstairs hall." He shook his head. "I'm sure it wasn't a beautiful heirloom like this one, though."

The air had been sucked out of the hall, and she was choking. She couldn't say anything—she could only force a meaningless smile.

The slant-top desk wasn't the family heirloom he obviously supposed it to be. She'd found the piece stuffed away in one of the sheds and refinished it herself when she was getting the inn ready to open.

Coincidence, she insisted. It had to be. The desk was a common style, and surely plenty of homes in the area had one like it.

"Rachel?" Tyler stared at her, eyes questioning. "Is something wrong?"

"No, not at all." She had a feeling her attempt at a smile was ghastly. "Nothing—"

She broke off at the sound of footsteps coming up the stairs. Sturdy footsteps that could only belong to Emma.

Emma rounded the turn at the landing, saw them, and came forward steadily. Rachel glanced at Tyler. He might not have noticed it, but Emma had been doing a good job of avoiding speaking with him. Now, it appeared, she was headed straight for him.

Emma came to a halt a few feet from them, her face square and determined, graying hair drawn back under her white kapp.

"I would like to speak with Tyler Dunn, *ja?*" She made it a question.

"Of course." Rachel took a step back. "Do you want to be private?"

"No, no, you stay, Rachel." She looked steadily at Tyler. "Mrs. Unger tells us that you are John Hostetler's grandson. That you might want to know about him. My Eli's mother, she minds him well. You come to supper Monday night, she will be there, tell you about him, *ja?*"

Tyler sent her a quick glance, as if asking for help. She tried not to respond. She'd already let herself get too involved in Tyler's search for answers, and look where it had gotten her. She'd been leading the trail right where she didn't want it—back to her own family.

"That's very kind of you, Mrs. Zook." Tyler had apparently decided she wasn't going to jump in. "I appreciate it."

Emma gave a short, characteristic nod. "Is *gut*. Rachel, you will come, too. That will make it more easy."

Not waiting for an answer, Emma turned and started back down the stairs, the long skirt of her dark-green dress swishing.

Rachel opened her mouth to protest and closed it again. Emma was bracketing her with Tyler, apparently assuming that she was helping him in his search. But Emma didn't know everything. Rachel carefully avoided glancing at the desk. She'd think that through later. In the meantime—

"Look, I'll understand if you don't want to go with me," Tyler began.

"No. That's fine. I'll be happy to go."

Well, maybe "happy" was a slight exaggeration. But like it or not, she seemed to be running out of choices. The circle was closing tighter and tighter around her family.

Staying close to Tyler was dangerous, but not knowing what he was doing, what he was finding out—that could be more dangerous still.

Rachel tried to focus on Pastor Greg's sermon, not on the fact that Tyler Dunn was sitting next to her in the small sanctuary. She'd resigned herself to the necessity of working with Tyler. She just hadn't expected that cooperation to extend to worshipping next to him.

Sunday morning with guests in the house was always a difficult time. She'd served breakfast, hoping she wasn't rushing anyone, and then scrambled into her clothes.

When she'd rushed out to meet Grams in the center hallway, Tyler had been there, wearing a gray suit tailored to perfection across his broad shoulders, obviously bound for church as well. They could hardly avoid inviting him to accompany them.

She took a deep breath, trying to focus her mind and heart. Unfortunately the heady scent of pine boughs sent her mind surging back to the night she'd faced fear in this place.

And Tyler had been there to help her. She stole a glance at him. His strong-boned face was grave and attentive. He didn't seem to be experiencing any of the distraction she felt.

Maybe he had better forces of concentration than she did. That was probably important to an architect. She wasn't doing as well. Because of the trouble he'd brought into their lives, still unresolved? Or whether because of the man himself?

She folded her hands, fingers squeezing tight, and emulated Grams, serenely focused on the pastor's sermon.

Grams would show that same attention and respect no matter who was in the pulpit. She hoped she would, as well, but Pastor Greg always gave her some sturdy spiritual food to chew on.

Today the topic was angels—not fluffy, sentimental Victorian Christmas card angels, but the angels of the Bible. Grave messengers from God, exultant rejoicers at Jesus's birth. Her wayward imagination caught, she listened intently, rose to sing the closing hymn and floated out of the sanctuary at last on a thunderous organ blast of "Angels We Have Heard on High."

The spiritual lift lasted until she reached the churchyard, where Sandra Whitmoyer grabbed her arm. "Rachel, I must speak with you about the open house tour."

Of course she had to. Rachel stepped out of the flow of exiting parishioners, buttoning her coat against the December chill.

"I thought we were all set. You received the brochures, didn't you?" Phillip had finally responded to her prodding and produced a beautiful brochure, which she'd dutifully delivered to the printer.

"Yes, yes, the brochures are fine." Sandra tucked a creamy fold of cashmere scarf inside the lapel of her leather coat. "But Margaret Allen wants to serve chocolates along with her other refreshments at The Willows. Now, you know we can't risk having people put sticky, chocolaty hands on antique furniture when they go on to the next house."

"It will be all adults on the tour," she pointed out. "I'm sure they'll be responsible about touching things."

Besides, she had no desire to take on the owner of a competing bed-and-breakfast. They'd had their runins with Margaret in the past, and she didn't want to reopen hostilities.

"You don't know that," Sandra said darkly. "Some

people will do anything. I won't have people touching the Italian tapestry on my sitting room love seat with sticky fingers."

Sandra was caught between a rock and a hard place, Rachel realized. She'd been the first to offer her lovely old Victorian home for the tour, but she'd been worrying ever since that some harm would come to her delicate furnishings.

"If I might make a suggestion—" Tyler's voice was diffident. She might have forgotten that he was standing next to her, he'd been so quiet, but she hadn't.

Sandra gave him a swift smile instead of the argumentative frown she'd been bestowing on Rachel. "Of course. Any and all suggestions are welcome."

Especially when they came from an attractive male. Rachel chastised herself for her catty thoughts. And practically on the doorstep of the church, no less.

"You might have each stop on the tour offer a container of hand wipes at the entrance. It's only sensible during cold and flu season, in any event."

"Brilliant." Sandra's smile blazed. "I don't know why I didn't think of that myself. Or why my husband didn't suggest it—"

"Didn't suggest what?" Bradley Whitmoyer slipped his arm into the crook of his wife's arm.

While Sandra was explaining, Rachel took another quick glance at Tyler's face. Could he possibly be interested in all this? His gaze crossed hers, and her heart jolted.

He looked so serious. Worry gnawed at her. If he'd found out about the desk—

But that was ridiculous. How could he? He'd hardly go around asking Grams or Emma about the provenance of a piece of furniture.

She'd asked both of them herself, cautiously, if they knew where the piece had come from. Emma had shaken her head; Grams had said vaguely that perhaps Grandfather had bought it at an auction.

Impossible to tell. The outbuildings were stuffed with furniture. Andrea had been after her to have a proper inventory made, but who had time for that?

Maybe she should be up-front with Tyler about the desk. After all, even if it had come from his grandfather's farm, that meant nothing. He could have sold it—

She was rationalizing, and she knew it. She didn't want to tell him because it was one more thing to make him suspect her father. First her grandfather, now her father. Where was it going to end?

She forced her attention back to the conversation in time to find that Tyler's suggestion had been adopted and that Sandra, thank goodness, would take care of it herself.

"I think we've kept these people standing in the cold long enough." Bradley nudged his wife toward the churchyard gate.

He was the one who looked cold. Maybe it went along with being overworked, which he probably was now that flu season had started.

Rachel turned away, feeling Tyler move beside her. She probably should have suggested that he go on back to the inn—after all, none of this would matter to him. But before they'd gone more than a couple of yards,

Jeff Whitmoyer stepped into their path, his face ruddy from the nip in the air.

"Hey, glad I ran into you, Dunn." He thrust his hand toward Tyler. "You have a chance to give any thought to my offer? I'd like to get my plans made, be able to break ground as soon as the ground thaws in the spring."

"I don't recall your saying what you planned for the property, if you should buy it." Tyler sounded polite but noncommittal.

Jeff glanced from one side to the other, as if checking for anyone listening in. "Let's say I have an idea for an Amish tourist attraction and leave it at that. When can we sit down and talk it over?"

"Not today," Tyler said. "I don't do business on Sunday."

Before Jeff could suggest another day, Rachel broke in. "Speaking of work to be done in the spring, Jeff, I'd like to get on your work schedule to get that gazebo in the garden moved."

"Moved?" Jeff looked startled. "Who told you that thing could be moved?"

"I did," Tyler said smoothly.

"Tyler is an architect," Rachel added. "He suggested moving the gazebo to the far side of the pond, and I'd like to do that. If you can handle it."

"Of course I can handle it," Jeff said, affronted. "I just don't see why you'd want to move it. I thought you told me last spring you wanted it torn down. Still, if that's what you and your grandmother want, I'll get it on my schedule. I'll stop by and take a look at it this week—maybe talk to you at the same time, Dunn."

Tyler gave a quick nod and took her arm. "We'd better get your grandmother back to the house." He steered her toward Grams, who broke off a conversation with one of the neighbors when she saw them.

Well, she'd gotten Tyler away from Jeff Whitmoyer for the moment, but she didn't know what good that had done. Sooner or later Tyler would settle for whatever truth he found about his grandfather. He'd sell the property and go back to his own life. He probably wouldn't care what use was made of the property after that.

They'd reached the curb when one more interruption intercepted them, in the shape of the police cruiser, pulling to the curb next to them. Chief Burkhalter lowered the window and leaned out.

"Some information for you, Dunn." He shook a keen, assessing glance toward her and Grams. "That lockbox we were talking about—it's turned up. You can stop by my office tomorrow, if you want, and pick it up."

"Thanks. I'll do that."

She caught the suppressed excitement in Tyler's voice, and tension tightened inside her. Box? What box? He hadn't mentioned this to her. She wasn't the only person keeping secrets, it seemed.

"I hope you don't mind driving over to the Zook farm." Rachel glanced at him as he held the door of his car for her, her soft brown curls tumbling from under the knitted cap she wore. "It's an easy walk from the path beyond the barn, but not in the dark. I'd hate to have you arrive with burrs on your pant legs."

"That wouldn't look too good, would it? Am I appropriately dressed?" He hadn't known what the Amish would consider decent attire for an outsider supper guest, so he'd settled on gray flannels and a sweater over a dress shirt.

"You're fine." She pulled her seat belt across. "One thing about the Amish—they don't judge outsiders by what they wear."

How did they judge, then? He closed Rachel's door, walked around the car and slid in. He wasn't nervous— the fact that his grandfather, even his mother, apparently, had been Amish was curious, that was all.

Rachel glanced at him as he started the car. "Relax. They'll be welcoming, I promise."

He turned out onto Main Street. "It's odd, that's all. If not for my grandfather's break with the church, my life might have turned out differently."

He stopped. Impossible to think of himself being Amish. Tonight's visit was going to be meaningless, but he'd hardly been able to refuse Emma's invitation.

Rachel seemed content with the silence between them as he drove past the decorated houses and shops. Or was *content* the right word? He'd sensed some reservation in her in the past day, and he wasn't sure what that meant.

"Looks as if your Christmas in Churchville committee is doing a good job. The only thing missing to turn the village into a Christmas card scene is a couple of inches of snow."

"It does look lovely, doesn't it?" The eagerness in her voice dissipated whatever reserve he'd been imagining. "This is exactly how I've pictured it. Like coming home for Christmas. Don't you think?"

It wasn't the home he'd known, but he understood. "That's it. You'll send visitors away feeling they have to come back every year for their Christmas to be complete."

He understood more than that. That her pleasure and satisfaction was more than just the sense of a job well done. It was personal, not professional. Rachel had found her place in the world when she'd come back here.

It wasn't his place, he reminded himself. His partner was already getting antsy, emailing him to ask how soon he'd be coming back.

He deserved the time off, he'd pointed out to Gil. And it certainly wasn't a question of Gil needing him in the office. They had a good partnership, with Gil Anders being the outgoing people-person while he preferred to work alone with his computer and his blueprints.

Baltimore is not that far away, a small voice pointed out in the back of his mind. It would be possible to come back. To see Rachel again.

Always assuming Rachel wanted to see him once this whole affair had ended.

Rachel leaned forward, pointing. "There's the lane to the Zook farm."

He turned. "The Christmas lights seem to stop here."

"No electricity." He sensed Rachel's smile, even in the dark. "The Amish don't go in for big displays, in any event. Christmas is a religious celebration. The day after, the twenty-sixth, they call 'second Christmas.' That's the day for visiting and celebrating."

He nodded, concentrating on the narrow farm lane in the headlight beams. "You certainly have a lot of different Christmas traditions going in this small area. I like your grandmother's Moravian customs."

"You'd see even more of that if you went to Lititz or Bethlehem. That reminds me, I want to run over to Bethlehem sometime this week to take more photos and pick up a stack of brochures before the next weekend guests come in."

The farmhouse appeared as they passed a windbreak of evergreens, lights glowing yellow from the windows.

"Just pull up by the porch," Rachel instructed. "The children are already peeking out the windows, watching for us."

While he parked and rounded the car to join Rachel, he went over in his mind what she'd told him about the family. Emma and Eli, her husband, now lived in a kind of grandparent cottage, attached to the main house, while their son Samuel and his wife, Nancy, ran the farm with their children. There was another son, Levi, who was mentally handicapped. Nobody seemed to be considered too young, too old or too disabled to contribute to the family, as far as he could tell from what Rachel had said.

The front door was thrown open as they mounted the porch, and they were greeted by five children—

blond stair steps with round blue eyes and huge smiles. The smallest one, a girl, flung herself at Rachel for a hug.

"You're here at last! We've been waiting and waiting. Maam says that you might hear me do my piece for the Christmas program. Will you, Rachel?"

Rachel tugged on a blond braid gently. "I would love to hear you, Elizabeth. Now just let us greet everyone."

The adults were already coming into the room. In rapid succession he was introduced to Eli, their son Samuel, and his wife, Nancy, a brisk, cheerful woman who seemed to run her household with firm command. If he'd imagined that Amish women were meek and subservient, she dispelled that idea.

"This is my mother, Liva Zook." Eli held the arm of an elderly woman, her hair glistening white, her eyes still intensely blue behind her wire-rimmed glasses. "She will be glad to talk with you about your grandfather."

He extended his hand and then hesitated, not sure if that was proper. But she shook hands, hers dry and firm in his.

"You sit here and talk." Nancy ushered him and Eli's mother to a pair of wooden rockers.

He nodded, waiting for the elderly woman to sit down first and then taking his place next to her. The room initially seemed bare to his eyes, but the chair was surprisingly comfortable, the back of it curved to fit his body and the arms worn smooth to the hand.

Eli pulled up a straight chair and sat down next to his mother. "Maam sometimes does not do well in English, so I'll help." He reached out to pat his mother's hand, and Tyler could see the bond between them. Eli's ruddy face above the white beard had the same bone structure, the same round blue eyes.

He'd begun to get used to the Amish custom of beards without mustaches, and the bare faces with the fringe of beard no longer looked odd to him.

"Thanks." Now that he had the opportunity, he wasn't sure how to begin. "If you could just tell me what you remember about my grandfather—"

For a moment he was afraid she didn't understand, but then she nodded. "I remember John. We were children together, *ja*." She nodded again in what seemed a characteristic gesture.

"What was he like?" Was he ever different from the angry, bitter man who had turned everyone away from him?

She studied his face. "Looked something like you, when he was young. Strong, like you. He knew his mind, did what he wanted."

He glanced from her to Eli. "The Amish church doesn't like that, does it?"

"He was young." Her lips creased in an indulgent smile. "The young, they have to see the other side of the fence sometimes."

"Rumspringa," Eli said. "Our youth have time to see the world before they decide to join the church. So they know what they are doing." His eyes twinkled. "Some have a wilder *rumspringa* than others."

Sensible, he thought. It surprised him, in a way, that the Amish would allow that. They must have a lot of confidence that their kids wouldn't be lured away by the world.

"*Ja,* that was John Hostetler. Always questioning. Always wanting to know things not taught in our school. Folk worried about him." She frowned slightly, folding her hands together on the dark apron she wore. "But then he began courting Anna Schmidt. They had eyes for no one else, those two."

It was odd, he supposed, that he hadn't even thought about his grandmother. "I never knew her."

"She died when her daughter was only twelve." Her eyes clouded with sympathy. "Your maam, that was."

"What was she like? My grandmother?"

Pert and lively like young Elizabeth, who was bouncing up and down as she recited something for Rachel on the other side of the room? Nurturing, like Emma, or brisk and take-charge, like Nancy?

"Sweet-natured. Kind." The old woman smiled, reminiscing. "She was very loving, was Anna. Seemed as if that rubbed off on John when they married. But when she died—" She shook her head. "He turned against everyone. Even God."

Something in him rebelled at that. "Maybe if people had tried to help him, it would have been different."

"We tried." Tears filled her eyes. "For Anna, for himself, for the community. Nothing did any good. He would not listen. He turned against everything Anna was." She shook her head. "She would have been so sad. You understand. She was one who couldn't stop loving and caring."

He nodded, touched by the image of the grandmother who'd barely entered his mind before this. Someone sweet. Loving. Dedicated to family.

He glanced across the room at Rachel, her face lit with laughter as she hugged the little girl.

Like Rachel. Loving. Nurturing. Dedicated to family. Emotion flooded him. He had feelings for her. What was he going to do about that?

"It was in his blood," Liva Zook said suddenly. "Rebellion. He held on to that adornment out of pride, hiding it away and thinking no one knew about it. It took him on a dangerous path, like his grandfather before him."

He blinked. "I'm sorry?" He glanced at Eli. "I don't understand."

Eli bent toward his mother, saying something in a fast patter of the Low German the Amish used among themselves.

She shook her head, replying quickly, almost as if she argued with him. Then she stopped, closing her eyes.

It was unnerving. Had she gone to sleep in the middle of the conversation?

"What did she say?" Eli must know.

Eli shrugged, but his candid blue eyes no longer met Tyler's so forthrightly. "Old folks' gossip, *ja*. She has forgotten now. That's how it is sometimes."

There was more to it than that. His instincts told him. Eli knew perfectly well what his mother meant, but he didn't want to repeat it.

He could hardly cross-examine an elderly woman,

but Eli was another story. "It was you who found him, wasn't it?"

Eli's face tightened. *"Ja,"* he said. "Heard the cows, I did, still in the barn and not milked. I looked inside, saw him."

Eli was the closest thing to an eyewitness he'd find, then. "Where was he?"

"Chust inside the door he was. I could see things was messed up—a lamp broke, his strongbox lying there open. I went for help, but it was too late."

His mouth clamped shut with finality on the words, and for a moment he looked as grim as an Old Testament prophet. Tyler would get nothing else from him.

He thought again of what the elderly woman had said, frowning. He hadn't expected much from this visit. But what he'd heard had raised more questions than it answered.

Chapter Eleven

Rachel leaned against the car window to wave good-bye to Elizabeth, who stood on the porch, her cape wrapped around her, waving vigorously until the car rounded a bend and was lost to her sight.

"She's such a sweetheart." She glanced at Tyler, wondering if he'd say anything to her about what Eli's mother had told him.

The conversation had been general during supper. His manner had probably seemed perfectly natural to the others, but she knew him well enough to sense the preoccupation behind his pleasant manner.

"She certainly is. What was the piece she was talking about? Something she had to memorize?"

So apparently they were going to continue on a surface level. They turned onto the main road, and the Christmas lights seemed to blur for a moment before her eyes.

"The Christmas program in the Amish school is one of the most important events of the year for the chil-

dren. The families, too. The kids practice their pieces
for weeks, and the day of the program you'll see the
buggies lined up for a mile."

"Do they ever invite non-Amish?"

She smiled. "As a matter of fact, we both have an
invitation from Elizabeth to attend. It's the Friday before Christmas."

"If I'm still here—" He left that open-ended.

Well, of course. He probably had a wonderful celebration planned back in Baltimore. He wouldn't hang
around here any longer than was necessary.

She cleared her throat. "I'm glad you had a chance
to try traditional Amish food tonight. Nancy is a great
cook."

"I thought if she urged me to eat one more thing, I'd
burst. I hope I didn't offend her by turning down that
last piece of shoofly pie."

"I expect she understood." She gestured with the
plastic food container on her lap. "And she sent along
a couple of pieces for a midnight snack."

"She obviously loves feeding people. She could go
into business."

They were passing The Willows at the moment,
and she noticed, as always, what her competition had
going on. The Willows looked like a Dickens Christmas this year.

"I wonder—" The idea began to form in her mind,
nebulous at first but firming up quickly.

Tyler glanced at her. "You wonder what?"

"What you said about Nancy's cooking made me
think. If we could offer our guests the opportunity to

have dinner in an Amish home, that might be really appealing."

"Sounds like a nice extra to pull people in. Why don't you go for it, if Nancy and her family are willing?"

"It's a bit more complicated than that." The light was on in the back room of Phil Longstreet's shop. He must be working late.

"Why complicated? Just add it to the website, and you're in business."

"Not complicated at my end. At theirs. Even if Nancy and Samuel are interested, they'd have to get the approval of the bishop first."

He turned into the inn's driveway, darting her a frowning look as they passed under the streetlight. "Don't the Amish have the right to decide things for themselves? Seems pretty oppressive to me."

"They wouldn't see it that way." How to explain an entire lifestyle in a few words? "The Amish way is that of humility, of not being prideful or trying to be better than their neighbors. If something comes up that is not already part of the local Amish way, then the question would be taken to the bishop, and they'd abide by his decision."

"Still seems restrictive to me." He pulled into his usual parking space. "Maybe it would have to my grandfather, too."

"Do you think that's why he left the community?"

For a moment he didn't answer. Her hand was already on the door handle when he shook his head. "No, probably not. Will you stay awhile? I'd like to talk."

"Of course."

He stared through the windshield for a moment. Warmth flowed from the car heater, and the motor sound was a soft background. The windows misted, enclosing them in a private world of their own.

"Eli's mother told me a little about my grandfather. And my grandmother." His shoulders moved restlessly under his jacket. "Funny that I never really thought much about her. But if Mrs. Zook was right, she was really the key to understanding him."

"How do you mean?" She put the question softly, not wanting to disturb the connection between them.

"The way she described her—loving, warm, gentle. It sounds as if she melted his heart. When she died, he apparently turned against everyone."

"That's the last thing she would have wanted."

He shot her a glance. "That's what Mrs. Zook said, too. How did you know?"

"If she was the person you described, then his bitterness was a betrayal of everything she was." Her throat tightened. "So sad. So very sad."

"Yes." His voice sounded tight, as well. He turned toward her, very close in the confined space. "I'm not sure I like knowing this much about my family. They didn't do a good job of making each other happy, did they?"

"I'm sorry." She reached out impulsively to touch his hand, felt it turn and grasp hers warmly. "Sometimes people just make the wrong choices."

He nodded. "Speaking of choices—" He hesitated, and she sensed a moment of doubt. Then his hand gripped hers more firmly. "I didn't tell you about the strongbox that Chief Burkhalter found. Apparently, it's been shoved in a storeroom all these years."

"Did it—did it give you any ideas about what happened?" She held her breath, half afraid of the answer.

"It had apparently been broken into the night my grandfather died. The police chief at the time must have asked my mother what had been in it. I found a list inside. In her handwriting."

She smoothed her hand along his, offering wordless comfort. How hard that must have been for him, still struggling with his grief.

He cleared his throat. "Apparently he'd kept money in there, but there was no way of knowing how much. One thing she seemed sure was missing, though. It was a medal, a German military decoration. There was a pencil rubbing of it, still fairly legible after all this time. Apparently it was something of a family heirloom." He glanced at her. "Seems funny, doesn't it? I mean, the Amish are pacifists, aren't they?"

"Yes, but I suppose it could date from a time before the family became Amish. Or from a non-Amish relative. He might have kept it out of sentiment."

"Or pride. I get the feeling my grandfather really struggled with the whole humility aspect of his faith."

"That's tough for a lot of people, Amish or not."

His square jaw tightened. "There's something else. Something Eli's mother said, about him being rebellious. She said it was in his blood. Talked about him keeping some adornment, keeping it hidden."

"She may have meant the military medal, then." She wasn't sure why that seemed to bother him.

"Maybe." He tapped his hand on the steering wheel. "I could be imagining things, but I thought Eli didn't like her mentioning that. He denied knowing what she was talking about, but I wasn't convinced. He was the one who found my grandfather. Did you know that?"

"You can't imagine Eli had anything to do with your grandfather's death." Her voice sharpened in protest. "He's the most honest, peaceful person I know."

"There could be more involved than you know."

"I know that's ridiculous." Who would he suspect next?

"Maybe so." He didn't seem to react to the tartness in her tone. "In any event, the medal, whatever it means, gives me something that might be traceable. Another road to follow."

"Good. I hope you find something." She also hoped it was something that led away from her family.

"Sorry." He smiled, a little rueful. "I guess I sound obsessed. I can't help following this wherever it takes me. But I do hope—"

"I know." He was very close in the confines of the car, and she could sense the struggle in him. "I know you don't want to hurt me. I mean, us." She felt the warmth flood her cheeks. Thank goodness he wouldn't be able to see in the dim light.

"You." His hand drifted to her cheek, cradling it.

Her breath caught. She could not possibly speak. Maybe there wasn't anything to say. Because his lips lowered, met hers, and everything else slipped away in the moment.

He drew back finally. "I guess maybe we should go in. Before your grandmother wonders what we're doing out here."

It took a moment to catch her breath. To be sure her voice would come out naturally.

"I guess we should." She had to force herself to move, because if she stayed this close to him another moment, they'd just end up kissing again.

She slid out, waiting while he walked around the car to join her. The chill air sent a shiver through her, and she glanced around.

Imagination. It was imagination that put shadows within shadows, that made her feel as if inimical eyes watched from the dark.

Tyler put his arm across her shoulders. The spasm of fear vanished in the strength of his grip, and together they walked toward the house.

"It should be down just a couple of blocks on the right." Rachel leaned forward, watching as Tyler negotiated the narrow side street in Bethlehem late Wednesday afternoon. "I don't see any numbers, but I'll look for the sign."

"It's a good thing we came together. I didn't expect this much traffic. I'd never have found it alone." He touched the brake as a car jolted out into traffic from a parking space.

"Christmas in Bethlehem. It's a magnet for tourists, and the shoppers are out in full force this afternoon."

They were several blocks away from the attraction of the Moravian Museum and the Christkindlmarket, the Christmas craft mart for which Bethlehem was famous, but the small shops in this block had drawn their share of people.

"Are you sure this is the same medal?" She'd been surprised, to put it mildly, when Tyler told her that an internet search had already turned up the medal, or one like it, in a military memorabilia shop in Bethlehem. Since she'd planned to come anyway, it made sense that they do the trip together.

"No, I'm not sure. The dealer had a blurry photo on his website, tough to compare with a pencil rubbing." He frowned, glancing down at the printout that was tucked into the center console. "Still, it's worth checking out—same decoration, turning up in the same general area."

She nodded, not sure how she felt about this. "If it is the medal—well, I suppose if he valued it as much as you say, he probably wouldn't have sold it. But if the medal was stolen that night, where has it been all this time?"

"Might have been in the dealer's hands for years, and he just now got around to putting it up on a website."

He might be overly optimistic about that. The chances of finding the object so easily seemed doubtful to her. But if it was the right medal, and if the dealer remembered who'd sold it to him—

"There it is. In the next block." She couldn't help a thread of apprehension in her voice.

Tyler flipped on the turn signal and backed smoothly into a parking space that she wouldn't even have attempted. "Good. Let's see what we can find out."

A chilly wind cut into her as she stepped out of the car, and she wrapped her jacket tighter around her. Tyler tucked his hand warmly into the crook of her arm as they hurried down the sidewalk, passing antique shop and a craft store.

Military Memorabilia, the sign read. Joseph Whittaker, Owner. Dusty display windows revealed little of what lay inside.

"It'll probably be mostly Minnie balls and shell fragments," she warned. "There are plenty of places where a Civil War enthusiast with a metal detector can come up with those."

"Nothing ventured," Tyler murmured, and pushed open the door.

The shop was just as crowded and disorganized inside as it appeared from the street. Wooden shelves and bins held a miscellaneous accumulation of larger items, while a few glass cases contained what might have been military insignia and decoration. A Union Army uniform hung from a peg near the door, exuding an aroma of wool and mothballs.

An elderly man sat on a stool behind the counter. He unfolded himself slowly, straightening with a smile, and pulled a pair of wire-rimmed glasses from atop scanty white hair to settle them on a pointed nose.

"Welcome, welcome." He dusted off his hands as he came toward them. "What are you folks looking for today? Anything in the military line, I'm bound to have it. The best collection in the county, if I do say so myself."

"I'm looking for a military decoration you have listed on your website." Tyler obviously saw no reason to beat around the bush. He'd be as straightforward in this as in everything else.

"The website." For a moment the man looked confused. "Yes, well, my nephew did that for me. I'm afraid I'm not really up on such things. What was it you were looking for?"

She could sense Tyler's impatience as he pulled the printout from his pocket. "This medal."

The man squinted at the image for a long moment. "Ah, you collect Bavarian military memorabilia. Quite a specialty, that is. I have several pieces you might care to see."

"Just this piece." The impatience was getting a bit more pronounced. "Do you have it?"

He peered again at the sheet. "Well, yes, I'm sure I do. Let me just have a look around." He moved along behind the counter, peering down through the wavy glass and muttering to himself.

Rachel tried not to smile as he vanished around the corner of the shelves, still murmuring. "The White Rabbit," she whispered.

Tyler's frown dissolved in a surprised smile. "Exactly. I suspect he hasn't the faintest idea—"

"Ah, I know." The shopkeeper popped his head around the corner. "My nephew took some things in the back when he photographed them for the website. His new digital camera, you see. Just a moment while

I check." He went through a door that was hidden by what seemed to be half of a medieval suit of armor.

"If he doesn't keep track of his stock any better than that..." she began.

"...he's unlikely to know where it came from. Well, all I can do is try." Tyler drummed his fingers impatiently on the countertop.

It couldn't be this easy. That was what she wanted to say, but it hardly seemed encouraging.

The shopkeeper hustled back in, something dangling from his hand.

"Here we go. I knew I had it somewhere."

Tyler leaned forward, his face tight with concentration. The man put the medal on the glass-top counter, where it landed with a tiny clink.

Dull silver in color, the shape of a Roman cross, with something that might have been a laurel wreath design around it and a profile in the center. Tyler turned it over, frowning at some faint scratches, and then flipped it back. "What can you tell me about it?"

"Fairly rare, I assure you. Early eighteenth-century Bavarian. I'm not an expert on the period, I'm afraid. Civil War is more my area."

Minnie balls, she thought but didn't say.

"How did you come by this?" Tyler's voice sounded casual, but his fingers pressed taut against the glass.

She held her breath. Suppose he said— Well, that was impossible. Her father could not have been involved.

"Came from the collection of Stanley Albright, over at New Holland. Quite a collector, he was, but after he passed away, his widow decided to sell some things off."

"And do you know where he got it?" Tyler's gaze was intent.

The man shook his head. "I'm afraid not, but I assure you it's genuine. Albright knew his stuff, all right."

Since Mr. Albright was no longer around to be questioned, his expertise didn't help. She didn't know whether to be relieved or disappointed.

"Do you think his widow might have any records of his collection?"

"She might," he conceded. "I'm sure I have her number somewhere." He looked around, as if expecting the number to materialize in front of him. "Now about the medal—"

Rachel watched, a bit dissatisfied, as Tyler agreed to the first price that was named. He wasn't used to the routine haggling that the shopkeeper had probably looked forward to. She could have gotten it for at least fifteen percent less, but it wasn't her place to interfere.

She couldn't help commenting when they were back on the street with the medal and Mrs. Albright's phone number tucked into Tyler's pocket. "He didn't expect you to agree to the first amount he named, you know."

"Didn't he?" He looked startled for a moment, and then smiled. "No, of course not. I was just so obsessed with getting it that I didn't think."

"You're convinced this medal is the right one, then." It all seemed too easy to her. Still, the dealer's account held together. Apparently the police hadn't even tried to trace the medal at the time.

He nodded, the smile vanishing. "It's identical to the rubbing, right down to the small chip on one of the points." He put his hand over the pocket containing the medal.

It meant something to him, that memento of the grandfather he'd barely known. Something other than a clue to the thief who'd stolen it.

She glanced at Tyler's face, his brow furrowed in concentration. Thinking about the next step, no doubt.

And where would that next step lead? If Mrs. Albright did indeed have a record of where her husband had gotten the medal, whose name would be it be?

Rachel came out of the second-floor office where she'd picked up the brochures she needed. After they'd been unable to find a parking place on Bethlehem's busy downtown streets, Tyler had dropped her off and gone in search of a lot.

At least this gave her a few moments to compose herself and think this situation through rationally. What did it say about her faith in her father, in her grandfather, that Tyler's discoveries disturbed her so much?

She was being ridiculous, letting his suspicions taint her own belief. Of course, her father, her grandfather, hadn't been involved with the theft of that medal, any more than Eli Zook had been. The very idea was preposterous.

Someone bumped into her, murmuring an apology, and she realized she was blocking traffic in the hallway. People had begun pouring from the display rooms toward the stairs. It must be a tour group, or there wouldn't be so many at once.

Clutching the awkward box firmly against her, she stepped back to let them pass, pressing against the nearest wall. She'd wait until they were gone, and then she'd go down.

She felt it then. The hair lifted on the back of her neck, as if a cold draft blew on her, but there was no draft. Someone was watching her.

She shrugged, trying to push off the feeling. She was in the middle of a crowd. Of course people looked at her as they went by, probably wondering why she was so inconsiderate as to stand there when they were trying to get down the stairs. She could hardly make an announcement, citing the awkward box she carried and the leg that was not always stable on stairs. She wouldn't if she could—she didn't care to let anyone know that.

But this wasn't just a sense of being frowned at by someone who wished she'd move. This was a return of the feeling she'd had that dark night in the sanctuary—the automatic response of the mouse that glimpses the hawk.

Turning a little, she scanned the crowd. Lots of gray heads—this was probably a seniors' tour group, come to enjoy a day of Bethlehem's Christmas celebration. A scattering of families, too—a father in a bright-red anorak carrying a toddler in a snowsuit on his shoulders, a pair of parents wrestling with a stroller and a balky preschool-age child. And a few students, laughing, jostling their neighbors even as they ignored them a bit too obviously. No one stared at her, and there wasn't a soul she knew.

But the feeling persisted, growing stronger by the moment. Then a fresh group swept around the corner, also headed for the stairs, clogging the corridor, and Rachel was carried along with it, helpless as a leaf in the current.

She struggled for a moment and then gave up and let herself be taken along. She had to meet Tyler downstairs in any event, and at least this would take her away from that feeling, whatever caused it.

Maneuvering through the crowd, trying to find something to hold on to, she reached the balcony railing just as she was pushed toward the top step. She grabbed the railing, clutching it with a sense of relief.

At least she had something to hold on to. She'd make it down the stairs all right. Goodness knew it would be impossible to fall—the packed bodies in their winter coats would certainly keep her upright no matter what she did.

An eddy in the crowd pressed her against the railing. It pushed uncomfortably into her side, sending the corner of the box poking into her ribs. She lifted the container, trying to get it out of the way, taking her hand from the railing for a moment.

The crowd lurched, for all the world like a train about to go off the track. Irrational fear pulsed through her. She hated this. She had to get out of it, get away from this feeling of helplessness.

Another, stronger push from behind her, this time

doubling her over the waist-high railing. The box flew from her hands, flipping into the air and then going down, down, until it spattered on the tile floor below.

She tried to hold on to the railing, but it was round, smooth, shiny metal, sliding under her fingers. She didn't have breath to cry out. Someone shoved her again, harder, she was going to go over, she couldn't stop herself, she'd go plummeting down to that hard tile floor, she glimpsed Tyler's startled face in the crowd below, looking up at her—

And then a strong hand grasped her arm and pulled her back. "Easy, now. Are you okay? Get a little dizzy, did you?"

A bronzed face, looking as if its owner spent most of the year on a golf course. He gripped her firmly, smiling, but with apprehension lurking in his eyes.

"Of course she got dizzy." His wife, probably, a small round dumpling of a woman with masses of white hair under a turquoise knit cap. "No wonder, with this crowd. Just take it easy, my dear, and Harold will get you down safely."

Harold was as good as his wife's word, piloting her down the rest of the stairs with a strong hand on her arm. It was a good thing, because it seemed her balance had gone over the railing with the brochures.

And then they reached the bottom, and Tyler's arms closed around her. She lost the next few minutes, hearing a jumble of concern, recommendations that she go somewhere and have a nice cup of tea, Tyler's deep voice assuring her rescuers that he'd take good care of her.

Somehow, in spite of everything that stood between them, she didn't doubt it.

Tyler held Rachel firmly as the helpful couple left, pulling her close against his side. His breathing wasn't back to normal yet, and he was torn between the desire to kiss her and a strong urge to shake her for scaring him so badly.

"Are you okay? I thought for a minute you were going to take a header all the way to the floor." He tried for a light tone, hoping to disguise the panic he'd felt in that moment when he'd seen her falling and been unable to help her.

"So did I." Her voice trembled a little, and she shook her head impatiently. "Silly to be so scared, but it's such a helpless feeling when you're losing control."

His hand tightened on her arm. "Are you hurt?"

"No, not at all." Her smile wasn't quite genuine. "But my brochures—"

"They're over here." He led her into the shadow of the soaring staircase. "About where you'd have landed if someone hadn't grabbed you."

His uneasiness intensified. Either Rachel was accident-prone, or she'd been having a surprising run of misfortune lately.

He gathered up the brochures, stuffing them back into the box, his hands not quite steady. Coincidence, that bad things seemed to be happening to Rachel since his arrival? But not entirely—her accident had occurred before they met. That didn't reassure him.

He kept a firm grip on her as they exited the building. The streets were still crowded, and a band played Christmas carols on the corner. In the glow of the streetlamp and candles from the windows, her face was pale. He read the tension there, and something jolted inside him.

"What is it?" Anxiety sharpened his tone, and he drew her into the shelter of a shop doorway. "There's something more, isn't there?"

She pressed her lips together, staring absently down the crowded street. "It… I must have imagined it." She looked up at him, the color drained from her face. "I thought someone was watching me, upstairs. And when I nearly went over the railing, it felt as if someone pushed me." She shook her head. "I must have imagined it."

The shop door opened behind him, and they had to move to let a couple come out. The irresistible aroma of cinnamon and sugar wafted out with them. The place was a bakery, with several small round tables, empty now.

"Let's get inside and have some coffee. We need to talk about this."

His heart seemed to lurch at her answering smile. The smile trembled for an instant, and her eyes darkened as if she saw right into his heart.

He cleared his throat. He couldn't give in to the urge to kiss her here and now, could he? He held the door, touching her arm to steer her inside.

For an instant she stopped, half in and half out, her eyes focused on the street beyond the plate glass.

"What is it?" He glanced in that direction, seeing nothing but the flow of traffic and the jostling crowds.

"Nothing, I guess." She shook her head, moving past him into the shop. "I thought I saw someone staring at us. I told you my imagination worked overtime."

"Man or woman?"

"Man—youngish, wearing a dark jacket."

He paused, holding the door, scanning the street beyond. Someone had knocked him out trying to break into the farmhouse—someone had frightened Rachel with that stupid trick at the church. Maybe someone had even tampered with the Christmas lights.

Still, why would anyone care what they were doing in Bethlehem today?

He led Rachel to a table, placed the order, ending up getting hot chocolate and an assortment of cookies, and all the while his mind busied itself with the answer to that question.

Someone might well care what they were doing in Bethlehem, because they were following up on his grandfather's murder. And if someone had tried to push Rachel over that railing, it was his fault.

She wrapped her hands around the thick white mug, lifting it to sip gingerly and coming away with a feathering of cream on her lip. She looked at him, eyes wide and serious.

"I might feel better if you told me that was a ridiculous fear, and that no one could possibly have pushed me."

He captured one hand in his. "I might, but I don't like the way things are going. Someone might be worried about what we found out at the shop today. Might think we're getting too close."

She looked down at the frothy liquid. "In that case, you'd think it would be you they'd try to push down the stairs. You're the one who's determined to learn the truth."

"Yes." That bothered him, more than he wanted to admit. "The attack on me seems pretty explainable. Thieves or vandals, hitting me so that they could get away. But you. Why would anyone want to frighten or hurt you?"

"I don't know. I'm not convinced that someone does, not really." Her brow furrowed. "Except— Well I still feel the Christmas lights could have been an accident. But someone was in the church that night." She shivered a little. "And I can't prove it, but someone did push me on the stairs."

"If so—" He felt in his pocket for the medal and pulled it out. "You'd think they'd have been better served by trying to pick my pocket if they're worried about this."

She nodded, watching as he unwrapped the medal. "Let me have a look at it."

He shoved it across the table to her, and she bent over it, studying the surface and then turning it over. Maybe the distraction was good for her. The color seemed to return to her cheeks.

She frowned, staring at the back of it. "Is this some sort of worn inscription, or is it just scratched?"

He held it up to the light, rubbing it with his finger. "I don't know. Maybe if I clean it, we'll be able to make it out." He fingered it a moment longer and then wrapped the tissue paper around it again. "If it could talk, it might give me the answers I need."

"Maybe it will anyway." She seemed to make an effort to meet his eyes. "I'll ask Grams the best way to approach Mrs. Albright. She knows everyone."

"It might be better if you and your grandmother didn't get involved in this. I don't want you put into any further danger."

"Assuming the danger is real, and not just a figment of my imagination or a series of unfortunate accidents." She shook her head. "If I went to Zach Burkhalter— well, he might take it seriously, but what could he do?"

His fingers tightened on hers. "I should move out. Not see you again. Make sure that anyone who's interested knows you have no connection with me."

"And what good would that do?" Her voice was remarkably calm. "If this incident was real, not yet another accident, then it means that the target isn't you. It's me. And I don't know why."

Chapter Twelve

"Thank you, Mrs. Albright, but I really don't care for any more tea. Now if we could just—"

Rachel's frown didn't seem to be working, so she silenced Tyler with a light kick on the ankle. She smiled at the elderly woman across the piecrust tea table, holding out the delicate china cup.

"I'd love another cup. What a nice flavor. It's Earl Grey, I know, but it seems to have extra bergamot."

Mrs. Albright beamed as if Rachel were a favorite pupil. "That's exactly right. I get it from a little shop in Lancaster. If you think your dear grandmother would like it, I'll give you the address."

"That would be lovely." Rachel could feel Tyler seethe with impatience, and she gave him a bland smile. He didn't understand in the least how to deal with someone like Amanda Albright. He undoubtedly saw her as a contemporary of her grandmother, but she was at least ten or fifteen years older, and as delicate and fragile as a piece of the bone china on the tea table.

Elderly ladies in rural areas had their own rules of proper behavior. What Tyler didn't realize was that if he'd come alone, he'd never have gotten in the door, let alone be having tea in a parlor that was as perfect in its period detail as its mistress. Only her own vague memories of having been taken to tea with some of Grams's friends as a child had come to her rescue.

"You're running a bed-and-breakfast inn at the Unger house now, I understand. Just a nice, genteel occupation for a young girl, and I'm sure your grandmother is delighted to have you there."

Normally she'd have choked at the prospect of being called a young girl, but in this case it was best just to smile and nod. "I'm glad to be settled at home again."

Mrs. Albright nodded, eyes bright and curious as she looked from Rachel to Tyler. "And you, young man. What do you do?"

"I'm a partner in an architectural firm in Baltimore. Now about the collection—"

Rachel kicked him again. "Tyler has family ties here, though. His maternal grandparents were John and Anna Hostetler."

"Ah, of course." One could almost see the wheels turning as she ticked through the possibilities. "John had his faults, no one could deny that, but generally good, sturdy stock. Very appropriate."

Tyler had his mouth full of butter cookie at the time, and a few crumbs escaped when he sputtered in response.

Rachel set her cup down, hoping the tiny clatter masked his reaction and trying to stifle a smile of her own. She'd known what was going on from the moment they'd sat down on the petit-point chairs. Amanda Albright was sizing up Tyler's potential as a match for her dear friend Katherine's granddaughter.

Explaining that she and Tyler didn't have that kind of relationship would only confuse the issue, and Mrs. Albright probably wouldn't believe it, anyway. She had her own agenda, and nothing would deter her. It was different probably, in Tyler's brisk urban life, but in country places like this, the gossip around any young couple would include the suitability of the family lines for several generations back.

"Tyler is settling his grandfather's estate, and in the process he's located a piece that originally belonged to the family." Now that she had firmly linked their mission to the personal, it was time to broach the subject.

She nodded to Tyler. Finally recognizing his cue, he took a tissue-wrapped package from his pocket and opened it to divulge the medal.

"The dealer said that he'd purchased it from your husband's collection." He held it out for Mrs. Albright to see.

She raised the glasses that hung on a gold chain around her neck. "Yes, indeed, that was part of my Stanley's collection." She shook her head. "I didn't want to part with any of it, but my niece persuaded me to begin clearing a few of the things that don't have personal meaning to me."

"Did your husband happen to keep records of the origin of the items he acquired?" Tyler sounded as if he had faint hope of that.

"Certainly he did." She was obviously affronted that he would think otherwise.

"That was very wise of him," Rachel soothed. "So few people are as organized as he was. Do you think we might be able to find out when and from whom he purchased this medal? It was certainly help Tyler in—" she could hardly say in investigating his grandfather's death "—in understanding his family history."

"That's very proper. I wish more young people took an interest, instead of leaving genealogical research to their elders." She rose with a faint rustle of silk. "Just come into my husband's library, and we'll have a look."

Tyler had sprung to his feet as soon as she moved, and he stepped back to let her pass. Behind Mrs. Albright's back, he clasped Rachel's hand for a quick squeeze.

She retrieved her hand and followed their hostess into the next room, hoping she wasn't blushing. Well, if she was, Mrs. Albright would just think—

She stopped, struggling with the idea. Mrs. Albright would think there was something between them. She already thought that. And there was certainly something, but the chances of it leading to a real relationship were slim, maybe nonexistent.

Mrs. Albright leaned over file cabinets against the wall, peering at the labels. "Your eyes are better than mine, young man. You check for it. He organized every item in his collection and each antique in the house by type, and kept a file with its provenance."

Tyler moved with alacrity, running his finger down the file drawer labels and then pulling out one of the drawers. He paused, glancing at Mrs. Albright. "Would you like me to look through the files, or would you prefer to do it?"

She shook her head, waving her hand slightly. "You find it. I think I'll just sit down for a bit."

"Are you all right?" Rachel grasped her arm. "Would you like me to get you something?"

"No, no, I'm fine." But she let Rachel help her to the nearest chair. "This was Stanley's province, you know. I can't come in here without seeing him sitting in that chair, his nose buried in a book, his pipe on the table beside him."

Rachel patted her hand. "It must be so difficult."

"Sixty-one years, we had." She sighed. "I never thought I'd be the one to go on without him."

"I'm sorry if our coming has been difficult. Perhaps we could come another time to look for it—"

"That won't be necessary." Tyler's voice had an odd note. "I've found it." He carried a manila file folder to her.

She took it, almost afraid to look. *Please Lord. Not my father. He couldn't have, could he?*

She forced herself to scan the page. The medal was listed, with a minute description. The date Albright had purchased it. Her heart thudded. A year after John Hostetler died.

And the seller. Phillip Longstreet, of Longstreet's Antiques.

Tyler came down the stairs, suppressing the urge to take them a couple at a time. The Unger mansion, even in its incarnation as an inn, seemed to discourage that sort of thing. Nothing wrong with that, except that at the moment his muscles tensed with the need to do something—anything that would resolve this situation and lead him to the truth.

Rachel came out of the family side as he hit the hallway, almost as if she'd been listening for him. Her green eyes were anxious as they searched his face.

"Did you talk to Chief Burkhalter? What did he say?"

His jaw tightened. There was nothing, he supposed, that dictated that he had to tell Rachel. But she'd gone out of her way to help him, in spite of what must have seemed like very good reasons to tell him to get out.

Besides, he'd gotten to like the idea that he wasn't in this alone. "I talked to him." He grimaced. "He pointed out that there could be several perfectly innocent ways for Longstreet to come by that medal."

"And one guilty one." She shook her head. "I couldn't believe it when I saw his name. And I still can't, not really. He's been a fixture in the community his entire life. Surely, if there was anything to be known, someone would have talked about it by now."

"People can do a good job of keeping a secret when their lives depend on it."

She paled, as if she hadn't considered that outcome. "Your grandfather died from a heart attack, but if it was brought on by the robbery, it could be considered murder."

"Exactly." He shrugged. "I can't blame Chief Burkhalter for moving cautiously. Longstreet is well-known around here. But I've had the sense from you that he's not entirely respected."

"I certainly never meant he was dishonest. Just— maybe a bit too eager to make a good deal. If there had been rumors of anything else—well, I haven't heard them. But Zach Burkhalter would have. He knows what's going on. You can rely on him."

"He said he'd investigate."

"But you're not satisfied." She seemed to know him as well as he knew himself.

"No." His hands curled into fists. "I can't just wait around, hoping he's asking the right questions. I have to do something."

Rachel put her hand on his arm, as if she'd deter him by force, if necessary. "What?"

"See Longstreet. Get some answers myself, before he has time to make up some elaborate cover story."

Her fingers tightened. "Tyler, you can't do that. The chief would have a fit. You'd be interfering in his investigation."

"That's probably true."

"But you're going anyway." She shook her head. "Then I'm going with you."

He frowned. "I don't want to be rude, but I didn't invite you."

"I'm not going to let you confront Phil Longstreet and get yourself in trouble." Her smile flickered. "It would reflect badly on the inn if you were arrested while staying here."

"Or on you? You've been seen in my company quite a bit."

Her eyes widened and then slid away from his. "All the more reason to keep you out of trouble." Her voice wasn't quite steady.

He resisted the impulse to touch her. What was wrong with him? He couldn't pursue a romantic relationship and confront a thief at the same time.

"I'm not going to be violent. Just talk to him."

"You should still have an independent witness," she said. "I'll get my jacket. Are you going to walk over?"

He nodded, waiting while she hurried off to get a jacket. He could leave without her, but she'd just follow him. And what she said made a certain amount of sense. If Longstreet let anything slip, it would be as well to have a third party hear it.

He heard her coming, saying something firm to the dog, who probably scented a walk in the offing.

"Later," she said, pushing an inquiring muzzle back and shutting the door. She turned to him. "I'm ready."

Outside, the air was crisp and cold. It was already dusk—they'd been longer getting back from their meeting with Mrs. Albright than he'd expected. Christmas traffic, Rachel had said.

"I hope Mrs. Albright wasn't tired too much by our visit." Rachel seemed to be reading his thoughts.

"She wouldn't have needed to turn it into a tea party." A few flakes of snow touched his face, and he tilted his head back to look up. "Snow. Are they predicting much?"

"A couple of inches by morning. Good thing we went over to New Holland today." She smiled. "As far as the tea party was concerned—you have to understand that's her way. She wouldn't have talked with you at all, probably, if Grams hadn't been the intermediary."

"Something else I owe to you and your grandmother. I appreciate it." Especially since none of them knew where this investigation would lead. Would it stop at Longstreet? Somehow he doubted it.

"About Mrs. Albright—" Rachel's mind was obviously still on their encounter with the elderly woman. The Christmas lights on the window of the florist shop they were passing showed him her face in images of green and red. "She jumped to some conclusions. About us, I mean. I hope that didn't embarrass you."

"No. But you look as if it did you." The rose in her cheeks wasn't entirely from the Christmas lights.

Her gaze evaded his. "Of course not. Setting young people up in pairs is a favorite local hobby of elderly women. I didn't want you to think—well, it's ridiculous, that's all."

Without a conscious decision, his hand closed over hers. "Is it so ridiculous, Rachel?"

She looked up, and a snowflake tangled in her hair. Another brushed her cheek. "We hardly know each other." She sounded breathless.

"Timewise. But we've come a long way in a short period of time." All the more reason to be cautious, the logical part of his mind insisted, but he didn't want to listen.

"Maybe too far." It came out in a whisper that seemed to linger on the chill air.

"I don't think so." He wanted to touch the snowflakes that clustered more thickly now on her hair. Wanted to warm her cold lips with his.

But they'd reached the corner. And across the street was the antique shop, its lights spilling out onto the sidewalk that was covering quickly with snow.

He'd come here for answers, he reminded himself. Not romance. And some of the answers had to be found inside that shop.

The bell over the door jingled, announcing their arrival. Rachel could only hope that Phil would attribute her red cheeks to the temperature outside, instead of seeing the hint of something more. He was usually far too observant about the state of other people's feelings—probably part of what made him a success as a dealer.

Still, in a few minutes he'd have far more to think about than the state of her emotions. Apprehension tightened her stomach and dispelled the warmth that had flooded her at Tyler's words.

As for Tyler—a swift glance at his strong-boned face told her he'd dismissed it already. Well, that was only appropriate. They had far more serious things to deal with right now.

"Rachel. Tyler." Phil emerged from behind the counter, a smile wreathing his face. He came toward them, hands extended in welcome. "How nice this is. I was beginning to think I might as well close early. The threat of snow sends people scurrying to the grocery for bread and milk instead of to an antique shop."

"We walked over, so the snow wasn't an issue."

She brushed a damp curl back from her cheek. Maybe she shouldn't have said anything, but she could hardly avoid greeting a man she'd known for years.

"Well, what can I do for you this evening?" He rubbed his hands together. "A little Christmas shopping for your grandmother? I have some nice porcelain figures that just came in."

She glanced at Tyler, willing him to take the lead. His face was taut, giving nothing away but a certain amount of tension.

"Actually there was something I wanted to talk with you about. A piece of military memorabilia that I ran across recently."

Phil shook his head, his smile still in place. "Afraid I can't help you there. China, silver, period furniture, that's my area. You'd have to see someone who specializes in military."

He was talking too much, being too helpful. The instinctive reaction was so strong she couldn't doubt it. Phil's normal attitude with a customer who expressed interest in something he didn't have was to try to turn them to something he did.

Did Tyler realize that? Probably so.

"I already know about the object. A Bavarian military medal, early 1700s. Sound familiar?" His tone wasn't quite accusing.

Phil turned the question away with a smile. "Sorry. As I said, not my area."

It wasn't, Rachel realized. That made it all the more unusual that it had passed through his hands.

"It came from the collection of Stanley Albright,

over in New Holland. You've dealt with him, I suppose?" Tyler would not be deflected or halted. He just kept driving toward his goal.

Phil's smile finally faded. "I knew Albright, certainly. Every dealer in the area knew him. Just like every dealer knows his widow is starting to sell off some of his things. I keep up with the news, but that's too rich for my blood, I'm afraid."

He tried a laugh, but it wasn't convincing. Rachel's heart chilled. Up until this moment she'd convinced herself that there was some mistake, that Phil would explain it all away.

He'd try, she knew that much. But she wouldn't believe him.

"You didn't sell him anything?" Tyler's tone was smooth, but she sensed the steel behind it.

"No, can't say I ever had the pleasure." Phil took a casual step back, groping behind him to put his hand on a glass display case filled with a collection of ivory pillboxes.

"Odd. Because Mrs. Albright says you sold him just such a medal about twenty-two years ago."

Phil was as pale as the ivory. "That's ridiculous. I tell you I never handled anything like that. Mrs. Albright must be—what, ninety or so? She's probably mixed up. She never knew anything about his collection, anyway."

He was talking too much, giving himself away with every defensive word. Tyler should have left this to Chief Burkhalter, or at least made sure Burkhalter was around to hear this. Zach Burkhalter would know Phil was lying, just as she did.

"That might be true." Tyler's voice was deceptively soft. "The thing is, I'm not taking her word for it. If you know anything about Albright's collection, you should know he kept meticulous records. It was there—his purchase from you, a description of the medal, even the date he bought it."

Phil turned away, aimlessly touching objects on the countertop, but she saw his face before he could hide his expression. He looked ghastly.

"I suppose you know what significance this is supposed to have, but I'm sure I don't. I suppose it's possible that the odd military piece might have passed through my hands at some point in my career. I really don't remember."

"Don't you?" Tyler took a step closer, his hands clenched so tightly that the knuckles were white. "Funny, I'd think you'd remember that. The medal belonged to my grandfather. It was stolen from his house the night he died."

He'd gone too far—she knew that instantly. He couldn't be positive the medal had gone missing that particular night, even if he were morally sure of it.

Phil straightened, grasping the significance as quickly as she did. He swung around to face Tyler, his face darkening.

"I've been accused of a lot of things, but this is a first. I doubt very much that you could convince anyone, including the police, that the medal was stolen, or that it disappeared the night he died. Your grandfather could have sold it himself."

"Are you saying you got it from him?"

"No, certainly not. But he could have sold it to someone else."

"He didn't. He wouldn't. It was important to him. He wouldn't have let it go."

Phil shrugged, seemingly on surer ground now. "We just have your opinion for that, don't we? The old man was on the outs with everyone, even his own family. Who knows what he might have done? All your detective work, running from Bethlehem to New Holland—"

Before she could guess his intent, Tyler's hand shot out, stopping short of grabbing the front of Phil's expensive cashmere sweater by an inch. Phil leaned back against the showcase, losing color again.

"I didn't mention Bethlehem. How did you know we went there?" He shot a glance at Rachel, but she wasn't sure he saw her. At least, not her as a person, just a source of information. "Could he be the man you saw watching us?"

Startled, she stared at Phil, certainty coalescing. "No. Not him. But I know who it was. I knew he looked familiar. It was one of those men who were loading the truck that first time we came. The men you said worked for you, Phil."

Now Tyler did grab the sweater. "Did you send him to watch us? Did he try to push Rachel down the stairs?"

"No, no, I wouldn't. If he—if he was there, it didn't have anything to do with me."

"You were involved. You had the medal. You sold it, months after my grandfather died. I suppose you thought it would disappear into a private collection and never surface again. But it did. Now, where did you get it?"

"Tyler, don't." Her heart thudded, and she tugged at his arm. "Don't. You shouldn't—"

He wasn't listening. Neither of them were.

Phil shook his head from side to side. "I didn't. I didn't do anything. I bought it." He glanced at Rachel, a swift, sidelong gaze. "I bought it like I bought a lot of little trinkets around that time."

"Who?" She found her voice. "Who sold it to you?"

"I'm sorry, Rachel."

He actually did sound sorry. Sorry for her. Her heart clutched. She wanted to freeze the moment, to stop whatever he was going to say next. But she couldn't.

He cleared his throat, looking back at Tyler. "I bought the medal from Rachel's father."

Chapter Thirteen

If her head would just stop throbbing, maybe Rachel could make sense of what everyone was saying. Her mind had stopped functioning coherently at the instant Phil made that outrageous claim about her father. The next thing she knew, she was sitting in the library at the inn, Grams close beside her on the couch, clutching her hand.

Zachary Burkhalter sat across from them. The police chief should look uncomfortable with his long frame folded into that small lady's armchair, but at the moment he was too busy looking annoyed with Tyler.

Tyler. Her heart seemed to clench, and she had to force herself to look at him. He sat forward on the desk chair that had been her grandfather's, hands grasping its mahogany arms, waiting. If he was moved by the chief's comments, he wasn't showing it. He simply waited, face impassive, emotionless.

That was a separate little hurt among all the larger ones. Such a short time ago, he'd said—hinted, at least, that there was a future for them. Now, he thought her father was a murderer.

"I told you I'd investigate." Burkhalter's tone was icy. "If you'd been able to restrain yourself, we might have been able to gather some hard evidence. You can't just go around accusing respectable citizens of murder."

"*You* can't." Tyler didn't sound as if he regretted a single action. "I'm not the police. At least I got an admission from him. What hard evidence do you expect to unearth at this point?"

"Probably none, now that you've jumped in with both feet and tipped Longstreet off that he's under suspicion. If there is anything, he had a chance to get rid of it before I could get a search warrant."

"Is Phillip under arrest?" Grams's voice was a thin echo of her usual tone, and her hands, clasped in Rachel's, were icy.

Burkhalter's expression softened when he looked at her. "No. The district attorney isn't ready to charge him with anything at this point. We're looking for the man who works for him—the one you thought was following you in Bethlehem. He may shed some light. And it's possible we might trace some of the things that have been stolen recently to him."

Rachel cleared her throat, unable to remember when she'd last spoken. Shock, probably. Anger would be better than this icy numbness, and she could feel it beginning to build, deep within her.

"What does Longstreet say now?" Impossible to believe she was talking about someone she'd considered a friend, someone she'd worked with and argued with on a project that had been so important to both of them.

And all the time—all those meetings when he'd sat across from her, when they'd shared a smile at some ridiculous suggestion from Sandra, when they'd talked plans for Churchville's future—all that time he'd been hiding this.

"He sticks to his first statement. Says he bought the medal, and some other small collectible pieces, from your father shortly before he left town. Claims to have been guilty of nothing more than not inquiring too closely where the objects came from."

Tyler stirred. "He knew. He had to."

"He's confident we won't prove it at this late date." Burkhalter turned to Grams. "I don't want to distress you, Mrs. Unger, but I have to ask. Longstreet implied that some of the things he bought might have come from this house. Did you ever suspect your son-in-law of stealing from you?"

Grams's hands trembled, and Rachel's anger spurted to the surface. "Leave her alone. Can't you see how upset she is? You have no right—"

"No, Rachel." Her grandmother stiffened, back straight, head high, the way she always met a challenge. "Chief Burkhalter has his duty to do, as do I." The fine muscles around her lips tensed. "We had suspicions, that summer. Things disappeared, perhaps mislaid. A silver snuffbox, an ivory-inlaid hand mirror, a few pieces of Georgian silver. My husband thought that my daughter's husband was responsible."

"Did he accuse Hampton?" Tyler was as cold as if

he spoke of strangers. Well, they were strangers to him. Just not to her. Her heart seemed to crack.

Grams shook her head slowly. "Not at first. He wanted to, but I was afraid."

"You're never afraid," Rachel said softly. She smoothed her fingers over her grandmother's hand, the bones fragile under soft skin.

"I was afraid of losing you and your sisters." Grams's eyes shone with tears. "I was a coward. I didn't want an open breach. But we lost you anyway."

"Not at first?" Burkhalter echoed. "Did there come a time when that happened?"

"Something vanished that my husband prized—a cameo that had been his grandmother's, supposedly a gift from a descendant of William Penn. He'd intended it for one of our granddaughters. That was the last straw, as far as he was concerned. But before he could do anything, Donald was gone. Maybe he guessed Frederick was about to confront him."

"Didn't people wonder about it?" Tyler asked. "Hampton disappearing so soon after my grandfather's death?"

Burkhalter shrugged. "I've done some inquiring. As far as I can tell, Hampton came and went so much that nobody questioned his leaving at that particular time. You don't automatically suspect someone of a crime for that."

"Of course not!" The words burst out of Rachel. She couldn't listen to this any longer. "This is my father you're talking about. My father. He wouldn't do anything like that."

Grams patted her hand. Tyler said her name, and she turned on him.

"This is your fault. You're trying to make yourself feel better by blaming all this on my father." She was standing, body rigid, hands clasped, feeling as if she'd go up in flames if anyone tried to touch her. "He didn't do it. He wouldn't do anything to hurt anyone. He was gentle, and charming, and he loved his children. He loved me." She was eight again, her heart breaking, her world ripping apart. "He loved me."

She spun and raced out of the room before the sobs that choked her had a chance to rip free and expose her grief and pain to everyone.

Rachel came down the stairs from her bedroom, glancing at her watch. Nearly seven and dark already, of course, although the lights on Main Street shone cheerfully and pedestrians were out and about, probably doing Christmas shopping. The house was quiet, the insistent voices that had pushed her to the breaking point silenced now.

She rounded the corner of the stairs into the kitchen. Grams sat at the table, a cup of tea steaming in front of her, Barney curled at her feet. He spotted her first, welcoming her with a gentle woof.

Grams looked up, her blue eyes filled with concern. "Rachel, you must be hungry. I'll get some soup—"

Rachel stopped her before she could get up, dropping a kiss on her cheek. "I'll get it. It smells as if Emma left some chicken pot pie on the stove."

"She sent Levi over with it. She knows it's your favorite."

Rachel poured a ladleful into an earthenware bowl, inhaling the rich aroma of chicken mingled with the square pillows of dough that were Emma's signature touch. "That was lovely of her. Please tell me the entire neighborhood hasn't found out about our troubles so soon."

"People talk. And I'm sure quite a few heard a garbled version of the police searching Longstreet's antiques and saw the police car parked in our driveway." Grams sounded resigned to it. She'd spent her life in country places and knew how they functioned. "Did you sleep any, dear?"

Rachel sank into the chair opposite her, pushing her hair back with both hands. "A little." After she'd cried her heart out—for her father, for the trouble that would hurt everyone she loved, for what might have been with Tyler and was surely gone now. "I guess I made an exhibition of myself, didn't I?"

"Let's say it startled everyone," Grams said dryly. "Including you, I think."

She nodded and forced herself to put a spoonful into her mouth, to chew, to swallow. The warmth spread through her. Small wonder they called this comfort food.

"I thought I'd accepted it a long time ago. Maybe I never did." She met her grandmother's gaze across the table. "This business of Daddy taking things from the house—did Mother know?"

"She never admitted it if she did." She sighed, shaking her head. "That was what precipitated her taking you away. She was upset and angry over your father leaving, and Frederick—well, his patience ran out. He said, 'At least we no longer have a thief in the house.'"

She'd thought she was finished crying, but another tear slid down her cheek. "You tried to stop them from fighting. I remember that." They'd huddled at the top of the stairs, she and Andrea, listening to the battle raging below, understanding nothing except that their lives were changing forever.

"It was no good. They were both too stubborn, and things were said that neither of them would forget." She took a sip of the tea and then set the cup back in the saucer with a tiny *ching*. "I thought all that unhappiness was over and done with, and that with you and Andrea back, we could just be happy."

"I guess the past is always ready to jump out and bite you. If Tyler had never come—" That hurt too much to go on.

"Perhaps it was meant to be. I know we can't see our way clear at the moment, but God knows the way out."

The faintest smile touched her lips. "When I was little, you told me God was always there to take my hand when I was in trouble."

"He still is, Rachel. Just reach out and take it." Grams stood, carrying her cup to the sink. "I believe I'll read for a while, unless you'd like company."

Rachel shook her head. "After I finish this, I'll take Barney out for a little walk. The cold air will do us both good."

"Don't go on Crossings Road, dear. Not after dark."

"I won't." Grams couldn't help remembering her accident. "We'll take a walk down Main Street, where the shops are still open."

Grams came to pat her cheek and then headed for the steps. "Look in on me when you get back."

"I will. I love you, Grams."

"I love you, too, Rachel."

Barney trotted happily at her heels a few minutes later as she pulled jacket, hat and mittens from the closet. He knew the signs of an impending walk, even if no one said the word.

She stepped outside, the dog running immediately to investigate the snow, not content until he'd rolled over several times in it. Must be close to four inches, but it had stopped at some time since she'd come back from the antique shop. The sky above was clear now, and thick with stars.

She whistled to Barney and started down the street. Grams hadn't mentioned Tyler's whereabouts, but his car wasn't in its usual spot, so he was probably out to dinner. Or even moving out.

She tried to ignore the bruised feeling around her heart. Tyler believed her father guilty of killing his grandfather. They could never get past that in a million years, so it was better not to try.

She tilted her head back. The stars seemed incredibly close, as if she could reach out and pick a frosty handful.

Why did You bring him into my life, when it was bound to end so badly? I thought I was content with things the way they were, and now—

God is always there to take your hand. Grams's words echoed and comforted.

I don't see my way through this. Lord. I don't know how many more hard lessons there are to learn. Please, hold my hand.

Comforted. Yes, that was what she felt. She didn't see any farther, but she didn't feel alone.

Barney danced along the sidewalk, dodging shoppers—some locals that she knew, a few tourists. The Christmas lights shone cheerfully, and in every window she saw posters for the Holiday Open House Tour.

Funny. It had occupied an important place in her mind for weeks, as if its success marked her acceptance as part of this community. Now it was almost here, and she didn't feel her customary flicker of panic. There were too many more important things to worry about. The tour would go on, no matter what happened in the private lives of its organizers.

She passed Sandra and Bradley Whitmoyer's spacious Victorian, ablaze with white lights and evergreens, a lighted tree filling the front window. Across the snowy street, Longstreet's Antiques seemed to be closed, the shop dark.

Would the police have searched thoroughly? She couldn't imagine Zach Burkhalter undertaking anything without doing it well, and he'd probably love to tie recent antique thefts to Phil. But he didn't think there was enough evidence to charge Phil with anything from the past. That had been clear from his manner.

It had also been clear that he pitied her. That he

agreed with Tyler's assessment. That her father had been guilty of that terrible thing.

She stopped, staring at the shop. Barney pressed against her leg, whining a little.

Odd. The shop was dark, but she could glimpse a narrow wedge of light from the office. Phil must still be there.

If she talked to him again—just the two of them. Not Tyler. Not the police. Just two people who had been friends. Would he tell her about her father? Would he help her understand this?

She shouldn't. Chief Burkhalter had been angry enough with Tyler for his interference. He'd be furious with her if she did any such thing.

It was her father. She had a right to know. And the idea of being afraid to talk to Phil, of all people, was simply ridiculous. Snapping her fingers to Barney, she crossed the street, her boots crunching through the ruts left by passing cars.

She reached for the knob, expecting the door to be locked, but the knob turned under her hand. She'd have expected Phil to stay open tonight, like the other shops, but if he'd closed, why hadn't he locked up?

She stepped inside, reassured by the tinkle of the bell over the door and the feel of the dog, pressing close beside her.

"Phil? It's Rachel. Can I talk with you for a minute?"

No answer. The door to the office was ajar, a narrow band of light shining through it, reflecting from the glass cases.

"Phil?" she shivered in spite of the warmth of the shop, starting toward the light.

And froze at a rustle of movement somewhere in the crammed shop.

Her hand clenched Barney's collar. She felt the hair rise on the ruff of his neck, heard a low, rumbling growl start deep in his throat.

Danger, that's what he was saying. *Danger.*

She held her breath, though it was too late for that. If someone lurked in the shadows, she'd already announced herself, hadn't she?

She took a careful step toward the outside door, hand tight on Barney's collar, trying to control him. He strained against her, growling at something she couldn't see in the dark.

A step matched hers. Someone on the other side of an enormous Dutch cabinet moved when she did. Fear gripped her throat. Scream, and hope someone on the street heard before he reached her? Let Barney go?

She hesitated too long. Before she could move, a dark figure burst from behind the cabinet, arm upraised. She stumbled backward, losing her hold on the dog, she was falling, he'd be on her—

Barney lunged, snapping and snarling. Something crashed into a glass display case, shattering it, shards of glass flying. Dog and man grappled in the dark, and she fled toward the office, bolted inside, slammed and locked the door, breath coming in sobbing gasps.

Barney— But she couldn't help him. She had to call—

She turned, blinking in the light while she fumbled in her bag for her phone. And stopped.

Phil Longstreet lay on the floor between his elegant Sheraton desk and the door. His arms were outflung, hands open. Blood spread from his head, soaking into the intricate blue-and-wine design of the Oriental carpet.

Tyler wrenched the steering wheel and spun out of the snowy driveway at the inn, tension twisting his gut. He'd come back to the inn from supper to find Katherine in shock. Phil Longstreet was in the hospital, and Rachel was at the police station.

Incredible. Surely the police couldn't believe that Rachel—gentle, nurturing Rachel—could harm anyone. But he doubted that the police made their decisions based on someone's apparent character.

Think, don't just react, he admonished himself. Katherine Unger had rushed to him the instant he walked in the door. Her incoherent explanation of events had been interspersed with Emma's equally hard-to-understand pleas for her to be calm, to go and lie down, to stop exciting herself.

Finally he'd gotten both of them enough under control to get the bare facts they knew. Rachel had gone out with the dog for a short walk on Main Street. A half hour later, just when her grandmother was starting to worry, a policeman had appeared at the inn with the dog, saying that Phillip Longstreet had been injured and that Rachel was at the station, helping the police inquiry.

Emma had to restrain Katherine from rushing out into the snowy night without even a coat.

"Go after her, please, go after her." She'd grasped his arm, holding on to him as if he were a lifeline. "Someone has to be with her, to protect her. Please, Tyler. She needs you."

He clasped her hands between his. "I'll take care of her." He glanced at Emma. "And you'll take care of Mrs. Unger."

"*Ja,* I will." Emma put her own shawl around Katherine's shoulders and drew her toward the library. "Come. You come. Tyler will do it."

Now he was forced to slow down, watchful of the small group of pedestrians who hovered on the edge of the street, trying to see what was happening inside the antique shop. He passed a police car and then pulled to the curb in front of the police station, heedless of the No Parking sign.

He raced across the sidewalk, up the two steps and shoved the door open. A young patrolman looked up from the desk, telephone receiver pressed against his ear.

"Rachel Hampton. Where is she?"

"She's with the chief." He glanced toward the door to the inner office with what seemed a combination of fear and excitement. "They can't be disturbed."

"Is there an attorney with her? Because if not, I'm certainly going to disturb them."

"Now, sir—"

The door opened and Zach Burkhalter came out,

closing it behind him, looking at Tyler with an annoyed glare.

"Mr. Dunn. Now, why am I not surprised that you've turned up here?"

"You're talking to Rachel Hampton. If she doesn't have an attorney with her—"

"Ms. Hampton isn't being charged with anything. And she said she doesn't want an attorney."

Tyler's eyes narrowed. "I'd like to hear that from her." Maybe it was better if he didn't look too closely at the emotions that drove him right now.

Burkhalter's annoyance seemed to fade into resignation. He opened the door. "Go ahead."

A few more steps took him into the room, and the sight of Rachel sent everything else out of his mind. She sat on a straight-backed chair in the small office, huddled into the jacket that was wrapped around her shoulders. It wasn't cold in the room, but she shivered as she looked up at him.

"Tyler." She blinked, as if she were close to tears. "Phillip…did you hear about him? About what happened?"

"Shh. It's all right." He knelt next to her chair, taking her icy hands in his and trying to warm them with his touch.

A sidelong glance told him that Burkhalter had left the door open, and there was no sound from the outer office. They'd hear anything that was said here.

"But Phillip—"

He put his hand gently across her lips. "Don't. Just tell me what the chief asked you."

The truth was that he liked Burkhalter—he judged him a good man and probably a good cop. But he *was* a cop, and that's how he thought.

"He wanted me to tell him exactly what happened." Her eyes were wide and dark with shock. "I told him. I was out for a walk with Barney, and I saw that the office light was on at the antique shop. I thought I should talk to Phil. Just as a friend, that's all, to try and understand."

"The shop was unlocked?" His mind worked feverishly. She'd already told this to the police, so it was as well that she told him, too. He had to understand what they were dealing with.

She nodded. "I went in, calling his name. He didn't answer. And then I realized someone else was there, in the shop."

Fear jagged through him. "Did he hurt you?"

"I'm all right." But she didn't sound all right. "Barney went after him. Gave me time to run into the office and lock the door."

"Did you see his face? Who was it?"

She shook her head. "I never got a look at him. And then I saw Phil lying on the floor. His head—" She stopped, biting her lip.

He smoothed his hands over hers. "What did you do next? Did you try to help him?"

"I was afraid of making things worse. I thought I shouldn't touch the things on his desk, so I used my cell phone to call the police."

If she hadn't touched anything else in the office, that

was good, but she'd undoubtedly been in there before, maybe touched things then.

Her fingers gripped his suddenly. "The paramedics wouldn't tell me anything, but it didn't look good. They took him to the hospital. Someone must know by now how he is."

Burkhalter came back into the office on her words, as if he'd been listening. For an instant he eyed Tyler, kneeling next to Rachel, as if he weighed their feelings for each other.

Well, good luck figuring that out. He didn't know, himself. He just knew that Rachel needed help and he was going to make sure she got it.

"What about it, Chief?" He rose, standing beside Rachel, his hands on her shoulders. "The hospital must have been in touch with you."

The chief's stoic expression didn't change for a moment. Then he shrugged. "Longstreet is in serious condition with a head injury."

"Is he conscious?"

"No." He bit off the word.

That meant that the police had no idea when or if Longstreet would be able to talk to them. He tightened his grip on Rachel's shoulders. "I'm sure Ms. Hampton has already helped you as much as she can. It's time she was getting home."

"If we went over her story again, we might—"

"She's told you everything. She's exhausted and upset, and she probably should be seen by a doctor. Is she being charged with anything?"

Rachel moved at that, as if it was the first time she'd

realized that she might be under suspicion. His grip warned her to be still.

Burkhalter leaned against his desk, arms crossed, looking at them. "Charged? No. But from my point of view, she quarreled with Longstreet earlier in the day. She was upset about his accusations against her father. She went to the shop."

"But I didn't—"

His grip silenced her. "She's not saying another word without an attorney present." Somehow he didn't think Burkhalter wanted to press this, not now, at least.

Burkhalter eyed him. "Actually, you had a quarrel with Longstreet today, too. And a reason to have a grudge against him."

"And I was at the Brown Bread Café having dinner this evening, which you can easily check."

The chief looked at him for a long moment, then he nodded. "You can go now, both of you. We'll talk again. Please be available."

He took Rachel's arm as she rose, but she seemed steady enough now. She looked at Burkhalter with something of defiance in her eyes.

"I won't be going anywhere, Chief Burkhalter. I have a business to run." She turned and walked steadily out of the office.

Tyler followed her through the outer office, holding the door while she went out into the street. It was dark, cold and still. The crowd had dissipated, so Rachel wouldn't have to endure their curious gazes.

"My car is right here." He piloted her to the door. "Your grandmother—"

Her knees seemed to buckle, and he caught her, folding his arms around her and holding her close. "It's okay," he murmured. "It's okay."

She shook her head, her hair brushing against his face. "I don't know what to do. Why is this happening?"

He pressed his cheek against her hair. "It's going to be all right. Don't worry."

Fine words. The trouble was, he didn't have any idea how to make them come true.

Chapter Fourteen

It took a gigantic effort to keep smiling when she felt that everyone who came through the door for the open house was staring at her. Rachel handed out leaflets about the history of the Unger mansion to the latest group, hoping that their curiosity was about the house, not her.

"Please enjoy your visit. If you have any questions, be sure to ask one of the guides."

A couple of her volunteer guides had, oddly enough, become unavailable today, probably as a result of last night's events. But Emma and Grams had stepped into the breach. She'd worried about letting Grams exert herself, but she'd actually begun to regain some of her zest as she talked to people about the house she loved.

And then there was Tyler. She was aware of him moving quietly through the visitors, lending a hand here, there and everywhere. They'd managed a few minutes alone to talk earlier, trying to make sense of all this.

If Phil feared that Tyler's investigations might reveal he'd bought stolen property, he might have a reason to try to stop him. But why would he have anything against her?

Everything that happened to her could have been coincidence. Accident.

Except that someone who worked for Phil had been there, in Bethlehem. And someone had attacked Phil and her.

Her head ached with trying to make sense of it. Tyler had listened to her attempts at explanation, but he hadn't offered any of his own. Because he believed her father guilty of murder? Even so, last night he hadn't hesitated to leap to her defense.

She'd been emotionally and mentally shattered, finding Phil in that state after everything else that had happened. Tyler had had every excuse to cut her adrift, even to suspect her of the attack on Phil, but he hadn't. He'd rushed to the rescue. Without him, she might well have stumbled into saying something stupid that would make Chief Burkhalter even more suspicious.

She smoothed out a wrinkle in the Star of Bethlehem quilt, trying to make herself think of something— anything—else. Christmas was only a few days away. Andrea and Cal would be back soon. She should call Caroline and urge her again to come home for Christmas. And wrapping the gifts—

It was no use. She could think of other things on the surface, but the fear and misgivings still lurked beneath. She was caught in a web of suspicion and pain, and she didn't see any way out.

The sound of the front door opening yet again had her turning to it, forcing a smile even though her face felt as if it would crack. Her expression melted into something more genuine when she saw Bradley Whitmoyer, bundled up against the cold, pulling his gloves off as he closed the door behind him.

She went forward, hand extended. "Dr. Whitmoyer, it's a nice surprise you could make it. I thought you'd be completely tied up helping Sandra with the visitors at your house."

"Bradley, remember?" The doctor managed a smile, but she thought it was as much a struggle as her own.

"It's all right," she said impulsively. "Maybe we should both agree to stop smiling before our faces break."

"That is how it feels, isn't it?" He seemed to relax slightly. "I thought I'd go mad if I heard another person say what a lovely tree we have. The only way I could get out of the house was to agree that I'd see how you're doing and report back to Sandra."

She'd take Sandra's interest as a gesture of support. That was better than assuming there was anything negative about her interest.

"As you can see, we're busy, but I think it's starting to dwindle down now. We've had a steady stream of visitors all afternoon, up and down the stairs, determined to see everything."

The fine lines of his face tightened. "I drew the line at that. Guests to our house may see the downstairs, that's all. The upstairs is strictly off-limits."

"Well, yours is a private house. We have to keep

business in mind, and some of our house-tour people may be potential guests."

She was faintly surprised that he was willing to stand here talking so long. The busy-doctor persona seemed to be in abeyance at the moment, but she suspected he'd been out early, checking on any patients in the hospital.

"Will you tell me something?" She asked the question before she could lose her nerve.

"If I can."

"Phillip Longstreet. Do you know how he's doing?"

His face seemed to close. He wouldn't answer. He'd plead professional ethics and say he couldn't. But then he shrugged.

"He's not my patient, so I don't know any details. But then, if he were, I couldn't tell you anything." His smile had a strained quality. "The police have a guard on his door, so I didn't see him, but I spoke with a resident who said he's stable. Not awake yet, but otherwise showing signs of improvement."

Something that had been tight inside her seemed to ease. *Thank You, Lord.* "I'm glad. Do you think, when he wakes up, he'll be able to identify his attacker?"

But there Bradley's cooperation halted. "I couldn't begin to guess. I understand the police think they can trace a few things stolen in the recent robberies to the shop, so it may have been some thief he was involved with." He took a step through the archway into the front parlor. "The *putz* looks very nice. Are you getting tired of explaining it to people?"

Obviously Bradley had been as indiscreet as he

would let himself be. "It does get a little repetitive after a while, doesn't it?" she said. "Refreshments are set out in the breakfast room. I hope you'll go back and help yourself, although people do seem to come to a halt there."

He nodded and disappeared from view into the back parlor. She turned around, the smile still lingering on her face, and drew in a startled breath. Jeff Whitmoyer stood behind her.

He didn't seem to notice her reaction. "Sending my brother back to have something to eat? He won't. He avoids sweets, along with most everything else that makes life fun."

"I should probably follow his example. I've already been dipping into the snickerdoodles." Nerves, probably. She'd had an irresistible urge for sugar all day. "Have you taken the tour of the house yet?"

"I'll pass. No offense, but I'm not really into admiring the *decor*." He exaggerated the word. "It drives my sainted sister-in-law crazy when I refer to her eighteenth century étagère as 'that thing against the wall.'"

"I can see how it would." Both Whitmoyer brothers were unusually talkative tonight. Jeff usually only talked this long when it was a matter of a job to do.

"I heard you were the one who found Phil last night," he said abruptly.

Probably everyone who'd come through the door had heard that, but no one else had ventured to bring it up. A headache she hadn't noticed before began tightening its coils around her temples. Jeff stood there, waiting for an answer.

"That's right. I'm afraid I can't talk about it. Chief Burkhalter asked me not to say anything."

Before Jeff could pry any further, Emma bustled up to her.

"Rachel, you are needed in the kitchen, please. I will watch the door." She took the handful of brochures and gave Rachel a gentle shove.

"Thank you, Emma." She gave Jeff a vague smile and escaped with a sense of thankfulness.

Nancy Zook was in the kitchen, washing dishes, her oldest daughter standing next to her, drying.

"Nancy, you needn't do those by hand. We can use the dishwasher."

"It makes no matter. We can be quick this way." She passed a dripping plate to her daughter.

"Your mother said I was wanted?"

"Oh, *ja,* Tyler thought we should stop putting more food out."

"Tyler?"

"Here." He leaned in the doorway at the mention of his name. "According to my watch, the house tour hours are about over. But if Nancy keeps feeding those people, they're never going to leave." He nodded toward the chattering crowd clustered around the table at the far end of the breakfast room.

She glanced at Black Forest mantel clock. "It really is time." Her whole body seemed to sag in relief. "Nancy, I agree. No more food for them. Take the rest of it home for your family, all right?"

"That will be nice for our second-Christmas visitors, it will," Nancy said. "You don't worry about the kitchen. We will finish the cleanup in here."

"But—"

"Don't argue." Tyler's hand brushed hers in a gesture of support that seemed to reverberate through her entire body. "When you get a chance, I want to show you the medal." He lowered his voice, stepping back into the hallway and drawing her with him. "Those scratches on the back—there was something there. Faint, but it looks like someone scratched a triangle with something else inside it."

She tried to focus her tired brain on it. "Does that mean something?"

He shrugged. "I'm not sure. The triangle is a symbol of the Trinity, of course. Maybe my grandfather felt better about having a military decoration if he added a Christian symbol." He frowned. "It doesn't have anything to do with the robbery, but I can't help thinking about what Eli's mother said. Wondering what she really meant."

"Maybe I can talk to Emma after everything calms down." If it ever did. "She might have some insight."

"Good idea." He touched her shoulder, a featherlight brush of his fingers. "I'm going upstairs to get that last group moving. Just sit down and put your feet up for a moment."

She couldn't do that, but she appreciated the thought. "Thank you."

For a moment longer he stood motionless, his hand touching her, and then something guarded and aware came into his eyes. He turned and headed for the stairs.

Rachel swallowed hard, trying to get rid of the lump that had formed in her throat. To say nothing of the hot tears that prickled her eyes.

No matter how kind and helpful Tyler was, the events of the past still stood like a wall between them. And she was afraid they always would.

It had taken more than a few minutes, despite Tyler's best intentions, to clear the house of visitors, but finally the last of them were gone. Nancy and Emma had insisted on cleaning up the kitchen. Rachel had intended to leave some of the cleanup until tomorrow, but her helpers wouldn't hear of it.

And she had to admit they were right. Dirty dishes left in the sink, chairs pulled out of their proper places, a glass left on a tabletop—all offended her innkeeper's sense of what was right. Andrea might consider her the least-organized person in the world where record-keeping was concerned, but the house had to look right or she wouldn't sleep.

Once the Zook family had taken their leave, chattering as happily as if they'd been to a party instead of working hard for hours, she tucked Grams up in bed, Barney dozing on the rug next to her.

She went back downstairs, knowing she couldn't go to bed yet. Sleep wouldn't come, and she'd just lie in the dark and worry.

She walked into the library, where the last embers of the fire were dying in the fireplace. She sank down on the couch facing it, too tired to throw another log on. Silence set in, and with it came the fear that was becoming too familiar. And the questions.

I don't know what to think, Lord. How could the father I idolized have done these things?

One of the words she'd just used stopped her. *Idolized.* That was not a word to be used lightly, was it? Natural enough for a child to love her father, even if he hadn't been what the world would consider a good father.

But idolize? That smacked of something forbidden in her faith. Thoughts crept out of hiding, images from the past. How often had she let her feelings about her father's abandonment get between her and a relationship with someone else?

Is that really what I've been doing, Lord? I didn't mean to. I just never saw it.

Before she could pursue that uncomfortable line of thought, she heard a step. Tyler came in. One look at his face told her this endless day was not yet over. It was set in a mask, behind which she could sense something dark and implacable moving.

"We have to talk."

She steeled herself. What now? "If this is about the attack on Phillip—"

He dismissed her idea with a curt gesture of one hand. "No. Not Longstreet. You."

"Me?" Her voice came out in a squeak. "What about me?"

His jaw was hard as marble. "Showing people around the house was educational. Very. One woman in that last group especially admired the desk in the upstairs hall."

"It's a nice piece." She had to struggle to sound normal.

"Yes. And you let me believe it had been sitting in that spot for a couple of generations. But it hasn't, has it?"

"I didn't—" The attack, coming on ground she'd totally forgotten in the sweep of other events, took her off guard.

"I told you it reminded me of one that had been in my grandfather's house. When that woman was babbling on about the style and finish, I remembered it. I remembered hiding under that desk while my grandfather and mother shouted at each other. I had a brandnew penknife that my father had given me, and I used it to carve my initials on the underside, in the corner, where no one would see. T.D. Guess what, Rachel? They're still there."

She could face this attack better on her feet. She stood, facing him. She wouldn't be a coward about it.

"I didn't know. How could I know that the desk came from your grandfather's house?"

"You knew that it hadn't been standing in the upstairs hall for a hundred years. You could have told me that."

She could have. She hadn't.

"Tyler, try to understand. I didn't know, then, what you—"

What you would come to mean to me. No, she couldn't say that. Not now.

"I didn't know whether it meant anything that it was here. I found the desk in one of the outbuildings when I was decorating the inn. You've seen those buildings—they're crammed with cast-off furniture. It was just another piece."

He wasn't buying it. "After I mentioned the similarity to my grandfather's desk, you had to have known it might be significant. You should have told me."

"And could I have trusted you not to make too much of it?" Anger and tears were both perilously near the surface. "You've been so obsessed with finding out the truth, that you haven't cared who got hurt in the process. Our having the desk could be perfectly innocent. My grandfather might have picked it up at a sale anytime."

"Or not. It could be confirmation that someone from this house was involved in my grandfather's death." He was armored against her by his anger and determination. "You didn't tell me the truth, Rachel. All along, you've only been helping me as a way of protecting your own family. Isn't that right?"

Her head was throbbing with the effort to hold back tears. "You can't believe that."

"I can't believe anything else." The words had an echo of finality about them. He turned toward the hall. "In the morning I'll look for another place to stay until all of this is settled."

He walked out, and she heard his steps mounting the central staircase. She listened, frozen, until they faded away. Then she sank back onto the sofa and buried her face in her hands.

Forgive me, Father. Please forgive me. I know that Tyler never will. I'll try to accept that. I was wrong. But I have to protect my family, don't I?

Tears spilled through her hands, dropping to her lap. *Do you?* The question formed in her heart. *Can you protect your family by hiding the truth?*

I need this, Father. The cry came from her innermost heart. *I lost my family, and I need to bring it back together again. Isn't that the right thing to do?*

The answer was there. It had been all along, but she hadn't been willing to face it. She couldn't go back and recreate the family that she imagined they'd been once. That idealized image had probably never really existed.

And she couldn't build a future based on a lie. Her heart twisted, feeling as if it would break in two. She'd already lost Tyler, and whatever might have been between them. She couldn't go on trying to cover up, trying to pretend her way back to an imaginary family.

I've been wrong, Father. So wrong. Please, forgive me and show me what to do.

She already knew, didn't she? If her father was guilty, the truth would have to come out. And if evidence of that guilt lay anywhere in the house or grounds, she'd have to find it.

She leaned against the couch back, too tired to move. She couldn't start searching attics and cellars now. Even if she had the strength, she couldn't risk waking Grams.

In the morning. She pushed herself wearily to her feet. She'd start in the morning, assuming the police didn't decide to arrest her by then for the attack on

Phil. She had the list of items that were missing from the farmhouse. If any of them were on Unger property, she'd find them, and let the truth emerge where it would.

And in the morning Tyler would leave. She rubbed her temples. Lying awake all night worrying about it wouldn't change anything. She'd take a couple of aspirins and have a cup of the cocoa Emma had left on the stove. Maybe, somehow, she'd be able to sleep.

Tyler had been staring at the ceiling for what seemed like hours. Probably had been. He turned his head to look at the bedside clock: 4:00 a.m.—the darkest watches of the night, with dawn far away and sleep not coming. It was the hour of soul searching.

He got up, moving quietly to the window that looked out on the lane and drawing back the curtain. It was snowing again, the thickly falling drifts muffling everything. The lights in front of the inn were misty haloes, and nothing moved on the street.

Was he being unjust to Rachel? He understood, only too well, her need to protect her family. She'd been eight when she'd lost all the stability in her life. Small wonder that she was trying desperately to protect what she had left of family.

But she'd lied to him. Not overtly, but it was a lie all the same. If she'd just told him, the day he'd talked about the desk—

What would he have done? He hadn't remembered, then, about the initials. He wouldn't have been able to identify it any sooner. But if she'd been honest, they could have searched for the truth together.

That was the worst thing about it. That he'd begun to trust her, care for her, maybe even love her, and she'd been keeping secrets from him.

He moved away from the window, letting the curtain fall. There was no point in going over it and over it. Facts were important to him, concrete facts, not emotions and wishful thinking.

The desk was certainly concrete enough. It had seemed huge to him when he was a child playing underneath it, imagining it alternately a fort and a castle. He'd needed a shelter during that visit, with his mother and grandfather constantly at each other's throats.

Giving in to the urge to look at it again, he opened his door and stepped out into the hall. No need to worry about anyone seeing him in his T-shirt and sweatpants—he was the only person in this part of the house tonight. When he moved out in the morning, it would be empty.

The thought didn't give him any satisfaction. He ran his hand along the smooth surface of the slanted desktop. Rachel had done a good job with it, as she had with everything she'd touched in preparing the inn. She'd taken infinite care. Did she even realize that she was trying to recreate the family and security she'd lost?

He stiffened, hand tightening on the edge of the desk. That sounded like the dog, over in the other wing of the house. But Barney never barked at night.

A cold breath seemed to move along his skin. The barking was more insistent. Something was wrong.

Someone—Rachel or her grandmother—would have silenced the dog by now. His heart chilled. If they could.

He was running, moving beyond rational thought, knowing he had to get to Rachel. Down the stairs two at a time, stumbling once as his bare feet hit the polished floor. The dim light that Rachel always left on in the downstairs hallway—it was off.

His fear ratcheted up a notch. He grabbed the door handle, already thinking ahead to how he'd get into the east wing if it were locked, but it opened easily under his hand.

Race through the library, pitch-black, stumbling into a chair, then a lamp table. Out into the small landing at the base of the stairs. Up the second set of steps, no breath left to call out, just get there. The dog's barking changed to a long, high-pitched howl, raking his nerves with fear.

Get to the upstairs hall, and now he knew his fears were justified. Barney clawed at Rachel's door, frantically trying to get in. From the crack under the door came a blast of cold air. One of the windows must be wide-open in the room. Or the door onto Rachel's tiny balcony.

Grab the knob. Locked. He'd known it would be. No time to analyze or plan. Draw back. Shove the hysterical dog out of the way. Fling himself at the door. Pain shooting through his shoulder. Throw himself at it again, wordless prayers exploding in his mind.

The lock snapped; the door gave. He stumbled into the room. The balcony door stood open, Rachel's slender body draped over the railing, a dark figure over her, pushing—

He hurtled himself toward them, out into the night, snow in his face, grabbing for Rachel, pulling her back, fending off the blows the other man threw at him, the dog dancing around them, snarling, trying to get his teeth into the attacker. Rachel struggling feebly, trying to pull herself back. But the man was strong, Tyler's bare feet slid on the snowy balcony, he couldn't get a grip, they were going to go over—

The railing screamed, metal tearing loose, giving way. He fell to his knees, grabbing Rachel's arm, holding her even as her feet slid off the balcony. Holding her tight and safe as the other figure windmilled on the edge for an agonizing second and then went over, a long, thin scream cutting off abruptly when his body hit the patio.

He pulled Rachel against him, his arms wrapped around her. Safe. She was safe.

She pressed her face into his chest. "Who?" Her voice was fogged with whatever had been used to drug her. "Who was it?"

He leaned forward cautiously, peering down through the swirling flakes to the patio. The man lay perfectly still, sprawled on the stones, face up. The ski mask he'd worn must have ripped loose in the struggle. It was Jeff Whitmoyer.

Chapter Fifteen

Would this never end? Rachel sat at the kitchen table, still shivering from time to time, her hands wrapped around a hot mug of coffee. The coffee was slowly clearing her fogged mind, but it produced odd things from time to time.

"The cocoa," she said now.

Tyler seemed to know what she meant without explanation. "That's right. He drugged the cocoa Emma had left on the stove."

"Imagine the nerve of the man." Nancy topped off the mug Tyler held. She and Emma had just appeared, as they always seemed to at times of crisis, and Nancy had taken over the kitchen, apparently feeling that food was the answer to every issue. She slid a wedge of cinnamon coffeecake in front of Tyler. "Eat something. You need your strength."

Well, the police who swarmed around the place would probably eat it, if they didn't.

Emma was upstairs with Grams, refusing to leave

her alone even though the paramedics had seen her and declared that she hadn't had enough of the drug to cause harm.

Tyler had dressed at some point in the nightmare hours before dawn. He wore jeans and a navy sweatshirt, his hair tousled. She'd put on her warmest sweater, but it didn't seem to be enough to banish the cold that had penetrated to her very bones when she'd been fighting for her life.

Not that she'd managed to fight very hard. "If it hadn't been for you—"

"If it hadn't been for Barney," he said quickly. "It was easy enough to drop something in the cocoa for you, but Barney had already been fed, so he had to take his chances that no one would hear the dog."

He didn't identify the person he spoke of. He didn't need to. They all knew.

The door opened, and Bradley Whitmoyer stepped inside. Usually he looked pale. Now he looked gray— as gray as a gravestone. He'd probably had to identify his brother's body.

She found her voice. "I'm so sorry."

Bradley shook his head. "I didn't come for that."

The words sounded rude, but she didn't think he'd meant them that way. He was just exhausted beyond reach of any of the conventions.

"You'd better sit down." Tyler didn't sound very happy at the prospect.

Bradley ignored the words. Maybe he didn't even hear them. "I have to tell you. I can't hold it back any longer. It will kill me if I don't speak."

She started to protest, but Tyler's hand closed over hers in warning.

"If this is something the police should hear, maybe you'd better wait until the chief comes in," he said.

"I'll tell them." He looked surprised at the comment. "But Rachel has the right to know first. And you. It was my fault, you see."

Tyler seemed to recognize the terrible strain Bradley was under. He looked at her, shaking his head slightly as if to say he didn't know what else they could do but let the man talk.

"I was home from college that summer." Bradley didn't need to say what summer. They knew. "I was desperate for money for my education, you see. I wouldn't have gotten involved with him, otherwise."

Her heart clutched. Was he going to name her father?

"Who?" Tyler's voice was tense.

"Phil Longstreet." He looked surprised that they had to ask. "He had this scheme—he would talk people, elderly farmers, mostly, into selling things, usually for a fraction of their value. While he was in the house, he would identify the really desirable items."

"And then you'd go back and steal them." Tyler finished it for him.

"We did." Bradley looked faintly surprised at the person he'd been. "I didn't...I didn't see any other way I could stay in school. I don't suppose Phil expected to get away with it for long. He was always talking about leaving here, he and Hampton both."

Her heart hurt. *Oh, Daddy. Why did you have to get involved in that?*

"They did all right, for a while. Then they tried it on John Hostetler." His gaze touched Tyler. "Your grandfather sold them some pieces of furniture. Then we went back when we thought the house was empty. He met us with a shotgun. He knew what we were doing. He was going to tell Phil's uncle, tell everyone—" His voice seemed to fade out for an instant. "There was a struggle. I don't know how it happened. I knocked him down. He lay there, clutching his chest. He was having a heart attack. I knew it, and I didn't help. I let him die."

His face twisted with anguish, and he seemed to struggle to control it, as though revealing his pain was asking for sympathy he didn't deserve.

"So you made it look like a robbery and you ran." Tyler didn't seem to have any sympathy to spare.

"The next day I was going to go to the police. I couldn't stand it. But I told Jeff, and he said he'd take care of everything. I couldn't ruin my future. So I kept quiet."

"My father?" She was amazed that her voice could sound so level.

"I heard he'd left town. The investigation died down. No one ever asked me anything. I went back to college, then medical school, and then I came back here to practice."

That was why, she realized. He'd come back as some sort of atonement for what he'd done, as if the lives he saved could make up for the one he'd taken.

Bradley's hands closed over the back of a chair. "I

kept expecting to be exposed. Sometimes I thought it would be a relief. But years went by, and no one ever knew. And then you came back." He looked at her, eyes filled with pity. "And Jeff told me you had to be taken care of. And he told me why."

She shook her head. "I don't understand." But she knew something terrible was coming, and she couldn't get out of its way.

"It was because of what you wanted to do. You wanted to get rid of the gazebo. He couldn't let you, because if you did, they'd find your father's body, where Jeff buried it the night he killed him to keep him quiet."

It was Christmas Eve before Rachel thought she'd begun to understand everything. Andrea and Cal had rushed back from their honeymoon, and Andrea's calm good sense had helped her get through all of the things that had to be done. Even Caroline had come, all the way from New Mexico, making light of it but seeming to feel that all of the Hampton girls had to be together at a time like this.

The police had superintended the removal of the gazebo, and the family had had a quiet memorial service for their father at the church. She'd only broken down once—when the police gave her the tarnished remains of a child's gold cross on a chain that had been in her father's pocket.

The numbness that had gotten her through the past week had begun to thaw, and she wasn't quite sure what was going to take its place. She looked around the faces reflected in the lights of the Christmas tree. Grams, Andrea and Cal, Caroline.

And Tyler. With every reason for him to leave, Tyler had stayed.

"Now that Longstreet is awake and talking, it sounds as if he's blaming everyone but himself for what happened." Cal, Andrea's husband, leaned back in his chair, a cup of eggnog in one hand. "According to what I heard, he now says that your father decided to go to the police instead of leaving town, as they'd agreed. Jeff Whitmoyer had been working on the construction project, so he knew it was ready at hand. And he wasn't going to let anyone spoil the bright future he saw for his little brother."

"We don't need to talk about it now." Andrea leaning close to her new husband, reproved him gently.

"It's all right." Rachel knew Andrea was trying to protect her, as she always did. "I'm over the worst of it." She couldn't suppress a shudder. "I guess I'm just lucky Jeff didn't do a better job of it back in the spring when he ran me down. I certainly never connected that to asking him for a quote on removing the gazebo."

Grams put a hand over hers, patting it gently. "How could you? I knew the man since he was a child, and I never suspected a thing."

"You seemed to give up your plans then, and I suppose they thought they were safe." Tyler rested one hand on the mantel, maybe too edgy to sit down. "Then I came and stirred them up again."

Caro brushed dark red curls back over her shoulder.

Her bright, speculative gaze went from Rachel to Tyler. "Good thing you were here the other night."

"Good thing Barney was here," Tyler said dryly. The dog, hearing his name, looked up from his nap on the hearth rug and thumped his tail.

"Longstreet won't get off scot-free," Cal said. "The police know he's been behind the recent thefts of antiques. I suppose he thought it worked so well twenty years ago that he'd start it up again, with a couple of hired thugs. He apparently got nervous when you two started nosing around and tried to dissuade you. But his efforts backfired when Jeff decided he was a liability."

"He's lucky to be alive." She remembered that pool of blood around him on the office floor.

"He may not think so after the district attorney gets through with him," Tyler said. "But he'll fight it every step of the way, unlike Whitmoyer. I understand Sandra's trying to have her husband declared mentally unfit to defend himself."

She could actually feel sorry for Bradley, in a way. He'd been trapped by what happened twenty-two years ago, and all his good works hadn't been enough to make up for that.

"So the medal really didn't have anything to do with it, except that it left a trail to Phil." She'd probably be trying to figure out all the ramifications of what happened for months, but it was starting to come a little clearer.

"Funny thing about that." Tyler set his punch cup on the mantel and pulled something out of his pocket. He walked over to put it on the coffee table where they could see it. The medal. "I had it professionally cleaned. The jeweler brought up what was on the back, and did a little detective work on it."

He turned it over. Rachel leaned forward, staring at the symbol incised on the reverse. "It looks like a triangle with an eye inside it."

"Not a triangle. A pyramid. Turns out this was a symbol used by a number of odd little groups back in the late 1600s in Germany and Switzerland. Rosicrucians, Illuminati, the Order of the Rose—apparently my grandfather's ancestor was part of one. Small wonder the Amish didn't want to talk about it. They'd consider that heresy."

"But surely your grandfather didn't believe in that."

He shrugged. "I have no way of knowing. I wouldn't think so, but—" He picked the medal up again. "Somehow I don't think I want this as a memento after all. It can go back into somebody's collection. We exposed the truth about his death. That's enough for me."

There was finality in his words. Did everyone else hear it, or was she the only one? This was over. Now he would go back to his life.

"I think that cookie tray needs to be refilled." She got up quickly, before anyone else could volunteer to do it. She needed a moment to herself.

She went through to the kitchen, and when she heard a step behind her, she knew who it was.

"Are you okay?" Tyler was close, not touching.

"I guess." Talk about something, anything, other than the fact that he's leaving. "You know, if Bradley had gone to the police right away, my father wouldn't have died. But he would still have left us." She tilted her head back, looking at him. "I'm not going to lie to myself any longer about who and what he was."

"I'm sorry." His voice was soft and deep with emotion. "Sorry he's gone, and sorry he wasn't the man you wanted him to be."

"I'm all right about it. Really. It's better to have the truth out. I can't find my happiness in recreating a past that never existed. It's the love we have for each other as a family that's important, not the mistakes our parents made." She took a breath, wishing she knew what he was thinking. "At least you fulfilled your promise to your mother."

"I found out more than she intended. Knowing something about her childhood, I understand her better. Her mother died, and then her father shut her away from the only support system she had left."

"It's sad. If he hadn't taken her out of the church, the Amish would have been family for her, no matter what he did." It was such a sad story, but at least now Tyler seemed content that he'd done what he could.

"Enough of that." His gaze seemed to warm the skin of her face. "I have a gift for you, and I'd like to give it to you without the rest of your family looking on, if that's okay."

She nodded, unable to speak. Her heart seemed to be beating faster than a hummingbird's.

Tyler took something from his pocket and dangled it in front of her. "I picked this up when I ran back to Baltimore yesterday. It belonged to my father's mother. I want you to have it. Not to replace the one your father would have given you, but because—well, just because it seemed the right gift."

She touched the delicate, old-fashioned gold cross, her heart almost too full for words. "It's beautiful. Thank you."

He fastened it around her neck, his fingers brushing her nape gently. "My grandmother was like you—loving, nurturing, filled with goodness. If my father knew, he'd be happy I found someone to give it to."

Her eyes misted as she traced the graceful design. "I don't know what to say."

"Then let me say it." He took both her hands in his, lifting them to his lips. "I know there are a lot of questions to be answered about the future, and I'm not sure how it will all work out. I'll move as slowly as you want, but I know right now that I want to share the rest of my life with you."

He was being careful, not pressuring her, but there was no need. She wasn't afraid anymore of what the future held. She reached up to pull his face toward hers, seeing the love blossom in his eyes.

She'd come back to this house to find something she'd lost years earlier. God had given her not only that but much more besides. She didn't have to look for home any longer. She'd found it.

* * * * *

Dear Reader,

I love coming back to my own beautiful rural Pennsylvania and the good, neighborly people who live here, especially that unique group, the Amish.

The Christmas traditions I've explored in this story come from a variety of sources, some from the Amish, some from the Moravians and some from my own Pennsylvania German roots on my mother's side. I hope you enjoy reading about them, and if you ever have a chance to visit Bethlehem, Pennsylvania, at Christmastime, you'll never forget the experience!

I hope you'll let me know how you felt about this story. I've put together a little collection of Pennsylvania Dutch recipes that I'd be happy to share with you—some from my own family, some from friends. You can write to me at Love Inspired Books, 233 Broadway, Suite 1001, New York, NY 10279, email me at marta@martaperry.com, or visit me online at martaperry.com.

Blessings,

Marta Perry

Questions for Discussion

1. Can you understand the need for family that drives Rachel to try to recreate the family life she remembers as a child? Have you ever thought you'd like to go back to a time when you felt cared for and secure?

2. Tyler feels driven to find the truth about his grandfather's death, even though he never had a bond with him. Do you sympathize with his need to do what he feels is the right thing?

3. Rachel has a close relationship with her older sister, but at times feels she can't live up to the standards Andrea sets. Do you have experience of the complicated relationships that can exist between sisters?

4. The struggle to expose the truth of the past is central to this story. Have you ever experienced the difficulty of learning a long-held secret that changes your view of the past? How does a person deal with that?

5. Rachel's injury gave her time to meditate on her relationship with God and develop a deeper relationship with Him. Have you ever found that God has used a difficult time to bring you closer to Him?

6. Rachel finds comfort and security through recreating the Christmas traditions of her childhood. What particular Christmas traditions are most important to you? Why?

7. Tyler attributes everything he knows about being a Christian man to his father. Did your parents provide a solid example of Christian life to you? If not, where did you find it?

8. In the scriptural theme, we see reflected the images of God as a stronghold and a refuge for the righteous. What particular incidents in your life are brought to mind by this verse?

9. Most Old-Order Amish keep their Christmas celebrations focused on the religious celebration and then on fellowship with family and friends. Have you ever longed for a simpler Christmas?

10. Have you ever felt that the busyness of Christmas preparations keep you from properly celebrating the birth of Christ? If so, how do you deal with that?

SPECIAL EXCERPT FROM

SUSPENSE

*When a woman's young child is abducted, can a man
with a similar tragedy in his past come to the rescue?*

**Read on for a preview of HER CHRISTMAS GUARDIAN
by Shirlee McCoy, the next book in her brand-new
MISSION: RESCUE series.**

"Just tell me what happened to my daughter."

"We don't know. You were alone when we found you."

"I need to go home." Scout jumped up, head spinning,
the room spinning. The knot in her stomach growing until
it was all she could feel. "Maybe she's there."

She knew it was unreasonable, knew it couldn't be
true, but she had to look, had to be sure.

"The police have already been to your house," Boone
said gently. "She's not there."

"She could be hiding. She doesn't like strangers." Her
voice trembled. Her body trembled, every fear she'd ever
had, every nightmare, suddenly real and happening and
completely outside her control.

"Scout." He touched her shoulder, his fingers warm
through thin cotton. She didn't want warmth, though. She
wanted her child.

"Please," she begged. "I have to go home. I have to see
for myself. I have to."

He eyed her for a moment, silent. Solemn. Something
in his eyes that looked like the grief she was feeling, the
horror she was living.

Finally, Boone nodded. "Okay. I'll take you."

Just like that. Simple and easy, as if the request didn't

go against logic. As if she weren't hooked to an IV, shaking from fear and sorrow and pain.

He grabbed a blanket from the foot of the bed and wrapped it around her shoulders then took out his phone and texted someone. She didn't ask who. She was too busy trying to keep the darkness from taking her again. Too busy trying to remember the last moment she'd seen Lucy. Had she been scared? Crying?

Three days.

That was what he had said.

Three days that Lucy had been missing and Scout had been lying in a hospital bed.

Please, God, let her be okay.

She was all Scout had. The only thing that really mattered to her. She had to be okay.

A tear slipped down her cheek. She didn't have the energy to wipe it away. Didn't have the strength to even open her eyes when Boone touched her cheek.

"It's going to be okay," he said quietly, and she wanted to believe him almost as much as she wanted to open her eyes and see her daughter.

"How can it be?"

"Because you ran into the right person the night your daughter was taken," he responded, and he sounded so confident, so certain of the outcome, she looked into his face, his eyes. Saw those things she'd seen before, but something else, too—faith, passion, belief.

*Will Boone help Scout find her missing
daughter in time for Christmas?
Pick up HER CHRISTMAS GUARDIAN to find out!
Available December 2014
wherever Love Inspired® books and ebooks are sold.*

Love Inspired®
SUSPENSE
RIVETING INSPIRATIONAL ROMANCE

THE YULETIDE RESCUE

by

MARGARET DALEY

MISTLETOE AND MURDER

When Dr. Bree Mathison's plane plummets into the Alaskan wilderness at Christmastime, she is torn between grief and panic. With the pilot—her dear friend—dead and wolves circling, she struggles to survive. Search and Rescue leader David Stone fights his way through the elements to save her. David suspects the plane crash might not have been an accident, spurring Bree's sense that she's being watched. But why is someone after her? Suddenly Bree finds herself caught in the middle of a whirlwind of secrets during the holiday season. With everyone she cares about most in peril, Bree and her promised protector must battle the Alaskan tundra and vengeful criminals to make it to the New Year.

ALASKAN
+SEARCH +RESCUE

Risking their lives to save the day

Available December 2014
wherever Love Inspired
books and ebooks are sold.

LIS44637

Love Inspired

An Amish Christmas Journey
by
Patricia Davids

Their Holiday Adventure

Toby Yoder promised to care for his orphaned little sister the rest of her life. After all, the tragedy that took their parents and left her injured was his fault. Now he must make a three-hundred-mile trip from the hospital to the Amish community where they'll settle down. But as they share a hired van with pretty Greta Barkman, an Amish woman with a similar harrowing past, Toby can't bear for the trip to end. Suddenly, there's joy, a rescued cat named Christmas and hope for their journey to continue together forever.

BRIDES OF
Amish Country

Finding true love in the land of the Plain People

Available December 2014
wherever Love Inspired books
and ebooks are sold.

Find us on Facebook at
www.Facebook.com/LoveInspiredBooks

LI87927

Big Sky Daddy
by
LINDA FORD

FOR HIS SON'S SAKE

Caleb Craig will do anything for his son, even ask his
boss's enemy for help. Not only does Lilly Bell tend to his
son's injured puppy, but she offers to rehabilitate little
Teddy's leg. Caleb knows that getting Teddy to walk again is
all that really matters, yet he wonders if maybe Lilly can heal
his brooding heart, as well.

Precocious little Teddy—and his devoted father—steal
Lilly's heart and make her long for a child and husband of her
own. But Lilly learned long ago that trusting a man means
risking heartbreak. Happiness lies within reach—if she seizes
the chance for love and motherhood she never expected...

Montana
Marriages

**Three sisters discover a legacy of love beneath
the Western sky**

*Available December 2014
wherever Love Inspired books
and ebooks are sold.*

Find us on Facebook at
www.Facebook.com/LoveInspiredBooks

LIH28290